AGAINST THE GRAIN

AUCKLAND MED. 4

JAY HOGAN

SOUTHERN LIGHTS PUBLISHING

Published by Southern Lights Publishing

https://www.jayhoganauthor.com

Trade Paperback ISBN:978-0-9951325-6-6

Digital ISBN: 978-0-9951325-5-9

Digital Edition published December 2020

Trade Paperback Published December 2020

First Edition

Editing by Boho Edits

Cover Art Copyright © 2020 Kanaxa

Cover content is for illustrative purposes only and any person depicted on the cover is a model.

Proofread by Lissa Given Proofing and Lori Parks- LesCourt Author Services

Printed in the United States of America and Australia

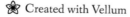 Created with Vellum

For my family who read everything I write and keep on saying they love it all, blushes included.

ACKNOWLEDGMENTS

I wish to acknowledge the direction, suggestions, and advice that I received from 'own voice' sensitivity readers who chose not to be named. These people helped ensure Miller's character, the book's language and terminology, and the depiction of events was a fair and sensitive representation. Any mistake is my own.

As always, I thank my husband for his patience and for keeping the dog walked and out of my hair when I needed to work. And my daughter for all her support.

Getting a book finessed for release is a huge challenge that includes beta readers, editing, proofing, cover artists and my tireless PA. It's a team effort, and includes all those author support networks and reader fans who rally around when you're ready to pull your hair out and throw away every first draft. Thanks to all of you.

CHAPTER ONE

SLAMMED FROM THE SIDE, MILLER HURTLED TO THE FLOOR, HIS embattled rugby chair strapped to his body like the shell of a fucking ninja turtle, the graunch of steel on steel echoing through the gym like a car crash. His shoulder took the brunt, the air whooshing from his lungs at the impact seconds before his hip crunched on the inside frame and pain jolted through his leg.

Son of a bitch.

"Fuck, Jimmy! What the hell was that?" Miller scrambled his weight sideways, using the momentum to rock back onto his wheels.

A beaten-up, solid wheelchair hub rolled into view and someone slapped him on the back . . . hard. "Aw, did you get an owie, pretty boy?" Jimmy flashed him a wicked smile. "Go big or go home, right, Tap? It's called murderball, not fucking tiddlywinks, you pussy. Besides, you're barely bleeding. I'll have to try harder next time."

"Arsehole." Miller shook the spasm from his pinned and plated wrist and checked the skin on his arm where the steel rim had caught. Felt worse than it looked. He wiped the blood off on his shirt and was ready to go. Spinning his chair to make sure he caught Jimmy's rims with his own, he shoved the cheeky fucker sideways. Jimmy might be on the opposing squad in this game, but he and Miller had been team-mates in the New Zealand Wheel Blacks for more years than Miller chose to remember.

Jimmy laughed, teetering on one wheel. "So that's how it's gonna be, huh? Better watch your back, Tap. You part-timers don't have the shoulder strength. Looks like that new-fangled offensive chair you got isn't worth shit. Should've stuck with the trainer wheels."

"Fuck you." Miller flipped him off, smiling at the good-natured ribbing aimed at those who weren't full-time in their chairs, but Jimmy wasn't wrong. Miller lacked the shoulder bulk of some others, but he wasn't about to own up to that shit. He'd never live it down. He hadn't put in years of weight training to compensate for nothing.

And damn, he needed that strength. Wheelchair rugby was a full-contact sport, often with more testosterone bullshit flying around these "friendlies" than in any professional game Miller had ever played back in his Super Rugby days. Wheelchair players tore across gyms like modern-day knights, steel clashing, bodies flying—the battle was real, and Miller loved every freaking bone-jarring, batshit second of it.

This was his jam, and he never felt more alive than when he was strung out on the floor after a huge hit, laughing his fucking head off while his team yelled at him to get his butt back in the game. On the wrong side of thirty-five, he was a little slower on the recovery than he used to be, but still, he could hold his own.

He headed back on court, calling for the throw from Amos, who was pinned down by two of the opposition trying to barrel him out of bounds. The ball headed Miller's way. He reached for it, shoved it into his lap, and sailed his chair ten metres through two defenders and a set of cones, to score a goal. A couple of teammates high-fived while the opposing team readied to in-bound, and then they were off again.

This time it was Vicki who intercepted the opposing team's throw, earning herself a sideways slam from Jimmy for her audacity and ending up on the floor in a screech of metal. She got her chair back upright and lost no time hoofing it down the court to return the favour to Jimmy, who'd snatched the dislodged ball after his well-aimed hit. On court, the two were like a red rag to a bull. Off court, they'd been cosy for five years and the sappy looks they shared were enough to make Miller's teeth ache.

Miller's team scored another two goals to bring them within a point of the opposition, and the concern in Jimmy's expression brought a smile to Miller's face. "Better dust off that credit card, Jimbo," he yelled across the court. "Drinks are gonna be on you, my friend." He caught another ball from Amos and headed for the far end of the court.

Jimmy barrelled up on him within seconds and nailed him on the side, upending them both. They stared at each other from their backs on the floor, laughing.

"Game isn't over till it's over, mate," Jimmy said drily as he was helped back onto his wheels. His gaze landed on Miller's arm and he smirked. "Well, look at that. What a shame. Guess you'll have to wait for those drinks, huh?"

Miller looked down at his arm and winced. *Bugger.* The small gash on his forearm had opened up, leaving a large smear of blood across the gym floor. "They don't need me to cream you lot," he huffed, getting back on his wheels. "You guys are going down. Rain check on that drink, buddy. I won't forget."

Jimmy snorted and headed off, shouting over his shoulder, "In your dreams, sunshine. Catch you next week."

The referee sent Miller off to get his injury looked at while someone cleaned the floor so the game could restart. The first aider took one look at his arm and said the last words Miller needed to hear.

"That'll need stitches."

Goddammit.

The team manager offered to drive Miller to the ER, but he was having none of that. He had a small laceration, not a damn broken leg. He could've gone to the local walk-in clinic, but he had work to pick up from his office anyway, so he wrapped a towel around his arm and headed to Auckland Med.

He grabbed the last accessible parking space outside the ER and briefly wondered who was on duty. With a bit of luck, he'd land Michael Oliver. The guy was gorgeous, and Miller sure as hell didn't mind those particular hands checking him out. Arrogant alpha males were a soft spot of his, and you didn't get more arrogant, alpha, or hot than Dr Michael Oliver. Except for maybe his husband, Josh Rawlins. The K9 handler was a tall drink of water and the two of them together were the stuff of any red-blooded gay man's fantasy.

Which was about as far as Miller usually got in terms of his own love life—fantasy and his right hand, plus the occasional discreet hook-up via an app if the stars aligned in his favour. Between his regional Freewheelers commitment, the New Zealand Wheel Black training programme, the fact he wasn't out in his sport or his job, dating didn't just take a back seat, it was relegated to the trailer hooked up behind, where the rest of his life was stored for some point in the future when he actually had time.

Miller grabbed his canes from between the seats and briefly debated making do with those alone, but immediately dismissed the idea. He was exhausted from the game and his leg was still giving him hell from the hit he'd taken. Not that he was going to mention that to anyone in the ER—they'd be all over him for an X-ray and he didn't need the grief. His pelvis had been shot for ten years from the accident, and another X-ray wasn't going to change that. But his forearm had soaked through the makeshift bandage and hurt like a motherfucker.

He pushed open the door to his Nissan X-Trail and pivoted in his seat to get his legs out first.

"Hey."

His gaze lifted to find a blonde woman in her forties with impeccably coiffed hair, pink trainers, and a furious expression, stabbing her finger at him.

"You can't park there. It's a disabled space."

"Accessible, actually." If he had a dollar for every fucking time someone decided to police his disability, he'd be rolling in it.

The woman remained unconvinced. "I'm going to have to report you."

For fuck's sake. "Go ahead."

She lifted her phone and moved to the rear of his car to take a snapshot of his number plate.

Meanwhile, Miller got to his feet and pulled his wheelchair out from behind the front seat. He unfolded it, sat down, and stowed his canes in the holder at the back.

"You didn't say you had a chair." She stared at him, clearly pissed at having her thunder stolen.

"It's none of your business."

A quick glance assured him she was still debating whether to push her case.

Her nostrils flared. "Why do you need a chair if you can walk?"

Miller looked her in the eye and fought to hold his temper. "Also none of your business, Ma'am, so I'd appreciate it if you'd take your attitude somewhere else or I'll be forced to call security."

Her eyes bulged and she stormed off to her car, muttering all the way, and Miller just knew he'd be getting a call to confirm his right to use the accessible car parks, again.

He made his way to the jam-packed waiting room, took one look around, and blew out a sigh. Saturday afternoon at the ER. Maybe he should've gone to the clinic, after all. But the woman at the front desk got him into a treatment cubicle quicker than he expected—mostly because he was beginning to drip blood all over the floor, but also, he suspected, because she clearly recognised him as a fellow employee. Considering he'd only been in his new role a little over a month, he was surprised, but he wasn't about to complain.

Snagging the Clinical Governance Coordinator's position at

Auckland Med had been a dream come true. Providing high-level support to all the various hospital sub-committees, but in particular the Credentialing Committee and the Serious Events and Disciplinary Committees, the job tested Miller's mediation skills to the max. Cliques, politics, ethical dilemmas, and strong personalities were the norm. Throw emergency decision making into the mix and a million things could go wrong. The job wasn't easy, or predictable, and that's just how he liked it.

"Well, look who the cat dragged in." Cameron Wano sashayed into Miller's cubicle and plonked himself down in a chair. The charge nurse of the ER was decked out in hospital scrubs, a rainbow gauge in his ear, and green eyeshadow with black eyeliner to accentuate those shrewd tawny eyes.

The whole makeup gamut had never been Miller's thing, but it suited Cam down to the last sprinkle of glitter in his infectious smile. He possessed a searing intelligence, quick wit, and scalding tongue to rival the best. There was only one side of Cameron Wano that you wanted to be on, and Miller scraped onto that approved list by the skin of his teeth.

"By all means, take a seat." He offered Cam a bemused smile. "We missed Reuben at the game today."

Cam's fiancé and Auckland Blues and All Black star, Reuben Taylor played for the Blues, just as Miller had done in his day. Age gap notwithstanding, they'd run into each other at various rugby and sporting events over the years and struck up a friendship.

"Yeah, I've got him building a play gym for Cory." Cam rolled his eyes. "You know, for a guy who plays professional sport at the top of his game, the man can't follow a sheet of instructions to save his life. Our back porch looks like a LEGO giant threw up on it. Just as well I'm working. So what did you do this time?" He eyed the blood-soaked bandage.

"To be honest, I'm lucky I got out of your damn car park. Some woman with a stick up her butt threatened to file a complaint against me for using the accessible park, again. Said if I could walk, I should. Even took a photo."

Cam's mouth dropped open. "You're kidding me. But you—"

"I know. I know. But you'd be surprised how often it happens. I've even been accused of faking, lying about needing the chair—like ambulatory wheelchair users don't exist."

Cam huffed and shook his head. "I guess it shouldn't surprise me. There's ignorant arseholes everywhere."

A nurse in her early twenties popped her head through the open doorway and Cam waved her in with a smile. "Marie's gonna clean up that arm of yours before the doc takes a look."

"Hi." The young nurse sent Miller a nervous smile and went to wash her hands, hitting the handle on the pump soap so hard it popped out of the holder and clattered in the bowl. "Shit." Her face drained of colour. "Sorry. I shouldn't have sworn."

Cam laughed. "Don't worry. He won't bite."

"It's not him I'm worried about." She narrowed her gaze. "This is part of my assessment, right?"

"You'll be fine. Bonus points if you make him squeal."

Miller snorted. "Good luck with that. The last time I squealed I was twelve and my brother had just skewered my cheek with a fishing hook. Be as rough as you like," he told her, then cast a quick glance Cam's way. "Is Michael on today?"

A wicked gleam lit up Cam's eyes. "No, he's off. He and Josh are on a dirty weekend down Napier way, minus Sasha. Some people have all the luck."

"I somehow doubt you're pining away from lack of attention." Miller eyed him pointedly. "That man of yours has been off with a hamstring injury for two weeks. All that bottled up energy has to go somewhere, I imagine."

Cam waggled his eyebrows and fanned his face dramatically. "Don't I know it. It's a tough job but somebody has to do it. Stocks in lube are on the up."

Miller snorted, and Marie flushed scarlet and choked back a laugh.

Cam continued, "There's a spot in the corporate box if you want to catch the next Blues game with me." He watched Marie carefully swab Miller's wound with saline and caught the excess run off with a spare paper towel before it hit the bed. He three-pointed it into the bin and grabbed another. "The team would love to see you, even if Reuben's not playing. You'll have the pleasure of his stressed-out may-as-well-be-on-the-field, company. I could do with the buffer to be honest. He's a godawful spectator."

"Pfft. It's hardly like I know any of the team, anymore," Miller protested. "It's been ten years."

Cam's eyes darkened. "That's crap and you know it. Most of the guys watch the Wheel Black games whenever they can. And if not, Reuben makes sure they know what you guys are up to."

Miller blew out a sigh. "Yeah, I'll admit he's a good ambassador for the game. And the guys love it when he turns up to training to get his arse kicked in a loaner chair. But isn't the All Black camp coming up?"

Cam scowled. "The week after the game. Right when I've booked the damn cake tasting and florist appointments."

"I'm sure he's devastated." Miller bit back a smile.

Cam side-eyed him. "If I didn't know you better, Miller Harrison, I'd think you were taking the piss."

"Who me?" Miller ducked the balled-up paper towel Cam fired his way. "So, when is the big day again?"

Cam glared and folded his arms. "You know very well when it is. You've got a damn invitation."

"I have a very busy social calendar."

Cam snorted. "You have zero social life, Miller. If it isn't work or sport-related, you wouldn't know what to do with it. But for your information, our *wedding* is four months, one week, two days, four hours, and"—he checked his watch—"forty-seven minutes away. But who's counting?"

"You're clearly very chill about it." Miller ducked again, but this time the paper towel ball caught him on the ear. He grabbed it and chucked it back. He'd been hearing about the damn wedding from Reuben for months as the poor man did his best to keep a lid on Cam's surprising bridezilla streak, not to mention keep himself out of the firing line.

"Don't try and be smart with me." Cam eyed him with suspicion. "I know Rube's been talking. I'm just trying to be . . . organised. One of us has to be."

Miller swallowed another laugh. "Mm-hmm. I'm not sure if those were the *exact* words he used."

Cam pinched his bicep.

"Ow. Yep, yep. That's what he said. His darling Cam was . . . organised. Now I remember."

"Yeah, yeah. You're lucky I like you, Tap. And by the way"—he grinned like a Cheshire cat—"I assume you're bringing a date? I kept a free spot next to you at the table."

Fuck. Miller looked everywhere but those tawny eyes. The last time he'd taken a date *anywhere*, he'd had a zit the size of Mount Fuji on his chin and his voice had barely broken. Even then it had been on the down-low because of his rugby aspirations. His "date" had been less than impressed, deciding Miller hadn't even rated a tongue down his throat. Fair to say the relationship hadn't progressed.

Ten years younger than Miller, Reuben had smashed through all those barriers as the first out gay All Black, with Cam in tow. And although Miller was cheering from the sidelines, he knew it hadn't been easy for either of them. In Miller's world, there were still very few who knew he was gay. His team and his workmates were certainly in the dark.

He didn't hide it as such, he just didn't talk about it. And since he didn't date, there'd never been a need. Between working full-time, playing a tough sport with a gruelling training schedule, and aiming to get another Paralympics under his belt, he had little time for relationships. Plus, it had always seemed enough to deal with one stigma at a time. It just made sense.

But Cam wasn't letting it go. "It's either a date or I find a job for you on the day."

Miller's eyes bugged. "God, no. Shit. I mean . . . Believe me when I say you wouldn't want to trust me with *anything*. I'm crap at all that shit. Just shove me in a corner with a drink . . . please. It'll be safer for all concerned."

Cam gave a sly smile. "Nah, I'll find something. Leave it with me. And I'll make sure you know *exactly* how it needs to be done."

Fuck. Me.

"All finished." Marie taped a temporary sterile dressing over the wound. "It's clean and the edges are reasonably approximated."

Cam got to his feet and patted her on the back. "Good work." He turned to Miller. "I'll stitch it for you, but Nate will wanna take a look first. He shouldn't be long."

"Have I got time for a bathroom break?"

Cam glanced at his watch. "Should be fine. Use the staff one. They've just finished the renovation to give us more lockers and they made the bathroom accessible. It'll be more private. You know where it is?"

"I do. Thanks."

"My pleasure, gorgeous. And remember, wedding date or wedding job. The choice is yours."

Goddamn. Miller watched Cam's saucy arse swish down the hallway toward the nurse's station, drawing the attention of most eyes in the place. He was a force of nature and Miller didn't know whether to envy Reuben or feel for the guy. Yeah, nah. Definitely envy.

Manoeuvring around the smallish staff change room would've been easier with his canes, but Miller opted for the chair itself. The loose dressing on his arm was a bit dodgy, plus his leg wasn't getting any better. He was gonna have to ice that sucker most of the evening to have any chance of walking tomorrow. Elbow crutches might've given him a more stable option, but Miller had always preferred the simplicity of his canes.

The whole mission took longer than expected, however, and he wasn't paying attention when he hurriedly wheeled out of the change room door and straight into a man talking on the phone, about to come in. He winced in sympathy as his footrest caught the poor guy on the shin through a pair of skinny dark-wash jeans.

"Ow! What the . . . ?" The guy hopped backwards, holding his leg until he hit the opposite wall. "Slow the h-heck down, why don't you?"

Miller bristled. "I could say the same to you, buddy."

His gaze travelled up the long, long, lean body of a strikingly attractive man, still rubbing his shin and regarding Miller with open-mouthed disbelief.

"You ran into me, remember?" the guy said in a soft lilt, then frowned. "Shit. You tore the denim."

"Let's see." Miller wheeled forward and peered at the material. "Pfft. Hardly a tear," he scoffed. "More like a small hole."

The man arched a brow. "And, of course, that makes it so much better."

Miller was finding it hard not to stare. The guy was just so . . . different, with a slightly intriguing androgyny to his features that had Miller captivated. He looked to be in his early thirties with sleek blond hair and fair, soft skin that likely never saw a lick of sun without protection. Sharply defined cheekbones you could slice a melon on, highlighted languid brown eyes above, and full lips below —lips that glistened with something Miller didn't want to think too hard about because . . . damn.

The guy was arresting, to say the least, and Miller could barely drag his eyes away long enough to get pissy again. Because, yeah, he'd been a little reckless in his chair, but this bozo hadn't exactly been paying attention either.

He took a breath. "If you weren't too busy on your phone, maybe you'd have seen me coming through."

The man's gaze narrowed and lifted to the Staff Change sign on the door, then back to Miller. "As it happens, that's not a public room, *sir*, and seeing as how I don't recognise you as staff, I'm going to have to ask what you were doing in there?" He folded his arms across the soft grey wool jersey and striped scarf he wore, revealing elegant fingers tipped in pearl polish, a singular index tapping in annoyance.

Miller tried and failed to get his eyes off those nails. Goddamn, they were pretty. Not to mention those long, long fingers. Everything about the guy was long and slender, and Miller's imagination couldn't help but go there. A thousand snarky replies sat poised on the tip of his tongue, but not one of them made it past the dry lump in his throat as he watched that silvery tipped finger tap its irritation.

Somehow, he dragged his gaze upwards and was once again struck by the man's curious beauty. Separated into his individual components, he shouldn't have worked on any hotness scale, but put together, he was simply breathtaking, at least to Miller. A feeling he was not at all familiar or comfortable with.

"Sir?" the guy prompted, spots of colour blooming on those pale cheeks. "I really do need to know what you were doing in there?"

The irritated tone sparked Miller's own frustration. He was so done with this day. "Using the bathroom. Do you want to know how many sheets of paper I used so you can bill me?"

The man regarded him with a cool stare. "We charge by the roll." His lips twitched at the corner in what could have been a smile, and Miller almost let it go, almost.

He should have. The guy had a legitimate point, but instead, Miller rolled his eyes and bristled further. "Funny guy."

"I try." Those pretty eyes ran over Miller bringing a heat to his cheeks he hadn't felt in years. "If you need me to show you, there's a public accessible bathroom by the door to the waiting room." The man indicated down the corridor.

Miller's jaw set. "I'm perfectly aware of that." After the woman in the car park, he was so done with this day. "Any further questions, or can I get on with my day?"

The guy flushed a lovely pink and Miller almost felt sorry for him.

"I'm questioning you because you've got no lanyard and your arm's dressed. Because of that, I have to assume you're a patient. Are you saying you're staff?"

"Well, you know what assume does." Miller's lips curled. "And yes, I am currently a patient. But that doesn't rule me out from being staff as well, does it? So, if you'd just get out of my way, I'll go get some stitches in this wound."

The guy stepped forward, not exactly blocking Miller but not making it easy for him to spin away either. And it meant Miller had to crane his neck to keep eye contact, something he hated having to do. His temper sizzled.

"I'd like to be able to trust you weren't up to anything untoward" —the guy kept his voice patient, which Miller kind of had to admire, and even added the barest hint of apology—"but we've had serious breaches in restricted access this year and I'll need to see some identi- fication. Please." He extended an open hand.

Oh, for fuck's sake. Miller raked his gaze over the striking man. "Step back."

The guy's brows knotted. "What?"

"I said, step back. I won't have you looming over me. That's intimidation. Who the hell do you think you are? And if we're really going to do this, how about you let me see *your* identification?" He held his hand out.

The man's jaw worked as he studied Miller a few seconds before holding his lanyard out for inspection. Miller leaned in and was immediately engulfed in the scent of orange, and maybe cinnamon, with an undertone of hospital antiseptic. He swallowed hard and focussed on the ID.

Sandy Williams. RN. Forensic Pathology Assistant. Auckland Med.

Sandy Williams. He committed the name to memory, telling himself it was only professional interest. For all that Miller was pissed off, Sandy was only doing his job, what all staff were encouraged to do. If you're not sure, check it out. Something poked at Miller's memory, then disappeared just as quickly.

"Well, *Sandy*—"

"Something I can help with, gentlemen?" Cam strode up the hallway from the ER proper, his curious gaze shifting between Miller and Sandy. "You both look like you swallowed something nasty."

"Nothing you need to worry about," Miller muttered.

Sandy rolled his eyes. "I caught this guy coming out of the change room and was just wanting to check he was legit. He implied he's staff. Still haven't confirmed that, as it happens." He eyed Miller pointedly.

Cam bit back a smile. "Oh, he's not legit in more ways than we have time to discuss, sweetheart."

Sweetheart?

"*But* he is legit to use the staff bathroom. Miller Harrison has been a hospital employee for a month. He's our new Clinical Governance Coordinator. God save us all. I sent him this way myself."

Sandy's eyes widened and he blushed brightly. "Oh. Shit. Sorry."

Miller tried and failed to keep the smug smile from his face, even though all he really wanted to do was lick every inch of that blush and . . . where the hell had that come from?

"Apology accepted," he said.

Sandy's scowl deepened. "How very generous of you."

"So, I guess offering to buy you a coffee would be a no go?" Miller really, really needed to shut his mouth. He didn't want to coffee with this guy. He didn't.

Sandy flinched, looking appalled. "Thanks, but you're not my type."

Cam snorted while still staring at Miller like a bug under a microscope, and Miller could guess why. Cue the earlier discussion re his social life. He shot his friend a glare, then refocussed on Sandy while trying to ignore the sting of the man's rejection.

"Too banged up for you, am I?"

Sandy's eyes never even flickered. "Too much of an arsehole."

Another snort from Cam, accompanied by a warning boot to Miller's chair that said *back off* in no uncertain terms.

"You know very well you could've avoided that whole misunderstanding." Sandy eyeballed Miller hard enough to make his toes squirm. "'*I'm staff*' springs to mind as an eminently fitting response that might've saved everyone some time. Sorry, if I offended you, in any way. It wasn't intended." He looked genuinely apologetic. "Enjoy your day, *Mr* Harrison. Catch you later, Cam."

He kissed Cam on the cheek, ignored Miller, and headed out the back doors of the ER, leaving a cloud of indignation in his wake that settled over Miller like an accusatory finger. *Fuck.* Way to go, dickhead.

He didn't need to turn around to know Cam had him in his sights. He could feel the heat of that pissy gaze burning into the back of his neck like a laser.

"Well, it didn't take you long to fuck off the locals, did it?" Cam crossed his arms and stared Miller down. "Sandy is good people, Miller. The best. Plus, he's a friend. Don't be a fucking arsehole to him, or you'll have me to answer to."

Shit. "I'm sorry. He caught me at a bad time. I've had a hellish day and then he was all over me, wanting my ID."

Cam's lips flattened into a thin line.

Miller threw up his hands. "I know, I know. It's no excuse. I'll apologise, okay?"

"See that you do. And you should know better. Sandy's got good reason to be suspicious after all the shit that went down the first half of this year, so cut the guy some slack."

And suddenly it all fell into place, the thing that had been tickling his memory earlier. *Shit. Shit. Shit.* Auckland Med's forensic pathology department had been embroiled in a murder coverup that had only come to light when the new pathologist took over at the beginning of the year. There'd been a break-in at the morgue and record tampering, and Sandy's boss had almost been killed. No wonder Sandy had pushed Miller for some ID. And Miller had been a total dick in reply.

So what else was new?

"I see I've made my point." Cam nodded sharply, those gold eyes flashing. "Now, let's get those stitches seen to. The doc's almost ready." He crooked his finger at Miller, who followed without question like the little lamb he so absolutely wasn't.

CHAPTER TWO

SANDY SLIPPED HIS GLASSES IN HIS POCKET, PUSHED THE elevator call button, and hauled up the waist on his skirt for the millionth time, cursing his decision to buy the thing online sight unseen. He'd fallen in love with the pretty butter-yellow colour of the wool print that ended just above his knees and left his common sense in the back of his wallet. With smaller hips than eighty per cent of most women, he needed a belt, elastic, or some means to keep the damn thing up or it ended up slipping down till it hung off his dick— generally *not* the look he was going for.

Normally he wore scrubs—the autopsy room being no place for fashion—but Ed had decided they needed a spring-clean admin day halfway through winter, and who was Sandy to argue with his boss? They both felt the need to exorcise the place of any demons left from the fiasco at the start of the year, and Sandy had taken great pleasure in rearranging his entire office space to a fresh new look, including potted plants. He'd even sneaked a couple into Ed's office to give the man some of that nature he so craved.

Ed had returned the favour, surprising Sandy with one of his stunning photographic prints to hang in his office. To say he'd been touched was akin to saying the Grand Canyon was a nice hole in the ground. Ed was . . . circumspect, careful both with people and his affections. The gift was a big thing.

But the Murder in the Morgue caper, as they were wont to refer to it when it was just the two of them, had blown through all those buttoned-up emotions and cemented their friendship. And when Ed had fallen for Mark Knight, the outgoing, playboy detective involved in the case, the relationship seemed to have softened any remaining edges on the pathologist quite nicely, although Sandy could do without all the cutesy eye fucking and less-than-subtle innuendo that went down between them whenever Mark visited his beau at work.

Was he jealous? Hell yeah. And he was man enough to admit it. It had been a long time between drinks for Sandy in the love stakes. But that was a whole other story. And fuck if he was going to ruin a perfectly good early dismissal from work by dwelling on the seemingly endless run of dipshits he'd dated over the last few years. Although the term, *dated*, was a stretch. Tolerated was a much more accurate verb.

Sandy had given each one the benefit of the doubt, hoping for more than lustful curiosity. Praying there was more to their interest than the fact he caught their eye in whichever mode of dress he'd chosen at the time. It was the both/and option that usually proved too complex for most to deal with. He always seemed to end up being "too much work." Or, "I never know where I am with you." Or, "Can you not wear just jeans today?" Or, "Do you have to make it such a *thing*?" "Does it always have to be about you?"

That last was a joke. As if none of them were thinking about themselves with any of those questions, particularly their discomfiture at having a guy in a skirt on their arm in public. Every single comment was a big fat "Don't embarrass me" warning. Well, fuck that. Sandy tolerated that shit for more years than he cared to remember. There had been some good ones amongst the timewasters, but not enough to float his hope.

His mind slipped to the irritating blockhead he'd literally run into down in the ER three days before. Sandy was still wearing the bruise on his damn shin. Miller Harrison. The name was forever burned into his brain, and not only because he'd been such an arsehole. He was also seriously hot.

Not in the magazine-cover sense—a bit too rough around the edges, maybe—but that didn't make a lick of difference to Sandy. With a mane of wild red hair to his shoulders, brilliant green eyes, a strong, square bone structure, including a slightly crooked nose, and a cute-as-a-button smattering of freckles—the only thing cute about the jerk—Miller Harrison was seriously attractive. Not to mention there were some impressive shoulder muscles flexing under that tight, sweaty T-shirt with the words Auckland Freewheelers stamped on the front.

His breath quickened at the thought. Miller Harrison ticked boxes Sandy didn't even know he had. But *handsome* was zero excuse for arseholery.

The elevator doors rolled open just as Sandy got his skirt rearranged and his pretty cream short-sleeved jersey settled over top. He pushed the button for the third floor and moved to the back of the car to rest his tired back against the wall. He was done. A wine and a Netflix binge sounded pretty damn perfect.

He groaned at the ding signalling a stop on the first floor, and when the doors slid open, Sandy barely held back a groan. Miller fucking Harrison. *Son of a bitch.* The universe was conspiring against him.

All those gorgeous fiery locks had been tamed and slicked back into a tail that only served to pop those green eyes further, and the close-shaved reddish scruff just did it for Sandy on all sorts of levels. He wanted to feel it against his skin, have it rub up against his thighs in that burn he so loved. And dressed in a dark suit, looking all kinds of serious and capable, the man certainly looked delicious enough to eat. Not that Sandy thought of doing anything like that. The guy was an arsehole, after all.

Miller's chair was halfway in before he even noticed Sandy

standing at the back. They locked eyes for a second and Sandy was about to give in and acknowledge the guy, when Miller simply spun his chair, looked at the lit third-floor button, lowered his outstretched hand, and grunted something unintelligible.

It was all Sandy could do not to laugh at the sheer rudeness of it all. But as they waited for the doors to close and Miller continued to fidget in his chair, Sandy just thought, fuck it.

"Look, about the other day," he started. "I hope—"

"Forget about it." Miller barely cast him a sideways glance.

What? Sandy blinked slowly. Of all the . . . "Just to be perfectly clear, I wasn't apologising." Sandy set the arrogant sod right. "I had every right to ask for your ID."

Miller spun to face him and seemed about to say something when his gaze landed on Sandy's skirt, and his mouth shut like a trap. Sandy tensed and waited, but Miller's lips remained a thin line, his eyes wandering over Sandy's outfit, his expression unreadable.

The longer it went on, the more annoyed Sandy became. *Arsehole. I will not adjust my skirt. Let him look all he fucking wants.*

The elevator dinged and its doors rolled open. *Thank Christ.* He was desperate to leave that confined space and Miller Harrison's judging eyes. He didn't need that shit. He'd worked at Auckland Med long enough for most staff to typically ignore his occasional . . . difference. And at the ripe old age of thirty-four, he was past explaining himself to anyone. His friendship with Cam had taught him a lot about claiming who he was without apology, learning from the Yoda of sass.

He waited for a second so Miller could leave first, but when the man just sat there, Sandy sighed and started to move past. *Whatever.* He wasn't into playing games. He'd just stepped through the doors when he heard the squeak of rubber and a warm hand wrapped around his wrist.

"Just hold on a minute, will you?"

"Let go." Sandy shook his wrist free and turned, his ire bubbling bright at what he fully expected to be some kind of snotty commentary about his dress. He'd fought that battle more times than he cared to remember in his early years at Auckland Med, until eventually the powers that be had simply given up and pretty much ignored him. It wasn't exactly approval, but he'd taken it. If this dipshit thought he was going to turn that around, he had another think coming.

Miller sat with his chair half-in, half-out of the elevator, both hands raised, looking decidedly flustered. "Sorry. It's just . . . I . . ."

Was that a flush to his cheeks? Sandy hesitated.

"I should . . ." The doors tried to close and caught Miller's chair. "Fuck." He shoved them back, looked up at Sandy and . . .

Hell yeah, that was a flush. Sandy bit back a smile as the doors tried to close once again and Miller angrily pushed them aside, even though it was clear he could wheel himself clear anytime he wanted.

"Do you need something?" Sandy asked, struggling to keep a straight face. "I'd grab them for you, but I'd hate to offend, just in case. Oh, for fuck's sake." He threw his hand over the cavity to stop the door having a third go at Miller's chair.

"I don't fucking need your he—" Miller stopped mid-sentence, dropped his chin to his chest, and his shoulders began to shake.

Was he . . . ? Surely not. Horrified, Sandy didn't know what to do. Staff and visitors passed, throwing curious glances their way as Miller just sat there. Sandy was about to suggest they at least move away from blocking the elevator door, when Miller's head fell back, his chest heaving in fits of laughter, tears running down his face.

"Goddamn, I don't know what it is about you," Miller choked out between laughs as he wheeled himself free of the doors and across to the windows with their view over downtown Auckland.

Sandy let the doors close and followed Miller to where he sat, still chuckling.

"We've exchanged no more than a half-dozen sentences." Miller wiped at his eyes. "And you've somehow managed to get me so tied up in knots, I'm getting trapped in damn elevator doors. That *never* happens to me, just so you know. *Never*." He eyed Sandy as though daring him to argue.

"I hope you're not about to suggest any of that was my fault." Sandy fired him a stern look.

Miller threw up his hands. "Of course not. What do you take me for?"

Sandy merely arched a brow.

To his credit, Miller looked more than a little sheepish. "Okay, fair call."

Sandy grunted. "So what's the problem? If it's about what I'm wearing, you can go—"

"What? No!" Miller looked genuinely horrified. "It's a very . . . attractive colour on you."

A pretty adorable crease formed between Miller's brows as his eyes roamed over Sandy, all those freckles standing bright on his crooked nose. It took a second for Sandy to remember he was supposed to be pissed at the guy.

"I'm serious," Miller pressed. "I can't say I'm familiar with the whole guys-in-skirts thing—"

"Oh my god." Sandy rolled his eyes and spun on his heels to leave.

Miller rushed forward. "No, please, hear me out."

Sandy pulled up, his toes tapping on the scuffed linoleum floor. If Miller made a single derogatory comment, Sandy was going to nail his balls to his comfy desk on the fourth floor.

Miller blew out a sigh. "Look, I'm not judging you, I promise. I was just surprised, that's all. It's different from how you looked on Saturday, and it simply . . . caught me off guard. Not worse, not anything. Just . . . different."

Sandy didn't trust himself to speak. *Different* was not usually a compliment in his experience. He knew he was an acquired taste to some, including those in the community who wanted to shove him into boxes they could understand, boxes they belonged to: NB, fem, fluid, trans. In his own mind, he fit none of them, but he'd learned to live with people's need to sort him. They could label him however they wanted as far as he was concerned. He tore that shit off most days of the week. Fuck 'em, basically.

"Maybe we should start again?" Miller stuck out his hand. "Miller Harrison. Pleased to meet you."

He stared at Miller's hand for a good few seconds before accepting it. "Sandy Williams. And the pleasure is yet to be decided."

Miller snorted but kept a firm grasp. His touch was warm and dry, the callouses on his palm lightly scuffing against Sandy's smooth skin, as their gazes locked for longer than entirely necessary before Miller let him go. There was an intensity to those cagey green eyes that startled Sandy, but the interest they held was undeniable.

"Was that a subtle flirt, Mr Harrison?"

Miller smiled. "Meaning, I'm either gay or I like to walk a dangerous road in handshakes for a straight guy, huh? I thought you'd have guessed by the fact I offered to buy you a coffee on Saturday."

Sandy sent him a level stare. "Forgive me for needing to confirm. It was a simple question."

"And the simple answer is, yes, I'm gay. Though I'm not exactly out; well, not everywhere."

Sandy cocked a brow.

Miller shrugged. "It's complicated."

"It usually is."

"How about you?"

Sandy eyed him warily. "You're blunt, I'll say that for you."

"I'm not the only one."

Sandy snorted. It really was hard not to like the guy. "Touché. And if you mean do I like to fuck men for sex, then yes."

Miller almost choked on his tongue.

"The rest is undecided," Sandy added. "And I like it that way."

Miller nodded and swallowed hard. "Good for you. But now we've got that out of the way, would you please let me buy you a godawful coffee from the cafeteria to apologise?"

That wasn't a good idea any way Sandy looked at it, primarily because the yes part of his inner response came way too quickly for his liking. He sensed the beginnings of a crush and those never, ever ended well for him. Miller might be interested, but the man screamed alpha, chip-on-his-shoulder, masc male to the fucking rafters. And Sandy's experience with those types was that they always *thought* they wanted him, found him titillating and intriguing . . . until they didn't. Behind doors was great. In the light of day, not so much, and he'd had his heart bruised enough times to steer well clear.

Or not, apparently. "One," he answered. *Goddammit.*

They made their way to the staff cafeteria in silence, and Miller felt regret pouring out in bucket loads from the man walking next to him. Sandy's demeanour became increasingly awkward and uncomfortable, and okay, Miller felt a certain amount of responsibility for that. He'd led with his mouth, as usual, and Sandy hadn't deserved the attitude.

Still, he'd surprised Miller. People didn't usually stand up to him without knowing him better. He was brash, cocky, and had no problem using his physical presence, including his chair, to push his point about something. It wasn't that Miller liked control and having the upper hand, but . . . okay, he liked control and having the upper hand.

Sandy simply ignored all of that or didn't see it. Either way, Miller was intrigued. Not to mention when he was with Sandy, he felt like Sandy didn't even see his chair, just the arsehole in it, and that was so damn refreshing. Plus, Sandy riled up was all kinds of appealing, and Miller wanted to bask in that just a little bit longer—hence the coffee.

Sure, the clothes had thrown him for a minute, and to be honest, he hadn't been sure what to think. It wasn't that Sandy didn't look good, because he did. He looked smoking hot, in fact, and Miller didn't know what the fuck to do with that. He was so out of touch with anything and everything to do with his community, he may as well have been straight. He didn't know any guys who dressed like Sandy.

After the accident, Miller hadn't believed he could do justice to both learning to live with a disability *and* coming out and opted to take only one bull by the horns at a time. Trouble was, ten years down the track, he'd nailed the first and almost completely ignored the second, and Grindr was growing old. Or maybe it was just that Miller was.

They got their coffees and found a quiet table at the far end of the cafeteria. At least a half-dozen people called out a warm greeting to Sandy as he passed. He was clearly well-liked, and Miller remembered Cam had said much the same thing. So yeah, Miller might've been a little harsh in his judgement. Like that was a surprise. He might be an excellent mediator in his job, but in his personal life, Miller generally sucked. Case in point.

He made room for his chair at the table, wincing as a stab of pain flashed through his hip and thigh, yet again, and realising he was going to have to get it checked after all, dammit. Sandy didn't jump in to help but took his own seat and waited, and Miller liked that he respected Miller's capability.

But the awkwardness returned as Sandy made zero attempts at initiating conversation; the ball left very clearly in Miller's court. It was a position he generally avoided. Negotiation 101—it was always better to respond than to lead. More control that way. But if the twitch at the corner of Sandy's slicked-up lips was anything to go by, he'd read the same playbook as Miller. *Fuck.*

"So," Miller began.

Sandy arched both brows in expectation.

"I might owe you an apology."

"Might?" Sandy took a long swallow of his coffee, and Miller absolutely did not follow the movement.

He rolled his eyes. "*Do.* I *do* owe you an apology. I perhaps wasn't at my best when you ran into me in the ER—"

Sandy coughed.

Miller sighed. "When we ran into each other?"

Sandy bit back a smile. "Close enough. I guess I could've been watching where I was going a little better as well."

"This is true." Miller flashed Sandy a wide grin and picked up his coffee for a taste. He immediately pulled a face. "God, this is awful shit."

Sandy chuckled. "You get used to it. How's the arm?"

"Fine. Half a dozen stitches, nothing more. Stung a bit for the first couple of days, but it's good now."

"Must pull a bit when you're wheeling?" Sandy held his eye.

Miller shrugged. "Actually, that's not so bad. It's worse with my canes."

Sandy's eyes widened but he said nothing, and because he didn't ask, Miller wanted to explain.

"I'm an ambulatory chair user. I use it when I need to travel more than a few rooms or when I'm tired or playing wheelchair rugby. But around home, in my office, or for any short distances, I do just fine with canes. When we met in the ER, I'd just come from rugby, so I was kind of used up for the day. That's why I was in the chair. Otherwise we would've tangled with my canes, and truthfully, you might've got more than a bruised shin."

Sandy laughed. "I'll consider myself lucky. Was that your team name on your shirt, Auckland Freewheelers? I couldn't help but . . . notice." A red stain crept over his cheeks.

The guy was pretty damn cute. Miller twirled his coffee cup on the table between them. "Yeah. There are three Auckland wheelchair rugby teams, or quad rugby, as some call it. There's a national competition, and then there's the Wheel Blacks, the international team I play in as well."

Sandy's eyes popped. "Really? I've heard that's a pretty hard-core sport. Reuben has something to do with you guys, right? You're in a rebuild at the moment."

Miller nodded and a warmth spread through his chest knowing Reuben talked about them. "Yeah, he's a big supporter, watches when he can, and comes to some of our training. And rebuild is a good word. We didn't do so well at the last Paralympics and we're still middling in the ranks, but we're getting stronger."

"I imagine it involves a lot of training. Must be hard with the new job?"

"It is, but I love the sport and I don't mind the hours. It helps that I wrangled a thirty-five-hour week from the hospital when they offered me the position. But nothing feels better than doing it hard on the court. Reminds me I'm alive. What I'm capable of. Having said that, I'm getting a little long in the tooth. I'd like to get another one, maybe even two Paralympics in, but who knows. I don't bounce back like I used to."

"I'd guess we're about the same age." Sandy studied Miller.

"Thirty-five."

"Thirty-four," Sandy shot back.

He looked younger. All that gorgeous, soft, pale skin with not a weathered wrinkle in sight. Miller shrugged. "The sport's tough on your body. Some people play into their forties at the top level, but it's kind of uncommon. It really depends on how your body holds up, as with any sport. And we've all got different body issues to consider, as well."

"You don't play in ordinary chairs though, right?"

Miller laughed. "Hell no. You can't manoeuvre for shit in those, plus there's not enough protection. We've got specialty chairs, five to ten grand each."

Sandy blew a low whistle.

It hadn't escaped Miller's attention that Sandy hadn't asked a single thing about *why* Miller needed to use a chair or canes, and it impressed the hell out of him.

"Yeah, it sucks if you're a bit strapped for money," he said. "But we fundraise for those that can't afford it. That's where people like Reuben really help."

Sandy worried his bottom lip for a few long seconds. "I wouldn't mind watching . . . sometime, if it was okay?"

Miller stared. He didn't know what to say. The idea was both flattering and terrifying. "Really?"

A crease formed between Sandy's brows. "Yeah, why not? Sounds an exciting game." He side-eyed Miller. "Just because I look like an uncoordinated ostrich doesn't mean I don't appreciate sports. There's a lot to be said for watching a bunch of sweaty men throw a ball around."

Miller laughed. "There is, indeed. And you don't look like an uncoordinated ostrich."

"Liar," Sandy scoffed. "Besides, it's true. I suck at hand-eye coordination and ball skills . . . on the field, that is."

Miller hadn't been flirted with in so long he'd almost forgotten how fucking good it felt to know someone might actually be interested. "Now who's flirting?" he fired back.

Sandy's brown eyes sparkled. "Just keeping the playing field level, so to speak."

Miller studied Sandy as he took a final swallow of his coffee and then pushed it aside. "In the interest of full disclosure, I feel it's important to warn you that wheelchair rugby has mixed teams. So there'll likely be some sweaty women throwing balls around on the court, not just men."

Sandy shrugged. "I'm sure I'll cope. And actually, that's pretty cool."

"It is," Miller agreed. "They're bad-arse players as much as any of the men, sometimes more so."

The conversation drifted onto other topics. Miller asked about Sandy's job and his boss. Sandy raved about both, and Miller felt oddly irked by the genuine appreciation Sandy held for Ed Newton. He clearly loved his boss, even though Miller had heard the guy was a bit of a cool fish and hard to get to know. Mind you, it was becoming obvious how very easy it was to like Sandy. He was a complex mix of friendly and kind, but also assertive and straightforward—a hard combination to pull off, but somehow, he managed it.

And as Sandy chatted on, answering the endless questions Miller threw at him just to keep him talking, Miller couldn't stop his gaze flitting between those elegant pearl-tipped fingernails, slick lips, and dancing brown eyes. Nor could he keep his head from running circles wondering what the hell was up with him.

Miller didn't do this. He didn't flirt. He didn't crush. He didn't get infatuated. Hell, he was lucky if he lusted. That part of himself was so buttoned-down, it needed a fucking vacuum to get the dust off its gears. And he'd never done any of the above for a guy who rocked a damned skirt—a skirt that, by the way, made said guy sexy as all fucking hell.

"Miller?" Sandy stared, having obviously asked him a question.

"Sorry, I spaced out for a minute."

"No problem. I said I need to get going."

"Oh. Right. Of course." He checked his watch. *Shit.* They'd been talking for nearly an hour. He should've left for training ten minutes ago. He pushed his chair back as Sandy got to his feet, and Miller was once again struck by how good Sandy's legs looked in the skirt, and also that he must shave them.

Sandy held out his hand. "It was good to meet you, Miller. I'll be sure to take you off my arsehole list." His mouth curved up in a lazy smile.

Miller took his hand and watched those long fingers wrap around his. "Likewise. Perhaps we could do this again sometime?"

Sandy cocked his head. "That would be nice. Let me know about the next game, and maybe I can watch."

Miller's gut clenched. "Sure. We should exchange numbers, I guess."

Sandy's shining smile could've lit up a room and Miller felt a twinge of guilt knowing he'd likely not follow through. He wasn't at all sure he was ready to have Sandy in his sports world in any way whatsoever. Considering he wasn't out to his teams, it had bad, bad idea written all over it.

But when Sandy donned a pair of black-rimmed glasses before taking Miller's phone, every doubt he had disappeared in a cloud of hitherto unknown fetishising, as Sandy morphed into every fucking nerdish wet dream Miller had ever imagined. *Damn.*

They exchanged numbers with Miller's gaze glued to Sandy's face, the hint of a smile tugging at the corners of Sandy's mouth as if he knew exactly what was going on in Miller's mind. Well, Miller sure as hell hoped not.

Then when they were done, he watched Sandy's lean body glide through the cafeteria like his feet didn't quite touch the floor. He exchanged words with a couple of staff as he passed, those shapely calves drawing more than a few interested glances from women and men alike, who, like Miller couldn't seem to take their eyes off him.

Yep, Miller was definitely in trouble.

CHAPTER THREE

"Do these make my butt look big?" Cam stared over his shoulder at his reflection in the full-length mirror of the fitting room.

Sandy rolled his eyes for the millionth time that hour. "You've got a bubble butt to die for and you're wearing a tiny frou-frou silk and . . . what the hell is that stuff?"

"Black taffeta."

"Jesus Christ . . . silk and *black taffeta* thong, with not nearly enough material to warrant that eye-watering price tag hanging off it. So yes, it makes your butt look big, but in the best possible way. Happy?"

"Excellent." Cam preened. "Exactly the look I was going for. Reuben's gonna cream his fucking tuxedo."

"Oh, dear god." Sandy dragged a hand down his face. "Let's hope he can at least wait until after the ceremony."

Cam flashed a wicked smile. "We made sure to order a backup."

Sandy's palm shot out in front. "Stop right there. I don't want to know. Bad enough I'm having to witness . . . this." He waved a hand up and down in front of Cam, who was naked other than the ridiculous jockstrap which, okay, looked really, really fucking hot, but still.

"If anyone had told me a month ago I'd be spending my Saturday afternoon helping to choose your fucking wedding lingerie, I'd have unfriended them on the spot for tempting the painful jaws of fate."

Cam pouted, or glared—it was a close call. "But you're the only one I trust. You understand this shit's important. It doesn't matter that no one but Reuben knows there's something special under my outfit; *I* need to know it's there, right? It's me."

He looked strangely vulnerable and Sandy wanted to wrap his arms around his friend and reassure him. His gaze softened. "I *do* know it matters and we'll get it right, okay? But can we just speed the process up a bit? I have to eat something this century."

"But there's sooo many choices." Cam gathered the pile of silk and lace rejects into his arms and threw them into the air much to the horror of the poor sales assistant who'd had the misfortune to be available over three hours ago when they'd first walked into the shop. She'd erroneously thought Cam might be buying a gift for his bride. Like, really? Did the woman have no eyes in her head whatsoever?

Still, Sandy made a mental note to send her a thank-you card and chocolates, *a lot* of chocolates. Because sure as hell this wasn't getting solved today.

Cam frowned at the mirror, then turned to the poor woman. "I'm gonna have to think about it."

The sales assistant visibly drooped. "Of course. You can't make these sorts of decisions lightly. When did you say the wedding was?"

"Four months," Cam answered, doing another spin in front of the mirror. "I'm just not convinced about this one, although I have to say it's close." He fluffed the gathered taffeta at the back of the thong. "But I'm still hung up on the possibility of going with leather. Maybe even a harness. You know what I mean?"

The woman's eyes bulged. "Absolutely." It was clear she had no idea what Cam meant, and Sandy wasn't about to enlighten her. "I can see it's a difficult decision," she continued, plastering on a thoughtful expression that got ten points for effort. "And you still have time, as you say. No need to rush. Maybe you could make an appointment with our *senior* sales manager next time. She might have more options for your . . . fit."

Sandy smothered a laugh. Oh, she was good.

"Excellent idea." Cam missed the sarcasm completely. He turned to Sandy. "Take a pic, sweet cheeks, so I remember this one. But for God's sake, don't send it to me. Reuben's been trying to get a peek at all my planning shit for the last week. If the man wants a look, he needs to be prepared to do the hard graft of research and shopping, and we all know how that ends. Reuben and shopping go about as well together as a drag queen in a suit shop. But I guess he has other skills, right?" He winked and shoved Sandy out of the change room.

"Oh, you're *that* Cam." The assistant's eyes widened in recognition. "I've seen you on TV. You're engaged to that scrumptious All Black."

Cam rolled his eyes. "Or he's engaged to me. You could always look at it that way."

She laughed. "Quite right. I imagine you're a bit of a handful."

"Don't encourage him." Sandy slammed the curtain closed before Cam's peacock tail fully unfurled and whatever outrageous thing he was planning to say escaped his mouth. They were all better off not knowing what that was. "If his head gets any larger, he won't fit in my car for the ride home."

The woman laughed. "Oh, believe me, I understand *everything* now."

Sandy snorted in amusement.

"I heard that," Cam fired from behind the curtain. "I *was* gonna buy you a coffee for your help, but it's your treat now, *Mr* Williams."

Sandy winked at the assistant and shooed her off. "I'll handle Madonna here. Hopefully, for your sake, it'll be your day off when we come back."

She grinned, shoved a business card into Sandy's hand, and called back over her shoulder, "Nah, now I know, I wouldn't miss it for the world. This is gonna be fun."

Sandy shook his head. "Your idea of fun and mine have a few

galaxies between them." The strains of "Witchy Woman" floated from Sandy's pocket and he pulled out his phone.

"Tell Lizzie, hey," Cam called from behind the curtain.

"Darling sister, how are you?" Sandy purred into the phone.

"You still have that damn ring tone, don't you?" Lizzie growled.

"I plead the fifth, and Cam says, hey."

"We don't have the fifth and tell him hey back. And also that I'm still waiting for him to text me the colour of that eyeshadow he wore to the hospital fundraiser last month."

"Did you get that?" I asked Cam. Lizzie's personal volume button was permanently stuck on full, a hangover from the years she suffered with glue ear as a kid.

"Tell her, I'll do it tonight," Cam answered.

"He better," Lizzie grumbled. "I've got a hot date this weekend and I need to sparkle."

"Who's the guy?"

"Not telling. If he survives the first date, I'll give you the deets."

Good luck to him. Lizzie was a handful at the best of times, and her dreadful taste in men—arrogant and edgy—coupled with her own high standards around manners and not being a fucking prick, meant ninety per cent of her dates ended in disaster. But Sandy held out hope. Lately she'd been experimenting with broadening her target market and the odd nice guy was actually getting a look-in. When she landed the right guy, he'd never know what hit him. Sandy had no doubt Lizzie would be an awesome partner, if not a teeny bit . . . headstrong.

"To what do I owe the pleasure, sis?" He could see her rolling her eyes as clear as day.

"Daddy Dipshit is back in the picture."

Sandy's stomach dropped to his knees at the sound of the nickname for their father. "Wh-what? How come? Is Mum okay? If he's—"

"Save your wrinkled brow. Mum's fine. Apparently, he's living just north of Auckland. Has been for five or so years. Can you fucking believe it?"

"That close?" Sandy did his level best not to let the thought kick him in the guts. That his father had been within an hour drive of them for five years and never made contact. "I thought he was down south?"

"He was for a while. Anyway, he and Mum have been *talking* . . . for a few weeks, or so she says."

"Talking? What the hell does that mean?"

Lizzie sighed. "Your guess is as good as mine, but if it doesn't involve a fuckton of apologies and a mammoth amount of arse kissing on his part toward us all, but particularly you, I frankly don't give a shit and neither should she. To tell you the truth, I'm so fucking angry with her right now, I can barely speak."

Sandy dragged a hand down his face as Cam stuck his head between the curtains looking appalled.

"What the hell? Your dad?"

Sandy managed a nod.

"You okay?"

He shrugged and shooed Cam back into the fitting room. Twenty years without a word from his father and then this out of the blue? Lizzie got the odd letter and Christmas card which she duly threw in the bin. Sandy had no idea if his mother had kept in touch or if this was something new.

"Sandy?" Lizzie's voice carried concern.

"I'm still here."

"Okay, well, I just wanted to give you a heads-up, you know, in case it all goes to shit. She's talking about meeting the bastard for a coffee, some bullshit about regret and him wanting to build bridges. I kind of switched off after the first bit. You regret a parking ticket or missing someone's birthday. Turning away from your own son? That deserves a hell of a lot more than bloody regret." She paused. "Sandy? You there?"

"It's . . . I . . . yeah, yeah. I'm here." It was the best he could do.

After so long, he had no idea what to feel other than the unwelcome sting of a pain he'd worked so hard to bury. He'd paid his dues in therapy many years before and thought he was done with it. But with one call, like a damn splinter, he could feel those memories shift and start to make their way to the surface once again. Well, fuck that.

"Did Mum say what he wanted?" he croaked out.

"No." Lizzie's voice softened. "And to be fair, she didn't exactly sound overjoyed about the meeting either. But I think she wants to at least hear him out, you know, just in case."

"In case what?" The shock had started to wear off and anger seeped in to take its place.

"In case he's serious, I guess. I mean, I know at the time you blamed yourself, but their relationship had been shit for a while, you know that. Hell, we both lived through those fights, but Mum still took it hard when he left. He walked away from *all* of us, not just you. Remember how devastated she was? If she gets an apology, or maybe if he even owns *some* of what happened, it might make a difference to her, give her some closure."

There was some truth in that. His mother had taken years to recover, years to feel confident enough to even date again. Floyd Williams had just up and left while she'd been at work, clearing his share of their bank accounts, taking the best car, and leaving a note that simply said he couldn't spend any more time stuck with a life he didn't want. He wished them all the best and fucked off out of their lives forever.

Wished us the best. What the hell? It had taken years for Sandy to come to terms with exactly how little his father thought of them and to accept that Sandy himself wasn't to blame. Because it hadn't been just any random day his father had chosen to leave. It had been the day after Sandy had come out to them all at dinner. The day after the most hellish fight between his mother and father that ended with his mother locking herself in her room and his father storming out to stay at a friend's.

The day everything changed and Sandy learned what living his truth could really cost. He might not have been the sole reason his father left, or even the main one, but he was definitely on the list. They'd all lost something that day, and Sandy had decided, then and there, that he'd be damned if any of it would be in vain.

As far as he knew, his parents had divorced without another word being said between them. So, if his mother could get an apology, he guessed she deserved it, but Sandy had a ball of fear and anger lodged in his throat that wasn't going anywhere.

"She can do what she likes, it's entirely her choice, sis," he managed. "But I don't want any part of it. If an apology from that arsehole will help her, then I'm all for it. But it won't make a shit show of difference to me, and I'll be damned if I'll do anything to ease that fucker's conscience. I don't want to know. Tell Mum whatever she chooses is fine with me, but keep me out of it, okay?"

"But Sandy—"

"*Okay*, Lizzie?"

She hesitated. "Yes. I'll tell her."

"Thanks."

"Are you still talking about me?" Cam flung the curtain open and broke the tension. "Because I totally understand if you are."

Sandy recognised a good distraction when he saw one. "I've gotta go, sis. Talk to you later." He hung up and eyeballed Cam. "How much of that did you hear?"

Cam's expression softened. "Everything. You wanna talk about it?"

Outside of Sandy's family, Cam was the only one who knew the whole fucked-up story. "Not particularly," Sandy told him. "Just get me out of here."

But Cam waited instead.

"Fine," Sandy huffed. "My dad has popped up out of nowhere wanting to make amends, apparently, and I couldn't give a shit. Can we go now?"

Cam pulled him into a hug that Sandy fought for about five seconds until he melted against Cam's shoulder and let himself be held. "Don't make me talk, please," he pled. "I just can't right now."

Cam squeezed him tight and then stepped back and straightened Sandy's jacket. "Okay." He hooked his arm through Sandy's and steered him toward the door. "Let's feed you instead, before you evaporate into a toothpick. There's not enough fat on these bones as it is."

Sandy elbowed him hard. "I'm fine just the way I am. But yes, please, and it's back to being your treat after what you've put me through this morning."

Cam rested his head on Sandy's shoulder. "Aw, don't be like that. You love me."

Sandy kissed him on the cheek. "I do. But that doesn't mean you're not annoying as fuck. Now, dust the cobwebs off that credit card, bitch, because I'm in the mood for seafood and a view over the water."

"So, word has it you and our esteemed new governance coordinator were seen canoodling in the cafeteria last week." Cam wiped a smudge of sauce off his lips and stretched out in his chair. "And then again yesterday, I believe, after end of shift on a Friday, no less, when every good little *single* gay boy should be heading home to jump on Grindr or dust off their sequins, not that I know anything about that anymore."

They'd snagged a table next to the window in the Viaduct Basin at Sandy's favourite seafood restaurant. Beneath them, a flotilla of boats bobbed alongside the pier, the brilliant sun dancing sparks atop the olive-green water of the harbour quay. Winter cool but pretty damn perfect.

"Canoodling is such a wanton word." Sandy pushed his plate with its three remaining prawns aside and patted his belly. "Who's been talking?"

"Who hasn't?" Cam scoffed. "I was pretty sure you two hated each other after your first encounter, which was even better in the retelling to Reuben, I might add."

Sandy shook his head. "We just got off on the wrong foot. I ran into him three days later and he offered to buy me a coffee to apologise."

"Aha. And the second time?" Cam waggled his eyebrows.

Sandy's cheeks warmed. "We get on . . . surprisingly well. And that second meeting was pure chance. I went to grab a sandwich for Ed, who was working late, and Miller just happened to be there. We barely talked five minutes. No need to make a big deal about it."

He refilled their water glasses to avoid Cam picking up on his slight fudging of the truth. He'd only *run into* Miller because he'd seen the back of his chair disappear into the cafeteria as Sandy was headed to the lab, and he'd followed. The sandwich for Ed was a last-minute excuse to offer Miller for Sandy being there. So sue him.

Miller Harrison was worth a detour for the eye candy alone. They'd chatted about the hospital car park being dug up, how good the lunch lasagne had been the day before, and how Sandy wanted to blow the fuck out of Miller's dick if he was given half a chance. Okay, that last part only happened in Sandy's mind . . . on repeat . . . most of the rest of the day.

Cam studied him for a good few seconds, making it clear he saw straight through Sandy's bullshit. "Riiiight. And hell yeah, I'm making a big deal about it. I've rarely known Miller to *get on* with *anybody* outside of his job, which he is remarkably good at considering his talent for keeping people at a distance in his personal life."

"He told me he was gay but not *out* everywhere. Whatever that means."

Cam sighed but looked relieved. "Yeah, well, I'll let him explain that. Reuben knows the guy better than me. All I can say is he doesn't hide it from us or his family, and I guess that includes you now as well. But that being said, I have never, and let me say that again in case you missed it, *never* seen him with another gay man other than us lot, or even heard him talk about a guy in that way, *ever*. Reuben thinks he's ace. I just think he's an arsehole on a good day, although I like him, a lot."

"Well, I don't know about him being ace, and you can keep your labels to yourself by the way." Sandy smiled over the top of his water glass. He loved guys in bed, exclusively, and was happy with he/him pronouns, but other than that, he was never quite sure where he fitted. "What I want to know is, apart from the fact he's a bit gruff, would you say Miller's an okay guy? I feel after so many deadbeats, I can't trust my judgement anymore."

Cam thought on that. "I think he'd disappear in a puff of mortified smoke if you said the words gay pride too close to him. And he wouldn't know a gay bar if he fell over the pile of ripped booty shorts outside."

Sandy laughed. "So he's not exactly active and political in the community?"

Cam choked on his water. "You might say that." He wiped his chin. "But he's safe, if that's what you're asking. Trustworthy. But Lord knows you have to be pushing his boundaries, sugar." He smiled conspiratorially. "Miller might be gay, but he's hardly a spokesman for our ever-expanding alphabet of genders and sexuality. I suspect he barely gets past the first two letters of LGBTQIA. He's not bigoted, just completely out of touch. Has he said anything, asked any questions?"

Sandy shook his head. "Not yet. Kind of surprising, to be honest, and I haven't offered. But I think there's still a dent in the floor of the elevator, from where his jaw hit it the first time he saw me in a skirt."

"Huh." Cam thought about that for a moment. "No questions. Okay, so maybe there's some hope for him yet." Another lengthy study from those tawny eyes. "I'd say go for it, especially if you like your eye candy with a fair whack of chilli on the side. It's more of a concern that he never does *anything* except work and wheelchair rugby. In fact, Reuben was meant to watch one of his games this afternoon, until he got called to a press thing."

Miller was playing today? Sandy tried not to take it personally that Miller hadn't told him in their conversation the day before. Maybe he'd just forgotten, or maybe he didn't want Sandy to feel obligated to watch?

Cam continued, "That damn sport is the love of Miller's life, or it may as well be."

"So, where do they play, his team, I mean?" Sandy did his best to sound casual, but yeah, epic fail.

Cam eyeballed him. "Peterstown Gym. Three thirty kick off. You can get there if you push it. And what the fuck, sweetheart? Does that mean you're genuinely interested?"

"Yes. No. Maybe." Sandy slid him a knowing smile.

Cam snorted. "Well, I'll say something for you. You don't make it easy on yourself. The man has the charm of a rattlesnake."

"He's challenging."

"He is."

"He's hot."

"He is."

"He's stimulating to talk to."

"He is."

"And he's funny."

Cam frowned. "He is?"

"Yes, he is. But yeah, he's also kind of . . . brusque and shut off at times."

"Hah." Cam stabbed a finger Sandy's way. "The fact you're even using a qualifier like *kind of* shows he's letting you in more than he lets most people, so that's promising."

"Really?" The idea sent a warm shiver through Sandy. "I just don't want another Ricky or Todd or fucking Jeremy. I am so over guys who just want to fuck me for the novelty and then move on."

"Preach it." Cam put his hand up for a fist bump and Sandy obliged. "Do you need to know anything more? He used to play for the Auckland Blues. That's how Reuben got to know him."

"Nope." Sandy didn't even have to think about it. Although it was interesting to know Miller hadn't always used a chair. "If he wants me to know, he can tell me. I want to see if he opens up. That'll determine my interest. I am so over babying guys through their puberty of emotional expression."

Cam sighed and stared out the window. "Yeah. Fucking men, right?"

Sandy followed his gaze. "Who'd fucking love them?"

"Us," they both said and clinked their glasses.

Miller stood at his office window, stared at the gorgeous day happening outside, and wondered for the millionth time why the hell he was spending yet more Saturday hours at work. He could've gone for a drive, a swim, had lunch somewhere, anything but bang his head against the brick wall of a misconduct complaint against the hospital's Chief Orthopaedic Surgeon.

The surgeon in question wouldn't even return Miller's calls, citing by text that patients came before any *administrative issue*. Miller was two breaths away from conjuring up some of that free time the man so clearly needed by recommending he was suspended until the hearing. But before making that rash call, he stepped away and decided it could wait until Monday.

It wasn't a competence/safety issue, after all. It was about the surgeon being an impatient arsehole to a stressed-out family who'd needed answers and understanding, not arrogant fob-offs and an argument with the patient's brother that came close to fists. Goddammit, Miller had to wonder at times if an even passable bedside manner ever made it onto the bullet points for medical school interviews. Some days, he couldn't see it.

His phone buzzed in his pocket with a text from Jimmy.

We've been bumped thirty minutes by a netball game running late. Kick off now at four. Team beer after the game.

Shit. Miller wasn't sure his leg would stand for any after-game shenanigans, and that was without the hits he was sure to take that afternoon. He'd even made an appointment with his specialist and team doctor on Thursday. He stared at the screen, then texted back. ***Not tonight, sweetheart. I feel a headache coming on***.

Pussy. Jimmy's standard answer to anything that wasn't what he wanted to hear. ***Better bring your A game. The Steamrollers have roped in Ascot.***

Bugger. Miller's stomach dropped. Ascot was a fellow Wheel Black. A young twenty-four-year-old with shoulders like fucking steel and zero fear. Miller could almost remember those days. A great guy to have on your team. Miserable to play against. Miller was in for a hard game.

He swallowed another couple of ibuprofens dry to get a level going so he'd survive the game and then tried to remember just how long he'd considered that standard operating practice. Too damn long. But the thought of giving up at any level, regional or Wheel Black, was unthinkable. This was what he did. It was who he was. You overcame, you persevered, you triumphed over adversity, you prevailed. You didn't let it beat you down, you didn't let it win. He couldn't keep going forever at Wheel Black intensity, but the reality of that day's approach was an expanding black hole he avoided thinking about at all costs.

Before he could pocket his phone, it chimed with another call. This one from his father. James Harrison might be a little intense, but he was Miller's number one fan and largely responsible for Miller making it through that first year after the accident without losing himself to the depression that threatened his recovery.

"Hey, Dad, what's up?"

"I can't get to the damn game because your mother double-booked a dinner with the Morton's."

Miller snorted. "Mr 'I can get you a good deal on a new Toyota' Morton?"

James snorted. "The same."

Miller laughed. "No problem. It's just the regional ladder, Dad. You don't have to come to them all."

"I know, but I like to be there. I wanted to see how you were looking out there. You've got that fitness test coming up. Can't afford to ease off the hammer now. Have you been doing that new weight regime I found to build your core strength? It should help—"

"Dad, stop. I got the email and I'm having my fitness guy take a look. I can't just add random things to my routine. It has to check out."

"I know but—"

"Dad, please."

"Okay, okay. I get the message."

The phone went silent and Miller let it hang. His dad meant well, but the constant pressure had grown old a long time ago. He was hugely proud of Miller, to the point that Miller sometimes wondered exactly who benefitted the most from Miller's sporting success. *Nope. Don't even go there.*

"Anyway, I just wanted to say good luck for the game, son. I wish I could be there. I hear Ascot's playing."

"Yeah. He'll keep me on my toes, metaphorically speaking."

Miller's father laughed. "You can take him. Just go hard. He's weaker on defence than you guys give him credit for. I think he needs to up the specs on his chair."

Miller kept his mouth shut. Ascot Prentice had very few weaknesses, and defence certainly wasn't one of them.

"Before I go, your mother wants to speak to you."

"No, wait—" But he'd already gone, and Miller held back the groan.

"Miller?"

"Hey, Mum." He brightened his voice. "How are you?"

"Fine. I just wanted to remind you about Dane's fortieth party next month. Check if you've ordered the wine."

Shit. Miller had, of course, completely forgotten. Of his two brothers, he was closest to the eldest, Dane, who ran a Greek restaurant in Auckland, along with his Greek wife, Chloe, and their two teenage kids, Nicole and Sam. The middle brother, Trent, owned a landscape business in Hamilton and only made it to Auckland every few months or so.

"No, of course I hadn't forgotten," he lied.

"Rubbish." His mother laughed. "I know you too well."

"To be fair, he forgot mine this year, so I refuse to feel bad about it. I'll get onto the wine tomorrow. What else can I do?"

"Nothing. I've had this organised for weeks. But keeping your brother from trying to cater his own party is doing my head in. He keeps sending me these *helpful* texts. So, if he says anything to you, tell him I won't be happy if he tries to turn up with *any* food. He can have a damn day off for a change."

Miller chuckled. "I'll pass the word. You sure I can't bring anything else?"

His mother hesitated. "Well, you could bring a . . . friend, if you'd like."

Oh, Lord. "A friend?" he teased. "Really, Mum?"

She flustered. "You know what I mean. A man. A date, for heaven's sake. After all, I'm not getting any younger."

"You're sixty-two, Mum. I'm only thirty-five. Not to mention, taking a guy to your parents' house for lunch, in no way and in no form, constitutes a *date*. A favour, a service to humanity, an obligation, a test of fortitude, a blatant attempt at impressing, but never a date. Besides, there's plenty of time for that."

His mother tut-tutted. "That's what you say now, but I'm ageing by the day. Before you know it, I'll be pushing a walker and incapable of babysitting those grandbabies you're going to supply us with, and then you'll be wishing you got started a lot sooner. Plus, your sperm are best before forty, everyone knows that."

Miller choked back a laugh. "What the hell? Who, Mum? Who knows that? No one. That's who. And who said I was supplying you with *any* two-legged mortgages? I may never roll that way, pun intended."

"Well, you won't if you don't start dating, that's for sure—"

"Oh, look at the time, I have to go or I'll be late for the game. Love you to bits, Mum. See you next weekend." He blew a couple of kisses down the phone and hung up on her laugh. Stubborn persistence was a Harrison trait, and the force was strong in his mother.

Before he left the office, Miller lodged a reminder in his calendar to buy a present for his brother and order the wine. Then he gathered his gear into the satchel hanging off his chair and headed out. If he was lucky, he'd have enough time to grab a snack from a drive-through on the way to the gym.

CHAPTER FOUR

SANDY WAS BEGINNING TO WONDER IF HE WAS IN THE RIGHT place. He was sure Cam said three thirty, but it was three forty and he was still watching the tail end of a netball game between two badly matched teams with a twenty-point difference on the scoreboard.

Thrilling, it wasn't, though if he were into women, he imagined a few on the court might've made the wait worthwhile. But none of them ticked the boxes currently lodged in his brain—green eyes, red hair and scruff, delicious shoulders, a sharp enough tongue to cut through most bullshit, and a hole somewhere inside that Sandy couldn't quite put his finger on.

He hoped he wasn't making a mistake turning up unannounced, but it was a public game, after all. Not like Sandy was breaking any team rules or anything. He was happy to just watch and leave. He didn't have to interact with Miller at all, especially since he wasn't out to his team, and Sandy definitely screamed gay from every mois-turised pore on his body. To that end, he'd picked a spot at the top of the bleachers, well out of the way, and waited.

The buzzer sounded the end of the game, and the netball teams cheered and did their huddles and were off the court in five minutes. A group of people then set up cones for what had to be the wheel-chair rugby coming up next. Sandy blew out a long sigh, his nerves spiking for reasons he didn't want to think too closely about.

He fucking liked this guy and there was no rhyme or reason for it. Sandy didn't chase guys, didn't turn up randomly at their sports games when he hardly knew them, didn't risk putting himself out there like this, didn't . . . well he just didn't. Miller was everything Sandy wasn't. Masc, hugely sporty, academic, brusque, uneducated in a lot of queer political shit, and somewhat closeted. Yeah, especially that last one. But Sandy couldn't help it. He just liked the guy. Go figure.

A minute or so after the cones were laid out, a hubbub of voices floated up from the locker room, loud, ribald, and full of swagger. Along with the clank of metal on metal, a dozen or so players then appeared on court, high-fiving and talking bullshit while bumping and shoving their low-backed, solid-hub sport chairs into each other with obvious amusement.

Miller drew Sandy's eye immediately, his wild red hair bouncing free as he struggled to wrestle it into a scrunchy. He stood out from the rest of the players like a damn beacon, and not just because of his hair. The effervescent energy he radiated was almost electric, magnetic. Team members circled him like a fucking sun, and Sandy got it. He couldn't take his eyes off him either.

Then, just as Miller finally got his hair tamed, a teammate flew past and yanked the scrunchy off again, haring up to the other end of the court with Miller in hot pursuit. Miller sideswiped the guy, sending him to the floor.

Sandy gasped in horror as Miller grabbed the scrunchy from the hand of his downed teammate and then flipped him off before leaving him flailing on the gym floor.

What the ever-loving hell? Was Miller just going to leave him there?

Sandy was on his feet without even thinking, ready to head down to the court and give Miller an earful, when the guy on the floor finally got his chair upright amid a string of profanities all directed at Miller who simply laughed along with everyone else on the court. The guy wheeled up to Miller, high-fived, and the two then jostled for position.

Sandy retook his seat and shook his head. Fucking jocks. They were all the damn same.

The two teams split the court to warm up, and then it was all on. Miller's team had two women on it: a tall blonde in her twenties who flew around the court like she owned it, and a heavier-set redhead whose role seemed to involve engaging and ramming opposing chairs out of the way if the Freewheelers had the ball. The opposing team had a single woman, also super slick on her wheels.

The remainder of both teams were a mix of size and varying physical challenges, but the way they all committed their bodies one hundred per cent to the full-contact game had Sandy hissing through his teeth and flinching in his seat. It was full-on, no quarter given, and fucking exhilarating to watch.

Miller was clearly one of the most skilled players: receiving impossible throws, rocketing up and down the court, blocking and slamming the opposition like they were chess pieces on a board, those massive shoulders flexing and bunching, sweat pouring off him, expression awash with pleasure, fully alive and sexy as fuck.

It was in stark contrast to the arrogant, prickly man Sandy had first met, and he was transfixed. But he knew Miller had to hurt at the end of a game like this; they all must. The injury to his arm also made a lot more sense as Sandy watched limbs tangling with chairs as they fell on the floor and scrabbled to right themselves—wheels, guards, and front bumper things connecting with naked flesh. Jesus Christ, they were lucky any of them could get out of bed the next day.

He pulled a bag of pineapple lumps from his satchel and popped a couple in his mouth, relishing the hit of chocolate and fruit.

"Impressive, isn't it?" A dark-haired woman in her thirties with deep blue eyes and a pretty smile took a seat close by. She threw out her hand. "Robyn Walker."

Sandy took it. "Sandy Williams."

"Pleased to meet you. I'm the wife of one of those fools down there, for my sins. If you don't mind me saying, you have that stunned mullet look of a virgin spectator." She chuckled. "I still remember the first time I saw a game. Thought I was going to be sick watching Beau crash out on the floor time and time again. You know someone down there?"

Sandy nodded. "Miller Harrison. Would you like one?" He held out the bag of pineapple lumps and Robyn helped herself to a couple.

Then she chuckled. "Tap, huh?"

"Tap?" Sandy frowned.

"His nickname. It comes from his hard-hitting approach to the game. If his chair hits your one, you know it. The players call them his love taps. That's where it came from."

Sandy laughed.

"Beau and he are teammates in the Wheel Blacks too. Your friend's the best on court today, other than maybe Ascot—he's the young guy on the other team, and also a Wheel Black, as is Jimmy, the big guy on the far side playing for the other team. Miller's been to two Paralympics and aiming for a third. He's a tough nut."

Miller chose that moment to connect with an opposition player, and Sandy cringed. The clash of steel on steel echoed around the gym as the man crashed out and Miller throttled past to score.

"So I see." He blew a breath of relief.

Robyn fired him an understanding look. "Don't worry too much. The best thing about watching them play this ridiculous sport is that it buries any and all inappropriate sympathy bubbling inside you. After that first game of Beau's, I never offer him help with *anything* unless he asks for it. Anyone who thinks this sport is fun won't appreciate anything more."

Sandy tucked that bit of advice away to mull over. As a natural helper, he usually didn't operate like that, so he took her point.

Another crash of steel accompanied by gutsy swearing from one of the women players only served to underline her point.

Robyn smiled his way. "Tough doesn't begin to cover it. You want a brief rundown on the game?"

"Please."

She shuffled closer. "Okay, it was first developed in Canada by athletes living with quadriplegia. That's why it's still called quad rugby in the States. And I guess you know its nickname, murderball? Most people do."

Sandy nodded. "And I'm beginning to appreciate exactly how it earned that name."

Robyn laughed. "Yeah, it can be pretty brutal. There's a maximum of twelve players on each team, but only four players are allowed from each on court at any one time, and each game has four eight-minute periods. Substitutions can only happen during a stoppage in the game.

"A goal is scored whenever someone carries the ball across the line marked by those cones. If you have possession of the ball, you have to dribble it or pass it every ten seconds, and you have twelve seconds to get it from your back court to the front court and forty seconds to score—that's what makes it such a fast-paced game."

Robyn suddenly sprang to her feet. "Callum, get your arse moving," she yelled. A curly-haired young man glanced up with a grin and flipped her off.

The woman was clearly a firecracker.

She sat and continued. "It's a full-contact sport as in chair contact but not direct physical contact, and there are rules around that. Chair hits are an integral part of the game—hence the shape of the chairs with those front bumpers or pickbars. There are offensive and defensive chairs, and there's actually an anti-tip device at the back. It doesn't always stop them arseing over, but the players *are* strapped in and the chair framework acts somewhat like a roll cage."

"Yes!" Sandy's gaze fixed on Miller, who'd just scored another goal, and it was all he could do not to leap up and fist pump the air.

"How do they make sure the teams are evenly matched? There's obviously a whole range of physical abilities reflected on court."

There were players with full arm and hand control and players without. Some living with amputations, some with spinal cord injuries, and then there was Miller, who didn't always use a chair.

Robyn groaned as the other team scored a goal, then answered. "There's a point system, but you need some loss of function in at least three limbs. Each player is assessed and given a point value based on their functional ability—0.5 being the lowest functional level to 3.5 the highest. The total classification level you can have on court for your team at any one time is eight points. How you get there is up to you. So if you have two three-point players on court, your other two can only add up to two points in total, get it?"

"Got it. What's Miller?"

She smiled. "Tap's a 3.5-point player. Since he can walk with other aids, it means he has great stability in the chair. He's a hugely important playmaker. But he takes up 3.5 points so the other three players on with him can only add up to 4.5 together. Anyway, there's a heap of other rules around fouls and possession and stuff, but those are the basics."

"Thanks. That helps a lot." Sandy held out the bag of pineapple lumps.

Robyn shook her head. "Do you mind if I stay and watch the rest with you?"

"I'd love it." Sandy turned back to the game only to find Miller had been subbed off and was now staring up at him with an unreadable expression on his face. *Shit.* He chanced a wave, which Miller answered with barely a lift of his fingers before turning his back to talk to a teammate alongside.

Sandy should maybe have taken Miller's less than exuberant acknowledgement as a signal to leave, but he wasn't scared off quite that easily. He'd told Miller he wanted to watch a game and he'd damn well watch a bloody game. It was a free country.

Robyn caught the exchange and shot Sandy a curious glance but said nothing.

After another two bone-crushing quarters, Miller's team took the win by a half-dozen points and Sandy gathered his things to leave. He'd seen what he'd come to. No need to poke the bear. He'd escape via the side door and leave Miller to it. But at the bottom of the bleachers, Robyn grabbed his hand.

"Come and meet the team."

Sandy jerked free. "No, but thanks. I wouldn't want to interrupt. I only stopped by to take a look. Miller didn't know I was coming. I'm not sure he's happy about it, to be honest."

"Rubbish. The boys love it when people come to watch. I'm sure Tap's delighted you came."

Sandy wasn't. Not at all. He caught a look Miller shot him and there wasn't much of a welcome in it as far as he could tell. Damn. He tended to go with his gut about stuff like this, but maybe he should've shown a little more caution this time. After all, he hardly knew the guy. But before he could get himself out of there, Robyn retook his hand.

"Come on." She pulled him toward the team before he could stop her. Most of the players had a water bottle jammed between their lips, including Miller. But unlike the others, Miller's eyes were locked on Sandy.

And no, Sandy wasn't going to run with that image . . . much.

"Hey, Tap. Look who I found in the bleachers." She dropped Sandy's hand. "Guys, this is Sandy. He was looking a little lost, so I schooled him up—wheelchair rugby 101. Shame you fumbled those couple of passes, Tap. Missed a chance to show off." Her eyes brimmed with mischief and Miller took a second from staring at Sandy to shoot her a glare, which she duly ignored.

The team immediately turned their attention to Sandy, mostly curious, but there were a couple of raised eyebrows in the mix and one decided sneer. Yeah, the almost see-through floaty orange shirt hanging loose over his tight black jeans was probably not typical spectator fare. He'd dressed to shop not to rough it in a gym.

He ignored the stares and focussed on Miller, whose gaze was also roaming the sheer shirt with a look Sandy understood only too well. Maybe it hadn't been such a bad choice after all. But then the crease between Miller's brows deepened as he checked out his teammates' reactions, and Sandy's hope evaporated.

Goddammit. Just when he was beginning to like the guy. He stepped closer and dropped his voice so only Miller could hear. "Hi. Cam told me you had a game today, so I took a chance on dropping in. I hoped it would be okay, but I'm guessing maybe not?"

Miller said nothing for long enough to classify as awkward and for his team to notice the tension between them, and heat rose in Sandy's cheeks. "Okay, well, I guess that answers that. You're back on the arsehole list by the way. I'll leave you to it—"

"Sandy, nice to meet you." A guy about Miller's age, with equally broad shoulders and an even bigger toothy grin, pushed forward to interrupt Sandy's big fuck-you exit and threw out his hand. "I'm Beau. And I'm sure I speak for all of us when I say we weren't really sure Tap had any *actual* friends other than Reuben, so you come as somewhat of a relief. He's a surly bastard, right?"

Sandy accepted Beau's hand, grateful for at least one person's welcome. "Nice to meet you. And yes"—he shot a glare at Miller—"he definitely is."

Beau cast Miller a teasing look. "We're not holding out hope for a girlfriend though. No one worth their salt would put up with his ornery arse."

Girlfriend? "Yeah, I can't imagine any woman tolerating his shit." Sandy arched a brow Miller's way and the man's cheeks pinked. The guy looked so damn uncomfortable it was hard not to laugh.

The team started packing up, and a few others came forward to shake Sandy's hand, but Miller remained rooted to the spot.

"Well, I'll leave you two alone." Beau shot one last look at them and then wheeled toward the locker room along with the rest of the team, leaving Sandy scrambling for composure under Miller's ongoing silence.

The man was behaving like a world-class dick. Not to mention rude as fuck.

He sighed and steeled his nerves. "I wasn't going to out you, in case you were worried."

Miller shook his head, his face still a mask. "I wasn't. It's not like I'm in the closet, anyway."

Sandy arched a brow pointedly.

"I'm not," Miller whispered.

"Really?" Sandy folded his arms. "Then why are you whispering?"

Miller's lips pressed in a straight line. "It's just never come up. Why should I have to share my sexuality with them?"

Sandy held up his hands. "I'm not saying you should. Believe me, I get it. That's totally up to you. All I said was, I wasn't going to out you if you were at all concerned. And to be honest, I'm not sure if you're unhappy about me being here—since you clearly are—because I stepped over a friendship line somehow, or because I'm so fucking *not* straight that I might get them thinking about you. Either way, you can rest easy, because I won't be coming again."

Miller opened his mouth and then closed it again as a teammate wheeled behind him. "I just . . ." His gaze swept the gym.

Sandy sighed to himself. He wasn't sure he was up for this.

"Okay, so maybe I'm more in the closet than I want to admit," Miller finally said.

"Ya think?" Sandy ferreted in his pocket for his car keys.

"But it's more habit than fear, I think."

"So you just take the girlfriend jibes on the chin?"

"Usually I simply tell them to mind their own business. But yeah, it's getting old."

"And the Wheel Blacks?"

His expression never changed. "Same thing. If I don't give them an answer, then it's up to them what they think."

"Riiiight." *Goddammit.* Those warning bells sounded in Sandy's head like fucking sirens. "You know, Miller, I came to watch you as a friend, that's all. It doesn't matter whether you're out or not in that regard, that's your business. But I also came because I'm interested in this game that you're obviously so damn good at, even though it's clear I shouldn't have.

"But if you hadn't wanted me to come, you could've just said so right back when we exchanged numbers rather than let me think it was okay. My being here clearly makes you uncomfortable, but if you're embarrassed to be seen with me, that's on you, not me, and I'm sure you'll survive. I don't apologise for who I am, and I don't waste my time on people who want me to be anything else. It was a good game. See you around."

He didn't wait for a reply, too pissed off at being let down by yet another guy finding him *too much* in public. He was as much angry at himself for expecting more, as he was at Miller for his disappointing reaction. Miller didn't seem the sort to let other people's opinions cramp his style, and since Reuben came to some of his games, the team had to have seen Cam at some point, so what the hell?

Plus, he and Miller were lucky if they even classified as friends. There was nothing to tell. That'll teach him for getting his hopes up again. He crossed the car park, briefly wondering where the morning's sun had disappeared to, the sky far more gloomy than when he'd arrived, and with the smell of moisture in the air. He'd just climbed into his much-adored decade-old Mercedes when Miller's voice boomed from behind.

"Hey, wait up!"

Ugh. Sandy ignored him and slammed the car door shut.

"Sandy! Fuck, will you just hang on a minute?"

He dropped the window, but kept his eyes straight ahead. "What?"

Miller rolled alongside, breathing hard. "Jesus Christ, those long legs of yours can cover some ground."

Sandy faced him but said nothing, and Miller squirmed a little in his chair. His gaze flicked down, those beautiful shoulders bunched and tense, every gleaming muscle defined.

"I'm sorry." Miller landed that persuasive green gaze back on Sandy. "I warned you, I was an arsehole."

"You did," Sandy shot back. "And that oversight is entirely on me. I should've known better."

"Ouch." Miller winced, resting his forearm along the open window.

Sandy said nothing and waited.

Miller's lips twitched. "Tough crowd." He took a deep breath. "I guess it's kind of my default position, although my family would say it never used to be. But it's done me well since . . . well, to get me where I am, after everything. But I now find myself in somewhat of a dilemma." He paused.

Sandy rolled his eyes. "Go on, I'll bite. Why is that?"

"Because for some reason, I don't want to be that . . . not with you." He glanced away and Sandy saw the internal struggle to open up. "But it's hard to simply switch it off, you know? And when I saw you watching the game, I didn't know what to think. I keep my life in nice little compartments . . ." He swallowed hard.

And Sandy was such a damn sucker. He rested his hand on Miller's arm and Miller startled at the touch. His gaze darted to Sandy and they locked eyes for a few seconds.

"There's work, and there's the rugby, and then there's family and friends, and mostly they don't interact," Miller explained, keeping eye contact. "But today they kind of collided and I felt ambushed, I guess. Not by you, but by the situation. Out of control. For instance, as much as Reuben is my friend, he's only ever met my family at the odd game, and I actively avoid making friends at work because I don't like people up in my business. I nearly didn't take the job because of Cam working there. I don't mix those worlds. And Beau's right. I don't rate much on the friend scale."

Sandy snorted. "That's possibly more about the whole arsehole thing . . . just saying."

Miller choked out a laugh and shook his head. A few drops of rain hit the windscreen and Miller glanced up but didn't move. "No doubt," he said, his shoulders relaxing a little as he slumped forward on his elbows. "I'm sorry if you felt I didn't want you there or that I was embarrassed—I wasn't by the way. You look—" His gaze travelled from Sandy's face down to the barely-there orange shirt. "—stunning."

And goddammit, Sandy was going to blush. He glanced away to hide it. "Thank you. And just for the record, I wouldn't normally have worn this to your game. I was out shopping with Cam and came straight from there. So . . ."

"Don't apologise. I'm glad you wore it. And I was actually pretty flattered that you came."

"Really?" Sandy cocked his head. "Because you sure as hell didn't look it."

Miller snorted. "Well, I totally wasn't going to invite you, you're right about that. Not because I didn't want you to watch me play, but because you don't seem to fit in any of my nice little life compartments, and I really don't know what to do with that. But when I saw you watching, I couldn't believe you simply came on your own, so yeah, I was flattered. *I* should've been the one to introduce you, and it's to my shame that I didn't. I hope you'll forgive me. There's no excuse and it's all my own making, but I don't want to lose your friendship because of it. I really enjoyed our coffee, enjoyed talking with you—"

"Me too." Sandy levelled a look at Miller, a warmth spreading through his chest.

Miller's mouth curved up in a slow smile. "That's . . . good."

Sandy shuffled onto his hip so he was looking out the window and Miller turned his chair to face him. "Does it help if I tell you that you don't fit in any of my nice little life compartments, either?" he admitted.

Miller's gaze turned wary. "Because of the chair?"

"No. And stop doing that. I don't give a rat's arse about your aids, and I don't need to know anything other than what you want to tell me about them. It's just that I'm cautious when it comes to guys. I've been burned more times than I care to remember, so I don't do this anymore. I don't jump in first and take risks like I did today. I'm all about slow and steady, except with you, apparently."

Those drops of rain grew closer together, one or two gathering on Miller's lashes, and Sandy had to smile at the fact that Miller either wasn't acknowledging them or didn't care. Either way, it sent a message Sandy didn't miss. Miller was serious.

"And so then I go and confirm your fears, right?" Miller admitted.

Sandy screwed up his nose. "At first. But then you did this, chasing me as well, so . . ."

They held each other's eyes for a long moment, then Miller reached out and gently tucked a few locks of Sandy's hair behind his ear and Sandy all but trembled, fighting the urge to turn his cheek into Miller's palm. The gesture was so intimate, so tender, so totally unexpected from this gruff man, it completely threw him.

Then, instead of simply dropping his hand, Miller brushed the back of his damp fingers down Sandy's cheek, and Sandy thought he might need a jump-start on that pounding thing in his chest, because holy fuck, if this was his reaction to all of two inches of Miller's body, Sandy was gonna need to up his vitamins.

He wiped his hands on his thighs and cleared his throat. "You've got a great line in apologies, I have to say."

Miller grinned. "I don't want to scare you away, but I'm in unfamiliar territory here, and I think it only fair to warn you I haven't 'dated' as such, well pretty much ever, really." His smile turned shy, all that brashness gone in a hot second, and Sandy ran out of room in his notebook for how complicated and surprising this man was proving to be.

"Is that from worry about being outed?"

Miller grunted. "I'd say I'm not really in the closet, but you pretty much blew that one out of the water already, so, maybe. But I also haven't had the time. I pretty much work, eat, sleep, and train. And can you maybe open the door? I feel like you're about to take off at any moment."

"It's raining," Sandy pointed out.

"It is," Miller deadpanned. "I'm so glad you reminded me. Now open up."

He reversed to give him room and Sandy obliged. Miller then wheeled his chair into the open space, bringing them almost knee to knee.

A glance at his pale hands and the quickening rain, and Sandy reached for the blanket he kept in the back seat. "Here, you must be freezing coming straight off the court. You're getting wet. You should get inside. It's not good for you." He threw the blanket around Miller's shoulders and tucked it over his legs. "There."

Miller watched him with a strange look on his face.

"What?"

Miller shook his head. "A thousand people could do that and I'd take offence at being coddled. You do it and my brain just says, mm that's nice. And that's what I mean about not knowing what to do with you."

Sandy eyeballed Miller. "I'm gonna take that as a compliment before you screw it up by adding an arsehole qualifier or something."

Miller chuckled. "I knew you were smart." He grabbed at the blanket edges on his shoulder and pulled it over their heads and the open car door like a tent.

Sandy tucked one corner behind the sun visor to keep it in place and held the other. He bit back a smile. "I feel like I'm twelve and we're having a sleepover."

"That could be arranged." The heat in Miller's stare stole any reply from Sandy's mouth.

He cleared his throat and turned to start the car instead, looking to warm Miller up and avoid that incendiary gaze. "So, how does it work, being out with family and friends but not at your job or rugby?" He ran a finger down the back of Miller's hand, which was resting on his thigh. Miller immediately covered it with his own, locking it in place.

He caught Sandy's eye and smiled. "Pretty damn easy when you don't date or mix your boxes. Nothing to see or explain, right? My family are well schooled in keeping quiet, a rollover from my younger rugby years. No one was out back then. Reuben was the first at All Black level, and he was ten years after me. I wanted that black jersey so bad, and being out wasn't gonna help me get it, or get me through the brutal world of high school rugby until I could throw my hat in the ring. It was just easier to keep quiet.

"Then after the accident, I was too busy trying to get my life back together, and coming out was an added issue I didn't want to deal with. Bad enough the press hounded me for interviews during my recovery, and then again when I started doing well in the chair for the Wheel Blacks. I never bothered setting things right. To be honest, I've been kind of surprised it never got out. But then, I've always been quiet about my family and social life in general, even when I played for the Blues. Grindr was about as risky as it got, not that I use it much."

Sandy's brain kicked into gear. "But you're not without some form then?" he teased. The rain fell steady around the two of them as they sheltered under the blanket roof. Their breath fogged together, adding another layer of warmth, and Sandy almost laughed at how ridiculous they must look, not to mention how wet the inside of his car was getting around the edges of the blanket.

Miller snorted. "I'm in no way a virgin, if that's what you mean? Unless you're talking about relationships. In that regard, I am completely clueless and inexperienced. Mum wants me to just stop mucking around, be honest, and bring a boyfriend home. Dad doesn't think past my sport and keeping me focussed."

Sandy bit back a smile and turned his hand, palm up, threading their fingers together. Miller squeezed them tight in return. Tucked up in their blanket bubble, it was so very high-school sweet and fucking delicious, it sent shivers down Sandy's spine and put his I'm-in-so-much-trouble radar on full alert. A ten-minute apology and he'd u-turned from leaving Miller in his dust, flown straight past interested, and was busy booking a vacation rental in besotted and crushing hard.

He pushed his knee forward to nudge Miller's. "I want you to know that I haven't avoided asking about this *accident* you keep mentioning because I'm not interested," he said. "I am. But I'd like to think we can have that chat somewhere other than a parking lot, if and when you're ready."

Miller nodded. "Agreed. And I appreciate you not pushing. For most, it's the first thing they want to know. Anyway, that's enough about my underused and overcautious sexuality. But just so you know, I'm currently rethinking that whole strategy."

Hope surged in Sandy's chest, but he tried to keep a lid on it. "Yeah? Am I allowed to ask why?"

Miller reached across to firmly cup his chin. "Come here." He drew Sandy forward and pressed the softest of kisses to his lips, barely more than a brush of air, but enough to send a cluster of butterflies soaring through Sandy's chest. "I like you. That's why." He rested their foreheads together as the blanket fort semi-collapsed and water dripped down Sandy's back.

He felt the icy run of it through his thin shirt, but he wasn't about to move a fucking inch. Miller had his rapt attention.

"And also, it's time," Miller continued. "Past time. I'm tired of hedging around. I want to be free to do *this* if I want. Ask a guy out. Kiss a guy. Build a tent with a guy."

Sandy snorted. "A particularly leaky tent, I might add."

"Shit." Miller unthreaded their hands so he could help support the blanket in a better position, giving Sandy more shelter, but not himself.

Sandy tried to extend the extra cover over Miller, but Miller stayed his hand. "I'm fine. I'm heading for the shower. I don't want you to get wet."

Dear god, chivalry. Sandy returned his hand to Miller's thigh, because, well, because he could.

"And further to that point of asking a guy out . . ." Miller hesitated and bit at his lips, and Sandy suddenly caught on.

He was nervous. Miller Harrison was nervous. And Sandy was charmed in a hot second. His heart tripped and his breath caught in his throat as he waited.

"Would you be interested in coming for a meal . . . at my place, tomorrow? Only if you want, of course." Miller's gaze flicked his way and then off again.

Sandy swallowed the smile threatening to break out all over his face. "Are you asking me on a date, Mr Harrison? Or should I call you, Tap?"

"Not Tap. I like the sound of my name on your lips."

They locked eyes and Sandy saw a million second thoughts vying for attention in that big brain. Miller was nervous as hell and Sandy was sold on that alone.

"As to the date question?" Now Miller looked genuinely terrified. "God, am I? I guess I am. How am I doing so far?"

"It needs a little work but yes, I'd love to come to dinner." Sandy leaned across to return the kiss, just as soft, just as fleeting, but with his other hand lingering on Miller's thigh, he squeezed lightly and Miller nearly shot through the roof. He arched a brow. "Hair trigger?"

Miller blushed brightly under those spattered freckles. "As I said, five years. I'm gonna need some practice."

Sandy bit back a smile. "I think that can be arranged. You want me to bring something?" A crack of thunder jolted him in his seat and he might've squealed. "What the hell?" He peeked out through the windscreen in time to see the heavens open and a deluge descended onto the parking lot.

Miller looked up and laughed as the blanket roof sank with the weight of the accumulating water. "No. I've got it. Just bring yourself. You better get going before we get washed away."

Sandy's brows hit his hairline. "Are you telling me you can cook?"

"I can." Miller flashed a smug smile. "It's something I actually possess some impressive skills in, unlike dating or weather forecasting." He pushed back from the car and closed the door before wheeling forward again and keeping the blanket over his head and the top of the car.

"That's doing fuck-all to keep my car dry." Sandy pointed out with a laugh as he leaned on the open window. "And you talk a big game there, Miller. You realise my expectations about the meal just shot through the roof."

"I'm confident. Does five thirty suit?" He still sounded nervous.

It was so fucking cute.

"We can have a beer on the deck first, if you like?"

Sandy couldn't stop the huge smile that broke over his face, which was why he *never* played poker. "Yeah, I like. Text me the address and I'll see you then, but *I'm* supplying the beer. You like a sour?"

Miller mimed sticking his finger down his throat.

Sandy groaned. "Right, no sours. IPA?"

Miller nodded.

"IPA it is." He tried to free his hands, but Miller lifted them to his lips and kissed the palm of each as Sandy watched, gobsmacked, until the blanket collapsed again and they both got soaked.

Who the hell was this man? If this was Miller's novice game, Sandy couldn't wait for the A version.

"See you tomorrow." Miller wheeled back a little, but Sandy was still stuck on the unexpected kiss and took a minute to realise. "And I think that shirt looks even better wet, just saying."

Sandy glanced down at the saturated wafer-thin material plastered to his skin. He may as well be naked from the waist up. The heat hit his face before he'd taken another breath. *Shit.* "I like to feel I go the extra mile." Cheeks flaming, he belted up and threw the car into gear.

Miller wheeled forward, hair sodden, the pelting rain a blurred sheet between them—so loud Sandy could barely hear his own voice. He was going to have to get the damn car detailed.

"I *am* sorry about today." Miller almost shouted. "I can definitely do better."

Sandy's palm still tingled from Miller's lips. "Well, you've certainly made a good start." He ran an eye over Miller from head to toe. "Kissing my palm, Mr Harrison? Who knew there dwelled a romantic under all that fuckery?"

Miller spluttered out a laugh. "Oh, you have no idea how deep those layers of fuckery go. Icebergs have nothing on me. There are an infinite number of ways I can screw this up, just you wait and see. See you tomorrow."

"I'll dust off my best frock." Sandy bundled the wet blanket inside, hit the electric window switch and pulled away, leaving Miller a soaking glorious mess in his rear-view mirror.

He grinned to himself. Oh yeah. This had all kinds of potential.

CHAPTER FIVE

MILLER SMILED AT THE BURNISHED CRUST COATING THE LAMB
as he turned it in the roasting pan. It was all he could do not to lick
his fingers. The smell was divine. He placed the root vegetables
alongside the meat, all except the blanched and roughed-up potatoes,
which were headed for a separate dish to get crunchy enough to
shatter like glass.

Remembering his conversation with Sandy the day before, he
smiled. Saying he could cook was like saying Tiger could golf, and
he'd spent some serious money renovating his kitchen to give him the
best access and ease of function that he could.

Mostly he managed with his canes, but for those days when he
didn't have the energy or when he wanted to spend hours simply
playing with recipes, he'd had a lower bench installed along one wall,
with space for his chair underneath, and a second set of utensils and
necessary equipment arranged close by.

For reason of the kitchen alone, he couldn't see himself selling the
house anytime soon. That and its open-plan living, flat section, which
wasn't always easy to find in Auckland, and its glimpse of the harbour

if you stood in the far corner of the deck and leaned sideways to peer between the two fir trees.

He was by no means a decorator but Miller knew what he liked, and the house was a mix of soft creams and greens, an interesting mix of modern portraits and seascape prints, oversized comfortable furniture to buffer his often-exhausted body, and a few mod-cons to make his life easier—electric window shades and a basic smart house operating system to name a couple.

His phone rang Uptown Funk and his nephew's name flashed on the screen.

"Hey, kiddo." He put the phone on speaker while he seasoned the vegetables. "Do you need a new pair of trainers? An upgrade to Witcher? Someone to buy all your chocolate bar fundraisers? Dating advice?"

Sam choked at the other end. "Hell to the no on that last one, Uncle Em. Considering I've *never* seen you date, I suspect those old pickup lines of yours are buried under that pile of cobwebs and failed club glory days you keep tripping over on your way to collect your pension. Not to mention we don't fish in the same pond."

Miller grinned. His nephew had a quick, sharp-edged humour that Miller loved. "Ouch. I'm barely thirty-five and you're seventeen. Things haven't changed that much. Different ponds, maybe, but similar rules, I suspect. Anyway, I can still be hip and cool."

"Sorry, but no, no you can't. Cool is a relative word, Uncle Em, and believe me when I say *no one* over thirty is cool. It's an antithetical proposition."

He was also hella smart.

"You start shedding coolness at twenty-five, and by thirty it barely registers on the vogue scale. In fact, you've already started elevating the embarrassing trying-too-hard-o-metre. You know, like trying to convince your nephew you're cool and shit."

Miller laughed. "Fine. I'll consider myself suitably chastised. Now, how can I help you, fruit of my brother's loins and unwelcome predictor of my lack of contemporary relevance?"

"Aw, but I love you, Uncle Em."

Miller's eyes pricked and he jagged in a shaky breath. "Love you too, kiddo. Now spill. I'd like to pretend you called just to hear the voice of your ancient but oh-so-wise uncle, but I wasn't born yesterday."

The ensuing silence ran deep with a gravity that immediately put Miller on edge. Sam didn't do quiet. He grabbed a seat at his small kitchen table. The vegetables could wait. "Okay, what's up? You've got my full attention."

"It's nothing bad."

"Uh-huh. Then why are my antenna flapping like windmills?"

"I promise." Sam hesitated. "It's just that I've got this friend I'm worried about."

Miller said nothing.

"I know what you're thinking, but it's not me," Sam insisted. "He's genuinely a friend."

"Okaaay." Miller was cautious. "So, you have a *friend*. I'm following so far, but I might need a little more detail."

Sam snorted. "Smart-arse. It's just that this friend needs some advice, or rather, someone to talk to. And I thought about you, actually."

Not a lot to go on. "You thought of me, why? Does he live with a disability? Does he want to play rugby—"

"He's bi."

Miller nearly choked on his tongue. "Right. And you thought of me because of my outstanding high-profile work in the LGBTQ community, right?"

Sam laughed. "Hardly. If you were ever a flag-waving member, I missed that half-second, and you wouldn't know a pride march if it bit you in the butt."

"Now who's the smart-arse?"

"I was hoping he'd maybe talk to you. He's really quiet and he's only just coming out. He kind of met someone, a guy, and well, I just thought . . . you know what, it doesn't matter."

Shit. Way to go, jackass. "No. Don't say that. It does matter, a lot. I'm sorry for the wisecracks. I just don't get why you think I'd be the right person. Isn't there someone else? Almost anyone would know more than me. I'm not even out in most of my life, you know that." And god, he could almost feel the disappointment at the other end of the phone.

"As I said, he's kind of quiet, at least when it comes to this. There's a pan girl in our group but she's all out and proud and rah-rah and that's fine, but Geo isn't like that and his dad is a total dick. I guess he needs an adult to talk to. I know you're not fully out, but you know Reuben and Cam, and I just thought—"

"Did you tell your dad you were gonna ask me about this?"

"Yeah, not that it was Geo, but yeah."

"What did he say?"

"After nearly choking on his beer, he smiled and said it was a cool idea."

Fucker. Miller's brother was dead meat. "Okay, I'll do it."

"Yeah? That'd be great."

"This kid's over sixteen, right? So he doesn't need his parent's permission to talk to me?"

"Yeah, he's seventeen, like me."

"All right. Then suggest it and we'll see what he says. I'm free next Saturday morning, if that works?"

"That'd be great, Uncle Em. I'm sure he'll say yes. He's a really nice guy and his dad is just being a humungous dick about it."

Miller laughed. "Yeah, well, parents have been known to do that on occasion. Let's see what he says."

"Thanks. You're the best."

"Does that earn me any cool points?"

"The fact you even have to ask completely negates any chance of a positive response."

"Damn."

"I know, right? Sucks getting old."

"Punk."

"Coffin dodger."

Miller barked out a laugh. "Be gone with you before I write you out of my will."

"Nah, you love me," Sam shot back. "And besides, I haven't told Dad why you paid for my volleyball trip last year. He still thinks I earned the money cleaning your backyard, not playing the latest Fortnite with you."

Shit. It had been money well spent; the kid was a wizard with a controller. Not that Dane would agree with Miller's strategy, but that's what uncles were for, right? "Okay, you win. You can stay in my will. I'll leave you my rugby chair."

"Cool. That thing's gotta be worth a few grand at auction."

"You wound me."

"As if. Catch ya later, Uncle Em."

"Bye, kiddo." Miller dropped the phone on the table and stared at it. What the hell had he just agreed to? He was barely contemplating outing himself in rugby at the ripe old age of thirty-five. What possible words of wisdom could he offer a seventeen-year-old? His own family had been brilliant when he came out to them. Surprised, sure, but they quickly got over it. He'd always felt safe with them.

His carefully crafted and predictable existence had suddenly taken a turn toward complicated and thorny. He'd gone from closeted social turtle to actually asking a guy on a bloody date, god help him, and offering to play Dear Abby to a struggling baby gay. How was this his life?

He checked the oven clock—five fifteen. *Shit.* Sandy would be here any minute. He stamped on the nerves threatening to strangle the air from his lungs and took a deep breath. Ridiculous didn't even begin to cover it. Sandy Williams had set up camp in Miller's brain and seemed in no hurry to move on. And Miller didn't get it. He didn't do this. He didn't crush or obsess about *anyone.*

Yes, the guy was hot, and nice, and . . . hot. So okay, there was a chance this was all about his dick, but Miller wasn't buying it. He'd seen more objectively hot male bodies in his lifetime playing high-level sport than most gay men could only dream about, and none affected him like the lean, fluid lines of this winsome nurse. And fuck if that wasn't the perfect word for the man. Charming, engaging, endearing, but with a flinty core and a snarky edge of humour that simply did it for him. There was a gentleness and a deeply rooted sense of self about the guy that was just so damn appealing.

Who'd have guessed? Miller had spent most of his rare forays onto Grindr checking out the husky athletes because . . . well, fuck if he knew why. Because that's what he thought he wanted? Wrong. So fucking wrong. What a waste of time. Then again, he'd never met anyone like Sandy, and Miller was . . . well, he was just so tired of being alone.

And then he'd nearly screwed it all up. What a chump. Seeing Sandy in the bleachers, he'd had a mild brain explosion. There'd been a flood of warmth and excitement just seeing the guy, knowing Sandy was interested enough to come watch Miller play. It had been a rush.

But then the fear kicked in, dislodging the only reaction that had truly mattered, to riddle him with insecurity instead. Fear of being outed—and since when did that matter anymore? It didn't. But it was mostly fear that Sandy's obvious interest in not just the game but Miller as well, might actually require something of him, something more than the locked down safe life that was slowly suffocating him.

Yeah, that was a bag of snakes Miller had avoided for a long time. And so, being the rational grown-up that he was, what did he do? Go and fucking ignore the only man, in too many years to count, who actually interested him, that's what. Hurt him. Piss him off. No wonder Sandy left Miller's arse in the dust.

But the minute he'd gone, Miller knew he'd made a mistake.

All of which brought him to this point—nervous as hell and fussing over his goddamn choices all day like any of it really mattered. From what to cook, to what cologne to wear, to what jeans made his slightly skinny arse look better, right down to whether to eat at the table or out on the deck with the brazier fired up. The latter remained undecided, and he'd set both spaces just in case. He shot a quick glance at the dining table. The plain white plates might've worked better. He still had time to change them out.

What the hell am I doing? He dropped his chin to his chest and groaned. *Worrying what some guy might think of my fucking table setting?*

The doorbell startled him back into action, and balancing on one cane, he shoved the two roasting pans back in the oven and slammed the door, setting the timer before grabbing the other cane and making his way slowly to the front door, the pain slicing into his hip and thigh. To avoid the worst of it, he altered his gait, reducing the normal outward swing he put into each step. But the swing helped compensate for the lack of flexion in his knees, and by reducing it, he screwed with his balance. Keeping upright was a fine line at the best of times.

Sandy waited outside, eyeing Miller's boring, middle-class suburban neighbourhood with a little dip between his brows. He looked . . . fucking gorgeous; a tall fresh lily in a field of dusty beige boxes.

He couldn't see Miller through the one-way glass alongside the door, and so Miller indulged himself for a few seconds, wondering what might have put that tiny frown in place and taking in the soft pink long-sleeved shirt Sandy wore, with its pearl buttons, and a pair of pale aviators hanging at the front. The billowy number floated over another pair of tight black jeans tucked into cream Doc Martens, with a short almond wool coat hung over his shoulders like a damn movie star, and a natural leather cuff on his right wrist to top the outfit off. He was the picture of chic, cool and downright beautiful.

Miller glanced at his dark-wash jeans and black T-shirt and winced. Too late now. He pulled open the door and Sandy spun at the sound, wearing a huge smile.

"Hi." Never let it be said Miller didn't have game.

"Hey. There you are." Sandy stepped inside and immediately caught Miller off guard with a brief kiss to his cheek. "I've been looking forward to this." He held Miller's gaze. "All day."

Miller's tongue did this silly dance thingy in his mouth, all dry and ridiculous, a dozen possible replies materialising only to be dismissed just as quickly. He had no answer to the unexpectedly affectionate greeting. Hell, he couldn't remember the last time anyone had even kissed his cheek, other than his mother, in . . . nope, he wasn't going there. He mumbled something inane like "me too," and waved Sandy into the house. Good god, he needed to seriously upskill his dating specs.

"Can I take your coat?" he offered, leaning one cane against the wall. Sandy turned so Miller could slip the coat off his shoulders, his citrus scent flooding the hall. It was only the definite creepiness factor that stopped Miller from pressing his nose to the man's neck.

"Go ahead." He waved Sandy down the hall while he followed, his eyes not glued to the way the silk of Sandy's shirt wafted around his lean hips, or the bunch and stretch of his tight arse in those fucking painted-on jeans, nope, not at all. This had been an epically bad idea, and Miller wanted to run for the hills. Except that no, no, he didn't. New page, new life.

"How badly are you freaking out right now?" Sandy spun to face him, a wry smile on his lips.

Miller snorted. "Busted. As I said, I don't do this much, as in never."

"Maybe this will help." Sandy opened his arms. "Can I hug you?"

Oh, god. No. Yes. Miller had nodded before he knew it.

And there was that warm smile once again as Sandy wrapped his arms around Miller in a soft embrace that went on a lot longer than he expected and not nearly long enough to satisfy. Sandy's scent drifted over him like a silk scarf and Miller breathed it deep, slamming a mental door on all those jangling bells in his head as he just tried to enjoy it.

It wasn't that he didn't like being hugged, it was that startling sense of surrender that jolted him, his body sucking up the attention like a starved child. He felt . . . vulnerable, something he'd avoided his entire life. And yet when Sandy finally let him go, he had to fight the fluttering in his stomach and the almost irresistible urge to fist Sandy's shirt and demand more, a lot more.

"And how exactly was that supposed to help?" he flustered.

Sandy reached for his hand and squeezed it. "Gets us over all that 'Do I, don't I, can I?' bullshit. I like hugging, Miller. And fair warning, I'm likely to do it a lot. So, if you're not comfortable, you better tell me now."

Was he comfortable? Hell no, he wasn't. But was he going to tell Sandy that? Like fuck he was. "It's fine." He ducked his head and turned for the kitchen.

Sandy laughed and followed. "Said like a man who just swallowed something nasty, but you get ten for impeccable dating effort. Shall I open a beer and put the rest in the fridge?"

Miller nodded, aware of Sandy's curious gaze flicking his way once or twice as he popped the bottles open and realised Sandy hadn't seen him on his feet before.

His cheeks burned and he cleared his throat, turning to adjust the oven temperature to hide his self-consciousness, and then mentally slapping himself for even giving a fuck. It doesn't matter what he thinks, what anyone thinks, dipshit. "I'll get the salad finished, then I'm free," he said, shifting to the counter by the sink. "Take your beer to the deck, if you want. The brazier's on."

"Now why on earth would I leave you alone less than two minutes into our first date?" Sandy stowed the remaining beer in the fridge and then peered over Miller's shoulder to see what he was doing.

Warm breath slid over his neck and Miller's skin blistered with need. Heat bloomed the length of his back as Sandy pressed close, and Miller nearly took his finger off instead of the cucumber end. "Fuck." He dropped the knife and took a breath. He was definitely losing his shit.

Sandy chuckled and reached around to put Miller's beer within reach, his arm gently grazing Miller's waist. "Sorry if I distracted you."

Miller snorted and shot Sandy a knowing glance. "No, you're not. I think you like putting me off-kilter."

"You're right, I'm not. And yes, I do." Sandy stepped to the side, took a long swallow of beer, and rested his back against the bench to watch Miller work. "I told you I've been looking forward to this all day and I have. I like you, Miller. And I like you *off-kilter*, as you put it, even more."

"Are you always this blunt?" Miller took a swig of his own beer and kept chopping, trying and failing to ignore Sandy's tempting willowy presence less than a foot away.

"Yes. Does it make you uncomfortable?" Sandy answered.

"Yes." He glanced sideways to meet Sandy's gaze. "But not in a bad way. Just in an 'I don't know what the fuck to do with myself' way."

Sandy threw his head back and laughed. "I'm sorry. I guess I'm just over all the bullshit and the dancing around that tends to happen when two people are getting to know each other. I figure I may as well be upfront so guys know what they're getting, and if people don't like it, then I haven't wasted my time and everyone can move on. Because, believe me, I've wasted a hell of a lot of time over the years. I'm not everyone's idea of eye candy, at least not in public."

Miller paused in his chopping. It might've been said as a throwaway, but he hadn't missed the sting in Sandy's voice, and he suddenly wanted the name of every person who'd hurt this sweet man. He turned and locked eyes. "Well, I think you're beautiful, and anyone who doesn't see that is a total wanker and not worth your time. Their loss, and a big one."

Sandy froze. His pale cheeks pinked and a small crease formed between those immaculate brows. He stared at Miller, eyes shining, a small smile playing at the corners of his mouth. "You might be better at this dating lark than you think," he said softly.

Miller's gaze slid back to the chopping board and he cleared his throat. "Beginner's luck. I wouldn't get your hopes up. This beer's good, by the way."

Sandy flushed with pleasure. "I'm glad you like it. It's one of my favourites."

Miller finished the radishes with Sandy's eyes on him the whole time. "So, this whole forthright thing?" he finally said. "Was that some kind of a test? You figured if I only wanted to fuck you, getting cuddly would out my motives?" He reached for his beer and downed another swallow.

Sandy shrugged. "When you say it like that, it sounds pretty bad, and I guess to a degree, it's true. But I *am* a toucher and a hugger— that's me. And I'm also at a stage in my life where I'm looking for more than a hook-up, and most guys who don't want more let you know pretty quick if you get . . . cuddly."

Miller sent him a sideways glance. "You really thought that was me?"

Sandy flushed but didn't deny it. "I don't really know you. And I'm not slut-shaming, because I have those days too." He raised his bottle in a mock toast and took a sip. "But that's not why I'm here, not tonight, not with you. I hope that's okay?"

"Yeah, more than okay. But I'm guessing that means I'm not going to get lucky tonight," he deadpanned.

Sandy choked on his beer and had to wipe his chin, and Miller scored himself a point.

"Well, that depends on what you mean by lucky." Sandy leaned in and brushed his lips across Miller's ear, adding a flick of his tongue, and Miller promptly lost half his iceberg lettuce to the floor. Return point to Sandy, goddammit. He fired him a pointed look, but Sandy merely smirked and raised his bottle.

"I'm happy to dial you in slowly on the whole hugging thing," he continued as Miller slid all the salad ingredients into a bowl. "Especially since you've been floundering in the minor leagues of the relationship stakes for a fair while . . ."

Miller made sure Sandy caught his epic eye-roll.

"But I'm never going to be the low-key, down-low PDA option, so you may as well know that now. If you're serious about coming out and we give things between us a go, then I'll likely hug, hold hands, and kiss you wherever we are. That being said, I won't be offended if you want to pull the plug now, while you still have your armour in place. We can share a meal, chat and still be friends."

Like that was ever going to be an option. Miller could barely keep his hands to himself as it was. He cut Sandy an amused smile. "I'll consider myself cautioned. And thanks for the offer, but I think I'll take my chances. Shall we agree to try and always be honest with each other?"

Sandy studied him for a minute. "Yeah, okay. But you can't say you weren't warned. Remember who you're asking? Blunt *and* honest? You're a brave man. Now, onto more important things, because damn, something smells amazing in here." He slid his empty bottle onto the countertop and stepped around Miller to peer into the oven. "Is that a roast?"

Miller nodded. "Lamb."

A hum of approval escaped Sandy's lips. "Wow. That's serious date cooking right there. Consider me suitably wooed in the food department. My mouth is watering. I hope there's dessert." He caught Miller's eye and winked.

Miller shook his head. "You're a flirt. I wouldn't have picked that about you."

"Well, most people don't piss me off within a minute of meeting me." He cocked his head.

Miller chuckled. "Fair point." He covered the salad and pushed it to the back of the counter.

"Plus, I'm very selective." Sandy ran a finger slowly down Miller's forearm to his cane and then off, leaving a trail of goosebumps and a southbound rush of blood in his wake. Then he pushed off the counter and strolled around the large kitchen, taking everything in while Miller took the moment to breathe through his arousal and knock some sense into his head.

"This is a great space." Sandy ran his hand over the rack of copper pots hung from the ceiling, setting them clanking. "You weren't kidding when you said you could cook. This is some serious equipment. Is that one of those hibachi grill things?"

Miller nodded. "Yeah, it's pretty cool. This room was my one big extravagance. If I'm stressed, I cook. I always have done. And although I can mostly cope in here with my canes, some days I need the chair, so it only made sense to push through a wall and get a small table and low bench option in here as well. Carrying plates into the dining room is definitely not my forte. Even with my chair, I've had more than one disaster, and I'm crap on my knees. On an everyday basis, it's better that happen in the kitchen where it's much easier to clean up."

"Well, after all that, I can't wait to eat your food." Sandy's eyes danced.

"Don't." Miller wagged a finger at him. "I'm hot and bothered enough without you adding to it. Now, how about we take a couple of fresh beers out to the deck? We've got about forty minutes till dinner. Do you mind grabbing them?"

Sandy's eyes popped and he fanned himself dramatically. "You're asking for help? Be still my heart."

Miller flipped him off. "Brat."

Sandy snorted. "Just so you know, I don't do any of that daddy shit, either."

Miller barked out a laugh. "Well, thank fuck for that. I can cancel that order I put in with Daddy Knows Best."

"Oh. My. God. Yes, do that immediately. Whatever turns you on and all that, but for me? No thank you."

Miller settled himself sideways on the outdoor couch and eased his legs up with a groan.

"You're in pain." Sandy moved a chair so he could face Miller, and handed him his beer. "What happened?"

He squirmed to get comfortable. "I crunched my hip last week, the same day we met, as it happens. It's just taking its own merry time to come right. I'm gonna see the doc Thursday."

"You want a massage?"

Miller snorted and eyeballed him. "Is that a trick question? Cos I gotta tell you, you're getting my hopes up here."

The blush started at Sandy's neck and travelled all the way up to his ears. "I say what I mean."

God almighty. Nothing in the world sounded better than Sandy's hands on him at that moment. "Even so, I doubt that's a safe option. Considering I'm not getting laid, remember?"

Sandy's lips twitched and Miller just wanted to kiss them and keep going.

"Your loss."

Undoubtedly.

They sat for a few moments, contemplating their beers and the heavy tread of first-date elephants in the room.

"So, I'm guessing in the spirit of getting-to-know-you etiquette, this is the mutual show-and-tell phase? Family, interests, work, that kind of thing." Miller broke the silence.

Sandy's brows crunched adorably. "You want me to start?"

"Nah. We agreed to wait till we had some time for me to explain this." Miller swept a hand over his body.

"You know you don't have to tell me anything. We can just chat about other stuff. First date, remember?"

"But I'd like to. I appreciate more than you'll know that you didn't ask about it straight away. It's kind of a novelty for me."

"I won't deny I'm curious, but I understand the whole nosy questioning thing, more than you might think. I deal with my fair share of raised eyebrows and people who think they're entitled to an explanation."

Miller could imagine. "You don't deserve that."

"Thanks, but unfortunately a lot of people don't see it that way. Today was a case in point."

He frowned. "Something happened?"

Sandy blew out a sigh and slipped down in his seat. "There were no autopsies scheduled and Ed and I were having a paperwork day, so I was in civvies. A mother and her adult son arrived to view a body.

Ed was busy on the phone, so I answered the bell in the visitor room and asked them to wait."

Sandy shuffled in his seat. "Well, let's just say eyes bugged and hackles went up the minute the wife and son caught sight of the skirt I was wearing that day. They let me know their feelings in no uncertain terms. Disgusting, sick, and perverted are a few of the words I remember. I made the mistake of trying to explain why I wasn't in scrubs and that it was only clothes, after all, but you can imagine how well that went down."

Miller's heart squeezed. "People can be ignorant dicks. Was that the reason for the frown on your face when you arrived?"

Sandy shrugged. "Probably. I didn't realise I was still carrying it around with me. I should've ignored them, but although I might not think people deserve an explanation, it's hard to shake the idea that if only I explain things, then surely they'll understand and everything will be okay."

"Let me guess, it doesn't work?"

"Give the man a balloon. Those who are going to accept me usually don't need an explanation, they'll accept me anyway. Those who don't accept me, in most cases, won't change their mind with or without an explanation. When I came out, my mum and sister were fine with it, including my dress choices. My dad? Not so much, and no explanation was going to help."

Shit. "I'm sorry you had to go through that. It's tough when people aren't there when you need them to be, especially parents."

"Yeah, well, my coming out wasn't the only thing my dad dropped the ball on in the family stakes. He'd mentally checked out from us a few years before, but the day after I came out, he fucked off entirely, never to be seen again."

Holy shit. Miller wanted to take names and hurt something. "A bastard then." It was all he could trust himself to say.

Sandy shrugged. "It was a long time ago. But it taught me that if your own parents can't be trusted to listen to your story and learn from it, then no one else deserves it from you just as a matter of curiosity. It hurts too much to have it argued or rejected time after time, so I only offer it when I really want to. There might be people who genuinely want to know to improve their understanding, but unless they're going to be a part of my life, I don't have to be their rainbow Wikipedia. And they aren't entitled to that from me any more than they would be entitled to answers on personal questions from a cis, straight person."

Sparks flashed in his eyes as he continued. "That right to privacy is something I'm big on, especially when I talk to kids at the drop-in centre Cam's involved in. We don't need to explain ourselves unless we want to, especially when you might not even understand it all yourself. And that applies to people within our community as well."

"Do you get a lot of that from the inside?"

"A little. Mostly because I won't commit to a label. My sexual preference is men, and I mostly identify as a man."

"Mostly?"

"There are days when I feel much more . . . *neutral* about it. I don't identify as a woman at those times, but I do feel like I'm in flux, floating if you like, more agendered, or demiguy, than anything. In that way I fit more in the genderqueer, gender fluid, or non-binary. There's always people more than willing to tell me what *they* think I am, but I don't always relate to those labels either. And I don't see why I need to."

"Please don't take offence, but you sometimes wear *very* feminine clothes?"

Sandy flashed him a broad smile. "I'm not offended. You want to understand and we're trying something here, you and I, even if I don't think I can explain it very well. It simply feels right. Maybe because it's the easiest form of dress to reflect the difference I feel on the inside, but then I also wear a lot of androgynous stuff as well or I mix it up."

He indicated the soft shirt and heavy boots, and Miller wanted to tell him he looked stunning. And so he did.

Sandy's cheeks blushed crimson. "Thanks. I've learned not to question and just go with it. Feminine clothes are only in the eye of the beholder, right? Basically, they're just clothes. I even wore a Samoan lavalava to work once."

Miller chuckled. "I'll bet that raised some eyebrows."

Sandy pulled a face and nodded. "It didn't go down well, let's just say that. Even though I do actually have some Samoan heritage on my great grandmother's side." He saw Miller's eyes pop and laughed. "I know, right? All this white skin, it's hard to believe. My father's Danish blood runs strong in me."

"That accounts for the height and colouring."

"Yeah, I'm a real mix. The worst days are when I want to wear an outfit in particular, but there's some reason I think I can't. I'm not immune to self-preservation. But there's a difference between choosing and being told what to wear. Or having it nicely suggested by boyfriends in case I offend their family or friends or embarrass them. I guess it's as good a time as any to check if any of this is likely to be an issue for you?"

Miller guessed his silence wasn't reassuring. But it was a serious question and he didn't want to blurt an answer he hadn't thought through. Sandy was objectively hot *any* way he dressed; Miller didn't have to think twice about that. But he guessed that wasn't really what Sandy was asking, and god, Miller was so fucking out of his depth.

Sandy waited, laser-focussed on Miller's face, no doubt deciding if he was going to turn out to be precisely the jerk Sandy had thought at the start.

Miller could hardly argue with that.

Sandy in a skirt in the hospital was one thing. Wearing one to watch Miller at a game? How would that be? Miller couldn't believe he was being *that* guy by even needing to think about it. But wheelchair rugby had its bigots as much as any sport, and he couldn't ignore the twinge of nerves in his belly.

Jimmy had even approached Miller in the locker room the day before, asking all sorts of loaded questions about who Sandy was and how Miller had met him. Questions Miller had deflected or ignored.

The behaviour had homophobic prick written all over it, but Miller hadn't called him on it and he should have. He wondered if Jimmy's girlfriend Vicki knew and what she thought about it. She'd never struck Miller as someone to agree with that rubbish. Coming out to his team had suddenly got very real. And with it, a whole lot of issues he hadn't had to face before.

Sandy stopped chewing on his lip and simply got to his feet, his expression a studied mask. "Don't feel badly." He shivered and folded his arms across his chest. "I get it. I don't have to like it, but I get it. Better we find out now—"

"Stop." Miller struggled to his feet and took Sandy by the shoulders. "Just . . . sit, please. Don't go . . . just . . . sit."

Sandy hesitated, the conflict evident in his eyes. Then he sighed and did as Miller asked, another shiver travelling the length of his body.

"Shit, you're cold." Miller grabbed the blanket from over the back of the couch and wrapped it around Sandy's shoulders.

"Thanks." Sandy gathered it at the front and watched with wary eyes as Miller took his seat and wrung his hands together. "Miller, we don't have to do this—"

"Just give me a minute." Miller took a deep breath and blew it out slowly. "Okay. I know you think I'm a huge dick for even having to think about it, and maybe I am." He hesitated. "But I thought you were worth more than a glib answer."

Sandy pulled the blanket tighter across his chest. "I'm listening."

"It's not . . . you, it's me—"

"Jesus, Miller." Sandy snorted and tossed the blanket off his shoulders again.

Miller threw out his hand to stop him leaving. "I didn't mean it that way. God, I really am fucking this up."

Sandy remained tense, but he was still sitting and Miller counted that as a win. One he didn't deserve. He dropped his hand and tried again. "What I meant was, I really like who you are."

Sandy arched a brow.

"I do. Jesus, Sandy, we wouldn't be here if I didn't, or have you forgotten that bit about me never dating?"

Sandy grunted. "That's currently under review."

Goddammit. "Well, maybe if you don't kill me in the next few minutes that possibility might go back on the table?"

Sandy side-eyed him in a way that was less than reassuring.

"Or not. Entirely up to you, of course. But maybe just hear me out? What I was trying to say in my blundering, entirely inappropriate, and evidently unforgivable and offensive way . . ." He paused.

Sandy's lips twitched. "Not bad. Keep going."

"Was that, when I thought about it, I realised this was more about my fear of coming out than anything to do with you. I couldn't give a shit what you wear or how you present yourself—"

Another raised brow.

Miller groaned. "Son of a bitch, you'd never guess negotiation skills were part of my job skillset. What I mean is, I like *you*, whatever package you come in, however you see yourself, I want to get to know *you*. Does that pass?"

Sandy bit back a smile and waggled his hand between them. "It'll do."

"Thank Christ for that. And that's what I meant when I said it wasn't you. I'd find myself in this position with whoever I wanted to date because I'm not out. I guess I've tried to avoid the double stigma whammy of being gay *and* living with a disability. And it's not like our community is always accepting of disability either, right?"

Sandy nodded. "Arseholes are everywhere."

"Exactly, and I just needed a minute to get that clear in my head." Miller wiped his hands down the front of his shirt. "Jesus, I'm sweating like a pig. Can we change the subject now?"

"In a minute. Can I ask if you're going to be okay coming out to your team? Is that something you really want? Because you can't just do it for me. We can stay friends."

Did I really want it? "Yes. It's time, regardless. I'm not saying I'm not worried—scared shitless might be a more apt description—but yeah, it's time. You're a catalyst, not the reason. I need to do this. And dammit all, Sandy, we cannot stay as just friends. If we try that, I'm gonna end up with my dick looking like a fucking pretzel, locked into my briefs with a semi-permanent hard-on every time I think of you, which will be All. The. Damn. Time."

Sandy's eyes grew wide and his hand flew to his mouth to stifle a laugh. "Well, we can't have that." He eyed Miller with amusement. "So, for the sake of your dick, I feel it only fitting that I do my best to prevent that happening. I'll consider it a service to humanity."

Miller gave a solemn nod. "You are an honourable man. Humanity and my dick and I will be forever in your debt."

"Just as I'd hoped." Sandy studied him with that piercing way he had that seemed to cut through all of Miller's well-practised bullshit. "Okay. Dating is back on the table. Next topic."

Miller laughed. "Thank God for that."

Sandy shot him a mischievous grin that didn't bode well and then relaxed back in his seat with the blanket tucked under his chin. He looked fucking adorable, and Miller wanted nothing more than to crawl under there with him.

"Which means it's your turn," Sandy pointed out. "I started that one, remember?"

Fuck. Adorable with sharp teeth.

CHAPTER SIX

SANDY WATCHED MILLER SQUIRM. HE SURE DID HATE TALKING about himself. Things had almost gone off the rails there for a second until Miller had pulled one out of the hat. Wily man. Even if Sandy wasn't totally convinced Miller understood his own thinking yet.

Sandy's fluidity might not be Miller's prime concern in his eyes right now, but there was no avoiding the fact it hadn't really been tested. You only had to ask Reuben about that. The All Blacks had been theoretically ready for an out gay player, but with Cam as his partner, there was no avoiding the additional press scrum because of his look and sass.

But Sandy was willing to give Miller a bit of rope. The man was adept at putting his foot in his mouth, but for some reason Sandy wasn't inclined to take offence. Maybe because it was mostly ignorance. Maybe because Miller owned it. And maybe because he was genuinely trying. Plus, Sandy believed Miller was genuinely attracted to him, more than physically. And that was a possibility Sandy liked a lot more than he should, since Miller came with no guarantees and Sandy had been burned too many times to count.

He watched as Miller pulled a second blanket over himself and slid down against the pillows, grimacing as he adjusted his hips. He was clearly in pain, but Sandy knew better than to raise it. He waited for whatever Miller decided to share and tried not to put too much stock in what that would be. Neither of them seemed big on trust.

"There's not a lot to tell about the accident," Miller began. "A fairly typical fuck up in lots of ways."

He paused but Sandy said nothing. This was Miller's show.

Eventually Miller continued. "I was playing for the Blues at the time, a promising number fifteen just like Reuben. Twenty-four years old and headed for the All Blacks with a bit of luck. But a night of drinking and a stupid decision to get in a car with my drunk mate driving and, yeah, turned out to be not so lucky after all. My mate ran a traffic light and ploughed into an embankment, then bounced back into a large SUV coming the other way. The SUV's bull bar ploughed into the front passenger door, and the rest is history—a jigsaw puzzle's worth of broken leg bones, a shattered pelvis, significant spinal damage that thankfully fell just short of being severed, a crushed wrist, and a man who's lucky to be alive let alone able to walk for short distances. No chance of making the All Blacks after that or managing any sport where being upright is required."

"Holy crap. What happened to your friend?"

"He died." Miller paused and sucked in a breath. "No seatbelt. Flew through the front windscreen like a fucking cannon."

Sandy gasped. "That's . . . shit, I don't even know what that is."

"Yeah." Miller drained his remaining beer in a couple of chugs.

Sandy refused to fill the silence with glib condolences. Miller had no doubt heard them all. Instead, he watched as Miller picked at the label on his empty bottle and wondered how much guilt Miller still carried.

"That's pretty fucked up." He pulled his chair closer, took Miller's bottle from him and replaced it with his hand. "And a lot to come to terms with. I don't imagine that happened overnight."

Miller flipped his hand and threaded their fingers together. "Not exactly. I should never have got in that car. I knew it at the time. If I hadn't, then Tony might not have been silly enough to drive. It was a long time until I could see clear of the depression that haunted me those first few months."

"You both made choices that night." Sandy rubbed his thumb over the back of Miller's hand. "He did as well."

"I know. But at the time I was so fucked up, I couldn't deal with it. It seemed I was forever having surgery or recovering from surgery: both femur necks replaced, multiple plates, screws, fusing of bones, tendon repairs, you name it. My left wrist's still a mess with limited flexion and couple of frozen fingers, but at least I have my hand, so that was a win. It could've been a lot worse."

He paused, and Sandy knew he was reliving the possibilities.

"For eight months I couldn't walk. Everyone is still shocked how much function I've actually got back, but it didn't happen overnight."

"You're pretty damn impressive on those canes," Sandy commented.

"It took a few years. I can even muddle around the house and my office without them most of time, although I'm not hugely stable. Sensation down to my calves is pretty good. Below that is hit or miss. Motor control is the same. Outside of the house or office, I use the chair, and my car has dual controls."

Sandy squeezed his hand "I can only imagine the rehab. It must've been a killer."

"Fucking agony. No other way to describe it. I used to call my physio Satan's spawn to his face."

Sandy chuckled. "I doubt it fazed him."

"Hah! As if. He considered it the benchmark of a good day if he got called that or worse at least once. He was great. Without him pushing, I doubt I'd be where I am. He was the one who introduced me to murderball—had a mate that played and thought it might be a good motivator for me. Best decision I ever made. The first time I got slammed to my side on the gym floor, I knew I'd come home, but more importantly, I knew I'd survive this."

Sandy leaned forward, bringing them eye to eye. He wanted to be sure Miller got the message. "I'm so fucking glad you did. That's no easy thing. You should be hugely proud of what you've achieved. There's no room in any of that for misplaced guilt."

Miller swallowed hard but held Sandy's gaze, and there was steel in his eyes. "I am proud. And I agree with you . . . now. But it took a long time until I felt I had a life again. I have a lot to thank my family for in that regard. Dad was freaking tireless making sure I had what I needed in those early days: support, equipment, transport, and anything else that might help. I was really lucky. He still comes to most games, googles up new techniques and training tips, and fundraises for the Wheel Blacks. He's my number one fan, a bit too enthusiastic perhaps, but he loves me. Mum just wants to see me happy. She watches my games, but she's not so keen on the full-contact and injury side."

Neither was Sandy. He debated whether to say anything but then decided to stick with the honesty they'd agreed on earlier. "I can see her point. It's pretty full-on. I had an idea what to expect, but I admit I was . . . shocked. It's one thing to see it on TV and quite another to hear the slam of those chairs and see the bodies on the floor. I don't quite know what I think about it. Do people get hurt often?"

"Come here." Miller shuffled over and Sandy moved to sit beside him, turning on his hip so they faced each other. The man was like a furnace and Sandy's slender body soaked it up.

"Mostly it's minor stuff," Miller explained, taking Sandy's hand again. "Muscle strains and lacerations. And predominantly in the offensive players."

"But that's what you play, right? Offence?"

Miller gave a wry smile. "You catch on quick. And yes, bad stuff *can* happen. Broken bones do occur, sometimes made worse if the player doesn't have sensation in that area and doesn't realise they've been injured. But on the whole, it's rough rather than dangerous."

Sandy was calling bullshit. "Hey, honesty, remember? I watched the game yesterday. You can't tell me it doesn't take a toll, getting hit time and time again."

Miller's eyes narrowed. "No more than any other full-contact sport. I bet you wouldn't dream of telling Reuben he should give up because rugby is dangerous. And that's where the comparison should lie, don't you think?" He eyeballed Sandy, who held his gaze without flinching.

"True," Sandy replied, hackles rising. He tried to slip his hand free but Miller simply tightened his grip, so he left it there. Damned hard to argue holding someone's hand, and he almost lost his train of thought. "But just to be clear," he picked up again, "I think the same about those sports, as well. And I *have* said the same to Reuben, especially about the head injury risk he faces on the field. I'm a nurse, for fuck's sake. It's a concern, not an indictment on your sport, or Reuben's, or whether either of you should play it or not. It's simply a statement of fact. A reminder to be careful and do all the right things to minimise the risk."

Miller's expression softened. "Sorry. It's just . . ."

Sandy took a slow breath in and calmed down. "Look, I get it. But I'm not that guy, okay? Shoot me down by all means if I deserve it, please. But maybe give me the benefit of the doubt first." His thumb drew circles on the back of Miller's hand.

Miller's expression turned sheepish, and he pressed a kiss to Sandy's cheek. "Yeah, I can do that." His head fell back and his gaze searched the deepening sky. "I told you I'd be crap at this."

Sandy joined him, their shoulders touching as they marvelled at the clarity of the emerging stars and a half-cut moon. Only a few wisps of cloud in an otherwise clear and icy winter evening.

After a few minutes, Sandy elbowed him gently. "You know, I'm hardly a shining example of relationship success myself. I guess we both need a bit of practice. Want another?" He reached for the two empty bottles, then got to his feet.

Miller stood as well. "I better get dinner on the table first or I won't be capable. How about we take things inside and you can drink and talk to me while I finish cooking?"

Sandy could get on board with that. "Sounds like a plan."

He sipped on a glass of wine and watched as Miller left his canes to the side and moved carefully but deliberately around his kitchen to finish the mouth-watering meal. Sandy's offer of help had been summarily dismissed, leaving him to take residence at the small kitchen table and feast his eyes on Miller as he worked.

It was a tough job but somebody had to do it, and Sandy was struck by the effort Miller was putting in to feed him. It was flattering, and damn if he didn't soak that up like a dry sponge. No guy had ever cooked for him like this. A few half-hearted attempts, sure, but none of Sandy's boyfriends had ever been what you'd call a cook. A meal out or ordering in was as good as it mostly got. But this? He watched Miller taste and adjust the silky sauce he was fixing to go with the lamb. This was special.

Miller chatted about his job and colleagues as he worked, and Sandy contributed here and there, somewhat amused at the familiar domesticity of it all. He wouldn't have picked Miller as being easy to talk to, but there you go. Under that prickly exterior, when he let his guard down, Miller could be . . . well, almost charming. It was an unexpected and promising chink in that buttoned-up armour he wore.

No surprise that Michael Oliver got a mention in Miller's account of his first month on the job. Auckland Med's ER trauma specialist, the doctor was a star attraction for any warm-blooded gay man, and Sandy had lived through a small crush of his own when he'd first arrived. The fact that Michael and his K9 officer husband were smoking hot as a couple didn't hurt either, and Sandy had grown to know them both during the whole 'Murder in the Morgue' affair earlier in the year.

"It sounds like you love your job," he commented, carrying their plates to the dining area where a table was beautifully set for two people. This man was killing him.

"I do." Miller followed. "It wasn't at all what I saw myself doing before the accident. I'd never looked past professional rugby even though I did manage to finish two years of a degree while I was signed with the Blues. But rehab gave me plenty of time to focus on a major and finish off. It was one of the things that kept my head on straight during all that. I'm good at committees and consensus and brokering arbitrations." He glanced Sandy's way. "Shocker, I know."

Sandy snorted. "I never said a word. But yeah, I can actually see that. There's a carefully shielded side to you that I imagine works well as a kind of professional neutrality."

Miller openly stared at him. "Huh. I'm impressed. Not many people see that. Most just call it arrogance . . . or arseholery." His mouth quirked up in amusement. "Take a seat." He waved Sandy to the chair at the end of the table. "I'm better with a bit of room to spread out. More wine?"

Sandy nodded and got himself seated. "Well, I can't deny at a social level, there are some edges that are perhaps a little . . . sharp."

Miller poured for them both and they clinked glasses. "I'll try not to read too much into that, like I'm maybe a cool and distant fucker."

Sandy almost choked on his first sip of wine. "Hey, I never said that." He put his glass down and drew a breath. "I only meant that you have this solid personal protective wall around you, at least with people who don't really know you. Good for professional objectivity though."

Another long stare and Sandy was starting to think he was royally fucking this up. "Sorry. I've got no right—" The rest of his sentence was lost to surprise when his eyes landed on the tiny vase of flowers set between them. "You picked flowers . . . for me?" He looked up in time to catch a blush make its way up Miller's throat.

Miller dropped his eyes and focussed on cutting his meat. "There's not much out at this time of year, but I love this viburnum carlesii, and I just thought you might like it. Their scent kind of reminded me of you . . . in a way."

Sandy lifted the small arrangement to his nose and breathed it in, aware of Miller's eyes on him. Daphne-like in aroma, sweet and spicy, he loved it.

He had no words to offer, just an effusion of warmth in his chest. He covered Miller's hand with his own to stop him lifting his fork and waited for Miller to look up. "They're beautiful. Thank you. I love them." He lifted his hand to brush across Miller's bright red cheek. "You're a bit of a puzzle, Miller Harrison. I think I'm going to enjoy getting to know you."

Miller took Sandy's hand and brought the palm to his lips, dropping a soft kiss there before letting it go. "Ditto, Mr Williams. Now eat your meal before it gets cold. And you're lucky it's the carlessi variety in my garden. The tinus variety stinks like a dead horse."

Sandy snorted his wine, spraying it across the pristine white tablecloth. "Oh. My. God." He dabbed at the spots with an actual linen napkin, and who the hell had those things lying around these days? "Well, thank Christ for that. A lesson in how to get rid of a first date."

Miller laughed and they stared at each other for a few seconds, his bright green eyes soft and inviting under that waterfall of red waves, and Sandy had to remind himself they barely knew each other. Because this? This didn't feel like any first date Sandy had ever been on. This felt a lot more, enough to have him worried. It had been a long time since his heart had fallen so fast for a man, if ever, and he could get hurt, seriously hurt.

The remainder of the evening flew by in a tumbling back and forth of general getting-to-know-you conversation, humorous teasing, and comfortable silences—the best date Sandy had been on in a very long time. And as if the roast wasn't delicious enough, Miller shocked Sandy again with a roly-poly pudding to die for, smothered in home-made vanilla bean ice cream. He didn't even attempt restraint, going back for seconds before slouching in his chair with a groan, ready to pop.

"You're gonna have to roll me to the Uber," he said, wiping his mouth with his napkin. "I can't possibly get there on my own. Death by suet and jam."

"But what a way to go." Miller, who'd shown a great deal more self-discipline than Sandy, regarded him with an indulgent smile. "Here, give me that." He took the napkin, leaned in, and dabbed at the corner of Sandy's lip, their faces so close Sandy thought if he leaned forward just a smidgen, he might very well tip over into the cool welcome of those green pools and be lost forever.

"You've got some jam . . . right . . . there." Miller's lips parted and their eyes locked.

Neither said a word as they both leaned into the kiss, the soft press of warm lips giving way to an urgency Sandy couldn't contain as his tongue licked at the seam of Miller's lips before sweeping in to claim a taste. Miller shuddered, then groaned, plunging into Sandy's mouth in return, fisting his hair to hold him close, their position awkward, but hell if Sandy was letting that stop him.

Miller tasted of raspberry, cream, and vanilla, and damn, he couldn't get enough, the kiss desperate and fierce and hot as hell. Sandy was about to light those damn no-hook-up rules of his on fire, when Miller tore his lips away and pressed their foreheads together, both of them gasping.

"Tha—" Sandy cleared his throat. "That was . . ." He blew out a breath. "So fucking hot."

Miller's face lit up. "Yeah . . . it was . . . yeah." He pulled back and glanced at the clock. Sandy followed his gaze.

Eleven!

He almost shot out of his chair. "Shit. I'm so sorry. We both have work. I shouldn't have kept you so long. Let's get these dishes done and then I'll go."

Miller raised his hands. "Slow down, it's fine. I've got a dishwasher."

Sandy started collecting their plates. "Then I'll pack it. You warned me how crap you were carrying plates, remember? It's just good occupational health and safety practice." He fired Miller a don't-mess-with-me look and Miller threw up his hands.

"Fine. You carry, I'll stack. I have a system."

Sandy chuckled. "Of course you do."

They worked as a team until everything was tidied away. Sandy wiped the benches while Miller cleaned the dining table, and it was so fucking domestic it made Sandy's teeth ache . . . and his cock perk up. Go figure. Dishcloth porn—who knew that was a thing?

He finished sliding the chef's knives back in the block and turned to where Miller had been working at the sink and froze.

Miller was standing with a cane in one hand and two pink viburnum flowers in the other, their stalks wrapped in foil. "I thought you might like to take them with you," he offered softly, a frown on his face like he couldn't quite believe what he was doing, either. "Since you seem to like them." He hesitated, and those creases grew deeper as his hand began to drop. "Sorry, I'm probably just being . . ."

"Shh." Sandy walked over and put a finger to Miller's lips. "I love that you did this. Thank you." He accepted the flowers and stared at them. "This has been a . . . surprising evening."

Miller nodded. "It has. In the best way. But don't be fooled. As evidenced earlier, when I said I will likely suck at this, I wasn't joking. I just hope you'll keep cutting me some slack when I do. Keep being honest. I'm ignorant enough to be completely unaware of my dickishness."

Sandy studied him closely. "So, you want to do this again? Another date?"

Miller blew out a long breath. "Yes, please."

Sandy couldn't keep the huge grin from his face. "Yeah, me too. Maybe we should have a secret code for dickish behaviour?"

Miller brushed a lock of hair from Sandy's eyes and Sandy turned his head into Miller's palm and let it cup his cheek. "You mean like a safe word when I'm stretching the limits of your patience?"

Sandy laughed. "Or me stretching yours."

"That's hardly likely," Miller scoffed. "How about arsehole? It's practically my middle name."

Sandy leaned close enough to feel the heat of their bodies connect. He had a good few centimetres on Miller, meaning Miller had to look up. But when he did, Sandy couldn't keep the soft gasp from his mouth as Miller's heated gaze met his.

"Except it contravenes one rule that's served me well for many years." He pressed the lightest of kisses to the corner of Miller's mouth. "I don't date arseholes. Ergo, Miller Harrison, you are not an arsehole."

Miller leaned forward and stole another kiss. "Then I stand corrected." He stepped Sandy back against the pantry door, his cane horizontal at Sandy's waist, holding him in place.

"Don't move."

Holy shit. Like Sandy was going anywhere. He'd quietly hoped things might play out between them this way. Miller obviously liked control, and Sandy was down for as much of that growly-voiced direction as Miller wanted to throw at him.

Miller dropped his cane to the floor and cradled Sandy's face, his eyes dancing. "Is this breaching those no-hook-up rules?"

Sandy slid his arms around Miller's waist and pulled him close. "Pfft. What rules? I think my virtue is in safe hands."

"Unfortunately true." Miller nosed his way up Sandy's neck, inhaling deeply. "Fuck, you smell so good. I've wanted to do this since the minute you arrived. That and rip this damn shirt off you. Do you know I can see your nipples?"

Sandy bit his lip coyly. "Possibly."

Miller snorted. "Fucking tease. Can I kiss you again?"

Sandy nipped the end of his nose. "I'd be hella disappointed if you didn't."

"Then get down here where I can reach you better." Miller fisted his shirt, and Sandy spread his stance to even up their heights. "Oh, yeah. much better. Finally." He covered Sandy's mouth with his own, the kiss tender and teasing, nipping, licking, breath mingling, soft murmurings of pleasure.

Sandy gave himself over, melting in Miller's arms. He trusted Miller to take them both where they wanted to go. The rumbling growl of approval rocketed south to Sandy's balls, shooting his arousal off the scale as Miller swallowed Sandy's moan and dragged his hard cock across Sandy's own.

"Fuck." Sandy's head fell back against the door as Miller's lips and teeth wantonly explored his neck, hard enough to leave marks, but not nearly hard enough to satisfy. His hand spread across Sandy's throat, gently holding him in place while leaving the other free to explore—fingers skimming Sandy's chest, brushing a stiff nipple, sliding under Sandy's arm and down to rest in the small of his back, tucking him tight against Miller's groin and eliciting another demanding growl from somewhere deep in Miller's throat.

The sound shot a shiver down the length of Sandy's body. Just a kiss and he was so fucking turned on he was shaking. He wanted more. Craved more. The sounds Miller made when he came undone, the stain in his cheeks, the arch of his body as the pleasure rushed through him, the feel of him inside, pushing, filling Sandy up, the scent of their release, the taste of his spill. Everything.

They were shoved up against each other, grinding and panting, their faces buried in each other's necks—Sandy moaning encouragement as Miller bit down hard on his shoulder. He was close, so fucking close, and then Miller was gone, all except for his fingers on Sandy's lips.

His eyes shot open. *What the . . . ?*

But Miller stood wavering on his feet in front of Sandy; eyes closed, face flushed, breath shaky, his fingers over Sandy's lips as if he needed them there to stop him going back for more. And holy fuck, Sandy couldn't blame him. He was a half-second away from throwing the man's arm aside and taking what he wanted—rules be damned— because, Jesus Christ, that had gone nuclear fast.

He kissed Miller's fingers and removed them from his lips. "Yeah, so, that happened."

Miller's eyes stayed closed, but something, possibly a chuckle, either that or a grumble of frustration, rolled from his lips. "Yeah. Unexpected. But good, right?" His eyes cracked open a smidge and he watched Sandy through red-fringed lashes.

Sandy blew out a long breath. "Very good. But tricky."

"Tricky?" Miller's brow creased as he leaned closer again to nibble on Sandy's ear. "You are so fucking sexy."

Yeah, nah, way too dangerous to start that again. Sandy leaned away, cupped Miller's face, and drew him front and centre. "Yeah, tricky. With that whole moratorium on first-date hook-ups thing still in effect."

A slow, sexy smile crossed that beautiful face, highlighting each and every tiny freckle. "Riiiight. No bending the rules?"

Lost in his eyes for a second, Sandy almost, almost . . . "Not tonight. But having said that, you are way too fucking tempting. I need to go before I say to hell with it and drop my clothes on this nice clean kitchen floor of yours and let you do whatever the hell you want to me over that low counter."

Miller's eyes grew black and his breath stuttered. "Jesus, Sandy. You can't say shit like that. You . . . fuck."

"And just for the record"—Sandy picked up Miller's cane and pressed it into his hand—"*that* was fucking hot."

Miller glanced down at his cane and back up at Sandy with surprise. "Right. Noted. You better get going before I think of other ways I can use it."

"Homework." Sandy licked his lips.

Miller shook his head. "I have a feeling I'm gonna regret this."

"I guarantee you won't." They locked eyes until Sandy broke it. Broke free before he broke every fucking rule in his book. "Walk me to the door. And don't forget my, what were they, daphne?" He winked and headed out of the kitchen, leaving Miller standing there.

"Viburnum. They're fucking viburnum." Miller's voice followed Sandy up the hall.

"You're pretty cute, you know that?" Sandy called back over his shoulder.

Miller grumbled, "I am *not* cute."

CHAPTER SEVEN

SANDY THREW HIS KEYS ON THE HALL TABLE, DROPPED HIS satchel to the floor, and headed for the fridge. Only Tuesday and he was already beat. Four nasty post-mortems, two court appearances accompanying Ed, a missed lunch, a screwed-up order from the med supplies company, and a blocked drain in the autopsy suite. *Ugh.*

A double sloe gin with loads of ice drowning in a sea of cold tonic was exactly what these hellish couple of days needed to set his head right. Then maybe a long bath, second gin in hand, while he took a little time to contemplate this whole new interesting thing he had going with Miller.

Because interesting, it definitely was. In fact—

"Sandy?"

"Holy shit!" Sandy's hand flew to his chest. "Mum! What the hell are you doing here?" He eyed his mother curled up at the end of his couch, coffee to the side, needlepoint in hand, looking particularly determined, something that never boded well.

"What do you think I'm doing here? Waiting for you. You're late, by the way."

"I'm *not* late. Late implies someone or something I should've been back for earlier. But, as it happens, I live in an apartment *by myself*, having had *nothing* on my evening agenda other than a bath and a gin. Ergo, I am *not* late. Which reminds me, I need a drink."

He kissed his mother on the cheek and glanced at her delicate handiwork—a scene from *A Midsummer Night's Dream*. "That's looking good."

"Just as well. I've been at it six months and the baby's due next week. Pour one for me, will you?"

Goddammit. There went his relaxing early night. Sandy headed for his postage-stamp-sized kitchen with its pretty view over the city skyline across to the Harbour Bridge. It might not have enough room to swing a cat, but damn, it had that view. Not to mention it hadn't bankrupted Sandy to buy it, which was a miracle considering the scorching Auckland property market.

Having said that, he'd almost outgrown the apartment before he'd even moved in, never being very good at calculating space to furniture ratios. Still, there was only him, so space wasn't really an issue. A yard sale at his mum's and a couple of trips to his favourite second-hand places and the problem was remedied.

He got the gin from the cupboard and pulled open the fridge, staring blankly at its contents for a moment, mostly to calm and prepare himself for the most likely reason his mother would be sitting in his lounge unannounced. His fucking father. Just the thought of the man boiled his blood.

"You realise you could've interrupted something." He grabbed the tonic and set it next to the gin and a couple of old-fashioned cut-crystal glasses from his grandmother. "I might've had a date. Just because you have a key—"

Shit. Sandy palmed his forehead in the weighty silence that met his comment. His mum had been nothing but a rock in his life, including when his dickhead of a father walked out on them.

He popped his head back into the lounge and winced at his mother's wide eyes. "I'm sorry," he said softly. "You didn't deserve that. It's just that sometimes . . . in some *situations*, I might not answer the door, even if I'm home . . . can we leave it at that?"

She accepted the olive branch gracefully. "You're right. It was naughty of me and I'm sorry. But you've been ignoring my texts about your father and I wanted to talk."

He nodded. "Fair call. Just give me a minute."

He finished making their drinks and joined her on the couch, kicking off his shoes so he could turn sideways to face her. "I'm sorry I didn't answer your texts, but I . . . I didn't know what to say without hurting you."

She rolled up her needlepoint and shoved it in her handbag with more force than was likely necessary. "I'm not sure you achieved your objective there, son. It hurts just as much being ignored."

Dammit. "Yeah okay, I admit it might not have been the best response," he answered carefully because there was no way he was laying claim to all the responsibility. His mum had made a choice that was hers alone. "But I did say I didn't want to be a part of this."

He took a deep breath and focussed on keeping his voice calm. "I still don't know what I think about him turning up like this out of the blue. I get why *you* wanted to see him, that you'd like answers, maybe even an apology. But personally, I'm not ready for any half-baked self-recriminations about how sorry he is for the pain he's caused. Sorry that he needed to go and fucking find himself because he was so damn unhappy.

"And screw the fact that he left the day after I came out without a single word to me, then or since. He might've been unhappy stuck in this family, but it was my queerness that tipped him over the edge; don't tell me that it didn't. Well, he can go fuck himself. There is *nothing* he can say that I want to hear. It took nearly ten years after he left for me to accept that it was okay to be me. That I didn't need his or anyone's approval, and that I wasn't to blame for our family breaking up. I'm not doing anything to jeopardise that acceptance now."

His eyes misted and he dropped his chin to his chest. "Fuck. I wasn't going to do this. I wasn't going to ever let him do this to me again." He wiped his eyes on his sleeves and scowled at his mother. "This is why I can't listen to his bullshit. I feel fucking fifteen all over again. He still has the power to make me cry, and I fucking hate it. Sorry for the language, but . . ."

His mother pulled him into a fierce hug and kissed his cheek. "I know, sweetheart. I know. And you're right, he did *fuck* us over."

Sandy snorted.

"*All* of us, but particularly you. What he did was inexcusable. Whether he deserves your forgiveness or not is entirely up to you." She let him go but held his gaze. "I'm not trying to influence that. We all have issues with him that we have to decide how to live with in our own ways. Your sister is different again from you. Yes, she lost her dad, but what he did to *you* affected Lizzie deeply as well. She tried so hard to make up that difference for you, to defend you. She still does."

It was true. Lizzie had always been more like Sandy's big sister than his little one, fiercely protective to the point of irksome. "I didn't ask her to, I did okay. She didn't need to worry."

His mother's eyes flashed. "Don't. Just don't."

Argh. What the hell am I doing? Sandy reached for her hand. "I'm being a little shit, aren't I?"

She covered his hand with hers and patted it. "Yes, but I understand why. I just have to put my teenager mum hat back on again."

Sandy gave her his best eye-roll. "Ouch."

She smiled. "I've still got it. But getting back to why I'm here, I know I'm asking a lot, but I want you to hear about my meeting with your father. I don't expect anything from you other than to listen. We're a family, the three of us: you, me and your sister. Your father is connected, but it's the three of us that matter in this instance. And I won't have any *one* of us out of the loop, understand. I won't fracture this family again. Do with the information as you like, but you need to at least have it. Please?"

It made sense, and Sandy hated that it did. "Have you talked to Lizzie?"

She hesitated. "I didn't need to talk to Lizzie."

No. His mouth fell open. "Jesus Christ, she went with you, didn't she?"

"Sandy, please." She pleaded with her eyes.

Goddamn you, Lizzie. I trusted you. "But she was just as mad at him, as I was. Why would she meet him? And why the hell didn't she tell me?"

His mother took a few seconds to breathe some calm between them. "She's her own person, Sandy," she reminded him patiently. "And she didn't change her mind until the last minute. Plus, you weren't answering any of my texts, remember?"

"But *Lizzie* didn't text or call me. I would've answered." *Never said I wasn't childish.*

His mother pursed her lips and scowled. "I'm gonna let that go and try not to take it personally. And she didn't text you for the same reason as she's not here today: she knew you'd do this."

Goddammit. Sandy slouched down in the couch and rubbed the back of his neck, avoiding his mother's gaze. "Do what?"

"Go off like a damn rocket."

His gaze shot up. "I'm not—"

She arched a brow.

"All right, maybe I am."

She patted his hand. "You've every right, of course, but she feels guilty, like she's betrayed you. And she shouldn't feel that way. She shouldn't have to feel guilty that she's letting you down just because she wanted some answers to get on with her life. She's not you, and she doesn't have to do what you want her to."

Fucking, fuck, fuck. He was being a jerk and he knew it. But was he really the only one who remembered what that bastard had done to them? As soon as the thought popped into his head he cringed. Of course he bloody wasn't. Just because his mum and his sister were apparently capable of being a damn sight more mature about it than he was, didn't mean they didn't remember every gut-wrenching moment of that time.

"No," he muttered. "No, she shouldn't feel guilty, and that's on me for making her think I wouldn't support her. She had every right. I just . . . I guess I just don't understand how the two of you can even stand to be in the same room with him."

"Who says we can?" His mother took a long swallow of her gin and Sandy followed suit. He saw another two in his immediate future at this rate.

"You don't have the monopoly on feelings of betrayal and anger," she added, cradling the glass in her hands and turning those guilt screws a little tighter.

Goddamn mothers.

She stared at her hands and shook her head as if remembering. "You don't think I wanted to spit on him?" She looked back up with surprising fire in her eyes. "He took off without a word, ignored his parenting responsibilities, left me with two hurt and angry teenagers to raise and a suffocating debt that his half-arsed contribution didn't exactly cover. And then I get divorce papers in the *mail* and learn he's marrying again? Do you think that didn't gut me to the core, Sandy? You think I didn't do my fair share of hating him? But I had two kids to raise, I didn't . . . I couldn't . . ." She choked up and her eyes welled.

Sandy's heart broke apart. He put both their glasses on the table and hauled her into his arms. "God, I'm so sorry, Mum. You were amazing for us, you still are. I don't know how you did it, and I'm sorry for being such a complete tosser about this. I just forget, you know. At the time it all seemed to be about me, and I forget he wasn't always like that. That you loved him once."

She wept against Sandy's chest and he buried his own tears in her hair. They stayed that way for a long moment until she finally wiggled free.

"I just needed to see him," she said, dabbing at her eyes. "And you weren't there to hear what was said, so you don't know how proud I am of your sister for laying it bare exactly what she thought of him. How proud you'd have been of her too."

Sandy perked up. "She did?"

His mother's eyes sparkled. "Called him an arrogant, selfish wanker who's lucky we didn't take a damn contract out on the remainder of his miserable life for what he did to us."

Huh. Go, sis. A swell of pride filled his chest, then another of shame. He ducked his head. "I *am* sorry I wasn't there to hear that. And I'm sorry for underestimating both of you."

She laughed and the sound set his heart to rest. "It was pretty awesome, and your father was, well, let's just say speechless. And don't be sorry, sweetheart. As I said before, we each need to do this in our own way. On that note, I'm just asking that you listen to what I have to say, and then you can decide for yourself what you want to do, no pressure from me. There's no right or wrong answer."

Sandy blew out a sigh. "Okay. I'm listening."

She nodded and squeezed his hand. "He still wants to meet with you."

Fuck. He'd known it was coming, but he was determined to hear his mother out, so he swallowed the spiteful reply dancing on his lips and took a breath. "Is there anything worth hearing?"

She shrugged. "Yes and no. He wanted to, in his words, reconnect, try to build a bridge."

His eyes rolled so far, the only thing stopping them falling down the back of his throat was the what-the-fuck coming up it.

His mother raised her hands. "I know, I know. It was all I could do not to slap him myself. And I'm not going to pretend he had any satisfactory answers to offer for what he did, but that was never going to be the case, right? I think you should ask Lizzie what she thought. I left still with a lot of questions, but *I am* going to meet him again. I need time to process this lot first, and then I'll call him."

"Lizzie said he was back up north of Auckland?"

"Yes. Apparently, his other marriage ended six years ago."

Shocker.

"There were no children. He said he'd been drinking too much at the time, although he's dry now. I guess we can count our lucky stars he wasn't doing that with us."

"Small mercies. But you're seeing him again?" Sandy could hardly believe it.

"I am," she answered flatly.

"You're not . . . I mean, you and he aren't . . . ?"

She barked out a laugh. "No, sweetheart. That's never happening. God, what a thought."

"So is this all part of that AA owning-your-shit stuff? Is he just visiting the people he's hurt in his life?"

She shrugged and reached for her glass. "I don't know. And even if it is, you don't have to be part of it. I just wanted you to have the information." But her gaze was hesitant.

"No." Sandy bristled, reading between the lines. "You think I should see him, don't you? You think it might help. That's what this is about, isn't it? Just because he's got you rolling over—"

"Sandy, enough!" Her eyes flashed a warning Sandy hadn't seen since he was a kid, and he instantly shut his mouth. "You don't get to talk to me that way. You know very little about my relationship with your father outside of a child's point of view. You *do not* get to judge me."

Sandy winced. "You're right, I don't. But goddammit, this whole thing has me so mad. He's done it again. Thrown a hand grenade into our lives and watched it blow everything to pieces again. He shouldn't get to do that. He shouldn't still have that power. He shouldn't . . ." Sandy slammed his eyes shut against the tears.

His mother reached for him, but he jerked away. "Don't . . . please. Just . . . not now. I need to think about things. I don't have an answer for you at the moment."

Her heavy sigh said it all. "He only gets to do what you allow him to, son. He doesn't deserve anything from you, certainly not the right to upset you again. Do I think it would be good for you to see him? To be honest, yes. He's a big bogeyman in your head, and I think that at the least meeting him might cut him down to size. But am I going to pressure you? No. This is the last you'll hear of it. And if you don't want to know what happens next time I see him, I won't push. But I wanted you to have this last opportunity. I'm sorry if it's painful or if you think I've betrayed you in any way."

"I don't think that, not really." He took her hand and let her tug him down so he leaned on her shoulder. "I'm just . . . ugh, I don't know what I am." He wished he could reassure her, but he just couldn't. He was still so fucking angry.

He felt her lips on his head.

"Call me when you're ready," she murmured. "Any time, it doesn't matter." She let him go and got to her feet, keeping a hand on his head. "None of this was done to hurt you, sweetheart. And no one will ever judge you for what you decide, least of all me. I love you so much, and I'm so proud of you. And I'll be careful using my key next time." She ruffled his hair and he looked up.

"I love you too, Mum. And I'm sorry for being such a prat. I'll call, I promise."

"Thank you. And talk to your sister." She patted his head once again, and the next thing Sandy heard was the click of the front door.

He thought about calling Miller, but they were too new. Miller didn't need to deal with Sandy's fucked-up family issues just yet. He clutched a cushion to his chest, fell to his side on the couch, drew his knees up to his chin, and let the numbness take him.

Goddamn his father.

Motherfucker.

CHAPTER EIGHT

THURSDAY AFTERNOON AND MILLER WAS ONCE AGAIN wheeling the length of the hospital corridors, headed for one of the numerous meeting rooms he spent most of his working life floating between. He whiled away more time in these bland caves than his own office, but that was the nature of the job—advise, consult, problem solve, and supervise all the key hospital working committees, particularly those riddled with ethical stumbling blocks.

His role wasn't as a functioning member of the committees, but a peripheral fount of knowledge both about correct process and the bigger picture. Committees got mired in their own shit more often than not, unable to see the forest for the trees. It was part of Miller's job to help them stay focussed and to act as a backstop to avoid procedural and ethical mistakes. To that end, he was about as welcome as you'd expect to a group of people who just wanted what they wanted and as quickly as possible.

He read all the committee minutes, but with the less crucial committees, he only attended if he was really needed or invited, dealing with most questions by phone. But in others, like any employment or discipline committees, attendance was often mandatory.

Like this one. He'd spent the first three days of the week back and forth along this hall, trying to get the surgical department to take another look at their shortlists for two senior surgeon positions about to become vacant. He was fighting for a better cross-section of applicants to be represented. You'd have thought he was asking for their damn firstborn. Now he was headed for the actual shortlist interviews. Normally he wouldn't bother attending these, the bulk of his directive done by then, but these bozos hadn't exactly inspired confidence to get any of this right, unable to see past their own prejudices.

He got into the elevator, nodding hello to a couple of physios he'd run into at different times through the Wheel Blacks, and rolled to the back thinking his week could've been worse. After his date with Sandy, Miller had been on a high that had somehow persisted throughout the entire shit show of a week, and that was saying something.

They'd even managed to synchronise a couple of shared coffee breaks early in the week which allowed Miller at least a taste of Sandy in his space again, but Sandy had been quieter yesterday, and as new as they were to all this, Miller hadn't been quite sure whether to push for the reason. In the end he let it go, the cafeteria not being the ideal place for any serious conversation. It was better than not seeing Sandy at all, but Miller begrudged the nosey staff and rowdy families.

Texting had filled the gaps—mostly mundane stuff like *how's your day going, don't eat lunch from the café today because they've rehashed yesterday's Bolognese into lasagne,* and *Cam's on the warpath so avoid the ER.* That kind of thing. But Miller was still struggling to get used to it. It was almost surreal, like he'd fallen down a rabbit hole he'd been neatly sidestepping his whole life, weird in a good way, having someone check in on him, care about his day. And every single remembered text brought a smile to his face he had zero control over.

Just like now as he thought of the raunchy gif Sandy had sent that morning.

"Miller? You want out at this floor?" one of the physios asked, jolting Miller from his musing.

Shit. He glanced at the floor panel. "Yes, sorry. Wasn't paying attention." He rolled out and took a right toward HR.

He'd never been this sappy guy. Never hung on the next call, the next text, the next—god help him—date. Welcome to the bright, new, and shiny world of Miller Harrison. Take an *aw* and a *golly gosh* with you when you go. For fuck's sake.

Those early months after discharge from rehab, he'd hated the constant check-ins from his family and well-meaning friends, his temper short and pointed. They'd soon got the message. Maybe too well. It was still rare for any of them to call unless it was for a particular reason. He had no one to blame but himself, and for the first time, he acknowledged that maybe he missed those random connections.

He made a sharp left turn into HR and waved at Clara behind the glass.

"We should charge you rent, you practically live here, Miller," she called out.

"You'd have to improve the service. I've heard the receptionist sucks."

She laughed and flipped him off. "It's the quality of the clientele. You're only as good as the ingredients, right?"

He headed for the meeting room, stopping for a water from the cooler on the way. Sam asking for his help had made him feel good in all kinds of ways. He'd spent breakfast thinking about Geo, still not sure he was the best choice for the kid to open up to. He was barely getting his own rainbow shit together. And as he threw his paper cup in the recycling, an idea struck him.

It was so freaking obvious. Why the hell hadn't he thought of it earlier?

He pulled out his phone and fired a text to Sam. **Would Geo mind another gay man sitting in on Saturday? I have a** *friend who knows a lot more than me about what support might be out there. Either way is fine.*

He got himself settled in the meeting room and exchanged a frosty hello with the two surgeons on the interviewing panel who made their displeasure at being *supervised* more than obvious. Tough cookies. If they'd had their acts together, he wouldn't need to be here. The HR rep was much more welcoming, although Miller suspected that was because he took the heat off her. They were still awaiting the arrival of two remaining panellists when Miller's phone vibrated and he pulled it out expecting to see Sam's answer.

Thought I'd check up on the 'cane homework' situation?

Not Sam. Miller couldn't stop his ridiculous smile, remembering Sandy's heated look when he handed Miller back his cane Sunday night. After a quick glance around the table, he texted back. *Are we talking the organic or inorganic variety of 'cane'?*

The answer came quick.

Both but I must admit the organic option has been taking up a lot of head space in my shower . . .

Miller's dick twitched. *You can't say shit like that when I'm in a meeting.*

You love it.

Miller so fucking did.

Besides you don't have to answer.

Touché. He stole another glance around the room, but no one seemed to be paying any attention, too busy going over their notes and gossiping. He took a deep breath and texted. *I'm studying hard. It's a lot to take in. Might have to cram.*

Miller stared at his phone, feeling all of sixteen. Shit, was he sexting? He'd never sexted in his life. All he knew was it was turning him the fuck on and his pale traitorous cheeks were likely blazing.

A few seconds later Sandy texted back.

Preparation is the key to success. Are we talking about this?

A photo of a pencil appeared on Miller's phone and he snorted.

Or this?

A sawn-off tree branch with a decidedly pornographic leaning popped up, and Miller had to swallow the laugh that threatened. He searched for a few seconds before he found what he wanted and sent it back. *You need to raise your standards . . .*

He stared at the image of the elephant trunk he'd sent and wondered if he'd gone too far, watching as the reply dots started, then stopped, then started again. A few seconds later, he got his answer.

We're gonna need a lot more lube . . .

The hoot of laughter was out before Miller could stop it and everyone in the room turned to stare.

"Sorry." He pointed at his phone, his cheeks on fire. "Kids." He shrugged. "What can you do?"

He fired a reply. *I just embarrassed myself in front of the entire surgical interviewing panel.*

I'd say I was sorry but I'm so not. I miss your lips.

Damn. Miller stared at his screen as every scrap of blood in his body headed south. A few seconds later, the door flew open and the last two people arrived. Just as well. *Gotta go.*

Think of me . . .

Jesus Christ, Miller wasn't sure he'd be able to think of anything else.

"You want the good news or the bad?" Art Spencer, team doctor for the Wheel Blacks and all-around bad-arse, shoved Miller's X-rays up onto the lightboxes and stepped back. The appointment had come immediately on the heels of the shortlist interviews, with no time for Miller to even grab a coffee between. After the X-ray part, he'd been poked and prodded and put through his paces as Art assessed his lower sensory and motor nerve function, grumbling to himself and taking copious notes.

Fuck. Miller had known to his core that the ongoing pain in his hip and thigh wasn't a good sign and wasn't only about the hit he'd taken during the game. He'd had the pain on and off for a while, though not as bad. Something had changed. Which was exactly why he'd avoided an appointment with the way too perceptive doctor for longer than he should have.

"Go on, just spit it out." He eyed Art warily.

"Come here." Art motioned him over to the lightbox. "See this." He pointed to a section of his vertebral column below the glare of plates and screws used to fuse an unstable portion of his spine following the accident.

Miller peered closer. "What am I looking at?"

"This." Art tapped his pen on the X-ray, pointing to the uneven greyed edge on a couple of the vertebrae. Miller's heart sank.

"Tell me." He hobbled back to his chair and stretched out his leg while Art returned to his desk.

"Your previous X-rays were taken at the end of the season last year. They showed a small amount of new degeneration since the accident, nothing unexpected, but these show it's advancing. The pain you're feeling isn't from your hip, Miller. It's referred nerve pain. The hit you took must have localised around these less than pristine vertebrae, and the nerves are irritated. The disc doesn't appear that happy either, but that's not new and may or may not be part of this particular problem. Have you noticed any other changes—mobility, sensitivity, erection issues, anything at all?"

Miller eyed him warily. "Nothing, just the pain."

"That's a good sign."

Miller didn't like how the conversation was going. "So, how many games am I going to miss?"

Art wrote on Miller's chart. "Your last game was Saturday, right?"

Miller nodded.

"Okay, then I want you out for another ten days."

Miller groaned.

"Or I can make that two weeks?" He side-eyed Miller, who instantly shut his mouth.

"Mmm. Just as I thought." Art tapped his pen on the file. "All being well, you can start back then and be right for the series with Australia next month. Because I'm nice, I'll let you participate in non-contact training to keep up for the fitness test, but no practice games and no hits, okay?"

Miller breathed a sigh of relief, but Art sat back in his chair, looking anything but happy.

"So this is the part where I need you to listen, Tap."

His stomach sank. "Okay, I'm listening."

Art nodded. "Bottom line? You got off lucky. The degeneration isn't going away and will likely get worse. Hardly surprising after the beating your body took in the accident. But as your doctor and physician for the Wheel Blacks, I'm putting you on notice. A few more hits like this, in the right place, and you could be looking at a lot less mobility than you enjoy at the moment."

Goddammit. Miller took a moment to let it sink in. A moment for the tentacles of fear to take hold in his belly. A moment to feel them and then bury them under that overwhelming determination not to let anything beat him, a determination he'd lived by for ten years and wasn't going to change now. "Okay. I hear you. I have to be careful. I get it."

"Do you? Do you really? Because this is serious, Tap."

"I know it is. But you're not cutting me, right? It's not bad enough to keep me off the team?"

Art's lips drew into a thin line and he sank back in his chair. "No, not yet. I'm not speaking to you as the Wheel Blacks' doctor, I'm speaking as your personal physician who's concerned about your overall health."

"But I'm fitter than I've ever been. I've got no other symptoms. I can do this, Art. I'll talk to Merv and we'll find ways to buffer the hits, adjust the strapping, whatever. Another Paralympics, then we'll talk, okay? Give me that much. Those risks you're talking about apply to every full-contact sport. You get hit in the wrong place in ambulant rugby and you can end up in one of these chairs. Fall off a racehorse and you can die."

Art's gaze remained steady. "That's all true, but in those cases, you're talking about bodies that haven't already suffered the kinds of injuries yours has. Your spinal column already has some dings in it, Miller, and this pain you're feeling is just another reminder. I take it you want to keep the movement and sensation you have?"

Miller narrowed his gaze. "Low blow. You know damn well I do."

"Then protect it. Draw a line in the sand for yourself before your body does it for you. You're only thirty-five. You've got a whole life ahead of you."

Miller snorted. "Tell that to my nephew. He thinks I'm already over the hill."

Art didn't laugh.

Miller's cheeks burned. "Okay, okay. I take your point," he relented. "I'll think about it. *And* I'll be careful."

"See that you are. Another episode like this and I won't hesitate to pull you for the season, understand?"

Fuck. Miller swallowed hard. "Understood."

"Good. Be back here in ten days for your clearance."

Miller nodded and spun the chair, suddenly desperate to get out of the office.

"I'm not the bad guy here, Tap."

He paused and looked back. "I know, I—"

"Just think about it, okay?"

"Okay." More nodding as he headed for the door. "I'll think about it."

"Do that." Art crossed to open it for him. "See you at training on Friday."

How he managed to get all the way back to his office and slam the door shut, before he fell apart was a damn miracle.

Fuck, fuck, fuck.

He freed his canes from his chair, got to his feet, and made his way to the window, spitting mad at the myriad of ambulant people making their way in and out of the hospital, not for one second appreciating the incredible gift they possessed.

Goddammit. He'd promised himself he wasn't going to do this again. He was done with comparisons and regrets long ago. Anything to do with feeling sorry for himself. He wasn't that guy anymore. He threw his canes across the room, bouncing them off his filing cabinet with an ear-shattering clatter.

But, son of a bitch, how was this fair? He'd thought he'd lost rugby once, he'd be damned if he was going to lose it a second time. Maybe he couldn't hold on to the level of the Wheel Blacks—maybe that simply wasn't possible down the track. He got that part. But if he had to learn a whole different way of playing, move from offence to defence, get another spinal fusion, Miller would do it, anything to keep the rest of his sport. He couldn't imagine his life without rugby in some form. He'd find a way. Pushing through was what he was good at.

A soft knock on the door broke Miller's downward spiral of anger. "Come in," he snapped, then mentally kicked himself.

"Miller?" The door eased open and Sandy slipped through in his hospital scrubs. The concern on his face said it all as his gaze landed on the jumble of canes at the foot of the dented cabinet. He shot Miller a questioning glance. "I thought I heard a crash. Whatever did the filing cabinet do to deserve that?"

Miller snorted and motioned him inside. "Close it again, will you?"

Sandy did, but rather than treat Miller with caution, he dropped the brown paper bag he was carrying onto Miller's desk, walked right up into his space, folded those long arms around Miller's waist, and pulled him close.

"Having a bad day?" He whispered the words against Miller's ear and Miller was lost again in that odd combination of scents he'd grown to associate with Sandy—citrus, often orange, but sometimes lemon, and usually a spice mixed in there as well. And while at work —a hint of antiseptic that undercut but never dominated the mix.

Miller drank it in, burying his face against Sandy's neck as he slipped his arms around his waist and felt the tension bleed from his body. His own personal stress leech. "You always smell so damn good. How do you do that?"

Sandy chuckled, the sound reverberating softly through Miller's chest. "I'm surprised I don't smell like thirty feet of four-day-old dead bowel, considering what we've been doing this morning."

"Ew. I don't think I even want to know."

"Wise choice."

"But that only makes it all the more remarkable."

"Will it destroy the fantasy if I tell you I spritzed before I came." Sandy pulled back to press a quick kiss to Miller's lips.

"For me?" Miller smiled.

"No. For the orderly who delivered our next body as I left." Sandy rolled those beautiful brown eyes. "Of course for you."

"And I am overwhelmed with gratitude." Miller nuzzled back into Sandy's neck, causing him to giggle and push him away. "Stop that. I feel like one of those scratch-and-smell T-shirts. Now tell me what's got your panties in a bunch."

Miller sighed. "Don't I at least deserve a proper kiss? I would've thought that would be in the first few pages of any dating-for-dummies manual. Always kiss your date upon meeting them, right?"

Sandy's lips twitched. "I believe I had that covered."

"Pfft. That wasn't a kiss." Miller leaned in so only a whisper separated their mouths as he brushed the tips of their noses together. "That was a tiny fart of the lips. Barely even felt it. And sub-clause B of the aforementioned meet-and-greet kiss protocol—" He licked the seam of Sandy's mouth. "—clearly states there are bonus points for tongue."

"Is that so? Well, far be it from me to fuck with sub-clause B."

Miller waggled his eyebrows and hooked a finger in the waist-band of Sandy's scrubs. "There's the can-do spirit I so love. Now let's see about those bonus points."

He let the wall take his weight and pulled Sandy forward, their mouths crashing together, the kiss hard and needy as Miller's tongue dove right in to sweep Sandy's taste back into his mouth where it belonged and banished his morning from hell.

It was everything he remembered, sweet and a little salty, just like the man himself. They made out greedily for a minute or so, Miller's hands tracing lines up and down Sandy's back under his shirt, cupping his arse and dragging him close, sealing their groins together. God, he felt good and Miller couldn't get enough. Hard and supple at the same time. Skin like a sweep of satin over flesh with the lightest scruff around the jaw. Legs like a fucking octopus, stamped on either side of Miller's, pinning him steady without a second thought. He gripped Sandy's hair from the back and tugged to expose his throat, and the groan that tripped from his lips when Miller sucked his way down Sandy's throat was about as filthy as they came.

"Damn, you have to stop." Sandy pushed back, flushed to his hairline, a hand on Miller's chest to keep him in place.

"As much as I'm enjoying this," he said breathily. "And I so fucking am, we only have fifteen minutes, and I brought lunch"

"I can do a lot with fifteen minutes." Miller pushed forward against Sandy's hand. "To hell with lunch. I want you."

A smirk stole over Sandy's face, and he looked particularly pleased with Miller's answer. "Understandably so. But be that as it may, we have food. And if you have anything like the afternoon I have ahead, you'll need to eat. Besides, it'll make you less growly. Eat lunch and save a filing cabinet. It's trending hard."

"I thought you liked me growly."

Sandy's eyes heated. "I do. But not when I don't know what's behind it. So, eat and talk. And hand me that rug you've got over there."

Miller passed the rug he kept for when his legs were bothering him and Sandy moved Miller's files to one side of the desk. Then he spread the rug over the rest and began setting out what looked remarkably like a picnic.

Miller stared in disbelief as his office was transformed. And just like that, all the angst, fear, and anger from the morning disappeared in the puff of a tall, scrub-clad blond miracle.

Sandy chatted as he laid out sandwiches, fruit, two tubs of ice cream, and a couple of fruit juices, but Miller barely heard a word, caught up in his expressive hands and easy charm. Even in scrubs, Sandy was captivating—tall, lean, and effortlessly graceful.

"You're staring at me." He gave a shy smile and Miller fucking loved those fleeting glimpses into a less collected version of the man.

"Sorry." He leaned across the desk and captured Sandy's mouth in another hard kiss. "Thank you for doing this. I've had a crap morning and this . . . well, in a few minutes you've turned my day from shitty to enjoyable, and I can't tell you how much I appreciate it. Plus I can honestly say I've never had an office picnic."

Sandy blushed prettily, that creamy skin, a pale and unforgiving canvas for the slightest emotion. "You're welcome. And everyone should have an office picnic at least once in their lives. But I'm not so easily distracted. Take a sandwich. We haven't got long, so you'll need to eat and talk at the same time. Aaaand . . . go."

Sandy ate and listened attentively as Miller filled him in on what Art had said about the degeneration in his vertebrae and the pain in his leg. It was, admittedly, a carefully edited version that left out the biggest issue around Miller's ongoing commitment to wheelchair rugby, but then Sandy and he were still pretty new as a concept, and Miller wasn't comfortable going there yet. Anyone who knew him would be gobsmacked that he was sharing even that much, so yeah, there was that. He was a little shocked himself. But then Sandy had presented Miller with a damn picnic at work. Who the hell did that?

Halfway through their picnic, he finally received a text back from Sam to say his friend was fine with someone else being there. Miller blew a very relieved sigh. He wouldn't carry the angst and responsibility on his own, *if* Sandy agreed, that was.

But when Miller asked, Sandy didn't even hesitate, looking surprised but also rather pleased.

"I feel a bit of a fraud, to be honest." Miller admitted.

"You're gay, Miller," Sandy answered flatly. "You don't have to be out, political, or a pristine role model, whatever the hell you think that is that doesn't actually exist. You'll share a lot of the same feelings and concerns regardless. And the fact you haven't been fully out puts you right where this boy is. You're relevant to him."

Miller snorted. "Not according to Sam. He thinks my relevance to youth culture is dodgy to say the least."

"Sam's a teenager," Sandy scoffed. "They're terminally ageist and drawn to shiny reflections of themselves. Best to take any deep life analysis they utter with a dumpster load of salt. So, tell me more about this degenerative change. What does it mean for your rugby?" He crumpled the paper bag that held his sandwich, three-pointed it into the bin, and reached for an ice cream.

Miller's jaw clenched. He should've known Sandy wouldn't drop it. Still, they'd promised honesty. "Nothing as yet," he answered, quick enough to have Sandy raise a speculative brow. "Art watches us like hawks. If he doesn't think our bodies are coping, he won't hold back. For now it's training, but no contact for a couple of weeks and then back into it."

"Mmm." Sandy looked less than convinced but he didn't push.

Which meant Miller's attention was instead free to focus on the spoonful of chocolate ice cream making its way to Sandy's mouth. Their eyes locked just as Sandy folded his lips over the melting mound of sweetness and pulled it ever so slowly inside. Then he flipped the spoon and ran it over his tongue to get those last drops, and Miller might have groaned.

Sandy smirked, ladled another mound of ice cream onto his spoon, and offered it across the desk. Miller leaned forward and took the spoon into his mouth and Sandy's brown eyes grew black. He licked his lips, withdrew the spoon, swallowed, then leaned in and fused their mouths together, plunging his tongue through that sugary, chocolatey taste, deep into Miller's mouth, making sure to get into every corner.

The remains of Miller's sandwich fell to the floor as he fisted the neck of Sandy's scrubs and joined the feast. He was seconds away from hauling the guy right across the desk and onto his lap when Sandy suddenly wriggled free and brushed off his scrubs with a knowing smile and a promise in his eyes that left Miller breathless.

He wasn't sure if it was the decade of limited carnal encounters of any description, or Sandy's intrinsic sexual appeal, or the simple fact that Miller just fucking had the hots for the guy like you wouldn't believe, but when he was with Sandy, Miller's brain fizzed and bubbled with a desire and urgency he struggled to control and sure as shit didn't want to.

Filed under miscellaneous for so damn long, now that his sexuality was back online, he didn't know how to turn it off, or even turn it down. Not to mention, it came with needs and wants and thoughts and feelings that he suspected had everything to do with Sandy and not just his dick. It was electrifying, breathtaking, and goddamn terrifying. He'd done perfectly well for ten years running his social life in first gear, second if he was feeling risky. He was in no way ready for this fuel-injected rollercoaster through his heart.

Sandy eyed him coyly, ran his fingers through his silky blond locks, and pouted. "Damn, look at that. You've got my hair all sticky." He pulled his bottom lip between his teeth, glanced at Miller, and winked. "I doubt it'll be the last time."

Aaaand nope, Miller had no more room in his "wild new feelings and experience" file for anything else, and so he left his jaw on the floor where it belonged.

Sandy took one look at the expression on his face and laughed. "Don't worry. I can tell by the whites of your eyes that you're hanging by a thread. I'll leave you to it. Thanks for . . . sharing lunch?" He retrieved Miller's canes from the floor and held them out. "I'll leave you to collect yourself, shall I?"

"Hey, Miller, what are you—" Cam pushed through the doorway and came to a sudden stop. "Oh. *Ohhhh.*"

Fuck. Fuck. Fuck. Miller dropped his head and counted to three.

"Sandy *and* Miller. In the same room. Would you look at that?"

And there it was. Miller glanced up to watch Cam's gaze shift between Miller, Sandy, and the canes Sandy still held out, and he saw the wheels spinning.

Then Cam spied the blanket on his desk and Miller's forgotten sandwich on the floor and his eyes sparkled with delight. "Ohhhh, a picnic lunch? How . . . romantic." Cam turned his focus on Sandy, who'd turned a spectacular shade of beetroot Miller wasn't sure he'd ever seen before.

"Sandy, sweetheart, *friend,*" Cam purred. "Something you forgot to tell me?"

Miller might've enjoyed watching Sandy squirm if it weren't for the fact he knew his was coming. There was no way to read the evidence in the room other than how it was, and he knew they'd just handed the Auckland Med diva of snark an early Christmas present.

Sandy pulled himself to his full height, towering over Cam. "There is nothing you need to know right now, *friend.*" He flicked the cane at Miller, who'd forgotten all about it, and promptly took it from him. "Miller and I are just getting to know each other, so you can keep your snarky commentary for another day, sweetheart."

Miller's brows hit his hairline. There was a clear warning in Sandy's tone which surprised him. Few risked telling Cam what he could and couldn't do, and Miller's respect for Sandy soared.

Cam chewed on his cheek and said nothing, although his eyes still danced. Whether in amusement or frustration, it was hard to tell, but the effect was obviously encouraging to Sandy, who stepped in and kissed his friend on the corner of his mouth. "I promise I'll talk to you later if Miller agrees." He flicked a reassuring glance Miller's way, then back to Cam. "But you know damn well this hospital is a cesspit of gossip, and neither of us need it."

Cam rolled his eyes but returned the kiss. "I won't lie to Reuben if he asks."

"I don't expect you to."

Cam turned to Miller. "And *you* better behave. If I have to juggle invites to social events for the next five years to keep the two of you away from each other, I'll be blaming you." He drilled Miller with a glare.

Miller's eyes popped. "Why me?"

Cam merely arched a brow.

Shit. "Okay, okay. I get it. It'll undoubtedly be my fault."

Cam grinned, setting off all the rainbow sparkles in his eyeliner. "Excellent. There's obviously hope for you yet. Which means I can just sit back and enjoy the show."

Sandy flashed Miller a pointed look that clearly implied he'd help Miller hide the body if necessary and then left him to deal with Cam on his own.

"Are you going to eat that?" Cam eyed the untouched tub of ice cream still sitting on Miller's desk.

"Yes." Miller grabbed it and threw it in the bin.

CHAPTER NINE

MILLER WATCHED WITH ENVY FROM THE SIDELINES AS THE Wheel Blacks broke into two teams and took to the court for a training game. Merv Tattersall walked alongside, then squatted next to his chair.

"For fuck's sake, Tap, if that lip of yours drops any lower, Benson's going to run over it in his new chair. He's moving that thing around the court like a fucking Ferrari. Somebody's gonna get hurt."

Miller laughed. "He's young and keen, coach. Remember when I was like that? Back in the days when I had the arms for it."

Merv patted him on the arm. "Aw, poor boy. You're holding up pretty well for an old dude."

"Fuck off." Miller elbowed him. "I can take that pipsqueak any day."

"I don't doubt it. But he's coming along nicely, don't you think? I think we should bring him up for the Paralympics next year."

A deafening graunch of steel spun their attention to the court where Jimmy's wheel guards had scraped along Benson's, tipping Jimmy sideways to the floor in a spray of creative expletives that rang around the gym like shotgun pellets. Benson hared off from the scene of the crime with a howl of laughter.

Miller turned back to Merv and arched a brow. "Really?"

Merv shrugged. "I admit he needs a little . . . finessing."

Miller snorted. "He's only nineteen. I thought we were just trialling him? You think he's ready?"

Merv's lips pinched together as he thought about it. "I think he could be. I thought I'd give him a run at the Aussie Steelers' games coming up next month. Give him a taste of playing with the big boys. He'll need some extra work, maybe some one-on-one to teach him some tricks? Know of anyone who could do that?" Merv's gaze stayed steady on Miller.

But Miller wasn't biting, yet. "Does that mean you're putting him into offence? With us?"

"It's where he belongs, you know that." Merv's gaze strayed to the sound of shouting on the court. "Ascot, take him on the left, for fuck's sake. You gave that penalty away," he yelled before turning back. "Benson's strong and hungry, and he's a 3.5 pointer like you, really stable in his chair."

Miller stared at him, the pieces falling into place. "You've been talking to Art, haven't you? You think I might not make it?"

Merv shrugged. "What I *think* is that we need options, Tap. And I'm also thinking you wouldn't disagree with that."

Fuck. Merv was right even if it galled Miller to admit it. He jerked his gaze to the court where Beau had Noel pinned on the far sideline with nowhere to go. "I'll pass that fitness test with flying colours, you'll see."

A hand landed on his arm. "I'm not worried about the test, Tap. You're the fittest guy we have. Don't make this more than it is. I simply want to make sure we have options if this nerve thing of yours causes problems. You're the best offence we have. If we lose you, we're screwed. We *need* a backup."

"What about Ascot? Or Jimmy? They're more than ready to take first spot. You can't just overlook them." For some reason Benson's age and obvious potential just rankled. Was he feeling threatened? Hell yeah.

"Jimmy's got a baby due in seven months. They just found out."

That was news to Miller.

"And Ascot has surgery in seven. The games are next year. If we're going to introduce a new offence option, it has to be now. Is there a particular reason you don't like Benson?"

Other than the guy could, like, replace me with room to spare after not too much more work, no. "No. He's great. Perfect for what you want."

"So you'll work with him?" Merv studied Miller closely. "I know what I'm asking of you."

Miller sighed. "Yeah, of course I will. I'm just a bit . . ."

"I know." Merv clapped him on the shoulder. "But I also knew I could count on you."

Fuck. Fuck. Fuck. He watched Merv walk away and tried to squash the mounting panic in his gut. Way to feel like yesterday's news. This week just kept getting better.

He was being ridiculous, of course. They needed options, young options. Even if he made the next Para's, which he bloody would, it could be Miller's last, and Benson was perfect for succession planning. Miller was just being sensitive, but it didn't make it any easier.

But fuck if he was being replaced anytime soon. He'd help the kid get up to par in his skills, but no one was claiming Miller's spot until he was ready to go, and that wasn't anytime soon. He'd be the leading offensive player for the Wheel Blacks at the next games come hell or high water. No one was hungrier than he was for that spot, and no one had worked harder for it.

His head jerked up as Benson's chair flew past, leaving a draught of youth, hunger, and muscle power in his wake. *Son of a bitch.*

Back in the locker room when training was done and they'd all showered, Miller sucked up his childish jealousy and approached Benson as he was about to leave.

"Hey, Benson, you looked good out there today."

Benson rounded his chair with a huge goofy smile on his face. Dear God, the kid looked like an over-eager Labrador puppy. Miller's hand almost shot up to protect his face from being licked.

"Yeah, you really think so?" Benson rolled closer, almost taking Miller's left cane out in the process. "Fuck, sorry." He rolled back, cheeks blazing.

Miller laughed and used his cane to push Benson's chair back further still. "An added buffer," he teased, and Benson's blush grew brighter still. "And yes, I really think so."

"Wow, that means a lot coming from you." Benson fidgeted in his chair, and yep, the puppy image was still hanging in there. It was damn hard not to like the guy. "I still suck at getting back up after a hit though. I'm too fucking slow. My right hip and leg may as well not even be there, I've got no control on that side. And so when I try to swing my weight, only the left side listens. I sometimes think I'd have been better with no motor control in either. Then at least they'd react the same."

Miller's brows crunched together. "Hey, don't ever wish away any of your function. That's a crap way to think."

Benson's gaze slid away. "I know. It's just so damn frustrating at times. Did you hear they're changing some of the international player point rules, which means some existing players won't be considered impaired enough to play in the next games? Graham Bolton said he's thinking of getting his other leg amputated so he'll qualify again. It fucking sucks. What the hell do they think they're doing? We should do something about it. Protest or something."

It did suck, but Miller had no answer to offer. "I think the coaches are getting a response together to file."

"Pffft. Like that'll make any difference," Benson dismissed the idea.

Miller shrugged. "What can you do? We have to work with the rules they give us."

"Maybe. And I get that committees are your jam and all, but we're the ones playing. We're the ones living with these shitty decisions. Why shouldn't we get a bigger say? Anyway, coach just told me he wants me to come regular from now on, be part of the team. Can you believe that?"

The abrupt change of topic was jolting, but Benson was practically vibrating out of his chair and Miller couldn't help but smile. "So I heard."

"Yeah? Yeah, of course you have. It's the best fucking news since I crashed off that wave. I can't wait to tell the olds. I just don't want to screw up, you know?" He looked suddenly concerned.

And oh, Miller knew the feeling like the back of his hand, and just like that he was over his little snit and keen to help the guy. "You won't," he reassured Benson. "And that's kind of what I wanted to talk to you about."

"Oh yeah?"

"Merv said you might appreciate some one-on-one coaching on your offence skills. I thought maybe we could set up a training session."

Benson's eyes almost bugged out of his head. "Really? I mean, you'd do that? For me? Because fuck yeah, that'd be awesome. Learning from the man, I'd fucking love it. Are you sure? I mean, of course you are. You said so, right?"

Miller nodded, and good Lord, had he ever been that eager? His lips twitched because yes, yes, he had. "Well, you've got my number, so how about you think about what days might suit and text me some options."

Benson's head was still nodding like a bobblehead. "Sure. Sure. I can do that. Fuck, what a day. Mum and Dad are gonna flip their wigs. Speaking of which, I'm supposed to head there after training. Better go. Catch ya later, Tap. And thanks, man. You're the best."

Miller stepped back with his canes to avoid getting sideswiped by Benson's chair yet again, and the young guy flew out the door like his wheels were on fire. It was all Miller could do to not burst out laughing.

"What's so funny?" Jimmy wheeled alongside, his gaze tracking to Benson's departing silhouette in the evening gloom.

Miller chuckled and slapped Jimmy on the shoulder. "Just remembering what it was like to be so freaking new at all this. It was so exciting, right? To finally have a space where we were actually a fucking asset and not someone to be worked around, you know what I mean?"

Jimmy grunted. "Yeah, I remember. I couldn't wait to get out of my house every damn day. Spent hours at the gym so I could play better, so I could make this team. Before I started this lark, you had to drag my sorry arse to work out or do my rehab. I was so fucking angry at the world. And now look at us. Old and battered, but still fucking Wheel Blacks, right? And kids like that"—he nodded toward Benson's car—"they want to be just like us. Who'd have fucking thought?" He raised his hand for Miller to high five.

Miller obliged. "Especially you. I mean, I was always role-model material, right? But you? This was probably your last chance."

"Fucker." Jimmy spiked his elbow into Miller's thigh. "But also, true." The smile slid off his face to be replaced by a frown. "So, I meant to ask you, who was the guy at the last game?"

"The guy?" *Shit.* It wasn't like Miller didn't know exactly what Jimmy was asking, but damned if he was going to make it easy for him.

"The one who came to watch you play. He looked a bit . . ." Jimmy rubbed the back of his neck and a flush lit his cheeks. "Well, you know what I mean."

Miller's throat squeezed tight, but he kept his expression neutral and his voice even. "No, I don't know, Jimmy. How about you explain it to me?"

Jimmy eyed him warily. "No need to take offence, mate. I was just passing comment. I mean, I know Reuben's your friend and all, and he's . . . gay, I guess, but that kind of makes sense with the rugby and stuff. I just didn't realise you had . . . others, like that, I suppose."

Son of a bitch. "Jesus, Jimmy. You almost choked on the bloody word. Have another go. *Gay.* It won't kill you. What fucking century were you born in? Let me take a look—" Miller leaned around the back of Jimmy's chair.

Jimmy flailed an arm at him. "What the fuck are you doing?"

"Just checking. And there it is. Fucking red neck all the way."

"Fuck off."

Miller came back around the front, folded his arms across his chest, and stared. "You got a problem with Sandy being gay? Cos I gotta tell you, Jimmy. I'm gonna be hella disappointed in you if you do."

Jimmy's cheeks blew bright red. "It was just a question. I've got no problem with whoever someone chooses to sleep with, I just . . . well, I guess I don't see why they have to make it so fucking obvious, all that makeup and shit. No one wants to see that. It just makes everyone uncomfortable."

"Everyone?" It wasn't that Miller was shocked. If he was going to pick anyone to have an issue, Jimmy's name would've featured high on the list, mostly because he tended to put his mouth in gear before he thought and could be a dumb-arse about this type of thing, but it was still grating.

"He didn't make *me* uncomfortable, Jimmy. He didn't make Robyn uncomfortable, so you want to be careful about those sweeping generalisations. And what about Vicki? I wouldn't have thought she'd feel uncomfortable, or maybe I'm wrong?"

Jimmy's cheeks flashed pink.

"Yeah, so maybe keep your opinions to yourself. And also, it's none of your damn business. Why the fuck do you care what he wears? He was there supporting us. We have few enough spectators as it is."

"Now you're twisting my words," Jimmy huffed. "I was only making an observation."

"Well, make it elsewhere," Miller growled. "He's a friend and I expect you to treat him exactly like I would *your* friends or any other spectator."

"Maybe we don't need those kinds of spectators," Jimmy shot back. Then his gaze slid away as he seemed to realise what he'd said. "And I'm not the only one who feels that way, Tap. Nothing personal."

Holy fuck. Miller's jaw dropped. Sandy's face sprang to mind—his kind nature and all that fucking courage. And Sam's friend that Miller was supposed to talk to tomorrow—dealing with a homophobic arsehole of a dad. And suddenly Miller was done with this.

"I'm going to pretend you didn't say that, Jimmy. Just this once." He loomed over the other man, something he never, ever did to a person in a chair, but the man was way out of line. "But only because we've been mates for eight years, we have to play together, and I don't want to break your fucking jaw before the next game. But if you *ever* say anything like that in my hearing again or within the ranks of this team, I won't hold back, understand? We don't need that sort of ignorant bullshit, and I really didn't expect this from a teammate."

Miller's white knuckles shook around his canes as he turned and made his way back toward the locker room. The squeak of Jimmy's chair quickly followed.

"Wait up," Jimmy huffed. "Look, I didn't mean shit by it. Tap, wait."

Miller ignored him, turned into the men's locker room, and bypassed his spot. Instead, he walked to the centre and rapped his cane on the wooden bench that ran up the middle of the room.

"Fuck. Tap, what are you doing?" Jimmy stopped a metre or so away and shook his head. "Jesus Christ."

Miller fired him a glare, then let his gaze sweep the curious expressions of his teammates lining up to hear what the hell he was so fired up about. He'd soon find out how many more Jimmys there were in the group.

"I have something to share with you that I would've told you a while back if the conversation had ever come up," he began. "Well, it's just come up." He flicked another furious glance Jimmy's way and a few frowns were added to the curious stares. People knew he wasn't one to grandstand or lose his temper for no reason. He played hard and kept to himself, but above all, he kept his cool.

"I'm gay," he said bluntly, half-surprised how easy the words fell out of his mouth even though his hands were shaking like damn leaves on his canes. "And if anyone has a problem with that or with anyone I might bring with me to the games, you can keep your bullshit thoughts to yourself or deal with me."

There were some rapidly exchanged glances and a few surprised faces, not least of all Jimmy's, whose jaw dropped like a fucking stone. The man sure as shit hadn't seen that coming. Well, fuck him.

When no one said anything, he continued. "I've been on this team for ten years, longer than most of you, and I don't give a fuck what you think in private. But I expect you to be a respectful team member when you're here, to me and to my friends."

He sensed a presence and turned to find Merv standing there with a deadly expression in place.

"I'll second that and go one further," Merv thundered, dropping his hand onto Miller's shoulder and squeezing lightly. "This team has a code of conduct that includes non-discriminatory behaviour of *any* kind. And considering the sport you play, I'd expect you to understand the importance of that more than most. Break that code, and you're off the team. Do I make myself clear?"

A rumble of agreement circled the room and Miller breathed a sigh of relief. He hadn't expected any different from Merv, but you just never knew.

"Good." Merv squeezed Miller's shoulder again and said quietly, "My door's open any time, son."

Miller nodded his thanks, and Merv left the room for Miller to face his team on his own. "That's all I have to say." He dropped his gaze and headed for his locker, feeling the heat of Jimmy's eyes on his back. But the man said nothing.

"Hey, Tap," Beau called from his seat on the bench.

Miller's stomach dropped. He turned and steeled himself.

"I'd say that makes it your turn to buy the beers then, right?"

Beau winked, and there was a clamouring of assent along with a banging of hands on the solid spoke guards of a dozen or so chairs—with one or two notable exceptions—Jimmy and one of the younger members of the team, David—a guy Miller had previously got on well with. Just showed, you never really knew someone.

Jimmy grunted and headed to his locker without a word while David brushed past Miller with the barely audible suggestion that maybe Miller would feel more comfortable with the girls down the hall. Miller let it go, this time.

"All right, you motherfuckers," he told the others. "I guess I'll spring for a round. The Irish pub in twenty? But nothing fancy. I might be gay, but I won't stand for those fucking umbrella drinks, got it?"

The locker room erupted in laughter and Miller grabbed a seat in front of his open locker, stared at its contents, and sucked in a shaky breath. *Holy shit.* He'd fucking done it. He'd catch the women later, but he was pretty sure they'd be fine.

He chanced a look to where Jimmy sat three lockers down. The man was staring at him, shaking his head. "I can't fucking believe it," he hissed. "What the hell, Tap? A fucking homo? You gotta be kidding me."

"I don't give a shit what you think, Jimmy, so keep your opinions to yourself or we'll have problems." Miller flipped him off and got his things together. The guy could go fuck himself. Although to be honest, Miller wasn't sure exactly what this might mean for them as a team going forward. Jimmy and Miller had always been the gruesome twosome when it came to the Wheel Blacks offence line. They *had* to work together. At some point he figured they'd need to talk. But fuck if that was gonna be tonight.

His phone buzzed and his dad's name flashed on the screen.

"You came out to your team?" Surprise, shock, confusion, concern.

Shit. Miller made his way to the showers for some privacy. "Hey,

Dad, good to hear from you too. And wow, I think that just broke the record for the fastest gossip ever."

His dad sighed. "Sorry. Nice to hear your voice, son. I just got a text from . . . look, it doesn't matter who it was from."

With all the fund-raising James did for the team, it could literally be anyone.

"I just thought we'd agreed to wait till after the next games so you could focus without . . . well, without getting distracted. Some people aren't going to like it, you know that."

"*You* suggested I wait, Dad. I never actually agreed even though I guess I didn't fight it either. Besides, it's done. And no, not everyone is going to like it, but I'm tired, Dad. It was time."

The phone went quiet and Miller let the silence sit until his dad broke it.

"Is there a particular reason you chose now? It's just . . . well, a guy was mentioned. Someone who came to watch you, and I just wondered."

Fucking hell. Miller sighed. "Yes, I've met someone. But it's kind of new, and I'm not ready to parade him in front of family just yet, okay?"

More silence. "But he's going to your games? Meeting the team?"

"Dad, please. You know what I mean. And to be fair, I didn't know he was coming that day. He surprised me."

"I just . . . well, I don't want you to be—"

"Distracted?" *God, how many times had I heard that?* "I know. And I won't be. I want to be at those next games as much as you want me to be there. More. But give me this, please. Don't make this a whole drama. After all this time, I deserve to have someone too, don't I?"

A huge sigh came down the line. "Yes, son, of course you do. I don't begrudge you that for a minute. I just don't want your training to suffer. You can't tell me you wouldn't be . . . disappointed if you didn't make the next games."

For fuck's sake. "Don't you mean I might disappoint *you*, Dad? I couldn't be an All Black but I could be a Wheel Black, right? So all wasn't lost." *Fuck.* The sharp intake of breath on the other end of the line said it all. *Goddammit. Could I be more of an arsehole after everything he'd done for me?*

"That's hardly fair." There was a shake in his father's voice that cut Miller to the quick, but this was a conversation that had been a long time coming.

His father drew breath. "You wanted the success just as much as I did for you. I did my very best to support you. I only ever wanted to help."

He wasn't being fair to his dad, Miller knew that. He ran a hand down his face. But it stung that his dad couldn't just be glad that Miller had found a guy and come out after all these years. "I'm sorry, Dad. And yes, you did help. I couldn't have done it without you, and I'll always be grateful. But I want this, Dad. I want more in my life. I like this guy, like him a lot. How about you try being happy for me?"

His father went quiet again, and Miller could almost see the deep frown lines on his face; the expression he wore whenever he was troubled, challenged, or backed into a corner. He was a good man, the very best to have at your back when the chips were down, but goddamn, he struggled to accept any decision, any answer, any direction that wasn't the one he'd envisioned.

He never intended to be overbearing, and to his credit, he'd mellowed a bit over the years, thanks to Miller's mother's dogged determination to have her own say in things. But for all his mellowing, Miller's dad was still a force to be reckoned with. But this time Miller wasn't taking the easy route.

And so he sat him out. It was the only way. He might not need his father's permission or approval, but he didn't want to hurt him either.

Finally he heard his father draw breath.

"All right, son. I'll try to be happy and not *bulldoze,* as your mother calls it. Will that do?"

Miller breathed a sigh of relief. "That would be much appreciated. And I'm going to ask another favour that you're not going to like."

"Don't push it. Keeping my tongue in check is like sitting on a bunch of hornets as it is."

Miller laughed. "Can I ask you to give him some space for a bit? Just a couple of weeks while this is all new. If you think you see him at a game, just leave him alone. And don't hassle me to meet him."

His father grunted unhappily. "It's your mother you have to worry about. I might be concerned, but she's going to start knitting booties, you know that, right? So, I'll tell you what. Just to show how *understanding* I can be, we'll both stay away from the next few games until the Aussie three-game series, okay? You've got another week on the bench anyway, and then it's just a couple of regional games. Plus I'm under instruction to get the backyard ready for Dane's birthday, so that'll give me an excuse to keep your mother in check. But you're gonna owe me."

A rush of gratitude filled Miller's chest. "Thanks, Dad. That would be awesome. And I promise I won't make her wait too long. At the moment we've only had one date and a couple of coffees. Early days."

"Okay. Well, good luck getting her to be as *understanding* about that as I am."

"Thanks."

"And son?"

"Yes?"

"Stay focussed. You need to pass that fitness test and train hard."

So much for backing off. "I will." Miller hung up and stared at his phone for a few seconds. Then he grinned and fired off a text to Sandy. ***Just came out to the Wheel Blacks.***

He didn't have to wait long.

Holy shit! How'd it go?

How *did* it go? Miller had barely given himself time to think about that or get past Jimmy's and David's arseholery. But then he pictured the faces of the rest of his teammates as they'd listened and felt some of the tension bleed from his shoulders. ***Mostly good I think. A couple of dicks as you'd expect. Coach was great. Beers are on me tonight. See you in the morning for Geo?***

I'll be there. And Miller . . .

What?

You are so getting laid tomorrow.

Holy fucking smokes. Miller now had an entirely different set of images in his head and a burgeoning semi to go with them.

Damn, tomorrow couldn't come soon enough.

CHAPTER TEN

MILLER OPENED THE DOOR SITTING IN HIS CHAIR. HE LOOKED good. Really good.

Sandy pushed inside, slammed the door shut, and shoved the chair back against the wall. He'd been waiting all morning.

"Should I be concerned?" He raised a brow at the low-profile, armless wheelchair, since Miller had said he didn't usually use a chair at home. "Is your leg hurting?"

Miller gave a brief shake of his head. "Just staying off my feet to rest it."

"Excellent." Sandy bit his lip and slowly worked his red woollen skirt up around his thighs as Miller watched, exposing the black stocking and suspender number he'd especially chosen for the occasion. A tiny snap-in-place leather jockstrap that did little to hide his more than interested cock, completed the outfit. He was taking a risk, but what the hell?

Miller's eyes bulged.

Bingo. Sandy smiled and tilted his head. "Tell me if this works for you?" He straddled Miller's lap and stared into his eyes. Thank god for long legs. It was still a bit awkward, the wheels digging into his thighs a little, but hey, Sandy could manage awkward, when it was sexy as fuck. The way it spread him for Miller's pleasure, if Miller chose to investigate was . . .yeah, hot.

He took Miller's mouth in a long leisurely kiss that involved a lot of squirming because Sandy had been horny as fuck for about twelve hours and Miller looked good enough to put on a sugar cone and lick from top to toe. When he finally pulled up for air, Miller shuddered beneath him.

"I, yeah . . ." Miller cleared his throat. "That, holy shit. Yep. That works just fucking fine." His hands slid under Sandy's skirt, over that garter belt, and wrapped around his arse, pulling Sandy down harder onto a nice thick cock that pressed up into his aching balls.

Damn, that felt good.

"Mmm. Then how about this?" Sandy peppered his face with kisses and ran his nose up Miller's neck and through his hair. He smelled of coconut and some kind of spicy liniment.

Miller groaned and pushed up under Sandy's balls once again, and Sandy almost came undone right there and then. Ever since Miller had texted the night before, Sandy had been planning exactly this. After a crap evening dealing with his fucking daddy issues and ignoring a bazillion missed calls and increasingly pissed-off texts from his sister, Miller's surprising text had given him hope, a reason to go to bed with much better thoughts than what his father hoped to gain by once again fucking them all sideways. Because Floyd Williams sure as hell hadn't come back into their lives for their benefit.

Miller pulled back and nipped at Sandy's chin. "And good morning to you, too," he murmured. "I've always been a fan of skipping the niceties of hello for a cute arse in my lap at eight o'clock in the morning. People should really do it more often. But did you miss the bit where I said Sam wasn't bringing his friend until ten?"

Sandy ground down, causing Miller to catch his breath. "Why do you think I'm here so early?" He nibbled at Miller's ear, drawing in more of that freshly showered coconut body wash, his fingers threading through all that glorious red hair, wrecking whatever style Miller thought he had going on.

"For breakfast?" Miller's head fell back, allowing Sandy better access.

And Sandy wasn't going to argue with that. He ran his tongue the length of Miller's throat and sucked on the dip at the bottom.

"I can whip you up something," Miller said in a thick voice.

"Mmm. Breakfast. That's what I'm here for," Sandy huffed out between kisses. Miller had a sexy-as-shit, heavy red scruff going on, and man, it looked and felt good. "You need to keep this." Sandy rubbed his cheek all over it and almost fucking purred. "You smell fucking delicious."

He kissed a path down Miller's neck, pulling aside his T-shirt to nip at his bulky shoulders. "I like my breakfasts sweet *and* salty." He leaned back and eyeballed Miller, who was well on the way to looking thoroughly debauched. "Do you think you can manage that?"

Miller snorted and cradled Sandy's face. "Jesus Christ, Dee, you've got me so bloody wound up I'm not sure I could boil fucking water. But if you're asking, can I *feed* you?" Those green eyes dipped to black. "Hell yeah, I can feed you. If you're sure that's what you want?" He watched Sandy closely.

Dee. Sandy ran the nickname through his mind and smiled. He turned his head to kiss Miller's palm. "Only you call me that, got it?"

Miller nodded. "So you like it?"

Sandy licked his lips. "I do."

"I see you wore a skirt." Miller eyed the red material bunched around Sandy's waist. "And not much else," he added with a smile.

Sandy wiggled back so Miller could get a better view and parroted Miller's earlier question back to him. "You like it?"

Miller's eyes never moved. "I so fucking do." His trembling hands ran over the black stockings and garter belt. "Holy shit, Dee. I'm never gonna be able to see a red skirt again without sporting a hard-on."

Sandy snorted. "Mission accomplished." He tipped Miller's chin up with a single finger. "You want more?"

Miller's eyes blazed, and a shiver ran the length of Sandy's spine. He leaned forward till his lips brushed Miller's ear. "You came out to your bloody team, Miller. And that is the biggest fucking turn-on. So touch me, dammit, before I lose my fucking mind."

Sandy gave him some room and Miller's hand slid between them. He hooked the thin leather jockstrap up and over Sandy's cock, ran his thumb over the slick head, and then raised it to Sandy's mouth.

Sandy wrapped his lips around Miller's thumb and sucked it clean, holding Miller's gaze all the while. Then he leaned forward and plunged his tongue deep into Miller's mouth.

Miller responded in kind, cradling Sandy's jaw to keep him in place with one hand while the other stroked Sandy's cock. He scavenged every inch of Sandy's mouth, sweeping through like his life depended on it, and between the filthy kiss and Miller jacking him off, Sandy was so fucking turned on he thought he might go up in flames if the man even looked at him sideways.

"Goddammit, I need more room." Miller pushed at Sandy, who slid off while Miller flipped his footrests up and pulled Sandy to stand between his legs. "Lose the jockstrap, hold your skirt, and spread your legs."

Sandy almost choked on a laugh and fanned himself. "Oh my, what every gay man hopes to hear." But as urgent as Miller sounded, Sandy was in no hurry. He took his time gathering the skirt material out of the way, unsnapping the leather jockstrap so it fell free, and then opening his legs with Miller's eyes locked onto every single movement, breath ragged. And when he was done, Miller reached out and trailed his fingers up and down the length of Sandy's sensitive cock, gently cupping his balls, before reaching behind to drag a hot and trembling finger through Sandy's crease to tap on his hole.

"You are so fucking beautiful, Dee." He caressed Sandy's balls, rolling them one by one in his hand, before giving a couple of short tugs on Sandy's desperate cock.

He grabbed Miller's wrist and counted to five.

"You close?" Miller caught his eye.

Sandy nodded, counting, counting, counting.

"You don't come unless it's down my throat, understand?" Miller caught his eye.

More nodding, because Sandy wasn't capable of anything more after an order like that. Interesting, since he didn't usually take to being ordered around at all, but hell if he might not have to change his mind about that, at least when it came to Miller Harrison.

"Put your foot up on my seat."

And oh fuck, yeah. Sandy was definitely rewriting his playbook. He lifted his leg and Miller spat on his finger and ran it behind Sandy's balls before leaning in and taking Sandy's cock down the back of his throat in a single swallow.

"Fuuuuuck." Sandy's head fell back as his dick was engulfed in a furnace of wet heat, his hips rolling forward to get Miller's finger . . . there. *Goddamn.*

Miller worked him hard, the tip of his finger sliding in and out of Sandy's hole, just enough to get him desperate but not enough to hit exactly where Sandy wanted it.

He groaned and wriggled and tried to get that damn finger deeper, but Miller resisted—sucking, licking, and wringing an obscene amount of noise from Sandy's mouth, but refusing to push higher.

Then just as Sandy was about to grab Miller's hand and shove that finger where it belonged, Miller swallowed around Sandy's cock at the same time he hit that sweet spot inside, and Sandy saw fucking stars—coming with a strangled shout and a wave of pleasure that coursed through his body. Miller sucked and swallowed every drop, then licked him clean, pulled back, and ran a hand across his mouth.

Sandy's foot fell to the floor as he backed up against the opposite wall and slid down the paintwork. "Jesus Christ, Miller. What the fuck was that? I'm too scared to check in case you fucking swallowed my cock along with everything that was in it."

Miller chuckled. "Come here."

Sandy crawled across the hall to kneel between Miller's legs, putting his hands on Miller's thighs. "Honestly. I think you've got shares in Dyson."

"Shut up and give me your mouth." Miller tilted Sandy's chin up and claimed his mouth in a thorough kiss that curled Sandy's toes in his stockings and left him wanting more, a lot more.

"I believe it's my turn." He licked his lips and eyed Miller speculatively. "Anything I need to know?" His gaze slipped to Miller's groin and back up.

Miller's mouth curved up in a slow, sexy smile and he shook his head. "All parts intact and functioning. Sometimes it takes me a little longer to get there than you'd expect, but that's it."

Sandy fired him a sultry look. "What a hardship. Having your dick in my mouth for an epic session? How ever will I cope? Call search and rescue if it's gone too long."

Miller choked out a laugh. "Should I be worried?"

Sandy smirked. "Are you familiar with the term gag reflex?"

Miller's lips twitched and he nodded.

"Well, let's just say, I'm not." Sandy waggled his brows. "It's my superpower."

Miller snorted. "I'll consider myself warned."

"You do that."

"But two things."

Sandy arched a brow. "Are you always this bossy?"

Miller's eyes twinkled. "I think you like it."

He so fucking did. "Maybe. So, what are these two things?"

"One, I want to stand. And two—" He trailed fingers down Sandy's cheek. "I want to come all over this gorgeous face, *if* that's all right with you?"

Miller's eyes blew black as ink, and it was all Sandy's dick needed to get fully back in the game. He blew out a shaky breath. "Oh, well, yeah." He cleared his throat. "I can do that, and yeah, more than all right."

"Then follow me." Miller wheeled back a little to free Sandy, who was still on his knees. "And hand me that ridiculous scrap of material you laughingly call a jockstrap."

Sandy's phone dinged in his bag. He pulled it out, swore, and switched it to silent before stuffing it back in his bag.

"You need to do something?" Miller watched him carefully.

"Nope. Just my sister."

Miller raised a brow.

Sandy grimaced. "Don't ask." He balled the jockstrap and threw it at Miller who laughed and caught it with ease before dropping it into his lap. Then, with his cock and balls banging free under his skirt, he followed Miller down the hall and into the kitchen.

"Not exactly where I thought we were heading," he commented drily.

Miller parked and pushed from the chair to his feet, dropping his chin to hide the sting of pain on his face. "Since your comment last Sunday about me having my way with you over this low counter, I haven't been able to get the damn idea out of my brain. Not that we're going there today, but fuck if I don't get a hard-on every damn time I walk into this kitchen. I'm hoping this might give me some decent imagery to go with it. You good with that?"

Sandy swept his skirt aside to let his dick spring free at half-mast. "Apparently, yes." He reached to the side to unzip—

"Don't." Miller croaked, then cleared his throat. "I . . . just leave it on, please."

Sandy pulled his lower lip between his teeth and angled his head. Well, well, well. Things just got interesting, not to mention sexied the fuck up. He rezipped and made his way over to where Miller stood with his back against the pantry door. He didn't stop until their chests almost touched. Then he nosed in against Miller's soft scruff and let out a slow breath.

"You *really* like my skirt, huh?"

Miller took an uneven breath and his hands trailed up Sandy's thighs, under the skirt. "Yes, I really like the skirt. I like the red. I liked the jockstrap. I like the fact you're now bare-fucking-arsed underneath. And I *really,* really like this damn garter belt." He snapped the elastic strap against Sandy's bare skin.

Sandy jumped at the brief sting, his cock plumping in Miller's other hand. Oh yeah, this was going places. "Noted." He ran his nose up Miller's throat, drawing the man's scent deep into his lungs. "There's more where these came from."

Miller shivered. "Get the fuck down here so I can kiss you," Miller growled. "I can't decide whether you being taller than me is a bonus or a curse."

"Having just established that when you're in your chair we're the perfect height for you to suck my cock, I'm going with the bonus option." Sandy nibbled Miller's ear, earning a groan of appreciation.

"That we are, baby. But right now I need your legs spread . . . for lots of reasons."

Sandy shivered, widened his stance, and Miller's answering kiss was hard and voracious. Fingers slid across his scalp, fisting his hair to tilt his head as Miller arched against him, seeking friction, moaning and gasping into Sandy's mouth as if he were the last drink on a blistering day. It was hot as hell and all kinds of sexy, but Sandy was on a mission.

He pulled off and dropped to his knees, tearing at the zip on Miller's jeans until he had it undone, the jeans shoved down, and Miller's dick in his hands.

"Damn, you have a beautiful cock." He looked up as he swiped the moisture from the head with his tongue, rolling it back in his mouth and swallowing hard while Miller watched with hungry eyes.

"Are you okay standing there while I suck this beauty off? I can guarantee you won't be disappointed." Sandy waggled his eyebrows, but it was true. For all that most of his boyfriends had lacked staying power, or sheer manners, as it turned out, they'd all been captivated by his mouth.

"Am I okay?" Miller snorted. "Jesus, Dee, I'll nail my fucking feet to the floor if I have to." He gripped the countertop with one hand and dropped the other to feather through Sandy's hair. "I wanna see this superpower of yours."

Sandy lifted up to snag a quick kiss, sharing Miller's salty taste as he did. Then he was back on his knees with Miller's thick cock in his mouth, his groans loud in Sandy's ears, and as close to heaven as he'd been in a long time. He fucking loved giving head.

And Miller didn't hold back. He was a vocal, active lover, and before long Sandy knew exactly what he liked and how he liked it. He moved Sandy's head where he wanted it, lifted his jaw, shoved a finger into Sandy's mouth alongside his cock, fisted his hands in Sandy's hair, pushed and pulled and guided. Sandy loved every filthy, bossy minute, and before he knew it, he'd begun working his aching dick.

In seconds, a hand cupped his jaw and Sandy looked up.

"I wanna see." Miller's eyes flashed.

With Miller's dick still in his mouth, Sandy lifted his skirt to show his cock leaking all over the kitchen floor. Miller sucked in a breath. "Get yourself off."

Sandy did, working himself with one hand while keeping balance with the other. He stilled his head in silent offer for Miller to take over, and Miller thrust gently into his mouth, careful, testing the limits. But when Sandy jerked Miller's thigh forward, he smiled and let loose.

The deeper Miller went, the faster Sandy stroked, and although his eyes watered and saliva ran from his mouth, Sandy's hand stayed firmly on the back of Miller's thigh, keeping him in place while Sandy doubled down on his suction. He hoped Miller didn't have a plan about who came first because there was no way Sandy was going to last. Two more strokes and his orgasm slammed through him, his back arching as he shot over the kitchen floor, his muffled groan of pleasure vibrating around Miller's cock.

Miller jerked his cock from Sandy's slack mouth and jacked

himself until he came over Sandy's face with a roar that Sandy hoped the neighbours would ignore. Hot come splashed his chin, cheeks, and lips, some even making it into his mouth, and Sandy greedily licked and swallowed every last bit he could reach before leaning forward on his knees to clean Miller's cock with a few long strokes of his tongue. Then he tucked Miller away, zipped him up, and got to his feet, dazed by the hottest fucking sex of his damn life.

Miller fisted his black blouse and pulled him close, licking every missed splash and drop of himself until Sandy's face was clean. Then, after one final caress of Sandy's garter belt, he flattened Sandy's skirt back into place, and Sandy made a note to hit his favourite online shopping boutiques stat. If a garter belt did this to Miller, he could only imagine what a corset might do.

"Superpower indeed." Miller wobbled a bit on his feet as he reached for his chair and collapsed into it. "Best fucking orgasm of my life. Get over here." He held out a hand and Sandy threw a leg over the chair to straddle Miller's lap, again.

"Did you get one of these sleek jobs with this kind of occasion in mind?" Sandy tapped the wheels that barely poked above the seat.

Miller laughed and tucked Sandy's hair behind his ears. "I would've had to plan on those long legs as well, I think. Not everyone can straddle one of these, low-profile or not. I bet you can still stand if you have to?"

Sandy pushed up on his feet, legs still either side of the small chair.

"Thought so. It's a custom design on an existing model. Too small to be efficient outside the house, but perfect for inside."

"Lucky me." Sandy took Miller's mouth in a slow kiss.

"I think I'm the lucky one." Miller returned the favour, then lifted Sandy's skirt for another peek and licked his lips. "Damn." He pulled Sandy down into his arms.

"I have no words," he whispered in his ear. "You're the sexiest man I've ever laid eyes on, and I'm not sure what you see in me, but I'm so fucking grateful you decided to give me a chance."

Sandy wasn't prepared for the way Miller held on, stroking his hair and rocking them together like they belonged, like it meant something. Tender and sweet and hopeful—Sandy had no idea what to do with it.

He was a good fuck, uninhibited, a novelty, even a challenge to some men. But to have a man say he was *grateful* for him? Before he'd even fucked him? That was new. New and scary, because it skirted the edges of that damn unicorn Sandy had been looking for his whole adult life. And those were dangerous, unforgiving, and disappointing waters to enter with a truckload of potential for hurt.

Miller's phone sounded with a call and it provided the perfect opportunity for Sandy to disentangle himself. He passed Miller his cell and leaned against the countertop.

"Yes, it is." Miller sounded pissed.

"That's correct." He gave an eye-roll which had Sandy even more intrigued. He mimed leaving the room, but Miller shook his head, and so he continued listening to the one-sided conversation.

"You seem to have the gist of it. I've nothing further to add."

"No comment."

"That's not any of your business."

"If I'm lucky to be picked. I'm looking forward to it immensely."

"I think the Australian team is on a roll and we'll have a battle, but we're up for it. We have some promising new players." More eye rolls.

"As I said, I've nothing further to add. In this day and age, I would've thought you guys were past this."

"I didn't ask to be a role model, but I don't see how it can be anything but good for the game and the sport. Thanks for calling."

"Goodbye." He slid the phone back on the countertop. "Fuck."

Sandy closed the distance and dropped alongside, pulling Miller close. "The press, I take it?"

Miller nodded, leaning into the embrace. "If my father heard in ten minutes, the press wasn't going to be in the dark for long."

Sandy froze. "Your father knows?"

Miller turned and popped a kiss on his lips. "Don't worry. He doesn't care about me coming out, other than the effect on my game. I've managed to get him to back off and give us some space before my mother demands to meet you."

"Oh, right. Good. That's . . . good." Sandy's heart slowed a little. He wasn't ready for mothers, not yet.

The phone buzzed again, and Reuben's name flashed. Miller took one look and swore, though it had little heat. He showed Sandy the text.

Figured you didn't need another phone call this morning but we need to coffee, soon. Congratulations and stop freaking out. They called for a comment. I said you play great rugby with an amazing drift in the corners. Talk soon.

Miller set the phone back. "Like the poor guy needs my problems added to his own personal media circus."

Sandy jumped as his own phone buzzed and he and Miller shared a disbelieving look. Then he held it out with a smile.

Miller laughed. "Cam."

Sandy held the phone out for Miller to read.

My office lunchtime tomorrow. No excuses. Bring donuts and details. Lots and lots of details ;)

"God help me." Sandy shook his head. "But if anyone understands, I guess those two do." He took Miller's hand. No use pretending he wasn't a bit nervous at the idea of the press knowing. "Is this going to be a problem?"

Miller shrugged and waggled his hand. "I wouldn't think so. It's not like the Wheel Blacks get mobbed on a daily basis, right? There'll be some interest, sure, but it should all blow over pretty quick."

But he looked worried, and Sandy ran his fingers through all those glorious red waves in an effort to soothe him while trying not to freak out himself.

"The thing is, from what the journalist said, they suspect or know there's a guy." Miller's gaze flicked over Sandy like he might run screaming from the room. "But they don't have a name, yet. I can't say how long that'll last though, so you could get a few phone calls. It might pay to be prepared."

Sandy sucked in a breath. He didn't like the idea, but he wasn't a runner. "I can handle a few calls if that's all it is."

"Are you sure? I'll understand—"

He pressed a finger to Miller's lips. "I'm sure. Now, I need to clean up and make myself respectable." He spun his jockstrap in his hand for emphasis. "I did bring jeans if you think that might be . . . better, what with your nephew and his friend? I wore the skirt because . . . well, I just felt this morning . . . I mean, I wanted to . . ." Jesus, how did he explain that hearing about his father had coiled Sandy tighter than a fucking spring. How he'd woken that morning feeling—

"Don't change." Miller grabbed his hand and brought it to his lips. "You're perfect as you are. Well, maybe the jockstrap wouldn't hurt."

Relief thundered through Sandy's chest. He was trying not to put too much hope into this thing he had going with Miller, but damn it was hard not to.

"Good idea," he answered, his voice thick with emotion. "I'm not sure this boy is ready for full-immersion treatment yet, at least not all in one shot."

Miller ran his eye over Sandy's outfit and grinned. "I suspect the skirt stockings and garter belt will be enough of an eyeful without you hanging free underneath."

Sandy brushed the front of his blouse into place and flipped his blond locks out of the way. "Excellent point. My dick nestled in a leather jockstrap has been known to make grown men swoon. You have to start them out slowly if you don't want to blow their little minds."

Miller brushed the back of his fingers down Sandy's cheek. "Very thoughtful of you. Now go get cleaned up and I'll tell you all about my coming-out party with the team."

"Deal. But I expect coffee first, lots and lots of coffee. I have a feeling we're gonna need it."

CHAPTER ELEVEN

SAM WAS PUNCTUAL TO THE BUTTON, A CHARACTERISTIC HE GOT from his father, and much appreciated by Miller. Dane ran his restaurant pass like the bridge of an aircraft carrier—everything timed to the second, perfect and in its place. He might've passed the trait to his son, but he hadn't been so lucky with his daughter, Nicole, who, like her mother, had a more fluid interpretation of the concept. It made for interesting family dynamics.

Miller invited the boys inside and then hauled Sam in for a hug, the similarity between father and son striking him yet again. Sam had Dane's lean body, angular features, strawberry-blond curls, and the Harrison freckles spattered over the bridge of his nose. But his eyes were definitely Chloe's—dark, intense pools of brown mischief.

"You came out to your team, Uncle Em! Way to go!" Sam was fizzing with the news and it was hard not to smile.

"How'd you find out?"

"It's all over social media." He handed his phone to Miller, who winced at the headline.

Wheel Black Star Comes Out!

Miller Harrison, star offensive player for the New Zealand Wheel Blacks, has admitted he is gay, according to Sport's Media sources within the sport. Miller, who has been the offensive linchpin in the Wheel Blacks for the last two Paralympics, has never been linked to a romantic partner, although there are rumours circulating of a current paramour who might be the reason behind his decision. Having come out to his team, Harrison has so far refused to comment publicly, but Sport's Media has asked various spokesmen of the LGBTQ and disability communities about the impact of this announcement. They were of one mind that it could do nothing but good for both groups . . .

Miller stopped there and handed the phone back.

"*Admitted.* Like it's something I've done wrong. Bloody journalists." It was the last thing he needed. Call him naïve, but he really hadn't thought the media would grab onto the news with quite such enthusiasm. *Just wonderful.*

Sam stepped aside and waved his friend forward. "Uncle Em, this is Geo."

A slight but startlingly beautiful teenage boy with dark waves, nervous hazel eyes, and a small intriguing divot in the centre of his lightly stubbled chin stepped forward with his hand outstretched.

"Mr Harrison. Thanks for agreeing to talk with me. And congratulations, on coming out to your team? It's kind of cool that some of this is new for you too, at your age, I mean."

At my age. Miller couldn't suppress the eye-roll as he shook Geo's hand. "Thanks, I think. But don't be too quick to buy me a plot. I've got a good five years left in me, yet."

Sam snickered. "Maybe three."

Miller fired his nephew a glare and swept the two boys into the lounge while he followed on his canes. "I've been out to my family since I was fourteen," he explained. "But sport was pretty unaccepting back then and I wanted to be an All Black. So, I kept it on the down-low and just never really corrected their impressions. I might make other choices today, but times were very different then. And you can call me Em. I keep telling Sam to drop the uncle, but I think he does it to piss me off and remind me that I'm old."

"You are old." Sam elbowed Geo. "Em's cool . . . -ish. Just don't tell him I said that."

"Brat." Miller ruffled Sam's hair.

"Hey, watch the do." Sam ducked away and then caught sight of Sandy standing by the couch and took a second.

Miller held his breath. He'd told Sam nothing about Sandy other than he was a friend and might be able to help.

"You must be Sandy." Sam recovered and stepped forward with his hand out.

Miller wanted to hug him.

Sandy flicked a glance Miller's way as he accepted Sam's hand, and Miller suddenly realised Sandy had no idea what Miller might've told Sam about him, or them. Mostly the them bit. *Shit.*

Geo also shook hands with Sandy, adding a long appreciative ogle at Sandy's outfit, which made Miller's mouth curve up in a smile and Sandy blush and dart his eyes to Miller for guidance.

Damn, he looked adorable. Still coming down from the high of their kitchen sexcapades, it was hard to equate this slightly discombobulated Sandy with the debauched man on his knees at Miller's feet, Miller's cock choking his throat. And goddammit, nope, he shouldn't have gone there.

He ignored Sandy's wide-eyed plea for help and got his aching body to the couch instead. Sandy could handle a bit of seventeen-year-old crushing without Miller's help. Besides, if anyone deserved a bit of ogling, in Miller's opinion, it was Dee. Warmth curled in his chest at the nickname. His alone.

"Take a seat." He gestured to the armchairs. "And pull them

closer so we're not sitting a mile away from each other. That's just so I can get my chair around."

Sandy squeezed himself into the far corner of Miller's couch, about as far away from Miller as he could possibly get, which had Miller biting back a smile. That left Sam and Geo the armchairs.

Sam's curious gaze flicked between Sandy and Miller, and Miller could almost hear the cogs grinding. It was killing his nephew not to know. Retribution.

He ignored Sam for the moment and focussed on Geo as the boy got himself comfortable. "As you may have gathered, other than being gay myself, I'm hardly a font of information on the subject of coming out. In my own family, it was relatively a low-key event, but since I haven't been open about it in the sports or work arena, I guess I still understand how scary it can be."

"I never knew you were gay, Mr . . . Em," Geo stumbled. "Sam never said anything. It's cool that you'll talk to me."

"My family's been good about keeping things quiet, although since the accident that blew up my All Black chances, there was really no reason. It was my dislike for drama, and also wanting to put a priority on getting my rehab sorted, that kept me in the closet. Although to be honest, I look back now and wonder if it might just have been an excuse to delay it."

"I get that," Geo said.

Meanwhile, Sam was still staring at Sandy. "What about you, Sandy? Were your family good about you coming out?"

Sandy rolled his eyes and crossed those long, long legs, revealing a tantalising glimpse of the suspender catches that lay just beneath that damn red skirt.

Sam's eyes bugged, Geo squirmed in his seat, and Miller drew a ragged breath. *Good Lord.* He wasn't at all sure his life was ready for Sandy Williams. Was anyone's? Regardless of how things went between them, he had a feeling nothing was going to ever be the same.

"Yes and no," Sandy answered with another glance Miller's way.

"How about I tell you my bullshit experience, Miller can share his much better one, and then you can tell us whatever you want about what's going on for you?"

And suddenly Miller realised that although he knew the bare basics—that Sandy's dad had been an arsehole—he hadn't heard the whole, deeply personal and painful story. Sandy had agreed to do this because Miller had asked him. And knowing how reluctant Sandy was to explain himself, it hit Miller just how much Sandy was risking here. And what was Miller doing? Being an arsehole by letting him hang.

He stretched out his hand. "Come here."

Sandy eyed him in that quiet way of his, a small notch deepening between his brows. Then his mouth lifted in a slow, shy smile and he took Miller's hand and scooted over, tucking himself against Miller's side with a pleased sigh, and Miller slung his arm around Sandy's shoulders to keep him there.

"Uncle Em?"

He was pretty sure Sam's eyebrows couldn't have reached any higher if they'd been on strings from the ceiling, while Geo stared google-eyed as if Miller and Sandy were the first gay couple he'd ever seen in real life. It occurred to Miller that maybe they were.

And that's when it really sank in. The phone call, the press, the way Geo was staring at them—

Son of a bitch. It was already too late. He was about to become a goddamn gay role model, like it or not. For a man who choked on the mere whisper of the words *pride parade*; who couldn't get the rainbow alphabet clear in his head to save himself; and who'd been shocked to learn that bears, cubs, otters, wolves, and pups existed outside the animal kingdom and inside actual gay bars, which also apparently existed, Miller's life had taken a sudden and decided turn to the unapologetically queer. Or maybe it was just a natural course correction after years of ignoring half his life. Either way, the universe was laughing its arse off.

"Yes, Sam. Sandy and I are . . . dating." Miller heard a soft huff of surprise from the man sitting next to him. He squeezed Sandy's hand, getting one back in return.

Sam fell back in his chair with a huge grin on his face. "Huh." He breathed the word like he'd found the corner piece of a jigsaw puzzle where he least expected it. "That's so cool. It's a good look on you, Uncle Em." His gaze flicked to Sandy. "Both of you. Does Grand—"

"They know there's someone but not who. No names," Miller jumped in. "You're the very first to meet him. It's . . . we're kind of new." Then he eyeballed Sam. "And I want to keep it that way, so you are sworn to secrecy name-wise, okay? I'm not ready to expose Sandy to the clutches of Grandma just yet."

Sam considered that for a moment, then he nodded. "Okay, done. But there'll be a price, yet to be decided."

Miller groaned. "Of course there will. Text me later and we'll talk."

"Yes!" Sam punched the air. "But when Mum and Dad find out, fu—far out, you realise they're gonna freak out, right? You've got an actual boyfriend, dude!"

God help me, but apparently, I do. Miller nodded. "I don't know how long till the press get hold of Sandy's name, but we'll deal with that when it happens."

"Holy crap, this is awesome!" Sam punched the air. "Nicole and I are gonna be in the clear for ages. Everyone's going to be too busy talking about you guys."

Sandy turned and dropped his voice. "Are you sure about this? It's not too late to back out."

Miller leaned in and kissed the corner of those pink glossed-up lips. "Absolutely. You?"

Sandy's brown eyes sought Miller's and lit up. "Bring it on."

Miller spoke first, thinking Sandy's more difficult experience might free Geo to talk after. It felt kind of strange talking about something that Dee hadn't yet heard in full either, although to be perfectly honest, it freaked Miller to be talking about this stuff at all.

His gay friends before Reuben numbered, oh, about zero. It was hardly the kind of thing you casually mentioned to straight friends or the occasional hook-up, and it struck Miller just how disconnected he really was. It wasn't only that he didn't have a gay life, it was more that he didn't have a life at all outside of sport and work.

It shouldn't have come as any surprise. Hell, his family had called him on it time and time again. He'd argued that his teammates were more than enough to tick his social boxes, and his days had little spare time for anything else as it was. But at a certain level, he knew he'd been using those as an excuse to not put himself out there.

In his small world of sport and work, he was safe, respected, valued. In this shiny new gay life, he was totally at sea. A part of him wondered if that was why he'd always gone for hook-ups that looked just like he did—athletic, muscled, stereotypically masc—mirror-images who never made him think. Sandy turned his world on its head.

But watching Geo and Sam hanging off Miller's every word—feeling the warmth of Dee's body alongside, his eyes tracking Miller's expression, supportive, understanding—Miller felt seen and heard in a way he never had in his small, safe world. But he was also scared to death.

He hadn't looked behind this door for a reason. He hadn't come out to his teams, for a reason. He wasn't out in his work, for a reason. He'd kept it all safe and quiet. He could tell himself he'd never had to because he didn't date, but he was coming to understand, part of that was a fucking crock. Not dating meant not having to come out, which kept his world smooth, which then became a reason to not date.

All this ran through his head as he told his very tame story about coming out to his family when he was fourteen. No big reactions, no shock and horror. No gnashing of teeth. Just surprise and then overwhelming support, bar the concern from his dad about his sport and professional rugby chances, hence the decision to stay closeted even though his mother hadn't been happy about it.

He told them everything, including how frightened he was about how things might change now that he was out. He wasn't sure if they needed to know as much as he told them, but once he started he couldn't stop.

He finished to a silent room and drew a shaky breath. A squeeze of his hand reminded him Dee was right there, his concerned eyes checking Miller was okay. He gave a thin, apologetic smile. He wasn't sure who this new Miller Harrison was or how he fitted into the world anymore. And Miller was so fucking tired of feeling like he didn't fit in or he had to fight to fit in with people who only saw him through his disability. He wasn't sure he had the energy to go through that all again with his sexuality. But he was on that roller coaster whether he liked it or not. He just needed to hang on for the ride and find a way to get through.

"Too much?" He glanced at the two boys. "I might've got a bit carried away."

Sam stood and launched himself into Miller's arms, almost knocking Sandy aside. "I didn't know hardly any of that," he said, strangling Miller around the neck. "I mean, I knew you were gay, obviously." He let go and collapsed back in his own chair. "And I figured out why you'd kept it quiet when you were with the Blues. But I guess I didn't think about why you'd never even brought a boyfriend home to us. And I'm sorry I didn't ask, Uncle Em. For what it's worth, I think it's really cool you're doing this now. It might suck people saying you're a role model, but it's important, right? For lots of people." His gaze darted sideways to Geo, who was wearing a worried frown.

"But do you think it was better . . . that you waited, I mean?" Geo asked softly.

Miller thought about that. "I think it made some things easier and some things a lot harder," he answered honestly.

"There's no *right* time to come out." Dee leaned forward to squeeze Geo's hand. At first he looked startled but then he put his hand over top. "There's only *your* time, the time that's best for you. Don't let anyone say otherwise. You've already told your family, I understand?"

Geo pulled a face. "Yeah."

"I'm gathering there were a few kinks in that then?"

Geo dropped his head back and blew out a sigh. "One or two."

"Well, mine didn't exactly go to plan either." Sandy freed his hand and Miller pulled him tight to his side. "My dad was struggling to be a father and husband as it was, and me coming out didn't exactly help."

He recounted his story about his troubled family and his arsehole dad, while Geo paid rapt attention and Miller's heart quietly broke. Miller had been unaware of the recent developments with his mother and sister meeting up with Sandy's dad, and he now wondered about all those missed calls from Dee's sister, but he said nothing.

Sam's eyes grew huge, and Miller knew the kid had just lost some of that untarnished naivety that came from having a loving supportive family at his back. He'd survive and be the better for it, but Miller made a mental note to check in with his brother to follow up with Sam later.

Geo had grown smaller in his seat as Dee talked, and by the end he was barely blinking, fixated on Dee's every word. Something was off, and Dee must've picked up on it too, judging by the increasingly concerned glances he shot Miller's way. If he had to guess, Miller would say things in Geo's house were worse than Sam thought.

When Dee was done, Miller asked Sam to give them a few minutes and organise cold drinks and something to eat while Geo talked. Sam's mouth opened to protest, but Miller quickly eyeballed him and he got the message. He wanted to give Geo the opportunity to tell them anything he might not want Sam to hear.

The story didn't take long, and Miller suspected Geo left a lot out. Geo was bi and in his first serious teenage relationship with a guy, a fellow student. He hadn't intended to come out to his family, but his dad had caught him texting his boyfriend and demanded to look at his phone. There were pictures and pretty obvious messages that outed him straight away. His dad *went ballistic*—Geo's words. His mum had left them years ago to return to her family in the UK.

Geo's father fought for custody, and rather than battle it out, his mum gave in. Geo saw her every couple of years and they talked monthly, but they weren't close.

"He thinks I'm acting out." Geo wiped his eyes as Sam returned and handed him a glass of juice and a box of tissues. "That if I'm really bi, which he doesn't believe in anyway, then I have a choice. I don't have to like dick." He drew a shuddering breath. "I can be *normal* and not a fucking queer. He said I make him sick to his teeth."

Miller wanted to find the man and slap him into next week.

"He said I have to dump my boyfriend and that if he ever finds I've been with another boy, there'll be consequences and I may as well not come home. He wanted Jacob's name, but I wouldn't tell him. I just had him as J in my phone."

He stared in earnest determination. "But I'm *not* giving him up. I don't care what my dad says. I won't stop seeing Jacob. He's . . . special. And I can't just choose not to like him. It doesn't work like that. You don't get to *decide* that shit. My dad's being a total arsehole."

And oh god, Miller's heart almost broke at the quivering lips and the well of emotion in Geo's eyes. The boy was in love—teenage, heart-wrenching, all-consuming love.

Dee again reached for Geo's hand. "You're right, we don't just decide this stuff. We like who we like, right? And that's okay."

Miller glanced up as Sam held out a tray loaded with glasses of juice and a plate of chocolate brownies Miller had picked up for their visit. He took a glass and waited until Sam had done the rounds and retaken his seat.

"Do Jacob's parents know?" he asked

Geo nodded. "It's just his mum. She knows he's seeing someone whose dad isn't supportive, but not my name. She's fine with him being gay. But I don't want Jacob to tell her who I am or have me over to his house, in case my dad finds out." He nibbled absently at his brownie.

Miller shared a look with Dee that said, what a fucking mess, and then asked, "So, what do you want?"

Geo shrugged and wiped his eyes again. "I want my dad to understand, but that isn't going to happen. I want to keep seeing Jacob, but I don't know if that's the right thing for both of us. I've only got eighteen months left of school before I leave for university and I'm out from under him. I don't want to leave home because he wouldn't help, and I'd have to give up school and get a job, but there's no one I can talk to. And if I stay home, I'm going to be miserable. There's only Dad's family in New Zealand and I don't know what they'll say. The school guidance counsellor is okay, but ally stuff isn't really her forte, you know? And then Sam suggested you."

Miller sighed. "Okay, so let's get the legal stuff on the table." He took a long swallow of his juice and put the glass down. "You're seventeen, which means your dad can't actually stop you seeing Jacob or talking to us or getting help on your own. You can get a job and leave home or school at sixteen in New Zealand without permission, although you do have to be considered in a safe place or social services can send you back. But . . ."

"Yeah, I know. But being legally able to see Jacob means nothing if Dad doesn't want me to, right?"

Miller nodded. "Pretty much. He can make things miserable for you, as he's already said. This is really complicated family stuff, Geo, and I think you know that."

He ran his fingers through his hair. "Pretty much. That's why it's been screwing with my head. I don't know what to do."

"And we can't tell you. You need to talk with someone who really knows what they're doing, a counsellor, so you can decide what you want and all the risks involved."

"I've got a suggestion," Sandy added. "I have a friend who works in an LGBT drop-in centre, Equal Paths, not far from your school, the next suburb in fact."

"Cam?" Miller caught on. "Great idea."

"They have all sorts of programmes and counsellors available. Do you think you could get there? It might be good for Jacob to talk to someone as well. It's a safe space and you'd be able to meet other people your own age to talk with. You don't need your dad's permission, but I guess you'd need to be discreet. Having a parent reject your sexuality is a really, really lonely place to be, Geo. I know how that is. I'll give you my phone number and you are welcome to call at any time, but I really think a counsellor would be a good idea, and Cam could help with that."

Miller could've kissed Sandy because the responsibility terrified him. This whole mess was complicated and had drama written all over it. Geo needed a professional. Someone who knew what they were doing. Sam was Miller's nephew, and things would fall at Miller's feet if shit happened. Talking to a teen, albeit of legal age, whose parent was so against his sexuality was still a risky thing. Things could so easily blow back on them. If someone asked Miller about the same issue at work, he'd be telling them to refer the kid to a professional as well. Not get involved in what could turn out to be a sticky mess.

Don't rock the boat. Don't draw attention.

Miller didn't do sticky messes. Even his job was to keep his employer out of sticky messes. But until now he'd never really appreciated how fortunate he was. He'd never faced anything like Geo, like Dee.

Because I hide the things that might count against me.

Geo was quiet as he thought about the suggestion. "I guess I could do that. I recognise the name and I think I know where it is. I'll talk to Jacob. Maybe he'll come too. I just want things to be okay, you know? Like they were before. I didn't think Dad was gonna be happy, but I . . . I never thought he'd . . ." He broke down.

Sam immediately set his glass on the coffee table and kneeled at Geo's side, putting his arm around his friend. "You've always got me and my family."

Miller was so damn proud of him. He caught Sandy's troubled

gaze and pulled him into a hug, knowing this had to be hitting very close to the bone.

Eventually Geo lifted his head and Miller caught a glimpse of steel and a flicker of resolve where there hadn't been one before. Geo scrubbed both hands down his face as Sam stroked his hair. "I'll go to the centre and talk to someone." He held his phone out to Dee. "Put it under E, but don't name it. But can I . . . ?" He drew in a shaky breath. "Would it be okay if I maybe came back sometime? It's been . . .really good."

"Any time," Miller answered.

"Do you want one of us to meet you at the centre for that first time?" Sandy checked, but Geo shook his head.

"It's easy enough to bike there," he answered. "And I won't know exactly when I can do it till the last minute. Maybe Jacob will come."

"Let us know if you change your mind. I can tell Cam to expect you if you like?"

"That would be good, thanks."

Miller watched Dee typing into Geo's phone.

"Add my number," he said, trying to ignore the curl of apprehension in his gut. For all that Geo seemed brighter and somewhat relieved to have a to-do list, Miller almost caved to the temptation to simply tell him to forget all about Jacob. To focus on keeping himself safe for another year and a bit until he left home for university. One more year wasn't too long to wait, was it? A boyfriend wasn't worth all that risk, surely?

Yeah, right. Sound familiar? Miller had been listening to that voice for more years than he cared to count, and the issues on both sides were anything but simple.

What would he do in Geo's place?

He had no answer.

Then his eyes landed on Dee and his pulse raced. Yeah, as if the heart could be so easily ignored.

CHAPTER TWELVE

SANDY SHOT UP IN HIS SEAT, THE CRUNCH OF STEEL reverberating around the gym like a shotgun followed by a cacophony of whoops and hollers. It was ten times louder on the gym floor than it had been up top in the bleachers, but he'd wanted to be closer to the action this time, closer to Miller.

"Holy shit." He patted his chest as his rattled nerves settled from the crash. His stress levels were no better than the first time he'd watched this crazy game, although at least Miller was only racing up and down the sidelines today, yelling out strategy, encouragement, and a fair bit of arse whipping to his team, who were down five points and not looking like recovering with only a couple of minutes left.

Sandy's dick sure as shit warmed to the glint of passion in Miller's eyes, hopeful for a little full-body contact of his own down the track.

Robyn shot him an amused grin from a few seats down. "Exciting way to spend a Sunday, right?"

"That's one word for it." Sandy blew out his cheeks.

"Hey, you." Miller rolled close to steal a pineapple lump. "Looking gorgeous today."

Sandy's heart ticked up. He'd chosen black jeans paired with another almost see-through silk blouse, in hot pink this time, and a cropped black jacket. Miller took another long look, winked, and it was all Sandy could do not to sneak a kiss before Miller rolled back to the sideline to shout at his team some more.

But he kept his lips to himself.

Miller's family might not be in the crowd, but Sandy was conscious of any potential media interest lurking close by and tried to keep his hands to himself—something that was becoming increasingly difficult. No one had yet mentioned his name in any of the news articles, but he guessed it wouldn't be long, and some of Miller's regional teammates playing today were already casting interested glances his way.

Sandy had arrived after the game started, so he didn't know whether Miller had talked to the team personally yet, but he did know Miller had contacted the coach the day before. Even so, unless the players had been hiding under a rock, they had to know. Wheelchair rugby was a small, close-knit sport. At least they hadn't made the six o'clock primetime news like Reuben and Cam had in their day.

Most of what had been written about Miller so far had been complimentary, especially his sporting achievements. But Sandy knew it was pissing him off big time that the whole thing was even an issue, especially for a sport struggling to get more mainstream. But also because it seemed the entire focus of the commentaries was around Miller living *both* with a disability and being gay, as if either or both of those were a hardship that deserved sympathy, and that together it made him some kind of superhero. If another person congratulated Miller on how amazing he was, and what a fabulous role model he was, Sandy thought Miller might lose the plot completely.

As the clock counted down, Sandy glanced at his bag. He'd packed a little surprise for later, just in case. His apartment was too tiny if Miller needed his chair to rest his leg, so they'd agreed to go to Miller's after the game instead.

He'd had a sleepless night thinking about Geo and reliving his own coming-out debacle, surprised at how deeply the boy's story had affected him. He thought he'd be past all that by now, but he guessed his dad's unexpected reappearance had stirred shit up. Hearing that familiar yearning in Geo's voice, the disappointment and shock, the sense of betrayal by someone you loved and trusted, brought everything crashing back.

Sandy remembered every heart-breaking, soul-crushing minute of it as a teen, not to mention all the years it had taken him to move beyond that day. He knew Geo wanted his dad's love and approval no less than he'd always done. Just like Sandy still did from his own nearly twenty years after the man had walked out on them without a word, goddammit. A part of Sandy was still that fifteen-year-old little gay boy trying to explain who he was and then blaming himself for breaking up his entire family and sending his dad running.

Five years of therapy and Sandy wasn't as impervious to the damage his dad had inflicted as he'd thought. And he didn't know what to think about that, or if he should even bother thinking about it at all. It would always hurt. The goal was to live through that, and not let it hold him back. But listening to Geo and thinking about his mother's words had got him wondering.

Should it be eating away at him as much as it was? Was she right? Sandy didn't give a fuck about his father. It had been years since he'd missed him. Years since he'd even thought about him too hard. The man could go fuck himself into hell for all Sandy could give a shit. He didn't care one little bit if he never saw the bastard again.

Goddam his fucking fuck of a motherfucking father.

Ugh.

So, maybe he gave more of a shit than he thought. The realisation made Sandy angrier than ever. But damn if all that anger wasn't landing on the people he loved. Lizzie. His mother. The ones who least deserved it. The ones who'd been there for him. None of it on the person who was the root cause of everything.

He carried his phone away from the court and hit the number he'd avoided all weekend. Miller's gaze followed him with a questioning look. Sandy gave him a thumbs up and turned away to buffer the crowd noise.

"Sandy? Oh my god, Sandy!"

"Hey, Lizzie."

"Jesus Christ, I thought you were never going to call back. I'm so sorry, Sandy. I just needed to see him and I didn't know how to tell you. I knew you'd be angry—"

"Lizzie, stop. It's fine. It's me who should apologise. I should never have made you think you couldn't tell me. You're an adult, more of one than me, it seems. You need to do what's right for you. Mum too. None of this is your fault. I . . . I've been so fucked in my head since I heard. I haven't been thinking clearly, and I took it out on you and Mum, and I shouldn't have."

Small gulping sniffs travelled down the line and Sandy's chest squeezed with shame. He dropped to a seat and cradled his phone to his ear. "I'm so, so sorry, Lizzie. I never meant to hurt you."

Her breath stuttered. "You didn't, not really. I was so worried I'd done the wrong thing, but I needed to see him for myself, you know? And it was . . . okay. There's never going to be a good enough reason for what he did, and to be fair, he didn't try and give one. We mostly just talked about what I was doing. It hurt. Seeing him. Being reminded what he did to all of us, especially you. But I guess I feel . . . calmer, so maybe it was worth it."

"Are you going to see him again?"

She hesitated. "I don't know. Can we talk face to face soon?"

A hand landed on Sandy's knee and he spun to find a pair of soft green eyes on his.

"You okay?" Miller whispered.

Sandy nodded, fell into those eyes, and let them do their magic. "Yeah, Lizzie, I'd like that. I want to hear what happened."

She whooshed out a sigh of relief. "I could come to the hospital tomorrow. You could take me to lunch."

"Deal." He'd put Cam off until later.

"Who's that with you, by the way? And *where* are you? It's really noisy."

"I'm watching a wheelchair rugby game."

"A what? What the hell?"

Sandy locked eyes with Miller. "I . . . might have met a guy . . ."

Miller pressed a quick kiss to Sandy's lips, then angled the phone his way. "Hi, Lizzie. I'm Miller."

Silence bore down the line and Sandy took his phone back. "Lizzie?"

"Get off the damn phone and put that Miller guy back on, oh . . ." She trailed off and Sandy imagined her brain ticking over. "Oh. My. God. He's that Wheel Black isn't he? The one in the news. And *you're* the romantic interest they're talking about. Holy shit. I can't believe this. You're seeing someone, *this* someone, and you're just telling me now?"

"Lizzie, settle down. It's only been a couple of weeks—"

"Get off the damn phone."

Sandy handed the phone to Miller just as the whistle blew on the court behind them, and the whooping and hollering started up again. He could only imagine the grilling Lizzie was handing Miller by his rapid-fire answers.

"Yes. ... No. ... Ten years. ... At the same hospital. ... Absolutely. ... I'll have to check with Dee. ... Dee, it's my nickname for him."

Sandy rolled his eyes and grabbed his phone back. "Enough, Lizzie. You'll scare the poor man away."

Lizzie laughed. "Riiiight, *I'll* scare him off. And really, Dee? A nickname?"

"Shut up."

"It's so fucking sweet, I'm almost gagging."

"Shut. Up. And you can't tell anyone about me."

"I'm gonna have to tell Mum."

"No one else. *Goodbye, Lizzie.*" He pocketed his phone.

Miller fisted his jacket and pulled him in for a long and thorough kiss.

"Mmm. What was that for?" Sandy licked his lips and leaned in to snag another taste.

"For being pretty damn cute." Miller let him go, eyeing him like a slice of apple pie with all the fixings.

Sandy lowered his voice and checked there was nobody close. "You need to stop looking at me like that before I wheel you into that empty locker room and have you fuck me in one of those shower stalls. Make all my jock fantasies come to life."

Miller raked his eyes over Sandy's body, making his damn toes curl in their polka dot socks. "That one's going on the to-do list."

Sandy raised a brow. "We have a to-do list?"

Miller smirked. "We do now."

Several throats cleared behind them, and Miller dropped his chin to his chest. "Fuck." Then he caught Sandy's eye. "Sorry."

And Sandy realised the bustle of voices and cheers had gone silent. He did a quick sweep of the immediate courtside to find every eye laser-focused on the two of them. His cheeks burned. "Oh god, I'm sorry."

"Hey, it was me who kissed you," Miller soothed, stroking his cheek. "They were gonna find out soon enough." He grabbed Sandy's hand. "Come on. Let's go feed the lions. Get it over with."

"That's not as reassuring as you think it sounds." Sandy fluffed his shirt, tugged at his cropped jacket, took a big breath, and stood tall. "You first."

He trailed Miller to where the two teams were gathered in a loose group, all trying to look a little less like they were bald-faced staring than a few seconds before. A few sucked on water bottles, some were packing their bags, others chatted to the refs and coaches. But all eyes turned as Miller approached.

Sandy bristled, sensing he was yet again about to be judged, categorised, and assigned a place in people's heads. And Miller's character was likely to be reassessed on whatever people decided that place was. Well, fuck 'em. It shouldn't matter that these were Miller's friends and teammates, but of course it did, and that infuriated Sandy even more.

He tried to ignore the appraising looks, but it wasn't easy. He met as many as he could with the best stare-down he could muster.

"Hey, everyone. I'd like to introduce my boyfriend, Sandy." Miller led right off the bat and Sandy had to give him ten points for balls. "He'll be coming to some of our games and training sessions, so I'd appreciate keeping your lies about me to a minimum. After the media shitfest, he hardly needs any more reasons to reconsider dating me. And I'd really appreciate Sandy's name being kept quiet for as long as possible. I know it's going to come out, but I'd rather it wasn't from my team. I trust you guys to have my back."

It might have sounded relaxed and joking, but Sandy caught the edge of Miller's nerves jangling beneath the words, the tightness to his smile, the uneasiness of his flickering gaze. This was a big deal for him. A big coming-out-of-the-sports-closet deal after thirty-five years gathering dust inside.

And Sandy suspected regional teams could be less forgiving than international ones who were playing to a political spotlight. Miller was taking a risk, socially as well as sporting. They might not boot him off the team, but they could make playing for them miserable.

But for all of that, Miller offered no explanations, no big "I'm gay" speech, and Sandy was impressed. It was all low-key, like any other partner introduction, and when Miller finished by lifting Sandy's hand to kiss the back of it, it was all he could do not to shove that chair up against a wall and maul the man. Instead, he took the prudent option of door number two and politely shook hands with everyone who came up to him. Not as gratifying, but pretty damn pleasing in its own way.

"Anyone who'd take on your sorry arse deserves a fucking medal, Tap." A big-shouldered guy with a huge smile rolled forward, his prosthetic hand outstretched. "Nice to meet you, Sandy. I'm Keller. Give me a yell if you need help to keep this one in line."

Sandy laughed and shook hands. "I'll keep that in mind, Keller, although I have a few tricks of my own up my sleeve."

Keller roared with laughter. "I just bet you do." He clapped Miller on the shoulder. "Looks like you wrangled a spitfire here, Tap. Been a big weekend for you, I take it?"

Miller grunted and rolled his eyes. "You might say that."

Keller grinned. "You can handle it. But I have to say, you with a boyfriend? Man, this is gonna be fun to watch."

"Yeah, yeah, yeah." Miller turned a nice shade of crimson and flipped the other man off. "Get the fuck out of my life, Keller. You're taking up too much oxygen as it is."

Keller let loose another boom of laughter and wheeled off to a young woman who cuffed him up the back of the head.

"Whaddya mean behave?" He playfully patted her arse, and she dropped a kiss on his forehead.

Only a couple of players ignored the chance to shake hands, and Sandy made sure to note those faces for any future interaction. Even most of the partners came over to say hello, including Robyn, whose whispered, "Love your shirt," into Sandy's ear brought a genuine smile to his face.

Of course, there had to be one or two dicks. One guy from the other team rolled straight past Sandy, nearly taking him off his feet. It was pretty in-your-face, but when he saw Miller about to call the guy on it, Sandy gave a silent shake of his head. Thankfully Miller let it go. Sandy didn't need help fighting his battles.

He was still talking with Robyn when shouting and the sound of running feet turned everyone's heads in time to catch the back of some guy with a camera legging it out of the gym with Miller's coach in hot pursuit.

Fuck. He turned to Miller who simply shrugged. "It's going to happen sooner or later, babe."

But later was definitely better in Sandy's mind. *Much,* much later. He had enough attention directed his way on a daily basis, he didn't need more. And Miller seemed overly blasé for a man who'd hidden his gay from the sporting world for twenty years. But when everyone left the locker room for their cars and there was only the cleaning crew to keep them company, Sandy watched Miller's frozen smile fall away and the tension finally bleed from those big shoulders.

Miller wasn't the least bit blasé.

Sandy flicked the footrests up and squatted in front of Miller's chair, his hands on Miller's thighs. His gaze roamed those cute-as-fuck freckles sparkling under tired eyes. Relief, exhaustion, and still that small edge of fear haunted Miller's face. Grabbing his gloss from his pocket, Sandy held Miller's eyes and took his time applying a thin sheen to each lip. Then he smoothed them together, ran the tip of his tongue along the seam, and blew Miller a kiss.

"You wanna take me home and do nasty things to me, handsome?" He ran his hands up Miller's thighs to just short of his dick.

Miller snorted, cradled his face, and pulled him up for a kiss. "Is that a trick question, beautiful? Let's ditch this joint."

Thirty minutes later, Miller realised with a shock he'd never had a man in his bedroom. Dating-app hook-ups stayed in the lounge. A blowjob, hand job, a quick fuck with the guy riding him on the couch, but no one in his bed, ever. No one stayed the night, no one chatted, no one got to see beyond the guest bathroom, and Miller had been fine with that, so fucking fine.

Following Dee's eminently delicious and fuckable arse on its jaunty passage down the hall and into his bedroom was, therefore, kind of surreal, and Miller had to pinch himself that this was, in fact, his life. In three days, he'd come out to both his teams and his world hadn't exploded. Not yet, at least.

And by the next day, he expected most of his work would know as well. Those that didn't, would catch up soon enough if the hospital grapevine ignited as usual. But he'd deal with that then.

Right now, walking in front of him, was a complicated guy Miller really, really liked and was about to get naked with. And wasn't all of that just a bloody fucking miracle?

Dee kicked off his shoes and threw his jacket on the chair before taking the small bag he'd brought with him into the bathroom. "Give me two minutes."

Miller parked his chair, ditched his shoes, socks, and jacket, and got to his feet, keeping just the one cane for balance. He didn't trust his dodgy leg not to give out on him, even if it had improved.

He'd almost made it to the bed when the scent of citrus washed over him and a pair of long arms slid around his waist from behind. Soft lips nuzzled the back of his neck.

"Let me." Dee unbuttoned Miller's jeans while kissing the back of his neck and slid them to the floor before lifting Miller's T-shirt over his head. Lastly, he pushed down Miller's rather pedestrian briefs. He really needed to switch things up.

He stepped out of his briefs, struck by the fact that Dee was seeing him naked for the first time, scars and all—another no-go zone with any of Miller's hook-ups. A flash of nerves rolled through his belly. His torso was cut and muscular from the hours he'd dedicated to core training, in order to be stable in his chair, but his legs, not so much.

As if he sensed Miller's concern, Dee leaned his head over Miller's shoulder, plastering himself against Miller's back. He felt . . . taller somehow, either that or Miller was so damn tired he'd slumped, which was quite possible. And Dee was also naked, at least Miller was pretty sure he was, and his cock jumped at the thought. It would be his first time seeing Dee, as well.

"I can hear you thinking." Dee's hand dropped to wrap around Miller's cock and give it a couple of firm tugs. "Touch me instead. I've been waiting to feel your hands on me all fucking day."

Miller turned in Dee's arms and almost dropped to his knees.

Black lace stockings, black garter belt, black high heels, and nothing else but a sexy smile and a hard-on to give thanks for.

Bloody hell. Any worries about whether Dee would like what he saw under Miller's jeans flew out the window. Dee wanted Miller, end of question. And he was standing there, looking like every fantasy Miller had never even known he had.

"Damn." He used his cane on Sandy's stomach to gently push him back so he could drink his fill, and holy shit, what a sight.

"Like what you see?" An uncertain flush painted those pale cheeks and Miller wasn't having any of that.

"Like it? Jesus Christ, Dee, I've never seen a more sexy, gorgeous man in my life, and I cannot believe I'm the lucky guy who gets to have you. Damn, you're beautiful."

Dee's chin dipped in shy pleasure, and once again Miller was struck by the ebb and flow of Dee's moods. One minute the sultry seducer, the next charmingly vulnerable, and then later again, outraged champion of justice. It just did it for Miller on so many levels.

"I'm beautiful? What about you?" Dee practically purred. "You never mentioned all this gorgeous chest hair, or I would've had that shirt off you a lot sooner. And damn, Miller, your chest is a fucking work of art." He wrapped his hands around Miller's cane, which was still resting on Sandy's stomach, and began a filthy stroke along its length, the heat in his gaze, fucking incendiary.

Miller threw his cane aside and stepped in, running both hands up Dee's thighs, tracking that garter belt, trailing around his waist, and then dipping back down over that shapely arse to jerk him close, bringing their cocks into cosy getting-to-know-you distance, albeit with a height difference.

"Drop down," he growled.

Dee's eyes blew black. "Fuck, yeah." He spread his high heels until their groins nestled together in a perfect fit, and Miller didn't think he'd ever been so fucking hard in all his life. Dee angled his head to the side, offering him the tempting curve of his neck, and

Miller wasn't about to say no. He ran his lips from ear to shoulder and back before teasing with a couple of bites, while Dee ground against him, moaning his approval. Miller bit harder, once, twice, licking the sting while his hands continued their trembling exploration of Dee's silken arse and all that satin and nylon, not a hair in sight.

"You waxed."

Dee pressed his nose into Miller's waves. "For you."

Miller grabbed a handful of cheek and squeezed. "I love it."

"That's good news." Dee kicked off a high heel and lifted his foot onto Miller's bed. "Now touch me like you mean it."

And oh god, everything was right there in reach of Miller's hand. Heavy balls, waxed and tight, a slick taint, and a . . . wet hole. *Holy moly.*

"You prepped?" Miller breathed the words against Dee's lips, slipping a fingertip inside, and damn, it felt good..

"I . . . fuck . . . yeah, I did. Just a little." Dee slammed his lips against Miller's mouth, shoving his tongue inside and squatting to get Miller's finger higher, get it where he wanted it.

Miller obliged, pumping in and out, before adding a second, while Dee groaned and grumbled in his arms that it wasn't enough, not nearly enough.

"On the bed." Miller pulled his finger free and Dee shot him a filthy glare.

"You better be replacing that with something a lot bigger in the next few minutes, or we'll be having words," he grumped, getting on his back on the bed and spreading himself wide, his hand dropping to his cock for a couple of lazy strokes as his eyes rolled back.

Lord help me. He looked like a cross between a Renaissance wet dream—all those acres of creamy sun-protected skin and blushing lips —and a pouty, filthy porn star ready to give Miller the ride of his life. Without doubt, he'd struck the fucking lottery.

What the hell Dee saw in Miller in return was likely to remain one of the great mysteries of the world, and one Miller was in no hurry to solve.

"How do you want me?" Dee opened his eyes and raised a questioning brow. "Whatever gets your dick deep enough to part the hair on the back of my head from the inside out works just fine for me."

Miller nearly swallowed his tongue. "Now there's an image I won't forget in a hurry. You on top. My knees are crap at the best of times. Supplies are in the drawer. I want you to ride me so I can see your face. I'm not missing a thing."

Dee kicked off his other shoe, reached into the bedside table, and threw a condom and lube on the bed. His dick bobbed in the breeze and Miller almost wept with the need to take it in his mouth. But he was already on the edge and Dee had barely touched him.

While Dee dropped to his knees on the bed, Miller stretched over onto his back and scooted up. He'd no sooner got into position than a wet heat engulfed his cock and he fell back and arched up into it.

"Fuck, your mouth is paradise."

Dee's languid tongue grazed the head of Miller's cock and a groan bubbled from deep inside his chest. Jesus, the man was good at this. Miller lifted his head to watch and did a doubletake, finding Dee's arse right there at his shoulder. His head dipped up and down on Miller's cock—one of his hands threading through Miller's chest hair, while two fingers of the other were jammed up his own arse, stockings and garter belt framing a spectacular and breathtaking view from Miller's front-row seat.

His mouth ran to dust, and he immediately lubed his fingers to join the action, batting Dee's hand aside to sink his own finger into that tight heat.

Dee hummed his approval around Miller's cock in his mouth, and Miller added another finger, which only ramped Sandy's rhythm. Seconds later, Miller's eyes flew wide as Dee's slick fingers found their way into his own hole. Knowing where they'd been just seconds before had Miller's cock dancing on the brink in Dee's mouth and he almost—

Fuck. He pushed Dee aside and blew a few fast breaths as Dee shuffled around to kneel between Miller's knees, swollen lips curved up in a smutty smile, his fingers still working Miller's hole.

"You feel so fucking good in there." Dee licked his lips and dipped his body to drag his cock up the sheets, the friction causing his eyes to roll back. "Gonna get my tongue in there next time." He eyeballed Miller, his fingers still working their magic inside Miller's body. "I'm gonna lick every inch till you're begging. Does that make you hot, Miller?"

Hot? Christ, they haven't invented a scale for exactly how fucking hot and turned on I am.

"Does it make you ache for me to fuck you?"

Holy crap, yes. And wasn't that a surprise? Anything for this man. "Yes, goddammit, yes. Now get your arse around my cock before I completely fucking embarrass myself."

Dee slid his fingers free and straddled Miller's hips, wearing a smug smile. "Hold yourself."

Miller did, as Dee positioned himself and sank down, taking Miller inside in a long, slow slide. A groan of contentment rolled through the room and Miller realised it was his.

Goddamn, it felt so fucking good.

Sandy fell forward on his hands, his face hanging over Miller's, those tousled blond locks tickling his brow. "Ready?"

Miller reached a hand around Dee's neck and pulled him down for a hard kiss. "Hit it."

Dee nipped his lips, then lifted himself agonisingly slowly up Miller's shaft, paused for a second, and then sank down and immediately set up an alternating rhythm. Hard and fast, slow and tantalising, deep and shallow.

It was all Miller could do to keep his eyes on Dee, but he wanted to see everything. The fire in Dee's eyes, the need, the desperation, the flash of his eyes as he drew closer to that edge. Miller hoped he could outlast him, but it was gonna be a close call. He could only hope his cock chose this time to be a bit tardy. Time would tell.

Dee's head lolled back and his eyes fluttered shut with pleasure as he upped the rate, shuttling up and down Miller's cock, and fuck but Miller was almost there. A hand white-knuckled Dee's hip, while the other found his cock and began a flurry of short strokes.

A buzz started at the base of Miller's spine and rushed down his legs, but he fought it off. "Dee, now, babe."

Dee's groans stuttered and his mouth fell open, his breath catching in his throat as he grunted, arched his back, and spilled hot splashes of come all over Miller's stomach and chest.

Miller couldn't drag his eyes away and pumped Dee slowly through until he twitched with enough. He looked fucking glorious—pupils blown wide, sucking in air, immaculate hair a scruffy, sticky mess, with rivulets of sweat marking that smooth pale chest.

He smirked, leaned forward, and thrust his tongue deep into Miller's mouth, then pulled back and braced. "You close?"

Miller could only nod.

"Go for it."

He didn't need to be told twice. Grabbing Dee's hips with both hands, he thrust hard. Once. Twice. It wasn't going to take long. Four more and he crashed over, the intense wave of pleasure almost catching him by surprise. His hands fell back as he let it take him, Dee shuttling slowly, milking him clean. In Miller's world, orgasms were unreliable and unpredictable, but this one hit like a thunderbolt.

He was vaguely aware of Dee easing to a stop, fingers stroking Miller's face, kisses crossing his cheeks and lips, and soft murmurings of contentment—the latter mostly his.

"Hey there." Dee smiled down from above. "That was pretty freaking fantastic."

Miller cradled his face, studying those deep brown eyes and finding nothing but sated pleasure. "It was. And you are. Stay tonight, please?"

A spark of delight lit up Dee's eyes. "Yeah?"

He drew Dee down for a lazy kiss. "Yeah. I want you in my bed. I want to wake up to this beautiful face in the morning. But I know we have work, so if you need to go, I won't take it personally."

Dee flashed him a wicked grin. "As it just so happens, I might've packed a toothbrush and a change of briefs. And, as you may have noticed, I kept my clothes clean."

"I did notice. But I hope you don't need the stockings because I have plans for those in round two. And you didn't happen to bring those sexy glasses of yours, did you?" He ran a finger through the come on his stomach and lifted it to Dee, who sucked it clean and smacked his lips.

Dee eyed him suggestively. "You like my glasses, huh?"

"I do. Very . . . Clark Kent meets sexy librarian. Who knew?"

Dee's gaze sparkled in amusement. "Well, how about we get cleaned up, grab some food, and then if you're a good boy, I'll blow you with my glasses on and then rim a spectacular orgasm out of you." He waggled his eyebrows. "It's my other superpower."

Miller's mouth fell open but nothing came out, so he closed it again, then opened it again. Still nothing.

Dee laughed, pushed himself off the bed, slipped his high heels on, snapped his garter belt, and with a sassy look over his shoulder, sashayed those long black-stockinged legs into the bathroom.

Hellfire and angels. Miller couldn't get there fast enough.

CHAPTER THIRTEEN

"You're getting crispy bits all through the bed." Sandy swatted Miller's hand from his paper parcel of fish and chips and pointed to Miller's own in his lap. "Stick to yours, mister."

Cleared by Art the week before and finally off the bench, Miller had played a game that Saturday morning and then they'd come back to Sandy's apartment and tumbled into bed. With Miller back on canes, Sandy's apartment was less of an obstacle course, but it was still tiny and the best place for them to stretch out was in Sandy's bed. Such a hardship.

Three weeks of watching Miller's team play and Sandy was becoming a bit of an expert. It was a fast-paced, brutal game—easy to get caught up in. In the Paralympics the games drew full crowds, and for the life of him, Sandy didn't know why it didn't do the same back home or at least be featured on television.

Miller had recognised a journalist and photographer in the crowd, so they'd been careful to keep the PDA down after nearly being caught that one time, but Robyn had remedied the problem at the first break by seating Sandy in a chair alongside one of the bleachers out of sight. A couple of generic photos had made it to social media over the previous couple of weeks—they weren't hiding, as such—but neither of them was clear.

The first caught Sandy side-on with his glasses on and a scarf bundled around his chin—thank goodness for winter—and the others were either taken from the back or in Miller's car. But the clock was ticking. Someone would recognise him soon. The fact they worked in the same hospital was a bonus, meaning they could meet regularly with no one the wiser. Even the staff, who might've been surprised at learning Miller was gay, didn't seem to connect the dots with Sandy, who just blended into the small social group Miller had going, which included Cam, Reuben, and more recently, Michael.

Anyone who knew Sandy well might've recognised him in those photos just like his mother—but the less said about her and Lizzie's dogged pestering to meet Miller, the better.

And as Miller had predicted, the Wheel Blacks were hardly front-page news. Even a gay boyfriend didn't appear to be worth too much effort to track down unless there was fuck-all else going on in the sporting world. They had it lucky compared to Reuben and Cam. How those two handled all the media attention, Sandy couldn't begin to imagine.

Having said that, a part of him would like his name to get out sooner rather than later. At least then they might start to get out more. Apart from the rugby, they hadn't been out in public together at all, and Sandy had to admit it was starting to bug him. Was Miller not as comfortable being out or being with Sandy as he'd said?

But today, at least, Sandy had been pleased to return to the privacy of his apartment and another opportunity to get the man naked. A couple of hours and some spectacular sex later, they'd ordered takeout and then decided, for some ridiculous reason, to have a naked picnic in bed. Like those ever ended well.

"You said you didn't want a potato fritter," he teased Miller. "If you did, you should've ordered one. We've barely known each other four weeks. Not nearly long enough for me to share my fritters." He took a large bite and released his best pornographic moan.

"You'll share your arse and ram your tongue up mine, but you won't share your potato fritters?"

Sandy grinned. "Damn right. There's arse . . . and then there are the most excellent potato fritters known to humanity." He waved it under Miller's nose, then quickly away.

Miller's eyes narrowed to slits. "How was I to know they'd be that good?" he grumbled. "Fritters are very hard to get right. Go on. Just that end bit."

"No!" Sandy lifted his parcel out of Miller's reach. "Oh shit, now look what you've done. I've got ketchup all over my chest."

Miller leaned over and licked a swathe through the middle of the tangy spill, collecting Sandy's nipple as he passed, swirling his tongue around the nub before sucking on it. Sandy's head fell back onto the pillow with a groan. "Damn, that tongue of yours is trouble. Maybe I should sit on that other packet of ketchup? Get that mouth where I really want it."

"Maybe you should," Miller murmured, still licking and making his way up Sandy's neck, much to his approval. Then he was gone, lurching sideways to snatch the fritter before scooting to the far corner of the bed and snagging a huge bite before Sandy could stop him.

"Why you little . . ." Sandy dropped his parcel to the floor, squealed, and launched himself on top of Miller, who fell back on the bed, fritter hanging out of his mouth. Sandy straddled his thighs, careful not to put weight on Miller's hip which was still a little sore, grabbed the remains of the fritter, and held it high while his other hand wrapped around Miller's dick and squeezed threateningly.

Miller swallowed his mouthful of fritter and froze. "You wouldn't dare."

Sandy waggled his eyebrows. "Try me, fritter-burglar." He wiggled his butt, going up on his knees and leaning forward until their cocks brushed and Miller's head fell back. "Ugh. Keep your damn fritter. I don't think I have another round in me. You wore me out."

Sandy smirked, staring at the spray of freckles across Miller's nose that he'd come to know so well. Had it really only been a month?

"Good," he said. "There's no room between all the fucking crumbs you've dropped for either of us to get comfortable for a third round without finding batter where we least expect it." He popped the last of the fritter in his mouth and leaned down to share it with Miller who took a good bite, their lips brushing in the process.

"So much better than spaghetti." Miller waited till Sandy had swallowed, then pulled him down for a kiss.

He tasted of salt, sweet ketchup, and everything Sandy had come to love about Miller. The sigh was out of his mouth before he could stop it. He was falling hard and fast, and he wasn't sure whether to be excited or terrified . . . but excited was so far winning out.

They lunched or shared coffee most days at the hospital, either in Miller's office or the cafeteria, talking easily about anything and everything. With training three nights a week, Miller didn't have a lot of free time in the evenings, but Sandy wasn't too bothered. They both had weekends off and spent nearly all of that time together.

Sandy went to some trainings and all the games, and most of Miller's team were cool about the two of them, with just a couple of exceptions. But so far those exceptions had kept their mouths shut, although Miller was upset about one in particular, Jimmy, who he'd thought was a friend.

Sandy hurt for Miller. He was well used to both subtle and in-your-face homophobia. He'd dealt with it all his life. For Miller this was new, and to come from within the sport he loved and had given so much to, it had to sting.

But there had been bright moments to help balance things. Cam had let them know Geo had turned up at the drop-in centre the week after their little talk, naming Sandy and Miller as contacts if Cam needed. Geo had talked to a counsellor and met a few of the regulars, and just knowing the kid had taken their suggestion and acted on it put a smile on both their faces.

Sam had texted Miller with the same information not long after, and Miller had talked to Dane, who'd checked his son's eyeballs were still in their sockets about how other less accepting families functioned. Dane pushed Miller for who the man in Miller's life was, pointing out the unfairness of his son knowing more than he did and Miller's blatant violation of the bro code, but Miller wouldn't have a bar of it.

They'd been in their own little bubble and Sandy had appreciated the time to get to know Miller without a million eyes watching. And what he'd learned had done nothing to dampen his attraction; just the opposite. He might be a bit acerbic with others, but with Sandy, Miller was kind, patient, funny, and keenly interested in what Sandy thought and what made him tick. The fact the sex was off the charts, as well, didn't hurt either.

He rolled off Miller and curled into his side, his fingers playing with all those sexy curls on that ample chest. "So, I've decided to see my father," he said.

Miller grabbed Sandy's twirling fingers in his own, causing Sandy to look up.

"Really?" His concern was clear. "I thought you'd decided against that after talking with Lizzie."

He shrugged and avoided Miller's eyes. He and Lizzie had mended things between them. And when they'd met up for coffee, she'd seemed much more settled, even talked of maybe seeing their father again. Sandy had been shocked but curious as well. But then his issues with their father were more complicated. He was a bastard over Sandy being gay, and he hadn't even seen Sandy's fluid dress yet. Because of that, Sandy felt even more vulnerable in some ways, and he didn't like it.

His initial reaction had been not to see his father. But it felt a bit like running away. And that made him rethink.

"I thought I'd decided too," he said, looking up to trace a line of freckles on Miller's face. "But I can't stop thinking about him, and it's driving me out of my mind. I feel caught between a rock and a fucking hard place, a father-sized piece of granite."

Miller caught his fingers and brought them to his lips. "I happen to like your hard places, particularly the *fucking* hard ones."

Heat bloomed in Sandy's cheeks. "Like I didn't know that." He tucked his chin and snuggled into Miller's neck. "But if I *don't* see him, I'm always going to wonder, and the questions will burrow under my skin like scabies, an itch I can't scratch, and I'll never get rid of him. It's already happening. Look at me. He's got to me without even trying and I can't seem to turn it off."

Miller's arm wrapped around and drew him close. "It sucks and I get what you're saying. But if you see him, it has to be your decision, no one else's."

"I know. But at the moment, it feels like he's controlling all my bloody emotions again and I won't have it. I won't let him. And that's why I'm going to agree to see him. It's the only way I think I can wrest that control back. I have to know. Even if it's really shitty, it can't be any worse than when he left, right?"

Miller kissed the top of his head. "I don't know the answer to that, but I know you're strong enough to handle *whatever* happens. There's no one stronger."

And that was all Sandy needed. Miller was right. He *was* strong enough, and he had nothing to prove. He had a life, friends, people who loved him, a job he adored, and now—he glanced at Miller and the worry in those bright green eyes—now he had a man at his back who believed in him. And if his bastard of a father tried to screw with him again, Sandy would simply walk away and get on with his life. And it was a good life. Lately, a great one. His gaze settled on the soft lines of Miller's face.

"Would you come with me?" The words were out before he even realised, but it felt right. Although it was hard to miss Miller's surprise.

"Sure . . . if that's what you want?" Miller propped himself on one elbow and stared down at Sandy. "I'll do anything to help, you know that."

Sandy did know that. There was a steadfastness about Miller that

blanketed Sandy like a soft shield. It was one of the things he lo—
Shit. Shit, shit, shit. He loved Miller. He fucking loved Miller. He
pushed the realisation aside. It was too fucking soon, goddammit.

"I . . ." He hesitated, regaining his mental feet. "I don't need you
with me, with me, but close, just in case." He swallowed hard. *How
had this happened?* "I'll tell him I want to meet in a café. He doesn't
know you, so—"

"I'll grab a table somewhere close or wait outside."

Sandy's whole body sagged. "Thank you. It means a lot to me."

Miller's gaze drilled into Sandy, causing a warmth to swell in his
chest. *"You* mean a lot to me."

Sandy didn't even have to think. *Oh, fuck. This was it.* "I feel the
same." *Safe. Safer than love.* His gaze slipped away. "Scary, huh?"

Miller leaned in and pressed his lips to Sandy's ear. "Terrifying."
He pulled back and ran a line of fairy kisses along Sandy's jaw that
made Sandy's toes curl. "But then if we're both on the same page—"
He tilted his head to catch Sandy's eye. "—then maybe we can hold
hands through the scary bits? What do you think?"

Sandy's heart settled from a gallop and he lifted his head to steal
a kiss. "I like that plan." His hand searched beneath the sheet for a
distraction from the intensity and found what it was looking for.
Miller groaned and his eyelids fluttered shut. "Oh, I thought that was
your hand," Sandy said coyly. "Silly me."

"Mmm." Miller shuffled onto his side with only the smallest
twinge to reveal any discomfort.

The change made it easier for Sandy to work his magic. He
pushed the sheet down, and then Miller added Sandy's cock alongside his own, and Sandy gave thanks for the blessing of long fingers.
He kept it slow and lazy, in no hurry to get anywhere, just enjoying
the delicious slide and the feel and scent of the man bundled against
him. Miller's eyelids stayed closed, and Sandy pressed a kiss to each.

"My brother turns forty in a couple of weeks," Miller said quietly.
"The family are having a *thing* for him. I'd really like it if you'd come
with me?"

Sandy's hand froze on their cocks.

Miller opened one eye. "Too much, too soon?"

No. No. But . . . shit. "Are you sure? Your mother and father and . . . everyone?"

Miller smiled. "As far as I remember, mothers and fathers are part of the whole family thing, so yes."

Sandy fell on his back and swallowed hard. He'd been waiting for this, wondering if Miller was getting cold feet, but still . . . fuck. He'd only met the family of one of his boyfriends and that hadn't exactly gone well. One look at his makeup and they'd pulled Harry aside for . . . *a word.* They'd barely lasted another two weeks after that.

"What if they hate me? I mean, I'd wear jeans and shit but—"

"You'll wear exactly what you want to wear," Miller said sternly, returning Sandy's hand to his cock. "It was getting cold," he answered Sandy's arched brow. "Anyway, this is *my* family we're talking about, and I want them to meet *you*, not some version you think is somehow more appropriate. I want you to be comfortable and relaxed, and you won't be if you don't wear what feels right. Jeans? A skirt? I don't care which."

Sandy swallowed. It was, of course, exactly the right answer. Hell, it's how Sandy had vowed to live his life, but these were Miller's parents they were talking about. Miller mattered to Sandy. His parents mattered. And Sandy wanted them to like him, really, really wanted that. But he also wanted them to like the real Sandy, and there were never any guarantees of that.

So, no. Miller was right. He'd wear what felt right on the day and pray. And oh god, he was so in over his head with the man.

"Yes, okay, I'll come." Said quickly, it didn't sound so scary. Except yes, yes it actually fucking did.

Miller's lips twitched in amusement. "Excellent."

"Mm-hmm. You sure, you're sure?"

"I'm sure."

Oh. He was sure. Okay, then. That was . . . fine. Sandy's heart skipped. *Shit, what did it mean that he was sure? Sure as in he can't avoid it any longer, or sure as in he really wants me to meet his parents?*

Miller pressed a finger to the spot between Sandy's brows. "You're gonna break something in there. Relax. It'll be fine. My mum will love you. And you've stopped jacking me, by the way. I'm getting all lonely." He thrust his hips forward into Sandy's hand.

Sandy snorted and idly stroked away. "You don't know she'll love me."

"Mmm, that feels so good." Miller nuzzled into Sandy's neck with a long sigh. "Look, she's been driving me crazy wanting to meet you ever since those glimpses of you in the paper. She thinks you look . . . sweet."

"Sweet?" Sandy squeaked and pulled away, brushing Miller's dick aside.

"Ugh, I give up." Miller fell to his back and dragged the sheet over himself.

Sandy sat up and shoved Miller's shoulder. *Didn't he get it?* "She thinks I'm sweet, Miller. Sweet! Oh shit. She thinks I'm one of those cheerful, twinky, go-shopping-with-your-girlfriend kind of gays, and I am *so* not that person. I'm six foot three of insecure, gangly, potty-mouthed confusion who struggles to find a dress size to fit. I'm going to be such a disappointment. By the time I leave, she's gonna think I'm anything but sweet."

Miller sat up and tilted Sandy's jaw so he could kiss him. "You *are* sweet. Like the best caramel. And just so you know, I happen to love your potty mouth."

Sandy stabbed his finger at Miller's chest. "That's because you think potty mouth means your dick in my mouth while my fingers are up your arse. I doubt your mother would think that was *sweet.*"

Miller screwed his eyes shut. "Please don't mention my dick in your mouth and my mother in the same sentence ever again."

"And what about your dad? He thinks I'm a bad influence on your sport as it is."

Miller hesitated and Sandy jabbed another finger at him. "See.

What was that? That eye thing. Oh god, he *is* gonna hate me, isn't he? I can't—"

"He's not gonna hate you, baby," Miller tried to soothe, but Sandy's train had left the station and was gaining steam. "He just . . . well, he can't see much further than my sport, so yeah, maybe expect a bit of hairy eyeball in that regard. He can be a bit . . . intense. He sees another couple of Paralympics in my future and he's worried I'll lose focus. But he won't have any other issue with you, I promise."

"Oh." Sandy hesitated, realising he probably hadn't given that side of things enough consideration. He thought of all their weekend time together when maybe, before Sandy, Miller would've been training. *And holy shit. He's definitely gonna hate me.*

He swallowed hard. "Okay, I guess I can understand that. You're an elite athlete, right? It's not like you're playing tiddlywinks. He just wants you to succeed." *And am I in the way of that?*

Miller eyeballed him. "Hmm. I wish I could read that mind of yours, cos I'm not sure I like where it just went. Don't go thinking I've dropped the ball on my training because of *you*. I wouldn't do that. Succeeding is important to me too. But my dad isn't being altruistic either. He's way too invested in my success as well, he just won't admit it. I've been planning to talk with him about that very thing soon."

"But—"

"Shh." Miller pressed a finger to Sandy's lips. "Not because of you. It's been coming for a while. I've given everything to my sport and my job, and I won't deny I've loved it." He tucked a lock of Sandy's hair behind his ears. "But I want this too, now. I want you. I want to feel *this*." He covered Sandy's mouth with his own and dipped his tongue inside for a quick taste, then pressed their foreheads together. "It's the most alive I've felt in a long time."

Sandy's heart picked up a beat and he pushed Miller flat, swinging a leg over his thighs before wriggling to a sit. "Okay. But please, please don't let him think it's because of me. Then he really will hate me."

Miller laughed. "I won't let him think that. And I'll choose my timing. Plus, I'll have Mum on my side. Just . . . be prepared."

Sandy cocked his head. "Prepared?"

"If you think my dad is intense about my sport, you have no idea how intense my mum is likely to get about me having a boyfriend. And my brothers are going to give me shit like you wouldn't believe. Sam wasn't kidding. Not to mention Sam's bugging the shit out of me to spill the beans so he can sit back and watch the feeding frenzy."

Oh. Oooohhhh. Sandy felt his cheeks light up again. "That could be okay, I guess. Are you nervous?"

Miller let out a slow breath and ran his hand up and down Sandy's thighs, popping goosebumps in their wake. "Yeah, I guess I'm a little nervous. Not because of you, but because it's a huge change in my life. I haven't quite got used to everything it means myself yet."

Sandy studied him for a few seconds, then dropped his eyes. They'd promised to be honest with each other.

Miller's hand landed on his. "What is it?"

He took a breath. "Can I ask if that's why we haven't gone out yet? I mean, we've had coffee at the cafeteria, been to your games and each other's houses, but not really a date . . . in public?"

Miller stared, a small crease forming between his eyes as if it hadn't even occurred to him, and Sandy's heart sank.

"I mean, I get that it's all new and everything," Sandy added. "But you're pretty much out now, and I just wondered . . . I mean, I hoped it wasn't because of . . . well—"

"God, no." Miller shot up on his elbows, then jerked to his side with a yelp, sending Sandy flying off the bed. "Ow, shit, sorry." Miller fell back again. "Fuck, my hip."

Sandy scrambled back on the bed and reached for Miller. "Are you okay?"

"Fine." Miller stretched his leg with a grimace. "Just cramped up." Can you pass me a couple ibuprofen from my bag?"

Sandy did, along with some water. Then when Miller was done, Sandy slid back alongside and ran his fingers over all the bumps and scars of Miller's surgeries, a map of Miller's recovery laid over his skin in graphic detail. He knew every scar by heart.

With gentle fingers he began to knead where he knew the pain was localised just above the top of Miller's thigh.

"You don't have—"

"Shut up," he ordered.

"Okay, I'll just . . . mmm, god, that feels good. Down a little—right there." Miller groaned with pleasure and relief. "You have the best fingers." He cracked an eye open. "For lots of reasons."

Sandy snorted and rolled his eyes. "I bet you say that to all the boys."

"Very few boys have had their fingers where yours have been, and none as talented."

Sandy's fingers dug deep into the joint and Miller closed his eyes with another groan.

"I'm sorry," Miller said. "About the not-going-out thing. It's me. Totally me. I'm still getting . . . used to things. I didn't think. Hell, I don't go out much myself, if ever, and I was enjoying getting to have you to myself. I'm a homebody at heart, and then we were keeping it quiet, and I just . . . damn. I should absolutely have thought of taking you out. I told you I'd be crap at this."

Sandy relaxed. "You're not crap at it. And I don't need anything to happen right now. I just needed to . . . understand, I guess, why it hadn't."

"No, you deserve better and I should've thought of it. Nearly a month and we haven't gone out? Not good enough."

Sandy leaned over and kissed him lightly on the lips. "I'm pretty sure I've already got *better*. And now I understand, I can wait."

Miller set his jaw. "You shouldn't need to, and you won't."

An hour later, he wheeled his way out of Sandy's apartment and into the elevator with more promises to work on a date, and Sandy waved him off, feeling lighter. He'd hoped to keep Miller in his bed for the night, but the man's cramps weren't getting any better and he needed a hot bath and an early night. Sandy's apartment barely had what passed as a one-person shower if you squeezed in sideways and held your breath, let alone a bath.

One thing was certain, if they ever got as far as moving in together, it wasn't going to be into Sandy's place. Besides, Miller's opened up a lot more possibilities. His mind went to being royally fucked in Miller's massive walk-in shower with Sandy straddling him on the tiled bench, still in his high heels. Thank god for all that core strength work.

He froze. *Oh. My. God. Living together?* Where the hell had that come from?

But he couldn't pretend. He was already in deep, in bloody love like the fool he was, even knowing the potential for heartbreak. Miller had the power to fuck Sandy up big time. He may not be like the other arseholes who'd let him down, but that didn't mean he'd stick around.

There was a lot going on in Miller's life, maybe too much for Sandy to claim a big enough space. Miller said all the right things, even wanting Sandy to meet his family, which, okay, had shocked the socks off him, but there were no guarantees. He didn't doubt Miller cared for him, but this thing they had was in many ways a novelty for Miller; he'd even said as much. And the sex was . . . well, fantastic, so there was that too.

Sandy needed to get his head out of his arse and try and keep some perspective.

Yeah, good luck with that.

Because even as he thought it, he knew it was already too late.

CHAPTER FOURTEEN

MILLER ROLLED INTO THE GYM TEN MINUTES LATE AND WITH his nerves jangling at full fucking volume. Whatever nerve he'd pinched in Sandy's bed the afternoon before was still digging its claws into Miller's hip and thigh. Between the extra effort it took to get his protesting body into the shower to loosen it up, allow time for his pills to work, and get something into his sour stomach, he simply hadn't been able to get clear of his house any earlier.

Merv gave him the hairy eyeball and he deserved that and more. As a senior player, he was expected to set an example. Add in the fact today was the big fitness test, and it wasn't a good look. He could only hope the fact he was normally a half-hour early had earned him some wiggle room.

"You look like shit." Merv sidled alongside Miller's chair, keeping his voice low. "Anything I should know about?"

Nope. Nothing to see here. "Just a bit stiff after the game yesterday," Miller lied. "I'll be fine."

Merv gave him a hard stare and shook his head. "Riiight. Well, I hope you're up for this fitness test today. I won't be offering it again."

He raised a brow. "To anyone, understand? It's only a couple of weeks till the Australian series and I'll be finalising the team after today."

"I'll be fine. As I said, just a bit stiff."

"How's Benson doing?"

Much safer ground. "Looking good. We've had a couple of one-on-one sessions and he's coming along nicely. You should notice an improvement at the next game. He's much sharper on those turns and blocks."

Merv gave a grunt of approval and moved away.

Miller wheeled over to correct Benson's form on a set of arm curls and then peeled off his sweatshirt to join the warm-up.

"No boyfriend today?" Jimmy asked without looking up from the weights he was working with.

"Fuck off." Miller wasn't about to pretend with the guy. Other than whatever they had to say to each other on-court to make things work, Jimmy had pretty much ignored Miller since the day he'd come out. It hurt, but Miller was more pissed than anything. Vicki still seemed friendly enough, so Miller wasn't sure whether it was just Jimmy and he kept his opinions quiet around his girlfriend or what. "I'm not discussing him with you."

Jimmy glanced up long enough to glare at him. "Hey, don't get mad with me. You're the one who kept the big secret."

Miller returned the glare. "What secret? I don't hear you putting your sex life up for discussion in the locker room or media. And if I chose not to talk about it, I wonder why that was, Jimmy? Maybe because I knew there'd be arseholes like you who couldn't get past their homophobic bullshit to just do the decent thing and be nice. Hell, garden-variety fucking polite would do. A few basic manners. Well, fuck you."

"Jimmy, shut your mouth," Beau snapped from a few metres away. "Before you look more of a dick than you already do."

"Yeah, what he said," Rosa added her voice, and Miller was pleased to see Benson nodding vigorously behind her.

"Keep your nose out of it," David snapped back at Rosa, holding up his hand for a high five as he rolled past Jimmy. "Everyone's entitled to an opinion."

"But that's where you're wrong." Merv stormed over, his face a thundercloud. "In this team and in this gym, you belong to me. And I'm the *only* one who gets a fucking opinion. And if I hear any more of this bullshit, especially from you two, Jimmy, David, you'll be stood down indefinitely, understood?"

Jimmy fired Miller a defiant glare.

"Is. That. Understood?" Merv's disapproving gaze slowly swept the group, pinning them in place. A sea of nodding heads greeted him. "Good. Then get back to work." He strode off muttering something about arseholes and fucking kindergartens.

Miller rolled closer to Jimmy and lowered his voice. "I can't do anything about the fact you're my teammate, Jimmy, but I'm not going to pretend it's anything more than that, not anymore. You've made that patently clear. See you on the court." He spun and left Jimmy and the rest of the Wheel Blacks staring at his back.

Which was just as well, as there was a distinct blur to his vision that he didn't want to think too hard about. *Goddammit.* This team had been his refuge and his passion for nearly ten years. Since when had it become this godawful battleground? And it was his fault.

Should he have kept his mouth shut? He thought of Sandy and mentally slapped himself. Of course not. He'd known there was a chance of this, going in. It would settle. He just needed to wait it out. But exactly how much would be left at the end of the game he loved, he didn't know.

He sucked in a deep breath and tried to focus on just getting through the damned fitness test before he lost his place in the team altogether.

Two gruelling hours later and he'd passed the test, thank god. At what cost, he wasn't sure, since he could barely feel his lower leg beneath the tide of pins and needles sweeping through it at regular intervals. But at least he'd passed. Not as well as the last time, and not without earning a concerned look from Merv after needing a second attempt on a couple of the stations, but still, a pass. He rolled into the locker room shower with a groan of relief and let the scalding needles of water work their magic.

When he finally shut off the water and headed to his locker, he was relieved to find Jimmy and David gone. He didn't want it to matter but it did. Over the morning the rest of the team had taken it in turns to touch base and reassure him they had his back, but he struggled with the idea that he should even need their support.

It was a sharp and unwelcome reminder of what he'd avoided most of his life and why he'd avoided it. Welcome to the real world.

He got dressed and was out of there before Merv took him aside for another heart to heart on the same thing or asked those niggly questions about his fitness that Miller had no intention of answering. He knew better than to think Merv wouldn't be taking his concerns to Art or that Art wouldn't be texting Miller for a catch-up. Oh joy.

He checked his messages and found he'd missed one from Dee and another from Sam. He read Sam's first.

Geo's dad being a dick again. Found some gay stuff in his search history and grounded him. I'm not allowed to visit.

Shit. Miller called his nephew.

"Hey, Uncle Em." He sounded low.

"Hey, kiddo. That sucks. Is Geo okay?"

"I guess. It happened yesterday, and he hasn't said much about it, just that he's grounded for the week. It's crap because he was really excited about talking to some counsellor dude at the centre tomorrow. He thinks Cam's really cool, by the way."

Miller smiled. Cam *was* cool. "Well, there's nothing he can do about it if he's grounded. How's the boyfriend situation?"

"The only place they can meet is at school or at the centre, but I think they're still tight. Jacob's a good guy."

"That's good. Well, tell Geo if he needs to talk, he has our numbers. And don't worry too much."

"Thanks, Uncle Em."

"Just Em, remember?"

"Got it, *Uncle* Em." He gave a half-hearted laugh and hung up before Miller could reply, so he flipped him off by emoji instead. He got an old man gif in response. Cheeky little shit.

He read Sandy's text next and let out a disappointed sigh.

Called in for a police autopsy. Sorry. Lunch tomorrow? How did the test go?

Damn. Miller had been looking forward to lazing on Dee's couch, ordering takeout, and fooling around, and not necessarily in that order. Though he wasn't sure just how much of the fooling around part he could manage with his leg screaming at him, so maybe it was better this way. Dee was far too smart not to notice when he was in pain, and Miller really didn't want to talk about that. He blew out a sigh and texted back. **Passed. No problem. Lunch tomorrow sounds good.**

A beer on his back porch sounded even better for right now, and that's where he was headed. Jimmy and David had gotten under his skin and weren't moving anytime soon. He was pretty much done with the day.

But when he got to his car, it became clear the day wasn't done with him.

Son of a bitch. The key gouge ran from behind the front tyre on the driver's side, all the way to the taillight. He threw his gym bag on the ground and swallowed the surge of rage that flared in his throat. *Fucking, fuck, fuck.*

He had no proof, but it was hard to pass on Jimmy's name as prime candidate, although he wouldn't have picked the guy for something like this. He might be an arsehole, but Jimmy was nothing if not in-your-face. If he had something to say, he usually said it straight up. Still . . .

Miller reached for his discarded bag and chucked it in the car. Then he groaned all the way to his feet and got the chair stowed as well before sitting behind the wheel and drumming his fingers. The idea of a beer had burned up in his fury. He didn't want to go home. He didn't want to be alone. He wanted . . . he wanted . . . hell . . . he wanted brown eyes and a sassy smile. He wanted long arms and a sexy-as-fuck mouth. He wanted Dee. Preferably to bury himself in, but failing that, one of the man's epic hugs would do.

He threw the car in gear and headed for the hospital. He might even get some work done while he was there.

———

Thirty minutes later he pressed the call button in the visitor room and waited. It was his first time in the dungeons of the Forensic Pathology Unit, and he'd only briefly met its rather quiet and intimidating head of department twice. Ed Newton had struck Miller as a particular and bookish guy, well respected and good at his job but difficult to get to know.

It was hard to equate with the friendly, quirky man Dee raved about, but then again, they'd gotten to know each other under fairly intense circumstances that happened to involve Cam and that whole group of friends. Uncovering a murder, being sent into hiding, and Dee helping the police to hunt down those responsible. And now Ed was apparently living with one of the detectives involved. It almost blew Miller's mind.

He looked around the room as he waited, chuckling at the Press Me label on the buzzer, the Eat Me label on the packaged snacks on the coffee table, and the Drink Me label on the water cooler. Somebody had a sense of humour, not to mention an eye for photography. The walls bore some stunning images.

Voices floated out from behind the closed door, and Miller suddenly hoped he'd done the right thing. Dee visited him plenty in his office, but that was entirely different to Miller turning up where Dee had a boss to answer to.

The door opened, and the surprise on Dee's face quickly morphed into obvious delight and Miller breathed a sigh of relief.

Dressed in the ubiquitous hospital uniform of loose green scrubs, and damn, those round black-rimmed glasses Miller loved, the saucy man still managed to look lickably gorgeous.

"Well, hello there." Dee leaned on the door jamb, looking somewhat amused. "Aren't you a sight for sore eyes?"

Miller peered around Dee's waist to check if he was alone. "Is this okay? I don't want you to get in trouble."

"It's fine. We finished up about ten minutes ago. I've got stuff to label and write up, but I can take a break. Come in. Do you want to walk or bring the chair?"

"Is it far?"

Dee shook his head.

Miller grabbed his canes and Dee frowned as he struggled to get out of his chair, offering a hand. "You're hurting," he said.

Miller accepted the help till he had his balance. "It's been a tough day."

"Come on, then." Dee led him down a short corridor. Country crossover played through speakers and more stunning photographic landscapes filled the walls. The place had a calm, inviting feel to it. Not at all what Miller had expected. No wonder Dee loved working here.

"I heard from Sam," Miller spoke as he followed Sandy down the hall. "Geo's dad found some gay stuff on his search history and grounded him."

"Oh for fuck's sake. After we talked with him, I got to thinking how in some ways I was lucky my dad took off. At least I didn't have to deal with the shit Geo's going through. Is he okay?"

"Sam thinks so."

Dee led him into a small office that was clearly his, judging by the tube of lip gloss on the desk and the bright green chiffon scarf thrown over the back of the chair and . . .

"Are those . . ." He pointed to a small vase holding what looked like two dried viburnum flowers, his heart skipping in his chest.

Sandy's pale skin turned an adorable shade of pink. "Damn.

Busted, I guess. I wanted a reminder. It was so sweet of you that night. It's not . . . I mean, I didn't think you'd see . . ." He sank back against the edge of the door. "Damn."

Miller was so fucking touched. And so deep, deep over his head. He reached for Dee's hand and pulled him close. "I love that you did that."

Dee grunted. "Well, I guess it's no surprise that I like you, right?" His lips turned up in a nervous smile.

"Just as well, since I guess it's no surprise that I like you too?"

Dee eyed him for a second, and then suddenly Miller was up against the noticeboard with Dee's tongue halfway down his throat. And damn, Miller needed this. He threw his canes aside and circled his hands around Dee's waist and under those scrubs till he connected with searing skin. The touch drew a sigh from his mouth, and when Dee finally pulled away, Miller growled and chased his lips, not nearly done.

Dee held back and snorted in amusement. "Problem?"

"I won't have if you get back here. And let me just say for the record, those glasses you wear are so fucking sexy."

Dee glanced into the hallway and then backed against the office wall and lifted his arms above his head. "I'm all yours, within reason."

Damn. Miller was there in a second, Dee's lips warm and hard against his own, Miller's hands racing under his shirt as Dee offered himself for Miller to indulge in a little personal therapy however he pleased—which was going to take at least a minute or two, maybe a year—it was a close call the way Miller was feeling. His arms snaked around that slim waist, holding Dee's warm pliable body right where it belonged. And just like that, Miller's crankiness faded, lost in the warmth and openness of this breathtaking man he was pretty sure he didn't deserve.

How long they kissed, he had no idea. Long enough to calm his heart and knit some peace into his day, but they were hardly hitting the workplace discreet button and he reluctantly pulled up and rested their foreheads together.

"Wow." Dee pushed him back a little to study him, a worried crease forming between his brows. "You can stop by anytime if that hello is anything to go by." His long fingers smoothed Miller's brow and trailed down his cheek. "Did something happen? I'd thought you were heading home for a hot bath and a beer."

Miller leaned forward and ran his nose up Dee's throat, earning a shiver from the man. "So did I," he said between nuzzles. "But I wanted to see you." He stood back. "The fitness test sucked even if I did pass. Jimmy was being a dick. And then some bastard keyed my car outside the gym."

Dee's brows crunched. "What? Who?"

Miller arched a brow.

"You think it was Jimmy?"

He shrugged. "Maybe. Not that it makes any difference. I just . . . wanted to see you."

"Well, I'm glad you came." He dropped his head to Miller's shoulder and Miller slid his hands up Dee's long back. "Fucking knobs. If it *was* Jimmy, I promise to walk over the damn hood of his car with my stilettos."

Miller barked out a laugh. "You bloody would, wouldn't you?"

"Bloody oath. Nobody does that shit to someone I care about and gets away with it."

He looked so pissed off and determined that it stole Miller's breath, and he didn't doubt for a second Dee would do exactly as he promised. "Come here." He fisted Dee's scrubs, hauled him close, and kissed him hard. "I like that you care about me. I care about you too."

"Good to know." Dee's hands found Miller's arse and yanked him flush. But just as their lips locked, a throat cleared beside them.

"Jesus, Sandy, I thought you'd already had lunch?"

Sandy startled in Miller's arms but didn't jump away, and Miller's gaze shot sideways to find a tall handsome blond wearing a huge grin. He recognised Mark Knight from a couple of Reuben's and Cam's barbecues, although they hadn't really spoken beyond introductions.

Sandy spun and flipped the detective's tie over his shoulder. "Like you can talk. Judging by the number of times I find Ed's office door locked when I know he's in there, and *not* alone, he should replace that damn door with a revolving one and put your name on it. You guys have a home, *together,* and plenty of time to do the nasty without exposing my delicate constitution to your wanton ways."

Mark laughed and Ed Newton appeared beside him from the room next door. "What's so funny?" Ed's gaze flicked between the three. "What did I miss?"

Mark turned and pressed a kiss to his partner's cheek. "Nothing, my sweet. I just caught your assistant in a lip- and hip-lock with who I'm guessing is the mysterious boyfriend we've heard whispers about."

"This guy?" Ed looked confused. "But you work here, right? Miller . . .?"

"Miller Harrison." Miller offered his hand and Ed and Mark shook it.

"Sandy has been very close-lipped about you." Ed eyeballed him, and Miller squirmed under the scrutiny. "You better be good to him. He has a lot of friends."

"Ed!" Dee scolded, flushing bright red.

"What?" Ed jutted his chin. "You threatened Mark when you thought he might screw with me."

"That was . . . different. Mark's . . . well, he's Mark." Dee waved a dismissive hand Mark's way.

Mark snorted. "I'm thinking I should be offended."

"And yet you're not," Dee shot back.

"You should bring him to our Friday thing." Mark feigned an innocent look while continuing to check Miller out.

"Friday?" Miller's curiosity piqued.

Sandy ignored him, folded his arms, and stared Mark down instead. "Don't cause trouble. And I wasn't being close-lipped. I just wanted some space before you lot got hold of him. Cam was bad enough."

"Cam knows, and I didn't?" Ed clasped a hand to his chest. "You wound me."

"Oh fuck off." Sandy shoved the two men out the door. "Go and make babies in your office. It seems to be its primary use these days."

"What?" Ed's face burned scarlet. "Oh, shit. That wasn't . . . I mean, we didn't . . ." He slammed his mouth shut and glared at Mark. "I told you we shouldn't—"

Mark clamped a hand over Ed's mouth. "Come on, baby. I think we should do what the nice man says. The world needs more babies, and with my looks and your brains, our kids should rule the world." He glanced back at Miller and Dee. "Don't do anything I have to arrest you for." Then he grabbed Ed's hand and dragged him protesting up the hallway.

Dee shot them a fond look, kicked his door shut, and turned all that focus back on Miller.

"So, Friday?" Miller cocked a brow.

Dee pulled a face. "A group of us were going to Downtown G for a few drinks. Cam, Reuben, Ed and Mark, Josh and Michael."

Oh. Miller's horror must've shown on his face because Dee sighed and quickly smoothed Miller's shirt.

"That's why I didn't mention it," he said. "I kind of guessed you wouldn't be interested. Not with all your training before the big game and your leg playing up. We can do it another time . . . when you're more comfortable."

Like *never*. Miller almost swallowed his tongue. He wanted to bury that idea under a pile of no-fucking-ways as soon as possible, but something about Dee's casualness didn't ring true. He remembered their conversation about not having been on an actual date outside their apartments and cringed.

Fuck. He was doing it again. Being a selfish prick . . . again. Dee considered Miller's comfort level all the time, while Miller was doing fuck-all about Dee's. But a gay bar? God help him. That had always been a no, on so many, many levels.

"Do you do that kind of thing often, as a group?" he asked, trying to keep the dread out of his voice.

Dee shoved his hair back from his face. "Sometimes, not often. Babysitters required and all that. But I love to dance, so yeah, every couple of months or so we try."

Shit. "Then we should definitely go." *Fuck, fuck, fuck.* "There's a reason I haven't been to a gay bar, but it's probably not what you think."

Dee couldn't look more sceptical if he tried.

"Okay, it's not *only* what you think. The fact is, I hate *all* bars. They're crowded and hard for me to get around, and I feel . . ." He hesitated, not wanting to go into all the different ways crowded bars and restaurants and clubs made him feel, and none of them good.

Sandy took his hand. "I get it. And we don't need to go."

Miller looked down and idly tapped his cane on the grey linoleum as he decided what size douche canoe he'd been too busy paddling to pay enough attention.

"But we do, in fact, need to go." He lifted his eyes. "For a lot of reasons. I've lived my life making a point of not being held back by my disability, and then what? I'm too scared to go to a gay bar? How much of a hypocrite does that make me? I'm not saying I'm gonna be any fun, so be warned. I can't drink and I can't be out too late. Hell, you probably won't want to ever take me again once I make a spectacle of myself, but I want to do this. I want to see you dance. We should go. And oh my god, I can't believe I just said that."

Sandy reached for Miller's hand and lifted it to his lips. "You've got nothing to prove to me, you know that?"

But he did have something to prove. "I'm not so sure. And even if I didn't, there's another reason to go—because *you* want to go. I'd be a piss-poor boyfriend if I didn't take you places you enjoyed. You come to my games to watch something *I* love to do. And I want to see *you*

enjoy yourself on that dance floor. Plus, I believe this would consti-
tute as a date outside our apartments, right?"

Sandy rolled those gorgeous brown eyes and eyed Miller side-on.
"I believe you'd be correct in that. But I have one condition?"

Miller waited.

"I want one dance with you."

Jesus fucking George. Worst nightmares and all that. Miller held
up a finger. "One. But if anyone tries to grind on me or feel me up,
fair warning, I'm going to beat them with my fucking cane." He
wasn't kidding.

Sandy laughed and slipped his hands around Miller's neck. "If
anyone tries to grind on *my* man, I'll beat them for you."

My man. Oh, Miller liked the sound of that. "I'll trust my virtue
to you, then."

"Foolish man. Now get those lips back where they belong."

Later—who the hell knew how much later—after a lengthy make-
out session involving mutual groping and a lot of tongue, Miller
headed up to his own office and called his car insurance company.
Then he managed a couple of hours work before the pain in his leg
forced him to pack up and take the rest home, where he'd just got
comfortable with a pie and a beer, and his laptop on his knee, when
Dee texted.

*I forgot to mention. I'm meeting my father a week
from Thursday at 4. Primo Café, just down the road.
Does that work for you?*

Miller checked his diary. *I'll be there.*

*Thanks. And thanks for dropping by. Lunch
tomorrow?*

Miller smiled. *Yes to lunch. I have a meeting that
should be done by 12.*

Then while he had his phone out, Miller texted Sam. *I'm
bringing Sandy to meet the fam at the fortieth. Keep
your dad sweating on the name.*

Sam replied instantly. ***Awesome. Will do.***

Finally, he took a deep breath and texted his mother. ***Red Alert. Klingons on the starboard bow. I'm bringing my boyfriend to Dane's fortieth.***

He took a long swallow of beer, threw his phone on the coffee table, and watched it blow up.

CHAPTER FIFTEEN

"You could've asked before just showing up," Sandy huffed, dragging the bazillionth shirt over his head, taking one look in the mirror, and then hauling it off to join the pile on the floor. Then he angled his glasses awkwardly on his nose to touch up his eyeliner.

"You would've just said no," Lizzie said before throwing him another from deep in his closet.

Sandy pushed his arms through the clingy material and unrolled it down his chest like Glad wrap. "Jesus, I can hardly breathe. And hell yeah, I would've said no. This is the first time we've been out in public on a date. I don't need you and Mum clogging up my mental space. What do you think of this?" He spun side to side, studying his reflection.

Lizzie turned her beautiful and deceptively innocent face toward him and positively beamed. "Aw, you're nervous. That's so sweet. Also, I hate the shirt. Take it off."

He fired her a glare while peeling the shirt from his back with no small amount of difficulty. "It's not sweet. It's humiliating. I don't do this with guys. I learned a long time ago, heading down that path leads to inevitable disappointment. Better to be cautiously pessimistic."

She flicked through another dozen coat hangers. Never let it be said Sandy was low on options. "But he's not just *any* guy, is he?" She frowned at a navy-blue skin-tight T-shirt he loved and then passed on it. "You're meeting his parents, Sandy. That's huge."

He fell backwards on the bed. "Fuck. It is, isn't it? Jesus, what am I going to do if they hate me? What if the thought of their son dating a guy who wears skirts makes them cringe in horror? What if—"

"Stop it." Lizzie tossed yet another floaty shirt on top of him. "Put that on. The colour is gorgeous on you. It'll look hot with that leather and makes your eyes pop."

He fingered the bright yellow material and instantly calmed. "It does, doesn't it." He slid to his feet and drew it over his head. The waft of chiffon against his chest as it fell brought a hum to his lips.

Lizzie stood back, folded her arms, and smiled. "That's it. You look bloody fantastic."

Sandy looked at himself side-on. "You don't think it's too much? It's practically transparent."

A rap of knuckles sounded on Sandy's bedroom door. "Can I come in?"

"No," they both shouted at once, then grinned at each other like fools.

"Jeez. All right. All right." Their mother wandered away muttering.

Lizzie ferreted through Sandy's dresser for a few seconds, then spun around with a triumphant look. "Found it." She got up on her toes and fastened the black choker around his neck. "Perfect." She stood beside him and stared in the mirror. "I'm assuming he's already fucked you silly by now?"

"None of your business," he grumbled unconvincingly. After all, oversharing was nothing new between them. Lizzie had been there from Sandy's first kiss with Tosspot Terry of the pouty lips and creepy long tongue; to his first head, both given and received with

Delectable Douglas of the I-am-so-fucking-not-gay fame; to his first bottoming gig under the not so skilled hands of Sexy Steve, who Sandy really should've given a miss if it weren't for his desperate desire to have his cherry popped before he left high school. A mistake all around as the experience left a lot to be desired. Enough that Sandy reinstated his cherry status immediately after the debacle, under the pretext of the "that couldn't possibly be all there is to it" gay sub-clause. Later with Handsome Harry, he'd been delighted to find it wasn't, and a whole world of possibilities had opened before him.

"Well, has he?" Lizzie elbowed him and waited.

Sandy couldn't keep the smile from his face. "All right. Yes. Yes, he has."

"Soooo fucking cute." Lizzie grinned up at him and added a cuff around his wrist.

"Shut up. And wasn't the choker enough?"

"No it wasn't. And all I meant was if you've already done the dirty, then what do you care if your shirt's laying your nipples out on display as a welcome mat?"

Sandy sat on the bed and pulled his shoes on. "He's quieter than me. More serious. I'm just worried he might find tonight, the club, the whole thing, *me*, I guess, a bit . . . crass."

She whacked him on the arm. "What the fuck? You have never been crass in your entire life. And if he thinks that, then fuck him, he's not worth your attention. You look hot, Sandy, and he's bloody lucky to have you."

He flicked her a glance. "I don't want to scare him off. He doesn't do clubs. Hell, he's barely doing *gay*. He only came out to his team a couple of weeks ago. He's still got bloody training wheels on his glitter, and here I am taking him to a club dressed like Lady fucking Marmalade."

She flicked him on the forehead. "You're wearing trousers, for Chrissakes. You want Lady Marmalade, we'll have to ditch that lot and go with the taffeta number at the back of your closest."

He snorted and she quirked an eyebrow at him. "That's better. Now come on, fix your hair and we'll see what Mum says."

He bent down and kissed her cheek. "Thanks, sis."

She patted his chest. "You're welcome. You really like him, huh?"

"Yeah, I really do." He lowered his voice. "Maybe more than like."

Her eyes widened. "Wow. I didn't see that coming. And he's okay . . . with everything?

For Lizzie to ask, he knew she was worried. "He is."

She relaxed. "Good. And so he fucking should be. You're gorgeous and I'm so happy for you. But holy shit, if he hurts you, I don't care if he uses a damn wheelchair, I'll kick his bloody arse."

"I'd expect nothing less."

His mother turned as they came out and her hand flew to her chest. "Oh, Sandy, you look beautiful."

He swore she wiped a tear. "What the hell, Mum?"

"Leave me alone," she snuffled. "It's like senior ball all over again, only this time you're going with someone you actually like, not that wanker who dumped you straight after."

"Mum!"

"Well, it's true. He was a toad. He only asked you on a dare."

Sandy threw up his hands. "Just what every kid wants to hear."

"Now, let me look at you." She circled around, straightening his shirt and turning the choker buckle to the back. "Certainly a bit risqué, but then you boys like that kind of thing I hear . . ."

Oh my fucking god.

Lizzie fluffed his shirt and Sandy twisted the buckle back to where it was.

Returning to the front, his mother nodded her approval. "I think you look lovely, dear."

He gave her his best eye-roll. "*Hot*, Mum, I look *hot*. Lovely is what your grandmother says to you and is definitely not the objective."

"Then you look hot."

"Ew, no, that doesn't work either. Not from my mother. And this is why you don't get invited to meet the guys I date until much further down the track," he grumbled.

"Stop complaining. I'll be on my best behaviour."

"Said every meddling mother ever."

"Be nice or I'll stop your pocket money." She hesitated and her face grew serious. "I hear you're going to see your dad."

Sandy flicked an irritated glance at Lizzie who threw up her hands.

"You know what she's like." She drilled her mother with a glare.

His lips drew a thin line because, yes, he knew only too well what his mother was like. Keeping a secret from Fiona Williams was an exercise in futility. She somehow always knew and was relentless in her pursuit. She'd have done well in the days of rendition.

"Well, since it's out of the bag, yes, I agreed to meet him," Sandy admitted. "But that's all. And only because I have to see for myself. I want a memory that isn't twenty years old that I can throw virtual darts at in my head, if that makes sense?"

His mother shrugged. "I don't think it matters what your reasons are, only that you satisfy yourself so you can put it aside if you want to. I said I'd support you whatever you decided to do, and I will. There's no turning the clock back for a happy ending here, not for any of us. It's too late for that. But maybe there can be a putting to rest, and surely that counts for something."

Sandy wasn't so sure. "I'm scared he'll fuck me up again in the head."

"Oh, honey." His mum took both his hands in hers. "He can't, Sandy. You're not that person anymore. You're strong, stronger than he is."

God, he hoped so. "I've spent all my damn life fighting just to be okay about who I am, Mum. I might not give in to the side of myself that wants to throw every skirt and dress I own in the bin so I don't draw any more judging looks, but the urge is still there. The only thing that stops me is the cost to my damn mental health. Get stared at and all the rest that goes with that, or get depressed. Great fucking choice."

"We all fight something, sweetheart. The point is, to fight as long as you have to or you can. Some people's battles are won and over in the blink of an eye. Some fight their entire lives without winning just so the next generation doesn't have to. Most fall in between. I'm so proud of you, and maybe I don't say it often enough. There's nothing about you I don't love with all my heart. The fact your father can't see it is absolutely his loss. And when you talk with him, you make sure to remember that, and be proud of who you are. No one can take that from you unless you let them."

"Goddammit." He grabbed a Kleenex, removed his glasses, and dabbed at his eyes. "I'll smudge my eyeliner." He pushed his face at his sister. "Is it okay?"

She tweaked his nose. "It's fine."

He replaced his glasses, turned, and wrapped his arms around his tiny pipsqueak of a mother with the heart of a fucking lioness. The woman who'd waved good riddance to their father even though it devastated her and then gave everything to her children to try and heal the damage.

"I love you, Mum. I'll never be able to thank you enough." He pulled her up on her toes and crushed her against his chest.

"This—" She patted his back, quietly chuckling. "This is all the thank you I need. Well, this and letting me gate crash your life in these moments while pretending you don't really want to throttle me."

She wriggled free of his grip so she could face him. "You don't need to wear these." She tapped his glasses. "I doubt you'll be reading anything."

He sighed. "They're bifocals, Mum, and Miller . . . likes them."

"Oh." She grinned. "Well, I'm sorry if you'd rather I hadn't come tonight, but I wanted to meet him, sweetheart. This man who's stolen my precious boy's heart, because don't pretend that he hasn't. I've never seen you like this. But fair warning, I have high expectations."

"It's fine, Mum. But please don't—"

"I won't embarrass you, I promise."

Like Sandy believed that for a second.

Miller rolled to a stop, smoothed his shirt, and did his best to calm his unravelling nerves before he knocked. He'd never been on a date like this, ever. And his last time to a club had been pre-accident days for sure. Not to mention both their weeks had been ridiculously busy, and he was itching to touch Sandy. They'd only managed a couple of coffees, one to celebrate the announcement of Miller's inclusion in the Wheel Black team for the Aussie series, but it hadn't been nearly enough time together for Miller's taste. Sandy had become an integral part of Miller's day, and he liked it that way.

Sandy answered almost immediately, catching Miller by surprise and sucking the oxygen from the entire hallway. With his jacket in hand, he looked like a million fucking dollars and Miller could scarcely breathe because, *damn.*

"We should get going." Sandy went to push past, but Miller grabbed his hand.

"Hey, slow down. I want to take a good, long look at you."

Sandy sighed and pulled a face, but there was a tell-tale quirk to his lips that showed he was secretly pleased. He held Miller's hand and did a twirl so Miller could drink his fill.

He looked drop-dead gorgeous in a canary yellow, virtually see-through chiffon shirt that showed off his nipples and hung loose over a pair of painted-on black leather trousers, so tight Miller feared for the health of the ample cock he knew lay trapped behind that zip. Black patent slip-ons with a matching leather cuff and sexy-as-fuck choker completed the stunning outfit. And those fucking glasses.

"You like?" Sandy grinned at Miller's obvious approval.

Miller had no words for just how very much he *liked.*

Sandy's blond locks framed his beautiful brown eyes lined in smoky black with soft beige shadow above. And there was a faint sparkle under his cheeks, which snapped all that sharp bone structure into focus. Not to mention, gone was the clear lip gloss and in its place a rich burgundy slash that Miller wanted to see wrapped around his dick as soon as fucking possible. The mere thought had him shifting in his chair.

"Holy shit, you look . . . stunning, exquisite, absolutely fucking beautiful." Miller lifted the back of Dee's hand to his lips, earning himself a bow and a delighted smile. "You sure you wouldn't rather stay here and mess up those sheets of yours?" he said, meaning every word.

Sandy's eyes flew wide and he quickly glanced sideways, but Miller was too stuck on how hot he looked to catch on.

"I see I should've made more of an effort." He swept a hand over his fitted black jeans and tight dark green button-down that he'd been told emphasised his shoulders and highlighted his red hair and green eyes. Okay, so his mother had said that, but whatever.

Sandy ran hungry eyes over him. "You look fucking hot. But sit forward a sec so I can straighten the back of your shirt."

Miller did and Sandy took his time running his hands down Miller's back and sneaking them under his arse on the chair. "I can't wait to show you off."

"Well, I think you both look fabulous."

Huh? Miller caught the roll of Sandy's eyes before he mouthed "sorry" and stepped aside.

"Miller, this is my mother, Fiona, and my sister, Lizzie. Mum, Lizzie, this is Miller."

Sandy's urgency to leave suddenly made sense, and Miller tried to remember what he'd said and just how badly he'd humiliated himself. *And, fuck.*

Fiona Williams came forward with her hand out for Miller to shake. "The pleasure is all mine, Miller. So glad to put a face and name to the man who my son is so enamoured with."

"Mum!"

Lizzie also shook hands, her expression falling somewhere between apologetic and wickedly delighted. The siblings shared the same blond hair and leggy height, not to mention cheekbones for miles, but Lizzie had deep hazel eyes and was a little heavier set.

"Pleased to finally meet you in person, Miller. Sorry for the ambush . . . not." She flashed a sly grin. "God knows when we would've got to meet you otherwise. As soon as Mum heard Sandy had been invited to meet your parents, there was no stopping her getting in first. You look very handsome by the way. And the bed will still be there when you get back, minus us, which is a definite bonus I'm thinking."

"Yes." Fiona shot a cheeky look at her son, then winked at Miller. "Anything that gets my son's sheets washed more often is a good thing in my books."

And, Oh. My. God. Blood shot to his cheeks in an inferno of mortification. He had absolutely no idea what to do with that and stumbled through some half-arsed apology.

"Pffft. Nothing to be sorry for." Fiona kissed her glaring son on the cheek and straightened his choker, again. "You boys have fun tonight."

With a glare at his mother, Sandy put his choker back the way it was and returned the kiss. "We will. And you two better be gone before we get back after you've done the dishes you messed up."

"Oh, we will," Lizzie assured him. "He's cute, by the way. You did good, bro."

"Leave it alone, sis."

But Miller didn't miss the pleased flush in his cheeks as he said it.

"And remember to play safe," Fiona said with a wicked gleam in her eye that instantly set Miller's cheeks to incendiary once again and had Lizzie doubled over in laughter.

"That's it, we're leaving." Sandy flipped his sister off, sent his mother a killer look, and then headed for the elevators at breakneck speed with Miller keeping pace in his chair alongside.

They caught one just before it headed back down.

"God, I'm so sorry about that," Sandy apologised as the door closed.

Miller laughed. "It's fine. They seem really . . . nice."

"That's because they don't belong to you. Now let's go have fun and screw this bullshit."

"Fun? Have you forgotten I can't dance? I keep telling you, you're gonna regret asking me to ever set a cane on that dance floor."

"Who said anything about dancing? I fully intend to prop that delectable body of yours up against the dancefloor wall and simply grind the fuck out of you till you come in those ridiculously tight black jeans you're wearing. Got a problem with that?"

Miller's hand shot under Dee's shirt and tugged on the waistband of his leather trousers, pulling him close. "No problem at all." He trailed his fingers across Dee's smooth, flat belly and then up to ghost a palm over his nipple, noting the shiver that ran through him. He pinched the nub and Sandy lowered his mouth over Miller's, sliding his tongue inside.

Miller sighed with pleasure. Like the first sweet taste of water on a hot afternoon, losing himself in the familiar scent and feel of Sandy's body close to his. His hands slid around to the swell of Dee's arse, relishing that taut curve caged under all that snug leather and wanting more.

"I missed you." The words rushed from his mouth as Sandy pulled away.

"I've missed you too." Sandy swiped his thumb over Miller's mouth. "You're wearing my lipstick."

"Like I could give a shit. By the end of the night, I hope to be wearing it somewhere a lot more interesting."

Dee's eyes glinted with mischief. "I like the way you think, Mr Harrison."

Swaying almost in time to the sultry voice of Harry Styles, Miller discreetly glanced down to check his watch. *Fuck.* They'd barely been in the club an hour and already he'd been kneed in his bad thigh, had a server trip over his cane with a tray full of drinks, and his foot stood on by a tiny twink in red sequins who wasn't watching where he was dancing. Not to mention he'd been exposed to more pert butts, tiny shorts, leather harnesses, wandering hands, and semi-naked grinding than he'd experienced in all of his thirty-five years put together. And he was going to need an eardrum replacement if the music cranked even a single decibel louder.

"Having a good time, handsome?" The aforementioned red-sequined twink appeared from nowhere and plastered himself to Miller's back, much to Sandy's annoyance who flicked the barely legal young man on the forehead.

"Leave him alone, Cheyne."

Oh, and Miller had been hit on more times in the first fifteen minutes of their arrival than he had in his entire life, something he had zero practise in handling. Awkward meet embarrassing. Sandy had merely looked amused, as if he'd been expecting the onslaught though god knew why. Miller hardly rated compared to the incendiary male hotness on display around him, but he couldn't help feeling a little bit tickled anyway.

Once Sandy had gently bullied him up onto the dance floor, he'd actually enjoyed it. Gazes raked over his body as he shuffled around, hands ghosting his arse and dick. He was caught between feeling flattered and wholly terrified. The place was packed to the rafters with gyrating bodies and handsy men, and Miller's senses gave up trying to make sense of any of it.

After all, what did you say when a random guy ten years your junior, cupped your arse on the dance floor and asked if you wanted to fuck him in the bathroom? While Miller was still dragging his chin off the floor, Sandy sent the guy off with a flea in his ear, then shoved Miller against the wall and almost made good on his promise to grind on him till he came in his jeans.

"You're the gay bar equivalent of Ebenezer Scrooge," Sandy shouted in his ear as they danced on the edge of the heaving crowd.

Well, Sandy danced. Miller was too busy trying to keep his canes from being knocked aside. The chair might've been easier on his legs, but it was almost impossible to manoeuvre around a crowded bar and dance floor. Without it and using Dee as a wingman, he at least managed a semblance of grace.

"If those frown lines get any deeper, they're gonna swallow the rest of your damn face and you'll look like a corrugated iron fence." He laughed and shimmied his way up and down Miller's front, a seductive feat that drew the interested stares of more than a few men dancing alongside.

And fuck, for a second those burgundy lips were right at cock level and Miller's cock was more than interested. A pink tongue darted out to brush his bulge on the way back up, and Miller nearly came there and then. For safety, Dee had ditched his glasses in the car, the only thing that might've made the sight any hotter.

"You two wanna hook up later?" An older man with stunning tattoos danced close and raked his gaze over Sandy's sinuous body before fixing on his lips. He had his arms around a young partner wearing a fluoro-green mesh bodysuit who watched the older man with adoring eyes.

Yeah, Miller had no illusions who the guy really wanted in his bed. "Not a chance," he shouted over the music, planting a possessive hand on Sandy's arse. He yanked him close, earning an amused snort in his ear for the trouble.

The man laughed and danced away and Miller relaxed his death grip on Sandy's butt.

Not that he could blame the guy for trying. Sandy was magnetic on the floor; lithe and seductive with rhythm to spare. Before the accident, Miller could've almost held his own, maybe, but now his balance was dodgy, and the canes made everything a little jerky. At home he occasionally risked cutting loose in his kitchen, but here he'd likely end up on his arse on the floor to be lost forever in the undulating swell of glistening bodies.

The best thing about the whole night? Sandy didn't appear to give a shit about Miller's canes, doing exactly as he'd promised—grinding up on him against a wall; or plastering himself to Miller's back on the floor with his hands sliding up under his shirt with devilish intent; or just as they were now—front to front, Dee's lips pressed to Miller's neck, his arms around Miller's waist to support him, while Miller's canes crossed behind Dee's back, caging him in, with the added advantage of keeping others at a distance unless they wanted a cane in the back.

He couldn't handle more than a couple of dances at a time, but Sandy made no complaint about being left on his own between, happy to drag Cam, Michael, Josh, Mark, Reuben, or all of them together onto the floor until Miller was ready to go again. Their table garnered a lot of attention. Partly because of its sheer level of hotness, Miller aside, of course, but mostly because Reuben always came with a spotlight of his own.

All Black and gay icon; everyone knew Reuben's face and that of his fiancé, Cam. But apart from a few autograph hunters, most left him alone. In this place, more than most, people perhaps understood his need to be free of all that attention and just enjoy being a gay man out for a night with his fiancé in an environment he felt comfortable.

It was good to see his friend get a chance to let his guard down, a pointed reminder of what Miller had missed by keeping himself so separated from this community. He knew nothing of this world, and he couldn't deny a wince of shame about that. It was uncomfortable at times, but there was also an undeniable sense of coming home.

In between their forays onto the dance floor, Miller relaxed at their table. The eye candy alone had been worth coming for. Cam and Sandy made a hot couple on the dance floor. The best dancers of their group, their sultry and eerily in-sync moves turned lots of heads.

Cam rocked a pair of skin-tight shiny black trousers with a solid peek of lace showing out the top, a matching shimmering black harness, and a chain collar and leash—the end of which mostly stayed in his fiancé's hand, although Reuben seemed at a loss what to do with it except blush and give it the occasional nervous tug. It cracked Miller up more than once. With the obvious dynamic between those two, Cam might've been wearing the leash, but hell if that was more than decoration.

Michael and Josh had their own admirers, both looking like they'd just left a modelling shoot, shirtless and hot as fuck—the chemistry between them a sizzling living entity.

But for all the hotness on display, Miller couldn't shift his gaze from Sandy. He might not like clubs, but Miller had discovered he fucking loved watching his boyfriend having fun. He'd come every week if it put that smile on Sandy's face. It was a side he wanted to see a lot more of, and he was determined to get out of his own rut and make it happen.

Mark turned out to be an amusing conversationalist, not to mention an outrageous flirt, which clearly wasn't news to any of his friends. Most people seemed to know him, greeting him like a long-lost friend and he was always in demand on the dance floor. On his own, Mark's extrovert cut loose and he worked the room with practised ease, leaving a trail of mischief and laughter in his wake. But he never drifted far for long, his gaze constantly seeking Ed's—checking in, smiling, blowing a kiss. Ed obviously trusted his man, chuckling at Mark's antics and returning the kisses. Mark might be a firecracker, but when they hit the floor together, they slow danced with zero room between them, Mark's face buried in Ed's neck, the quieter man holding him tight, like they were alone in the room.

"How are you holding up?" Cam twirled alongside Miller and Sandy, dragging Reuben in his wake. "I must admit, I never thought you'd come." He eyed Miller up and down. "But you're looking good. Who'd have guessed?"

Miller rolled his eyes. "No one. And they'd still be right. I'm merely a prop for this one." He kissed Sandy's cheek. "And I'm keeping the wolves at bay."

Sandy laughed and threw his arms around Miller's neck. "It's you they're after, hot stuff."

"Yeah right."

"He's right." Reuben chimed in, his lips buried somewhere in Cam's hair, which was spiked high on his head with threads of gossamer silver chain threaded through it. "Fresh meat, fit and built like you mean it, and fucking hot. You're the talk of the club, Tap."

"Their bar is set very low then," Miller shouted back.

"Hey." Sandy sandwiched Miller's face between his palms. "No one talks you down in front of me, not even you, understand? Look around. Everyone's watching us."

Miller took a quick look and yeah, there were a lot of eyes on them, but Miller suspected it was the men around him that drew the attention.

"That's your fear talking, not you," Sandy added forcefully. "You think I lie about what you do to me?"

Miller winced. "No."

"Then look like you believe it and lift your head like you do on that court in a game. This is the dance floor equivalent of murderball. Believe in who you are and never show the whites of your eyes." He grinned and nuzzled into Miller's neck. "Now wrap those canes around me, mister. I'm done with randoms cruising my man. One more dance, then we'll leave."

"You don't have to," Miller protested, trying to keep his balance as someone dipped their partner beside him and knocked his cane. "I'll have to head off soon, but you can stay as long as you want."

"Thanks, but I'm about done anyway." Sandy nibbled his ear lobe. "I want to get my lips around your fat cock before we go to sleep. How about I carve a path for you to the table, grab Cam for one last fling, and then we're out of here?"

Yes. Miller was totally on board with that idea. He let Sandy plough the road to their table, where Miller collapsed in a chair next to Ed with a sigh of relief. His own chair was more of a liability than an aid in this environment. But man, he was done, his hip and thigh on fire. But worth it. So fucking worth it.

Ed slid an iced water his way. "You're hurting."

Miller fired him a look. Damn doctors. He'd already taken a bollocking from Michael about looking after himself, which no doubt had come from Cam. He took a welcome swallow of water and measured his reply. "I took a bad hit a few weeks ago. It's still healing. It's fine."

"Doesn't look fine." Ed grimaced and held up his hands in apology. "Sorry. It's the doctor in me. It's none of my business, but you athletes and your injuries do my head in."

"No problem. But you're right. It comes with the territory." He took another guzzle. "We're heading off after this song. How about you two?"

Ed snorted and pointed to where Mark was dancing with a drink in one hand while doing a not-too-awful impression of John Travolta. "Could be a while yet. He needs to blow off some steam. His team just closed a nasty murder. It's good to see him like this."

"He has a tough job."

Ed caught his eye. "He does. I worry, but what can you do? The dogs keep us sane."

Miller wasn't sure what to say to that, so he just nodded. Being a cop's partner had to suck. He liked Ed, and they'd quickly become comrades-in-arms, neither particularly comfortable in the club scene but happy to watch their men and chat while the others did their thing. It struck Miller that the evening hadn't been terrible after all. Far from it. He'd even enjoyed it, mostly.

Ten minutes later and Sandy was leading him out the front door and back toward their car, the two of them laughing about Mark getting swatted by a drag queen's silver lamé purse for mistakenly taking her drink.

At the car, Sandy backed Miller against the driver's door and took his mouth in a lengthy, thorough kiss, tinged with rum and a promise for the night ahead. They'd barely pulled apart when a flash spot-lighted them, pinning them in place.

"Is this your boyfriend, Miller? Is he why you came out?"

"Get in the car, Sandy," Miller ordered, and Sandy fled for the other side while Miller threw his canes in the back.

"Sandy?" One of them raced over. "How long have you known Miller?"

Shit. Miller had just handed them Sandy's name.

"Can we get a statement from you, Miller? Is Reuben here with you, Miller?"

Miller slammed the door shut and started the engine. He should've realised that where Reuben went, cameras went. Catching a pic of himself and Sandy would've just been icing on the cake for the journos.

One of them knocked on Miller's window as he slowly backed out. "What's it like being gay *and* having a disability? What would you say to young kids just like yourself? Do you think you have a chance against Australia?"

"Motherfuckers," Sandy hissed under his breath.

Miller got out of that parking lot as quickly as he could, and then, a kilometre up the road he pulled over.

"You okay?" He reached for Sandy's hand and squeezed. "I'm so sorry. Your name came out before I could think. They were here for Reuben, not us."

Sandy gave him a reassuring smile. "I'm fine. We knew it was coming. I'm gonna text Cam and warn him."

Miller waited until Sandy was done. "Home then?"

Sandy flashed him a filthy look. "Absolutely. Your dick and my lipstick have an appointment to keep."

CHAPTER SIXTEEN

"Do you need to get that, Mr Harrison?" The chairman of the medical disciplinary committee paused his sermonising to fire a disapproving glare Miller's way. "I'd hate to think this meeting was interfering with more *important* responsibilities you might have." The accompanying look implied the obnoxious man's scepticism about the very idea. "Or maybe it's your adoring fans on social media."

For fuck's sake. The photos from the club on Friday had hit the news on the Saturday morning, highlighting Sandy and Miller in an admittedly salacious embrace. Miller hardly recognised himself. Sandy's name, fully capitalised, had made the first line of type alongside Miller's, and the rest was history. It was B-grade sports news at best, and already running out of steam, but it still irked to have his sexuality and relationship thrown up for public debate.

But as a way to come out to your work, it certainly made a statement. Thank god Sandy had been good about it, joking how they'd at least captured his good side. Which was a better response than Miller had expected, considering Sandy's looming meeting with his dad in two days had him wringing his hands more often than not. But maybe that was exactly why he took their couple outing in his stride.

By Monday, the hospital grapevine had run hot and not always in approval. A day later and they were still top billing, drawing a variety of looks in the cafeteria and hallways, some good-natured teasing, and the odd puzzled look, disappointed stare, and even pointed glare. The chairman definitely fell into the latter category when Miller had arrived for the meeting Tuesday morning.

"*Mr* Harrison." The chairman shot another glare at Miller's phone which was busy juddering its way across the table, again.

Shit. Miller returned the man's stony look because . . . just fuck the prick with a cactus and be done with it. Miller's job required him to be available at all times. The chairman was simply an arrogant wanker and Miller wanted to slap him. How anyone thought a dickhead like that could lead a sensitive committee was beyond him. But the guy had been there for more years than most could remember, and no one seemed able to shoehorn him out.

Well, Miller loved a challenge.

He glanced at the caller ID and the first twinge of worry hit. A second attempt from Sam. Miller had ignored the first. Sam knew the drill when Miller was in a meeting. Miller would call back when he could. Whatever he wanted had to be important.

He pushed his chair back from the table. "I need to take this outside. I doubt I'm going to miss anything vital at this stage, so you don't need to wait. Fire me an email with the minutes if I don't return." The comment was greeted with a sharp intake of breath from the chairman and muffled snorts of amusement from a couple of the other committee members who couldn't stand the guy either and no doubt wished they could leave as well.

Miller couldn't get out of the room fast enough. Sam answered on the second ring.

"Uncle Em, thank god. We're at your house," he blurted. "Mum and Dad are busy with lunch service at the restaurant and I didn't want to pull them away, but Geo's hurt and I didn't know what else to do. I'm sorry if I did the wrong thing, I—"

"What? Wait. Slow down. You're at *my* house?"

"Yes. I didn't know where to go and he wouldn't come to mine. He didn't want to get me in trouble cos we're not supposed to be meeting. I thought you wouldn't mind. Please, Uncle Em, he won't go to a doctor."

"Okay, okay. Take a breath and tell me what happened."

Sam sucked in a deep breath. "His dad saw him sneak out to the drop-in centre yesterday, to see that counsellor I told you about. Anyway, he followed Geo and dragged him home before he got there, and then . . . and then . . ." Sam choked up. "Jesus, Miller, he hurt him."

Fuck, fuck, fuck. "All right. I want you to stay there. I'm on my way. Ask Geo if I can tell Sandy?"

"He's coming and wants to know if he can tell Sandy and Cam?" Relief flooded Sam's voice as he passed the information on to Geo. "Geo says that's fine, Uncle Em. Thanks so much. I'm sorry I got you out of work—"

"Don't be. You did exactly the right thing. Now stay where you are and don't answer the door until I get there, okay?"

"Okay."

Miller pocketed his phone and dragged his hand across his jawline. *Holy shit.* This was way out of his league. He called Dee but it went straight to voicemail. He was likely in an autopsy. Miller left a message.

He wheeled back to his office, packed up his bag, and told his boss he had urgent family business. Then he headed for the ER and cornered Cam in his office.

"Geo and Sam are at my place," he told him from the doorway. "Apparently, Geo's dad grabbed him before he got to the centre yesterday and there was some kind of altercation. I don't have details, but Geo's refusing to go to a doctor. I'm headed there now."

Cam shot to his feet. "Bloody hell. I just thought he'd changed his mind with everything going on. I didn't want to push."

"Is Michael on?"

"No, but I'll give him a heads-up."

"Do you think he'd be willing to come to my place to take a look at him? Could you?"

"I'm sure he would. And we're swamped at the moment, but I can get there later. Have you called the police?"

Miller hadn't got that far in his head. "Let me talk to him first, find out what's happened and whether he wants to press charges or —" He shook his head. "Fuck, how does that even work when it's your damn father?"

"I'm sure Josh or Mark will help if you need advice, as long as Geo agrees."

Miller didn't know either of them well, but it was better than nothing. Damn, he'd known this was going to be a shitshow. "Thanks. I'll let you know. I left a message on Dee's phone. Could you—"

"I'll go down and see him."

"Thanks. I've gotta go." His shaky hands fumbled the phone in his lap and it skittered to the floor.

"Hey, hey. Slow down." Cam picked up the phone and wrapped his arms around Miller. "You don't have to handle this alone. We're here if Geo or you need us." He stepped back. "Are you sure you're good to drive?"

Miller nodded. "Fine."

"Okay, you've got this." He kissed Miller's cheek. "And we've got your back. Call me, okay?"

Miller nodded again, his throat thick with emotion—some of it fear for Geo and Sam but also gratitude for these multiplying men in his life. He'd been such a fool looking at his queer community like a damn liability, a flag pointing to where he was vulnerable instead of seeing its strength.

The drive home took too damn long, every red light a test in patience he increasingly failed. He called Dane as he drove. His brother needed to know and it helped keep his head together.

It took a few minutes, but eventually he got Dane pulled from the restaurant kitchen and on the line. He wanted to drop everything and head to Miller's, but Miller stalled him. He wanted to know exactly what state Geo was in first and who the kid wanted involved before a mass of adults descended.

He told Dane to talk to Sam instead and make sure he was okay. Then wait until Miller got a clearer picture of things. Maybe Miller could send Sam back to school or home in an Uber, and Dane and Chloe could take it from there. Either way, Miller promised to keep them informed. It took some convincing, but Dane finally agreed.

Miller's vehicle had barely pulled into his garage when the inner door to the house slammed wide and Sam almost fell on the car, ripping the driver's door open.

"How could he do that?" Sam's distraught question ricocheted around the large space. "How could that bastard beat him up? It's his fucking son, Uncle Em. It's . . . you don't do that . . . you don't . . ." His voice buckled and he collapsed into sobs.

Miller twisted in his seat and pulled Sam into his arms. "There's no excuse," he said, fighting back his own tears against Sam's mess of strawberry-blond curls. "And I hate that you have to see this sort of ugly at your age. There are shit parents in this world, as well as wonderful ones like yours. But you did the right thing and I'm so proud of you for being there for Geo. Now let's get inside so I can talk to him." He pulled back and cradled Sam's face. "Did your dad call you?"

Sam nodded and wiped at his eyes. "I said I'll call him back as soon as there's something to say, but I'm not going back to school." His jaw set in the same steely way that Dane's had when there was no budging him.

Miller bit back a smile. "Okay. How about you call your dad and tell him to ring the school and excuse you?"

Another nod. "Geo told them he was going home sick. His dad

doesn't get home till six, so he won't know Geo's not there until then. But he's supposed to be grounded, so when he finds he's not home . . ."

Miller glanced at his watch. Just after eleven. That left a seven-hour timeline to decide what to do next. But whatever they decided, it was going to be a fucking mess. Geo might be legally able to leave home without permission, so no one could force him back, but that didn't stop his father from creating merry hell if he wanted to. He was going to have to make sure every *t* was crossed and *i* dotted to protect everyone involved, including himself.

Damn it to hell. Since when was this his life? He felt the overwhelming urge to crawl back into his cave and pull down the walls. Things like this didn't happen when you kept your world nice and neat. When you didn't get involved. When you passed the buck to the professionals or just ignored half your life.

Too late now.

Right at this moment, he wasn't going anywhere except inside his house to try and help a young man who needed it. Dee or Cam would've been a much better choice, but they weren't here, so Geo would have to make do with the B team.

Miller squeezed Sam's hand. "Hand me my canes, will you?" And while Sam was doing that, Miller tried to get his shit together and look like the mature adult he needed to be before he faced Geo.

That lasted until he hit his living room and found the boy curled under a blanket on his couch looking about as lost and frightened and vulnerable as it was possible to get. One look and all Miller's well-practised words of reassurance died on his tongue. Instead, he sat on the coffee table in front of Geo and ran his fingers through the boy's hair.

"Hey there," he said softly.

Geo turned his head, wide-eyed and fearful but trying to hide it.

"First off, I want to be clear that you're safe here. And you're welcome to stay while we get things sorted, okay?"

The relief on Geo's face was instant. "I can stay?" His eyes filled. "You mean it?"

Jesus Christ, what had happened to this kid? "Of course I mean it."

Sam almost threw himself into Miller's arms. "Thank you, thank you. I knew you'd know what to do."

Miller tried to remember the last time he'd had two hugs from his nephew in one day. "Don't get too excited. I'm hardly an expert in this kind of thing, but I know people who are. We'll look after Geo, if Geo's okay with that?" Miller looked over Sam's shoulder to Geo.

"I . . . yeah, that would be awesome," he answered. "I didn't really know what was going to happen." He blinked rapidly and rubbed at his eyes, relief and fear spilling down his cheeks. "I didn't expect . . . I . . . I just didn't know what to do. I thought you might be mad that Sam brought me here."

Mad? Lord help me. Miller had the ridiculous urge to haul the kid into his arms. Geo was the same age as Sam and royally screwed over by a father who should be in fucking jail. Miller had never felt so grateful for his own parents and made a mental note to tell them at the first opportunity. He'd been so damn lucky.

He reached out to rest a hand on Geo's shoulder but instantly dropped it when Geo jerked back. *Shit.* What the hell had the kid's father done? "I'm not mad in the slightest. I'm happy Sam brought you here. You're safe. But I'm going to need to know what happened so we can make a plan, all right? And that plan is going to depend on what *you* want. I'm not going to tell you what to do, Geo, but I am involved now, as is Sam, so I need to know exactly what I'm involved *in*, okay?"

After a few seconds, Geo nodded and swung his legs to the floor so he could sit, the blanket still wrapped around his shoulders.

"Sam said your dad hurt you?" Miller's gaze swept Geo's face, seeing no obvious bruising. He shot Sam a questioning brow.

"Show him," Sam said.

Geo fired Sam a disappointed look but Sam's jaw set. "He has to know, Geo. Don't you dare cover up for him."

Miller held up a hand. "Sam, how about you take a seat and let Geo do this his way?"

Sam bristled. "But he can't let—"

"Sam." Miller copied one of Dane's best don't-mess-with-me father looks.

Sam plopped down next to Geo with a grunt.

Whaddya know, it worked.

Geo reached a hand from under his blanket to latch onto Sam's, and Sam immediately dragged both onto his lap, which dropped the blanket from Geo's arm, and that's when Miller saw it. A parade of angry mottled bruises encircling Geo's wrist and reaching as far as his elbow.

Miller couldn't hold back the sharp intake of breath, and Geo's gaze jerked down to his arm and then back up to Miller. He flushed and tried to pull the blanket back to cover the marks.

"Can I see?" Miller asked gently.

Geo hesitated, then nodded and let the blanket drop from his shoulders. He lifted his school shirt and turned so Miller could get a look at his back as well. Bruising bled across his ribs in a tapestry of colours that spoke to maybe more than one incident. Miller's gaze flicked up. Shame stared back at him, and Miller badly wanted to hurt something.

"This is *not* your fault," he said, mustering every bit of resolve he could find. "Don't ever think it is. There's no one to blame here but your father."

Geo nodded unconvincingly. "It looks worse than it is. He just pushed me around a bit. I got most of these when I fell over my study desk and bookcase."

Yeah, Miller wasn't buying that, but he let it go for now. A shit-load of therapy lay in this bright young man's future. *Goddammit.* Miller wanted that son of a bitch, coward of a father, in front of him right the fuck now. But that wasn't what Geo needed, and so he buried his anger as best he could to share with the others later. For now, Geo needed Miller calm and composed, and he could do that. He had to. Decisions needed to be made.

"Don't excuse him, Geo," he said. "None of this is okay, understand? Not a single bruise, not a single slur, nothing."

Geo didn't say anything for a minute, avoiding Miller's eyes and fingering the edge of the blanket. Then he almost seemed to collapse in on himself and the tears erupted.

"He was furious," he sobbed. "He was following because he thought I was going to meet Jacob. But when he saw I was going to the centre, he realised I must be talking to people there. He grabbed me off the sidewalk before I got to the steps and completely lost it in the car. I know I shouldn't have gone since I was grounded, but I really like the counsellor. We were going to talk about my options. I didn't want to miss it. I thought I could get away without him . . ."

"But those bruises aren't just from yesterday, are they?" Miller let the question hang between them.

Geo's gaze flicked sideways to Sam, then back to Miller. "No," he whispered.

Sam spun in his seat, eyes bugging out. "But you never said anything. He's done this before? Why didn't you tell me?"

Geo flushed. "What could you do? And it was never like this."

"But—"

"Sam," Miller cautioned. "How about we let Geo talk?"

Sam sat back, still grumbling.

Geo rubbed his friend's arm, then took a deep breath and finally opened up.

After the initial blow up when Geo came out, his father had been okay, thinking Geo was toeing the line. But then he'd found the websites and a few texts with Jacob, and things had gotten ugly. And when he caught Geo outside the centre, it was the last straw. He dragged Geo home, shoved him into the house, yelled and screamed a lot of homophobic bullshit, then trashed his room while Geo had to watch. Unfortunately, he found condoms and lube hidden in Geo's wardrobe, which only made matters worse.

That was as far as they got before Miller's front door rattled on its hinges and everyone jumped, including him. He spun to check the driveway and told Geo and Sam to relax.

Sandy flew into the lounge and went straight to Geo, wrapping him in his arms. "Ed sent me packing as soon as he heard. Thank God, you're okay." He pulled back and cradled Geo's startled face, taking a good long look.

Miller had never been so pleased to see anyone in his life. His heart settled in his chest and everything felt a little less overwhelming.

Considering Geo's panicked reaction to Miller simply touching his shoulder earlier, the kid seemed more than comfortable with Sandy's concerned affection. But then, of course, he was. This was Sandy. Not that Sandy exactly gave Geo a choice, but Geo sank back into his arms anyway, leaving Miller to marvel.

He'd thought it might be just him. But clearly this was the *Sandy effect* on people in general, and Miller couldn't find it in himself to be jealous. The world could do with a fuckton more Sandys.

"We're with you, sweetheart," Sandy said with absolute resolve. "All the way."

Geo's cheeks tinged pink and he smiled shyly. "Thank you."

But when Sandy stepped back and got his first look at the bruises on Geo's arms, his hand flew to his chest. "That son of a bitch."

He examined Geo's arm with the tenderest of care, turning it this way and that, before peeking under his shirt with Geo's permission. When he was done, he rolled Geo's sleeves down, drew the blanket around his shoulders, and kissed his head. Then he turned and flung his arms around Miller, whose knees almost buckled at the familiar scent.

"I'm gonna fucking kill that man," Sandy whispered in his ear.

"You'll have to get in line," Miller whispered back, then kissed him firmly on the lips. "I'm so fucking glad you're here."

Dee flashed one of those brilliant smiles that went a long way toward righting things in Miller's world. "Always for you, you know that."

They locked eyes for a moment, and something huge settled in Miller's heart that needed revisiting later. Things needed to be said between them.

Dee turned and squeezed Sam's hand. "Hey, kiddo, you did good. Now somebody, please catch me up. We have wagons to circle and plans to make. And I think it would be wise to have something in mind before Cam arrives and wants to change everything. Although I personally think we should just let him loose on your dad. What do you say?"

The first hint of a smile cracked Geo's face and Miller wanted to kiss Dee all over again.

Sandy's expression grew serious. "We're here to try and make sure what you want happens, Geo. Understand? No one is going to tell you what to do. But we're here to help."

"Mr Harrison said that too," Geo pointed out.

Dee flashed Miller a huge smile. "Of course he did. He's a smart man. He chose me, after all."

Another smile from Geo and even Sam chuckled.

"So Cam's coming?" Geo asked, checking through the window as if the nurse might appear at any moment.

"Would you like him to be here?" Miller checked.

Geo worried his bottom lip. "Yes . . . if that's okay. I mean, you guys are great . . ."

Dee waggled his eyebrows. "But we might need the big guns, right? Let loose the hound of hell, eh?"

Geo's lips twitched. "Maybe."

"Does Jacob know?" Miller worried what Geo's boyfriend's reaction might be. The last thing they needed was the teen trying to play hero and maybe confronting Geo's dad.

Geo looked like he might cry again. "I told him I'd left home but not why. We've been texting, but he doesn't know where I am. I don't want him to get in trouble. If he goes to my house . . ."

Smart kid. "No, we don't want that," Miller agreed. "How about you let him know you're safe and that friendly adults are helping you work things out. He can maybe visit after we have a plan, okay?"

"You'd let him come here?"

Miller shrugged. "I don't see why not. But let's give it a day or two, okay?"

"If he can wait that long." Dee nudged Geo's knee with his own. "Believe it or not, we remember what teenage hormones are like."

Miller laughed. "Speak for yourself. I wasn't out at school. My hormones were bottled and tightly capped, thank you very much. There was none of that 'running off-leash with an actual guy' stuff."

Dee ruffled Miller's hair. "Poor boy."

Geo picked at a thread on the blanket around his shoulders. "My dad's not really a bad guy."

It was only with supreme effort that Miller stopped from rolling his eyes.

"Before I came out, he was fine. Not perfect. He was always . . . tough, after Mum left." His eyes skittered away.

Miller studied him for a second. "Has he hit you before?"

"No." Geo was quick to answer, maybe a little too quick, and his gaze slid over Miller's shoulder to the sunny winter's day through the glass behind. "He slapped me . . . once or twice." He looked back. "But he's never punched me before. Mostly he just shouts. I don't always do so well at school. And I'm not into sports so . . . he gets angry."

Fucking hell.

"Does he drink?" Sandy added.

"No. Never that."

And for some reason, Miller believed him.

"When I got to school, I thought about talking to someone, but I still hadn't got things clear in my head. And then Sam found me throwing up in the bathroom and . . .called you." He gave Sam a small smile. "He wouldn't take no for an answer."

"Bloody oath," Sam grabbed Geo's hand and Miller had never been so proud of his nephew.

Geo said nothing, just covered Sam's hand with his free one, looked at the floor, and stayed quiet. Miller let him breathe through whatever was going on in his head without interruption, but when he did finally look up, there was steel in those eyes for the first time.

"I'm not going back," he said, soft but determined.

Relief swept through Miller.

"Not ever," Geo added.

The room fell silent.

"I've only got just over a year left at school before university, and I'll do whatever I need to, but I don't want to stay with him. Not now."

Everyone exchanged looks and Miller wanted to fucking cheer. "Well, alrighty then." He sent Geo a reassuring smile he wasn't sure he felt. There were a lot of hurdles to jump through first. "I guess that gives us a place to start."

Dee blew out a sigh of relief and stood. "I'll let Cam know he can come." He headed into the kitchen for some privacy.

Miller stretched his aching body in the chair and sent Sam for a couple of ibuprofens and some water. His hip and thigh were crucifying him, but he also wanted Geo alone for a moment. "That's a courageous call. But if that's what you want, we'll support you all the way."

"I'll have to talk to the police, won't I?" Geo suddenly looked very young and very frightened.

Miller kept his voice even. It had to be Geo's decision. "It's your call. But it could be wise, even if all you do is talk to them. Cam and Dee know a couple of police officers who can help, if you'd like. Then at least they won't be total strangers. And we should get you checked by a doctor. He can come here. We happen to know one of those as well, and he's gay also." Miller smiled. "You know you're going to need some help, don't you? This is too complex to try and manage on your own."

Geo seemed to grow smaller in his seat if that were even possible. "Yeah, I know. The doctor thing is fine, and the police too, if you know them."

Miller nodded at Dee, who was standing at the kitchen door, phone in hand. "Cam's on his way. I'll get Josh and Michael," he said and disappeared again.

"At seventeen, you might be able to leave home without him stopping you," Miller continued to explain to Geo, "but that doesn't mean he has to help you do that in any way, financial or otherwise. And social services can actually require you to return *if* they think you're at risk wherever you are. Your father has a legal duty of care in that regard until you're eighteen. Therefore, it's helpful to have on official record exactly *why* home isn't safe for you. Hence, the police."

"They can send me back?" Geo asked, horrified.

Miller raised his hands. "In theory. But it's unlikely a court would ever force you based on your age and your story, but your father could make it complicated if he chose to. Proving you're in a safe environment even temporarily is simply the prudent thing to do. Head him off at the pass, so to speak. And then there's all the changes that will need to be made for school records and all that. We want you safe, Geo, and we won't stop until you are. It's a big deal, no use pretending it isn't, but if you decide it's what you want after you hear all the options, then we'll be there for you."

Dee sat on the arm of the couch next to Geo and rested a hand on his shoulder. "And by we, he means all of us."

CHAPTER SEVENTEEN

"I HAVE NO IDEA WHAT THE FUCK I'M DOING," MILLER HISSED IN Sandy's ear while peering around him into the lounge where Josh and Mark were talking with Geo and filling in forms.

They'd ended up with both their cop friends attending—Mark and his best friend and dog handler, Josh Rawlins, who'd arrived with his doctor husband, Michael. Josh's police dog, Paris, was doing a fine job of keeping Geo distracted and loved up, so Sandy considered that a win.

But the figure of Cam strutting around, threatening to rain down fire and brimstone on Geo's father, was maybe less so. And with Reuben doing his best to calm Cam down, even Miller's quite spacious home was beginning to reach maximum tolerance. Thank god Dane arrived and whisked a reluctant Sam home, following promises to let the boys communicate via their phones as much as they liked when things settled.

"You're doing just fine," Sandy reassured Miller, pulling him back into the kitchen and into his arms where he belonged. He was pretty damn proud of how Miller had handled everything, especially for a guy thrown in the deep end. "Where else was he going to go?

You couldn't put Sam or Dane's family at risk, and the only local family Geo has is on his father's side. It was the right thing to suggest he stay with you."

"Was it?" Miller's eyebrows drew together. He scrubbed a hand down his face and sighed. "It's a bloody mess, and I . . ."

"Don't do messes." Sandy smiled. "I know. But hey, you're doing okay with me, right?" He elbowed Miller lightly.

"You're not a mess."

"No? Maybe not. But I sure messed up your nice little life pretty damn quick, didn't I? Any regrets?"

Miller didn't hesitate. "None. I might even like it better this way."

"Really?" That was pretty hard to believe.

Miller nipped his nose. "I'm working on it."

Sandy laughed, knowing that was likely closer to the truth.

"I can't believe how my life has changed since I left that godawful meeting this morning."

He tipped Miller's chin up for a quick kiss. "Not everything has changed, babe." He resisted the urge to bundle Miller into his bedroom and tuck the poor frazzled man in for some sleep. "And I'm not going anywhere. You're stuck with me for the night."

"Oh, thank god for that." Miller's eyes brightened. "I didn't want to ask you to stay."

Sandy's brows notched. "Why not? That's what we do, right? Be there for each other. It's in the boyfriend handbook."

Miller nuzzled into his neck. "Right, the handbook. I really should read that thing. I'm used to having to deal with everything on my own."

"Me too," Sandy admitted. "But I think we're doing okay." He slanted his mouth over Miller's and let the man's taste drown out everything else.

Miller caged him against the counter with his cane. "I couldn't have done this without you." His warm lips tracked Sandy's neck from top to bottom. "You being here means everything."

"I wouldn't be anywhere else."

Miller searched Sandy's eyes and then rested their foreheads together. "Look, I know it's not the right time or place . . ." He hesitated.

Sandy froze, his heart lodged in his throat, waiting, hoping, as Miller searched for what he wanted to say.

Miller's freckles danced across his cheeks as his jaw worked in concentration. "Shit, I'm making a mess of this," he said. "What I'm trying to say . . . what I *want* to say is that . . . I think I'm in love with you, Dee." He paused nervously. "Oh god, I actually said that, didn't I?"

Sandy gasped. "Yes, and you can't take it back."

"I know it's probably too soon— What?"

Sandy pressed a finger to Miller's lips. "I said you can't take it back, and no, it's not too soon. I feel the same way. I'm in love with you too, Miller."

"Oh. *Ohhhhh.* Really?"

Sandy grinned like a fool and nodded. "Really."

"Wow. Fuck. That's awesome. And thank god." Miller flashed a brilliant smile and leaned in for another kiss.

"Ahem." Cam cleared his throat and popped up beside them wearing a wicked grin. "Not that I don't like a bit of voyeurism as much as the next guy, but I think your young man over there is about to turn into a pumpkin, and I need to get Reuben home to cuddle Cory before he sends a lynch party out for this kid's arse-wipe of a father. Rube has zero tolerance for this kind of fuckery." He spun back to the room. "Come on, babe. I see popcorn and a millionth rescreening of *Frozen* on the cards. Cory's gonna be pumped."

Sandy cast a worried glance at Geo, who was starting to look more than a little frayed around the edges. "You're right. He's about done in. And he's hardly touched the pizza we ordered. Thanks for everything, Cam."

"Not a problem. I'll get that counsellor Geo likes to clear time for an appointment. She'll come here if he wants. She's good like that."

"I'll let you know what Geo says." Sandy handed Miller his other cane and headed for the lounge. "Have you got enough for tonight?" He directed the question at Mark and he nodded.

"We've got everyone's statements and we should have a protection order in place by this evening which we'll serve immediately to Geo's dad. He'll know Geo is safe, but not where he is."

"I thought it took longer?" Sandy asked.

Mark shook his head. "No. If we can satisfy the judge, which we should be able to, a protection order isn't the same as a restraining order. Its effect is immediate, and we'll be submitting a request to keep his whereabouts unknown for the moment. His dad will get the chance to be heard by a family court judge before they decide whether to make the order permanent after three months. We'll get a restraining order in process as well, just in case."

"Let's pray he uses common sense and stays the hell away." Sandy's gaze shifted to Geo, who looked more than a little worried. He reached for Geo's hand. "It'll be okay."

Geo squeezed tight. "He's going to be mad."

"We can't do anything about that. But you're not with him. You're with us."

"I've encouraged Geo to think about pressing charges." Mark glanced Geo's way. "But he's not feeling quite ready to do that yet, and with no witnesses or history, it makes it tricky for us to push ahead without him. We don't have mandatory reporting legislation here, but with Geo's statement, we can at least get the information in the system and he can change his mind any time by just calling me. The protection order should be enough to make his dad think twice, but I'd warn Sam and the boyfriend to keep their eyes open just in case, and to report any attempt at contact."

Fuck. Sandy hadn't even thought of that. He met Miller's worried glance.

Mark continued, "I'll call to confirm when the protection order's in place. The restraining order takes twenty to thirty days and there has to be a hearing for that. Geo might be of legal age for consent and to leave home, but I recommend you get him set up with a lawyer."

"I don't have any money," Geo protested, his eyes flying wide.

"Let *us* worry about that." Sandy slid his other hand into Miller's and squeezed tight. And just for a second, he was struck by the picture they made, the three of them holding hands, and he wasn't as freaked out as he might've expected.

"We'll get you someone good," he reassured Geo. "But they'll need to be independent of ours."

Mark nodded his approval. "And you might want to talk with Miller and Sandy about calling your mum, Geo. Plus, it would pay to notify Family Services and ensure they're in the loop just in case he decides to make trouble. They might want to come and check things out here."

Miller's mouth fell open. "You mean like a house inspection?"

Mark shrugged. "More of a safety check."

"What about the fact I'm . . . single and gay? Will that matter?"

"Shouldn't make any difference. Geo's of legal age and you're not in a relationship with him anyway; plus, you have us to speak to your good character. This isn't like the fostering checks. Geo can legally choose to leave home. This is just a tick box in case Geo's father tries to challenge and say he's not safe."

Jesus, Sandy hadn't even thought of that. He stole another sideways glance at Miller, knowing all this had to be rattling his cage in a big way. Miller hated having his business waved around in public. He was barely out, and this? This was big in-your-face, homophobic, queer politics come home to roost.

Mark turned to Michael, perched on the arm of Josh's chair. "We'll need those medical notes for the judge as soon as you have them. Photos as well. It's still Geo's word against his, but it should help get the order at least."

Michael tipped two fingers in salute. "All organised. I'm heading to the hospital from here. Miller's bringing Geo in tomorrow for check X-rays. I don't expect to find anything, but they'll be good for comparison or to look for any old stuff." He flicked a glance at Geo whose eyes fluttered closed.

"Then let's all get out of here and let these people get some rest." Mark squatted in front of Geo and waited till he opened his eyes. "You did the right thing, Geo. It's not going to be easy, but you've got friends to support you, all of us. Get some rest and we'll talk tomorrow."

Everyone said their goodbyes, and when the door closed for the final time, Sandy pushed Miller into a chair and collapsed on the floor beside him.

Geo watched them from the couch, looking gut-wrenchingly miserable. "I'm so s—"

"Don't say it," Miller cut him off. "Do not say you're sorry. We *want* to help."

Geo deflated.

"And I think you've done enough talking for a while, don't you? How about you take a shower and I'll get the spare room set up for you. Then you need to try and eat something, and after that, sleep. Sound like a plan?"

Geo breathed out a long, troubled sigh. "I guess." He got to his feet, took two steps, and then stopped. "Can I borrow some clothes?"

Shit. Sandy shot to his feet and waved Miller back into his chair before he collapsed. "I'll find something for him. You stay there."

Miller flashed a grateful smile and turned back to Geo. "I called in a personal day at work tomorrow. After we get you to the hospital and anything else the police might want from you, we'll get some clothes and stuff sorted out. At least you have your school uniform with you, right?"

Geo snorted. "The one item of clothing I hate. Do I have to go back tomorrow?"

Miller shook his head. "Let's give it a couple of days. If you agree, we can both talk to the school after Mark's provided them with the protection order, decide together when to start back. Cam thinks that counsellor you like might be able to talk to you tomorrow instead. How would that be?"

Something close to relief passed through Geo's eyes. "I'd like that. I'll go take that shower then."

"One thing before you go." Sandy waved him over, unable to ignore the hopelessly lost look in those teenage eyes a minute longer. "I don't know if you need a hug, but I sure as hell do." Nothing but the truth.

Geo's surprised gaze flicked to Miller, who simply shook his head. "I generally find it easiest to take the path of least resistance."

Geo only hesitated a moment before stepping into Sandy's embrace, his head falling against Sandy's chest, shoulders shaking. Sandy strengthened his hold, shushing and consoling while Geo let the enormity of the day out in a gush of feeling.

Miller got to his feet and wrapped his arms around them both, and yeah . . . another Kodak moment for the "holy shit, where is this going?" folder, along with a powerful sense of rightness, and a surge of hunger in Sandy's belly for something he'd never considered. It had his heart damn near beating out of his chest, but as he was too tired to tease it out, he let it float instead on a sea of questions. It would keep.

And when Geo finally made his way to the bathroom, Sandy took a minute to appreciate having Miller to himself and let him know in an avalanche of kisses, just how well he thought he'd coped with the crisis he'd been handed. Maybe he'd get time to show his true appreciation later.

But when he returned to the lounge after handing Geo some fresh clothes and getting his room ready, Miller was asleep in the chair. He gently slid a leg over Miller's lap and rested his head on those big shoulders. Warm hands found their way under his shirt and around his waist, a murmur of sleepy contentment bubbling free as Miller pulled Sandy against him.

"Please stay." Miller's lazy hands roamed Sandy's back, the ebb and flow of his breath hot on Sandy's neck.

"I already said I was." He fell into the fluid warmth of Miller's caress, letting his hands smooth the sting off the day. Sandy wasn't going anywhere.

Two hours later, after defrosting a container of Miller's awesome lasagne, the three of them shared a quiet meal on the couch watching some mindless superhero movie that no one paid attention to while continually checking their phones. Ed had texted Sandy to take the next day off, much to Sandy's relief, and everyone else was checking in to see how they were doing, including Sandy's mother and Lizzie.

Geo's boyfriend, Jacob, was . . . dealing . . . somewhat. Hearing only one side of the conversation, Sandy figured the guy was, one, mad as hell at Geo's dad and wanting to beat the man senseless; two, pissed off and crying that Geo hadn't told him; and three, desperate to rush over and protect Geo. None of which were gonna fly in Sandy's eyes tonight. He eventually took the phone from Geo and after a long conversation, talked the kid down to being patient and not giving Geo yet another thing to worry about.

Both Geo and Miller had stared at him with something akin to awe, and he curled up like a cat at Miller's side with Miller's arm draped around him. "Let's just say I'm not unfamiliar with dramatics," he clarified.

Miller mouthed the name *Cam* at Geo, and they both burst into laughter. It was so fucking cute Sandy didn't know what to do with himself.

About seven, Mark finally called to say the protection order was in place and a copy had been given to Geo's dad, who'd been less than thrilled, to say the least. But he'd also been left in no doubt of the severity of penalty should he break the protection order.

It was like a stay of execution had been delivered and the collective sigh of relief in the house was almost deafening. Not long after, Geo excused himself to bed with his phone in hand and Sandy collapsed in Miller's arms.

"Are you okay?" He slid his hand under Miller's shirt, basking in the warmth of his skin.

"I think so." Miller stroked Sandy's cheek. "I didn't realise how worried I was that the order wouldn't be signed off."

"Me too. Come on." Sandy got to his feet and held his hand out. "We could both do with a hot shower and some sleep." He helped Miller down the hall, out of his clothes, and into the shower. Then, shucking his own clothes, he pushed Miller down onto the tiled seat, soaped his hands, and washed every plane and crevice he could get to; smooth palms alternating with kneading fingers until Miller was loose-limbed and blissed out.

He batted Miller's half-hearted wandering hands aside, content to climb behind on the seat and jack him off in long, lazy strokes until Miller arched in his arms with a loud groan and spilled over Sandy's hand. But when he tried to scoot free for some towels, Miller pulled him between his legs and bent down to drop a kiss on Sandy's aching cock.

"Well, look what we have here." Miller glanced up and Sandy's heart welled with concern. There might've been humour in Miller's words, but those earlier waves of sadness, edged with anger in his bright green eyes, had now pooled into a flat sea of exhaustion.

"I want you inside me, please." Miller struggled to his feet and angled the showerhead aside.

Sandy held back, sensing something was up.

Miller reached for the grab bar with one hand and flattened the other on the tile wall. His head dropped to his chest. "Please, Dee."

A well of emotion lodged in Sandy's throat as he covered Miller's body with his own and wrapped his arms around from behind. "Are you sure, sweetheart? Can you go again?" Sandy topped on occasion, but it wasn't something the two of them had yet done.

"It doesn't matter if I don't come." Miller turned to stare at him, his face still flushed and with warm hope in his eyes. "I just need to feel you."

It was enough. Sandy wasn't going to second guess the man or play games. He trusted Miller to know what he wanted, and Sandy would give him exactly that. Whatever Miller needed.

He peppered Miller's back with kisses and long strokes all the way down until Sandy was on his knees. Then he elbowed Miller's legs apart a little more and ran the flat of his tongue over Miller's hole.

"Oh god." Miller shuddered and Sandy dived in for more, sliding a finger alongside his tongue until Miller quivered with need.

"I can't . . . you need to . . . my legs . . ."

Sandy got the message and grabbed the supplies they kept in a coffee mug on the tiled shelf and took a deep breath. "How long has it been?"

Miller chuckled. "Think Jurassic."

Hah. "No pressure, then."

Miller turned his head. "You'll be fine. I want you, babe."

Okay. He could do this. He squeezed an Everest-sized mountain of lube onto his fingers and slid them into Miller's arse, figuring more was always better. He worked him for a bit until he was happy and then slid his dick into Miller's crease until it caught.

Miller groaned. "God, yes."

Sandy wrapped an arm around his chest, pushed against his hole, and after a bit of resistance, popped through the ring of muscle and slid just inside. Miller tensed and held his breath, and Sandy waited, wondering if it was too much for him. But Miller quickly relaxed and turned awkwardly for a kiss. "Ready?"

"Always for you," Sandy answered, pushing all the way inside until he was fully seated, pausing so they could both catch their breath.

"Damn," he hissed over Miller's shoulder. "You're like a fucking molten clamp. I'm not sure my dick's gonna ever look the same."

Miller chuckled. "Quit complaining and fuck me."

"Are you okay standing there?"

"I won't be if you don't quit talking and start fucking."

Sandy set up a slow pace to start, keeping one hand on Miller's back, pressing him into the wall for support. "FYI. I hope your dick isn't going to have one of its slow days," he warned. "Cos I'm not sure I've got two minutes in me, let alone twenty."

Miller choked out a laugh. "It's a lucky dip, babe, you know that. But like I said, I don't need to come. But you could up that tempo to lower the odds."

Sandy did, his hand sliding around to find Miller's cock plumping nicely. He coaxed it back to hard, trying to stave off his own orgasm in the process, but to no avail. Miller's arse was just too fucking delicious and Sandy's cock happy danced all the way to a thunderous orgasm only a few thrusts later.

Well, fuck that. He manhandled a laughing Miller flat onto the bench, shoved a fuckton of lube up his own arse, and then rode the man till his laughter turned to desperate groans and he filled Sandy's arse, righting all the wrongs in his world, at least for a bit.

But when his spasming hole settled and he pulled off Miller's softening cock, he almost fell to his knees. No condom. Miller came to the realisation about the same time.

"Fuck." Sandy stared down at Miller in horror. "God, I'm so sorry. I didn't think. I just . . . fuck." He slid to the floor against the tiled wall. He'd never done anything like that. He was always so fucking careful. "I'm negative, I promise."

"Hey, hey, hey." Miller swung his legs over the side of the wide bench and planted a kiss atop Sandy's head. "It was my fault too. I should've realised and I didn't. I'm negative as well, by the way."

"It doesn't matter. I don't . . . we shouldn't have. It's too risky. And I'm the one with the experience. I was topping. It was my responsibility. You don't know me well enough to trust—"

"I know enough to know you wouldn't put me in harm's way, not deliberately. You're not selfish, Dee. It was a genuine mistake. It's fine. I fucking loved it."

But Sandy was still mortified. "It's not fine. I should've been more careful. I'm on PrEP, but I don't imagine you . . ."

Miller shook his head.

"See! Goddammit. I put you at risk. I wouldn't blame you if—"

"Stop right there." Miller put a finger to Dee's lips. "I trust you. Should we have gone bare without talking about it? No. But it wasn't as if we meant to. Besides, I've been thinking about it myself and I was planning to have that conversation with you soon. Guess we don't need it now."

"It's still not all right . . ." Then it hit him. "Really? You were going to suggest ditching the condoms?"

Miller grinned. "Really. Now come here. I love you." He wrapped Sandy in his arms and kissed him thoroughly.

"I love you too."

They cuddled under the spray until they were warm, and then Sandy dried Miller off and the two of them checked on Geo, who was sleeping soundly.

Finally in bed, Sandy curled his long body around Miller and ran his fingers through that fiery hair, counting the man's breaths until he fell asleep.

Sandy wasn't so lucky, kept awake till well past midnight by thoughts of Geo's shattering assault mixed with memories of his own father's betrayal and abandonment and his upcoming meeting with him. Not to mention the unsettling awareness of how deep his feelings ran and how exposed his heart had suddenly become.

They'd said they loved each other.

That was enough.

That was everything.

Wasn't it?

CHAPTER EIGHTEEN

"He's still asleep. I said we should've waited. He won't be happy with you."

"Nonsense. Nothing I haven't seen before."

"Oh shit. He's not alone. I'm shutting the door."

"What do you mean he's not— Oh. *Ohhhhhh . . .*"

Miller shot up in bed, blinking madly to clear his vision, because there was no fucking way he'd heard—*holy fucking fuck*. He hadn't been dreaming. Framed in the doorway of his bedroom stood one very sheepish brother and his incredibly smug—*goddammit*—mother.

"What the hell?" he hissed, dragging the sheet up to cover his dangly bits, the move alerting him to the presence of a long, smooth leg stretched over his thighs and an equally long arm wrapped around his waist, both attached to a gorgeously lean and currently entirely naked torso. *Shit.* Sandy.

He tried to fling the sheet over Sandy's bare arse, but it caught on something and fell significantly short of the desired effect. Plus Sandy was beginning to wake and wriggle out from under whatever modesty it did offer, with a purr that Miller knew only too well, and which absolutely, under no circumstances could be allowed to develop into anything further. If Sandy had yelled "fuck me now" at the top of his voice, it couldn't have been any clearer.

"Mmm, morning babe." Sandy's hand trailed south to—

"No!" Miller shoved it aside before it hit his cock, and Sandy jumped in surprise. "Mum, Dane, what the hell are you two doing here and, more specifically, *in my bedroom?*"

"Mum?" Sandy lifted an eyelid, peered around Miller's back to the doorway, and froze. "Holy fu—udge. Miller is that—"

"Yes. But not for long because I'm gonna kill both of them."

"You must be Sandy." Miller's mother smiled at Sandy and Miller wanted to kill her . . . very slowly.

"Not the time, Mum," he interrupted any reply Sandy might be about to make. "All parties equally dressed would be a desirable beginning to this conversation, I'm thinking."

"Hello, Mrs Harrison," Sandy peeked from Miller's back. "Nice to meet you."

"No." Miller turned to Sandy. "Do *not* reward her for this. She doesn't deserve it."

"Hello, son," his father's voice drifted from the other end of the house. "Please notice I was not involved in that particular incursion."

Miller's eyes bugged. "Dad's here too?"

"And Sam," his mother added with a sweet smile that suited her about as well as braces on a vampire. "They're in the lounge keeping Geo company. I think it's all just hitting the poor boy."

Shit. He glared at his mother while still trying to shield Sandy as the poor man attempted to scramble under the sheet at the speed of light. It was nowhere as easy as it sounded since most of said sheet was tangled around Miller, who couldn't seem to get the fucker free.

"Your mother?" Sandy hissed under his breath as he squirmed. "What the hell is your *mother* doing in your bedroom?"

Miller gave up trying to get the sheet free and thrust a pillow at Sandy, who immediately shoved it over his groin and fell back on the bed with his hand over his face, muttering, "I can't believe this. Your *mother.*"

Miller eyeballed Dane with what he hoped contained a threat worthy of Miller's current level of mortification, and by the speed at which the colour drained from Dane's face, he'd succeeded. There were going to be bodies.

"Yes, yes, we're going." He backed up quickly. "Come on, Mum, let them get dressed." Dane tugged at his mother, who seemed in no rush to move. "We'll get breakfast ready," he added, pulling the door shut on his mother's smiling face.

So many bodies.

"It better be in Wellington," he shouted to their departing backs. Goddamn, his nosey fucking family. He turned to grovel and apologise, only to find Sandy with his hand over his mouth, shaking with laughter. He whipped the hand away and planted a kiss on his lips instead, after which they both fell back, chuckling till their sides ached.

"God, I'm so sorry." Miller wiped his eyes and struggled to his feet.

"It wasn't your fault." Sandy rubbed a hand up Miller's thigh. "But I guess that was it, right? The dreaded meet-the-parents moment done and dusted. Not much I can do to top that epic tragedy, is there?"

Miller threw Sandy's jeans at him. "They're gonna love you. Come on. Let's face the music. Can you throw me that bottle of ibuprofen? I'll cover if you want to shower first."

"Nah. I'm clean enough from last night. Here, catch."

Miller caught the bottle and downed a couple of tablets straight off.

Sandy's eyebrows bunched. "You're taking a lot of those lately."

He shrugged. Not like he could deny it. "I just need to get through this Aussie series, and then the training will drop back and I can rest and let it heal."

"Mmm." Sandy was clearly unconvinced. "With the Paralympics coming up next year, I thought Merv was about to up the training, not drop it." He fired Miller a challenging look.

"Yeah okay, smart-arse. Can we maybe deal with one crisis at a time?"

Sandy grabbed Miller's dick, twisted it gently, and Miller froze. "Promise we'll talk about it after the series." He stared up at Miller.

Miller pulled a face and sighed. "Yes, yes, I promise."

"Excellent choice." Sandy let go of Miller's dick and got to his feet. "So, shall we get this done? Meet the parents—practicum. At least there are no soul-searching wardrobe decisions to make. I can't possibly match that first impression."

Miller stepped close and cradled his face. "Don't do that. Don't doubt yourself. I'm so fucking proud of you in any and every thing you wear. Just be you."

They locked eyes and Miller caught the soft edge of approval and gratitude in Sandy's. He tucked an errant blond lock behind Sandy's ear and kissed him.

The teeth-gnashing continued throughout breakfast as Miller's mother not so subtly interrogated Sandy, hovered over a very quiet Geo, and teased Miller mercilessly. Sandy held his own admirably, at least once he realised Miller's mother wasn't in the least bit offended by finding them in bed and that she enjoyed the robust banter that came so naturally to him. Every now and then he caught Miller's eye and threw him a secret smile.

His parents, kept in the loop by Dane, had come armed with a load of clothing, toiletries, and other necessities for Geo, all overseen by Sam. For that, Miller could forgive them a lot, especially seeing the look of gratitude on Geo's face. The supplies were welcome and one less thing on the list.

Another thing crossed off the list was any concern about Dee and Miller's parents getting on. Miller could only sit back and watch with wonder as Sandy charmed both of them. He'd only ever imagined this moment, introducing a boyfriend, and it still didn't feel real. His mother was always going to be the easy one, desperate as she was for Miller to have a love life, *any* love life. But even Miller's father didn't take long to bow to the magical Sandy offensive, regaled by Sandy's description of all the special plays they'd missed while Miller had banned his parents from coming. He also appeared suitably horrified that they'd been banned at all. If he'd known, he would've nipped that rubbish in the bud, he'd told Miller's father.

Miller almost choked on his toast.

There had been only one awkward moment when Sandy first appeared dressed in his jeans with that gorgeous shirt worn loose over top and a freshly applied layer of lip gloss. James Harrison's eyes had definitely bugged for a moment, and he'd even sneaked a second look before shooting a questioning glance Miller's way. Miller had fired back a silent warning and continued with introductions. His mother had discreetly elbowed her husband in the ribs and whispered something that bled all the colour from his face.

Miller had made a mental note to take his mum for lunch.

If Sandy caught the exchange, he hadn't let on, but his grip was fierce when Miller took his hand. Thankfully the awkwardness didn't last. Sandy immediately began chatting about Miller's wheelchair rugby, and Miller's dad was quickly impressed by Sandy's knowledge —even though Sandy was still running a little light in the shorts in his understanding of the finer rules. He made a couple of mistakes, which Miller's father let go with a wink Miller's way. Sandy's enthusiasm more than made up for it, and Miller's dad only mentioned Miller's need to focus on his training, oh, about half a dozen times.

But Miller also had his eyes opened for the first time regarding just how devious his boyfriend truly was when he listened in jaw-dropping wonder to Sandy explaining to Miller's father exactly how important it was for Miller to train well and eat right and that Sandy would be personally monitoring Miller's diet from now on. *Fucking hell*. Miller's dad looked like he wanted to kiss Sandy's feet, and it was all Miller could do not to burst into laughter when Sandy turned and shot him a wink.

But for all that things had gone well, Miller could've kissed his brother when Dane herded everyone out the door as soon as breakfast was done with a promise to Sam he could see Geo later and a worried glance Miller's way. While Sandy stayed back with Geo, Miller saw his family to the door. Dane hugged him hard in appreciation for what Miller was doing for Sam's friend. Physical affection was rare between them and Miller decided that was going to change. But Dane was also concerned Miller was taking on a lot—a concern his parents shared if their frowns were anything to go by.

It *was* a lot, Miller knew that. But he also knew it was the right thing to do.

His mother kissed his cheek and took him aside. "He's lovely, Miller. You've done well. Please don't be a stranger. We'd like to get to know him better. And about this morning—" Her eyes twinkled. "Sorry, not sorry. Made my day."

He pulled her close and she gave a snort of surprise before hugging him back. It seemed to be the day for it.

He waved them off with a relieved groan.

Back in the lounge Geo looked like he'd been hit by a truck: quiet, withdrawn, and pale. He'd eaten no more than a few mouthfuls of breakfast and was constantly on and off the phone with his boyfriend. The sooner the counsellor saw him, the better.

———

"I'm thinking Thai takeout for dinner," Miller suggested as Sandy battled rush-hour traffic on their way back to Miller's.

He'd handed his keys over saying he'd had enough of driving, but Sandy wasn't buying it. Miller's hand had been constantly massaging his right thigh whenever he wasn't wheeling his chair. Plus, he'd asked Sandy if he minded getting his chair in and out of the car so he could transfer without using his canes—something he never, ever did.

Sandy was worried.

If he knew anything about Miller, it was the man was fiercely independent and would rather chew off his arm than ask for help. He was in a lot of pain, the bottle of ibuprofen rattling in his jacket pocket paid testament to that, but Sandy knew better than to call him on it, again.

Instead he got busy making things easier for Miller as they'd ticked off the hospital, police station, Sandy's apartment, the drop-in centre for Geo's counsellor appointment since they were already out and about, the mall for some underwear for Geo, and finally Geo's school, before heading home.

Home. How quickly that idea had settled in Sandy's heart, but not without a flicker of worry. With most of the day spent waiting for Geo and Miller, he'd plenty of time to think, and regardless of how close they were growing, not all those thoughts had been positive.

If Sandy thought Miller's life was full before all this happened with Geo, how the hell was he going to claim a part of it if Geo became a full-time addition. Miller might not be talking permanent with Geo at the moment, but that was just the man hedging. Sandy wasn't fooled. He could see it in the set of Miller's jaw. If Geo wanted to stay, Miller would take him on for the next eighteen months. And although Geo was seventeen and pretty independent, he was still going to need a lot of time and understanding as he dealt with what happened. And where did that leave Sandy?

They loved each other, but this was a layer of complication neither had anticipated.

"What do you think, Geo? You up for Thai?" He caught Geo's eyes in the rear-vision mirror and the boy nodded. "Okay, we'll stop on the way home."

Geo had been quiet since his session with the counsellor other than saying it had been good. The woman offered to talk with Miller as well, alone and with Geo, if Geo agreed, which he did. Miller asked if Sandy could join, and she'd been surprised but agreeable.

Sandy tried not to read too much into Miller asking, but he worried all the same. Even if the two of them didn't make it long term, he'd always be available for Geo. It was a good idea. Maybe Miller hadn't meant it to be more than that.

Miller directed them to his favourite Thai restaurant and Sandy went to order, grateful for a bit of space. It had been a huge day, but they were on track. The counsellor had suggested keeping Geo home from school for the rest of the week, although if he wanted to go, that was okay too. He'd have daily sessions with her, talk to social services at some point, a meeting Mark had also promised to attend, and it would also give Geo's dad some cooling-off time so he wasn't tempted to search out Geo at school.

The school had been excellent, going so far as to distribute an action plan to staff in case Geo's dad showed up. Geo was still understandably nervous, but it seemed less about his dad and more about kids maybe knowing what had happened, and Sandy couldn't blame him for that.

The Thai didn't take long, and twenty minutes later they were turning onto Miller's street. The delicious aroma wafting through the car, in addition to knowing the difficult day was coming to an end seemed to lighten everyone's mood. Miller was instructing Geo on his ten favourite '80s Kiwi bands while Geo mocked him mercilessly, horrified at Miller's woeful lack of contemporary music knowledge.

The good-natured teasing lasted as long as it took to reach Miller's driveway and lock eyes on the words spray-painted in white across his dark grey garage door.

Fags Paedophiles

Sandy froze with his hand on the door opener. "What the hell?"

"Holy shit." Miller leaned forward in his seat, his face pale.

"What an arsehole." Sandy couldn't help but turn to check the surrounding houses, noting a couple of faces at nearby windows. "I hope no paparazzi did a drive-by."

Miller's eyes bugged. "Fuck. That hadn't even occurred to me."

"It's Dad, isn't it," Geo said quietly.

Miller turned to face him. "Possibly. How would he know where you were? Do you have phone track on?"

"No. The phone's under my own name and account, and I changed the password. But look." He held it up showing a pic of the three of them at the mall just a couple of hours before.

"Where the hell were those posted?" Miller took the phone and flicked through another four or five just like it.

"Sports Jam. It's a fan site."

"I'm on a fan site?" Miller stared at Geo in disbelief.

"Like, yeah. Of course."

Miller shook his head. "People really need to get a life."

Geo took his phone back and pocketed it. "It probably wouldn't matter. He knows you're Sam's uncle. He had a bit to say when you came out a few weeks ago. It was one of the reasons he stopped Sam coming over. And he'd have to guess Sam had something to do with me leaving; he's my best friend. It's not a huge leap, right? If he's been watching the school or Sam's house or the drop-in centre, he'd have seen us for himself."

Fuck. The idea that Geo's dad might've been watching freaked Sandy out big time. But not as much as those words on the garage door. That was personal and a big fucking message. *I know where he is.*

"I guess that answers whether he's going to just let things go, right?" He reached for Miller's hand and squeezed it.

They shared a worried look. "I'll call Mark," Miller said, reaching for his phone. "Could you maybe get some photos while the light's good? And then, I'm going to check with my neighbours whether they saw anything and soothe any ruffled feathers. Geo, can you get my chair for me? We'll leave the car parked in front of it and rope a tarp over the door once the police are done."

"I'm so sorry," Geo's small voice came from the back seat.

"Not your fault, Geo." Sandy turned to squeeze Geo's hand. "We deal with it and move on, okay?"

Geo drew a shaky breath. "Okay."

Three hours later and they were finally able to cover the offending slurs with a tarp and eat their Thai. Mark had come and gone, taken statements, spoken to neighbours, and a technician had dusted for prints. Not that there was much hope in that regard. It wasn't like the culprit needed to touch the door to spray it. No one had seen anything and there were no security cameras close by—a situation Miller intended to remedy much to Sandy's relief. And although Mark promised to drop in on Geo's dad and issue a warning, there was no hard evidence he was even to blame.

Geo had returned to his shell and was back to barely talking. The only upside: he hadn't retreated to his room, seemingly happy enough with their company, and that said a lot. But Sandy was gutted for him. The increasingly genuine smiles they'd gotten after his counselling session had now vanished.

It had been a day of two steps forward and one back. And with both of them heading back to work the next day, neither wanted to leave Geo alone. With Geo's permission, they'd organised to drop him at Miller's parents, and his counsellor would see him there. Sam would keep him company after school until Sandy and Miller could pick him up. That was, of course, *after* Sandy's meeting with his father.

Fucking hell. His bloody father.

He'd thought about cancelling but Miller talked him out if it. "Get it over with," he'd said, and he was right. But with everything happening with Geo, Sandy wasn't feeling remotely generous toward bigoted fathers. If his dad had any fuckery up his sleeve, it was going to be a very short meeting.

He put his empty plate on the coffee table and nudged Miller's foot. "I thought you had training tonight. The first game's only four days away. There was a thirty-second interview with the coach of the Australian team on the news while you were saying goodbye to Mark. Oh, and I got another call from that sport's journalist about us. Guess the Australian team's arrival has sparked renewed interest."

Miller's brows furrowed. "What did he want?"

"Asked how you were feeling about the game and had we been together long."

Miller's eyes almost hit the back of his head.

Sandy rubbed Miller's arm. "Let it go. I told him to be at the game on Sunday cos you were gonna kill it, and none of his damn business to the latter—in the nicest possible way, of course. They'll get their fill of photos at the game anyway. Hell, me and your parents sitting together? Holy shit. We'll be married and applying for adoption by the morning papers." His laugh hid a surge of yearning, which was getting harder to deny. Jesus, when had he become *that* guy? Married? Kids? He'd hardly known Miller a month, but hell yeah to both. Sandy wanted exactly that. Wanted that with Miller. He just wasn't sure if that's what Miller wanted or could even imagine.

"Can I come watch?" Geo perked up.

Miller's cheeks brightened, sending his freckles into a frenzy, all vying for attention. He was obviously chuffed and shot a questioning look Sandy's way.

Sandy nodded, resisting the urge to kiss Miller senseless for being so fucking adorable. As far as distraction went, taking Geo to the game was a great idea. All Miller's family was going, including Sam. Geo would be fussed over and taken care of.

"Yes, I don't see why not."

Geo's face lit up and he immediately pulled out his phone.

Miller turned back to Sandy. "I had to give Merv at least the basics of what was going on. He's okay with me missing this one as long as I make it Friday. Benson's taking my place at tonight's practice. It'll be good for him. I'll get some gym time tomorrow to make up. Geo is more important."

He was, obviously, but Sandy was still kind of surprised. "You know I can be here any time if you need to go."

"I know." Miller brushed the hair from Sandy's face. "But it's just a night. It's fine."

Geo's phone buzzed and he leapt to his feet. "I'm gonna Face-Time Jacob, if that's okay?"

Miller waved him off. "You guys can catch up Saturday if you want."

Geo returned a shining smile, the best they'd seen all day, and something in Sandy's chest cracked open a little with thoughts he had no business thinking. He stomped down on it fast. One step at a time.

"Hell yeah." Geo almost ran to his bedroom.

"Ah, young love." Sandy chuckled and snuggled close to Miller, alone at last.

"Not just young love." Miller tugged him around and onto his lap and Sandy wasn't arguing. "I still get excited when I see your name on my phone."

Sandy laughed. "Me too. Does that make us ridiculous?" He wiggled his groin against Miller, who immediately grimaced. Sandy slid to the side. "Fuck, I forgot. It's getting worse, isn't it?"

"It's fine." Miller moved to kiss him, but Sandy pushed him back.

"Liar. And stop trying to distract me." He sent Miller a pointed stare. "I've been watching you all day. You're throwing back ibuprofen like damn candy."

Miller cupped his cheeks and stared deep into Sandy's eyes like there was no one more important, and Sandy almost forgot what they were arguing about, almost.

"I got the all-clear," he soothed. "Pain is part of what we sign up for. Ask Reuben. But I promised we'd talk after, and we will. Is that enough?"

Not really, but Sandy doubted he'd get much more before then. "It's a start."

"Good." Miller pressed their lips together and Sandy sank into the kiss.

He wanted desperately to believe that Miller was okay, but he just wasn't feeling it. About stuff like this, Miller was still maddeningly closed off, which meant they had some work ahead of them, because if they were to have any future together, Sandy wasn't about to be shut out of something so incredibly important in Miller's life, in both their lives.

"So . . ." Miller tucked Sandy against his side. "Tell me how you're feeling about this meeting with your dad tomorrow?"

A strangled groan escaped his throat. *Terrified. Furious. Numb.* He settled on "Confused. I just want it over with. But knowing you're going to be keeping an eye on me helps so fucking much. Although if you feel you need to be with Geo, I'll understand, you know that." *Please don't say that.*

Miller didn't hesitate. "No. Geo's seventeen. He'll be perfectly fine with my parents. I belong with you."

You do. He melted into Miller's arms and let himself be held. "Thanks." He said nothing for a minute, happy simply to sit and enjoy the rise and fall of Miller's chest and the strength of his arms. "You're going to offer Geo a permanent home with you for as long as he needs it, aren't you?"

Miller sat in silence and Sandy kept count of his breaths, in and out, in and out.

"Yeah, I am."

Six breaths. Six breaths for Sandy to ponder the next question in his mind because the answer to the last was never in question.

"I haven't mentioned it to him," Miller was quick to add. "It's too soon. And maybe he won't want to. He might have relatives—"

"He'll want to," Sandy said evenly. He had no doubt. "For a lot of reasons, but mostly because he knows his sexuality is safe here. *He's* safe here. And that's a lot after what's happened to him. Possibly the most important thing."

"I know." Miller nuzzled Sandy's hair, sending a shiver racing through him. "But I wanted to talk to you first."

"Me?" Sandy was pretty sure it came out a squeak because Miller including Sandy in his thinking meant everything right then. Maybe there was room for him in this new world of Miller's, after all.

"Of course, you. Boyfriend handbook, page fifty-four. No life-changing decisions without consultation. And I'm pretty sure this classifies as a life-changing decision, at least temporarily. But I guess there's no pretending things aren't going to be . . . different."

Sandy turned his cheek to Miller's chest and heard the solid thump of his heart. "I can do different. But I want you to know something first." He tipped his head back till they locked eyes. "I'll still be here for Geo even if we don't . . . you know. I won't walk out on him."

A dozen questions passed through Miller's eyes and fell into the deep crease that formed between them, but he didn't ask a single one. Instead he stroked Sandy's cheek like he was gentling an anxious horse. And maybe he was.

"I'd expect nothing less," he finally said. "Although I'd very much prefer it if we did . . . you know." His troubled eyes smoothed and twinkled. "In fact, I'd be particularly grateful if we . . . you know-ed as soon as possible—down the hall in our . . . you know."

Our. And oh god, Sandy was so gone for this man. He licked a stripe up the side of Miller's throat, earning himself a shiver of appreciation. "I think that can be arranged."

Laughter floated from Geo's bedroom, bringing a smile to both their faces. "Do you think he'll be okay?" Sandy rested his chin on Miller's shoulder and looked back to Geo's closed door.

"Yeah, I do." Miller turned to follow his gaze. "He's strong. Strong enough to get out. Strong enough to accept help. So as long as we can keep his arsehole dad from getting to him, I think he'll be okay."

"Strong enough to accept help, huh?" Sandy couldn't resist the tease. "There's a lesson in there for the quick of mind."

"Such a funny guy." Miller pushed Sandy to his feet. "But I can think of much more interesting uses for that smart mouth of yours."

"Oh, can you now?" Sandy licked his lips slowly. "Then it's just as well there's a couple of rooms between the bedrooms, isn't it? And maybe we should make a list of all those uses for my smart mouth. I'm suddenly not the least bit tired."

Miller struggled to his feet and popped a kiss on his forehead. "Mmm, perhaps we should consider the benefits of a gag, just to be on the safe side."

Sandy swallowed hard, more than a little mortified at his cock's response to that particular suggestion.

But Miller hadn't missed a thing. "One for the list?"

Sandy narrowed his gaze. "You're very sure of yourself tonight. Let's just say we'll see." Which was infinitely less embarrassing than the, *hell yeah*, that first sprang to mind.

Miller nudged Sandy into the hall with one of his canes. "I doubt there's enough ink in all the world for what I want on that list, but I'm pretty sure we can wing it in the interim. Now, get moving before I forget which . . . you know, to put my . . . you know, into."

Sandy snorted, turned, and wiggled his butt invitingly. "I doubt there's a wrong choice in any of those options."

CHAPTER NINETEEN

SANDY PICKED THE LINT FROM HIS FITTED FOREST-GREEN JERSEY and hammered at the pleats on his smart red, green, and black tartan skirt with the palms of his hand, just like he'd been doing for the last hour. He was going to have a word with his dry cleaner. Somewhat satisfied, he wrapped his cream merino scarf tight around his neck and shoved his arms into his black leather jacket, almost going straight through the lining in the process.

Okay, so he was a little on edge.

Maybe a lot.

Fuck it to hell and back. He was in no way prepared for this meeting with his father, not after twenty years of hating the guy. But he wasn't about to run scared either. He refused to give the man the satisfaction.

Knowing Miller would be watching from a table inside was the only reason he wasn't completely freaking the hell out. An understanding ear and some excellent sex were exactly what he was going to need after, and not necessarily in that order. Of course, that depended on Geo's day and where his head was at. Sandy didn't begrudge the teen for putting a small dent in their sex life at the moment. Miller was worth the wait.

Which got him thinking about Geo, again.

After his session with the counsellor, the teen had texted them both to say he was thinking of going back to school the next day—good news for everyone. Hanging around with nothing to do but think wasn't always the best option. Plus, it would take the pressure off their weekend if he wasn't worrying about going back on Monday. The fact he'd texted them both did funny things to Sandy's heart, and the images in his head of the three of them together as some kind of interim family were getting worse.

Geo's dad had denied any knowledge of the tagging, shocker, but Mark had officially warned him anyway and they had to hope that would be enough. But he had said he was getting legal advice over his son. Good luck with that.

Both Lizzie and his mother were keen to help with Geo in any way they could. Sandy expected nothing less but was still incredibly grateful. They'd also offered to go with him to meet his Dad, and maybe that would've been the sensible option, but Sandy wanted to do this on his own. Miller was all the support he needed.

But Sandy wasn't about to make things easy on his old man just to avoid a confrontation, hence the skirt. If his father genuinely wanted to build bridges, then wearing a skirt would soon determine the truth of that. Either that or Sandy just wanted to fuck with his father. And yeah, okay, there was a little of that in there too. But the bastard deserved it.

Was Sandy going in with the best attitude? Maybe not.

But then why the hell should he?

Regardless of his reasons for the skirt, when Miller arrived in the morgue at lunchtime to give Sandy a kiss and wish him well, his endorsement of Sandy's choice of attire was plainly evident. His sharp intake of breath as he trapped Sandy against the desk, followed by a hand up Sandy's skirt and down his black tights and briefs, made that approval abundantly clear. But a comment before he left showed it hadn't escaped him that Sandy was throwing down a direct challenge.

It was kind of hard to deny.

But then an hour before he was due to leave for the meeting, he was handed another reason for wearing his favourite skirt. He glared at the official email on his computer for the millionth time.

Fucking donkey balls.

An official complaint.

About *him*.

In all his years of working, no one had *ever* complained about him for *any* reason. And now this; calling him unprofessional and an embarrassment to the hospital. Claiming Sandy was an inappropriate representative to meet with grieving families, especially children. And wanting an explanation about why taxpayer money was being used for the salary of a person setting a dangerous example to vulnerable youth.

And why?

Because he'd been wearing a bloody skirt.

There was no need to guess who'd made the complaint: the grieving mother and son from a month ago. The ones who had loathed Sandy from the minute they'd laid eyes on him. They hadn't even approached Ed, going straight to the hospital management so it couldn't even be handled quietly within the department.

When he'd shown the letter to Ed, who hadn't yet opened his own copy, his eyeballs nearly exploded, and he stormed upstairs to give HR an earful. He still hadn't returned, not that Sandy thought it would do any good.

He'd met the family while on the clock, and dress code was always a grey area in departments like theirs. He normally wore scrubs for all clinical work, but if he and Ed were catching up on office chores or doing court prep, Ed let him wear civvies, never questioning what that entailed.

The thought of answering about his choice of dress to a fucking committee, dissecting his gender and sexuality yet again, had bile surging up the back of his throat. He doubted he'd be fired for it, but he saw a fuckton of drama headed his way like a damned freight train. It was the last thing he needed, and in the back of his mind, he couldn't help but remember Miller saying how much he hated drama, again. Between Sandy in his life, Geo arriving on his doorstep, and Miller coming out in his sport, how much more drama could the poor guy handle?

So yes, Sandy was pissed at the world.

Especially today.

Especially going to see his arsehole of a father.

And yes, he was wearing a damned skirt and his father could go fuck himself.

He was purposefully five minutes late, not wanting to be the one kept waiting. He pushed open the door, sending the merry bells chiming, and let his gaze sweep the room. Primo was one of his favourite cafés, and he briefly wondered if he should've chosen somewhere different rather than sully its place in his heart. But he felt comfortable there. It was his space, his territory, and that seemed far more important.

Only a few tables had customers, which offered Sandy some solace if things went tits up. The café also closed in less than an hour, so more would surely leave soon. The timing had been a deliberate ploy on his part in order to keep their time together to something manageable. If things went okay, Sandy could choose to see him again, or not. Most likely the latter.

He recognised the arsehole straight away, which kind of surprised him—sitting in a corner booth nursing a coffee. The jolt ran through him like an electric shock, followed by an onslaught of painful memories. His knees almost buckled and he spun away before his father caught any hint of distress.

From behind his giant espresso machine, Tony gave a wary smile and asked if Sandy was okay.

No.

Sandy nodded and ordered his usual caramel frappé, taking the time to digest the effects of that first glimpse, calm his nerves, and try to settle his roiling gut.

He hated that the man could still do this to him.

Twenty years since he'd seen Floyd Williams, but other than a shit-ton more wrinkles, appreciably less hair, and about ten additional kilos in bulk—most of it around his gut by the look—his father hadn't changed that much, not where it counted. There was still that slightly supercilious smile, a sprawled posture that implied he owned the fucking place, or if he didn't he should, and a piercing gaze that left trails of stinging disdain the length of Sandy's body once he'd looked his fill. Which, to be fair, had taken more than a few seconds, something Sandy took a great deal of satisfaction from.

Fuck you and the horse you rode in on.

He grunted. Things weren't boding well for a happy reunion.

"Here you go, sweet cheeks." Tony handed Sandy's credit card back. "I'm here if you need me, sugar." He sent a meaningful glance over Sandy's shoulder.

Sandy's gaze met Tony's and he nodded. "Thanks." Then he took a deep breath and headed for his father's booth, adding a deliberate swing in his hips just for sheer piss-off value. He felt rather than saw Miller's gaze trained on him and glanced sideways to see him about three tables away. Miller smiled and winked, and something settled in Sandy's belly. They'd agreed he wouldn't tip off his dad by acknowledging Miller, so he kept going.

When he got to the booth, he ignored his dad and simply slid in opposite. Only then did he look up. "You wanted to see me?"

His dad looked surprised and vaguely amused by his blunt words. "You set the time and place, so I presume you wanted to see me as well. I'm still your father, after all."

Sandy narrowed his gaze and took a minute to really look at the man. He noted the thin line of his lips, the slightly anxious flicker to his eye, and the way his fingers nervously shuttled up and down the handle of his mug. *Huh.* His father wasn't nearly as together as he was pretending, and that made all the difference.

He steeled his resolve and answered, "You scrape by that title on the basis of genetics alone. But you are *not* my father, at least not in any manner you're implying. If that's the approach you're going to take, we may as well end this now."

His father ground his teeth, looking anything but happy, which was fine with Sandy. The man wanted to meet for a reason, and Sandy wasn't giving him a thing until he knew exactly what that was.

Floyd took a mouthful of what Sandy suspected was barely warm coffee and swallowed with a grimace. He was playing for time, and Sandy was more than happy to give it to him, feeling stronger by the minute.

"So why *did* you agree to meet me?" his father finally asked, lounging back in his seat as if he couldn't give a fuck. "You avoided it for long enough. Was it to shock me with this?" He indicated Sandy's outfit. "Watch me squirm? I already knew you were gay. The fact you're wearing a dress is just . . . ." He looked like he was struggling to find the words. "Whatever, it doesn't matter." His gaze slid away.

Sandy's hackles went up. "No. Finish that sentence. Finish it or I'm leaving right now. The fact I'm wearing a dress is just what?"

Floyd's attention skittered around the room before landing back on him. "Unexpected. Unnecessary. You only did it to bait me, shock me. Well, I'm not shocked. Surprised, sure."

"You hate it," Sandy challenged, jutting his chin. "That look on your face when you saw me, you were disgusted—"

"I wasn't . . . disgusted." His voice trailed off.

Sandy eyed his father with caution. That had been . . . unexpected. His father had never shied away from his contempt of people like Sandy. But for all that Sandy wanted to call him on a lie, there was something about his father's sheepish discomfort that stopped him.

"I'm not saying I understand or that I like it . . . but . . . but maybe it's my problem—"

He broke off as Tony appeared at Sandy's shoulder and set his caramel frappé in front. The break in conversation was a godsend as Sandy tried to make sense of what he was hearing. Was his father actually owning that he had issues? Sandy wasn't buying it, not yet. But he was perhaps more inclined to give the man a little more rope.

Tony flicked a curious gaze between him and his father. "Everything okay?"

Sandy nodded. "This is my . . . father," he explained. "He's in town for a drag show; he's top billing."

Sandy's father choked and promptly sprayed a mouthful of coffee down the front of his AC/DC T-shirt.

Tony's eyes popped out on stilts and he hauled arse out of there while Sandy made a mental note to fill him in later. He didn't even try to hide his smirk as he handed his father a serviette to mop up the mess.

"Okay, so maybe I did wear it to bait you, but only partly," he explained. "And because you deserved it. I'm not the one who came looking to reconnect, and you don't get to lay the rules down any longer.

"But if you think I borrowed this? I didn't. If you think it's the only one I have in my wardrobe? It's not. I wear skirts and dresses when I fucking feel like it, *Dad*. I wear jeans and trousers too. And T-shirts and frilly blouses and any fucking thing that I want to. And you don't get to say a thing about it because you're not in my life, and I don't give a shit what you think."

Floyd winced, his gaze darting to the tables close by. "Keep your voice down."

Sandy rolled his eyes. "Really, *Dad*? Am I embarrassing you? Let me solve that problem for you." He got up to leave, but Floyd grabbed his wrist.

He froze and spoke through clenched teeth. "Let me go, now." The scrape of a chair alerted Sandy to Miller getting to his feet. His gaze flicked over to stay him. He could handle this on his own, and the realisation changed everything.

"Sorry." Floyd released him and sat back. "Just . . . don't go."

As tempting as it was to ignore him and be done with it, something kept Sandy's feet in place. "Touch me again and I'm gone, understand?"

Floyd nodded and went back to playing with his coffee cup.

Sandy slid into the booth once again. Movement out of the corner of his eye told him Miller had also taken his seat.

He took a slow breath and eyed his father. "You asked why I agreed to see you?" He pushed his cup to the side. "Okay then, I'll tell you. Call it curiosity. Call it wanting to look you in the eye and tell you what a total bastard you are. But don't even think of calling it anything more than that. I'm here because I wanted a sharper image of the man who fucked off and abandoned his family. Sharper than the one my fifteen-year-old self remembers."

He dropped his gaze and paused for a second to gather his composure so his voice didn't crack. His father didn't get to see that ever again. Then he eyeballed him again. "That kid was too fucking devastated by what you did to see you clearly for the manipulating arsehole you are. You knew exactly how it would affect me—you leaving when and how you did, so don't pretend you didn't. You're not that brainless. You *wanted* me to blame myself. And maybe that young kid did, for a while."

He leaned forward, arms on the polished wood table.

"But this *man* in front of you has no such illusions. I didn't need you to raise me, Mum did a far better job of that. I didn't need you to help me become a good and decent person. Someone who's respected and great at his job. Who has friends and people who care about him. And I certainly didn't and *don't* need your approval for *anything*. So, let's be really clear about this, *Dad.* Unless you start telling me things I'm actually interested in hearing, I'm done here. I've achieved what I came to do."

His father squirmed in his seat looking a lot less sure of himself than he did a few minutes before. Good fucking job. Sandy was done wasting time.

"So, *Dad*, how about you start by telling me exactly *why* you're here. Not the half-arsed excuse you gave Mum and Lizzie about wanting to *build a bridge* between us—what the fuck does that even mean?—or some such shit, because you don't come across as particularly repentant, I have to say. I want the real reason." He dragged his glass back in front and took a long swallow of his frappé. Then he sat back, folded his arms, and waited.

His father's face ran a gamut of emotions from bluster to irritation and eventually resignation. Okay, so maybe they were getting somewhere. Sandy stole a quick glance Miller's way to find him watching intently. The sense of being under vigilant protection was both strange and exhilarating.

"I've met a woman," his father began, jerking Sandy's attention back.

Huh. Hardly what he'd expected as an opener. "And this affects me how?" he countered.

"She's . . . one of your . . . lot." His father's gaze slid away.

Which was just as well. Sandy's eyebrows shot up so fast, Tony would surely find them waggling atop his espresso machine the next morning and Sandy would be condemned to drawing them in place for the remainder of his life like some Jean Harlow wannabe on a bad day.

"One of *my lot?*" he coughed out. "You're going to have to give me more than that."

His dad pursed his lips. "You know exactly what I mean. LGBT people."

And Sandy wasn't sure what shocked him more. The fact that his father was dating someone from the community or the fact he even knew the freaking letters, or at least some of them.

"Which one of those in particular," he pushed, enjoying his father's obvious discomfort while realising in the same instant that whoever this woman was, she meant enough to Floyd Williams to bring him cap in hand to his family. "There're some major differences between them in case you hadn't realised."

His father shot him a pointed look that said he knew Sandy was fucking with him.

Sandy shrugged. "Just saying."

"She's bisexual." He almost whispered the word and then did a quick scan of the café as if checking whether someone had heard.

Sandy barked out a laugh. "Boy, how did that feel? You need a minute there, Dad? Maybe get a glass of water?"

"Shut up."

"No. I'm going to enjoy every fucking minute of this, so get used to it. And that still doesn't explain why you're here."

His father shuffled and stared out the window. "I didn't know at the beginning, all right. I just liked her."

Sandy snorted. "We *can* be likeable, you know? We're not the fucking undead."

Floyd glared. "Are you going to let me tell you or not?"

Sandy slouched against the booth cushions and waved his hand. "Go ahead."

His father studied him as if deciding if it was worth it and then sighed. "We'd been seeing each other for about six months when she told me, and to be honest, I didn't really care. I mean, she was with *me*, right? So it wasn't like it was . . . a thing, and the idea of the . . . other stuff was kind of . . . okay." His cheeks flushed bright pink.

And Sandy didn't know whether to laugh or fucking slap the guy on behalf of bisexuals everywhere who had to deal with those shitty double standards and erasure all the fucking time. But he kept quiet, thinking there'd be time for that later.

"She knew I didn't get it, the whole—" He waved another hand Sandy's way. "—gay thing, or whatever. That's why she didn't say anything up front. She didn't think we'd last, I guess. But we did. We get on really well." He paused, shifting his gaze to stare out the window for a moment before looking back. "So anyway, when she told me, she was really clear that she wasn't going to pretend she was something she wasn't—"

Sandy raised a calculating brow.

His father flushed. "Yeah, yeah, okay. She said she was willing to give me a chance not to fuck it up, but I had to stop saying shit about . . . you know. I mean I don't have a problem with women . . . together, just the men . . . thing." He turned back to face the window.

"Oh, I bet she just loved that enlightened comment." Sandy couldn't resist. It was like fucking Christmas.

"Glad you think it's so funny," his father grumbled. "But I've been *trying*. It's hard. It's not how I was brought up."

"I don't think it's funny, actually," Sandy shot back. "I think it's rude and disrespectful and just plain ignorant, but you're not my problem to deal with. And it still doesn't explain why you're here."

He sighed and slumped in his seat. "When she found out what I did—"

"You told her?" Sandy couldn't believe it.

"She, Cara, found some . . . pictures of us all."

Fuck me. Sandy didn't know what to do with that. His father had kept some photos of the family he didn't appear to give a shit about? He didn't trust himself to speak.

"She said I either came back and fronted up, or we were done."

"And you decided to come?"

He locked eyes with Sandy. "I . . . I love her."

Jesus Christ. This was the fucking rabbit hole to end all rabbit holes, the worst soap opera script ever written with his father in a starring role. Sandy scrubbed both hands down his face and tried to get a grip.

"Why should I give a flying fuck if you love her? Why should I even *believe* that?" he blurted. "You were *supposed* to love us, and look how that played out. Maybe you and Mum had issues, but we were your fucking kids, Dad. Your kids!"

Floyd chewed on his cheek. "I know. I know. I don't have any excuses and I'm not giving any. If you've talked to your mum and Lizzie, you'll know I didn't try to give them any either."

"Do they know about this woman?"

He hesitated, then shook his head. "I . . . I didn't think it would help."

Sandy's heart pounded. "You mean they'd see that you were only really in this for you, again, like always? That you wouldn't be here if you didn't need something from us. You weren't going to tell me either, were you?"

Floyd hesitated, then shook his head.

Sandy threw up his hands. "Fucking hell. So how was this supposed to work? You take some selfies with us so she can see you did what you were supposed to and then you disappear again to get your happy ever after while we all sit here wondering what the hell happened?"

"No." He held up his hands. "No. It's not like that. I know I should've told your mother and Lizzie. Cara told me I needed to, but I thought they wouldn't hear me out."

"Oh, I wonder why?" Sandy hated the derision in his voice, but he couldn't stop it.

"Okay, you're right," his father admitted softly. "I thought I could just see you guys and then go back to how things were."

Sandy scoffed. "You mean the life where you pretend we don't exist and that you're not a homophobic arsehole who abandoned his kids?"

Floyd sent him a look that said he wasn't helping. Like Sandy had a single fuck left to give about that.

"No. I *was* all those things and I'm not pretending I wasn't. But I *am* trying to change. When I took off back then, I was really unhappy. Learning you were gay was just an excuse. I'd been wanting to leave for ages. Your mother's a good woman, but I never really loved her. And yes, I was about as selfish as they come. I don't pretend it was right or forgivable, and it certainly wasn't your fault; it was entirely on me."

"Fucking oath, it was," Sandy spat, barely able to contain his fury. "But you let me believe that it was because of me, you fucking coward."

Floyd dropped his chin to his chest and took a long, slow breath, then let it out and looked up. "I'm not looking for forgiveness."

"Just as well."

His father grimaced. "I admit I was a homophobic arsehole and I probably still am. But I'm *trying* to see things differently, God help me. Even my son in a . . . dress. I'm trying."

"A skirt," Sandy corrected, his lip curled up in a sneer he wasn't proud of. "And you're only trying because you want to be with *her*," he said flatly.

His father threw up his hands. "Yes. So I can be with her. Is that so bad? Don't we all need a reason to change?"

Fucker. Sandy couldn't disagree, so he said nothing. He tried to find the manipulation in his father's words so he could salvage some righteous anger, but they sounded disappointingly honest. "So what do you want now? Are you saying you're not going to run again?"

His father scratched at his face, avoiding Sandy's gaze. "To be honest, I don't know." His eyes scuttled back. "I thought the best thing was to leave whatever happens next to you, Lizzie, and your mother to choose. Maybe you want something from me, maybe you don't. I'll go with whatever you decide. I know that sounds like a cop out—"

"It does. And I won't be backed into giving you an answer straight away. My instinct is to say I want nothing to do with you. I've been hurt enough, and I couldn't give a fuck about you and this woman. But I want to think on it. And while that's happening, you need to tell Mum and Lizzie everything, or I will. And it won't be in your favour."

He blew out a long sigh, then picked up his phone and played with it while Sandy waited.

"Okay, I'll tell them."

"I hope they tear fucking strips off you."

Floyd snorted. "They already have. But can I say one thing before you go?"

Sandy gave him a wary look, mentally preparing himself. "What?"

His father's gaze was steady for the first time. "You're a lot . . . stronger than I expected."

Sandy hardened his stare. "To survive you, I had to be."

He slipped from the booth and left the café without a backward glance.

Motherfucker.

———

Miller's text arrived the minute Sandy settled himself behind the wheel of his car. **You okay?**

He answered straight away. **Good. Exhausted.**

I'll see you at home?

Home. God, that sounded good. **I'll be right behind you.**

Miller replied. **Look to your left.**

Sandy did, to find Miller leaning against the open door of his car, those sexy-as-fuck freckles scrunched up in the creases of his huge grin. Sandy's heart did a ridiculous floppy thing in his chest as he shoved open his door and ran across. He flew into Miller's arms and let himself be engulfed in the warmth of his solid presence.

"I'm so fucking proud of you." Miller's lips brushed his ear. "Are you okay?"

Sandy nodded, not trusting himself to explain further. "Kiss me."

And Miller was right there. The firm warmth of his lips grounding Sandy, the reassuring slide of their tongues, the promise, the care, the reminder he wasn't that fifteen-year-old kid anymore. He had a place in this world. He'd fought for it. He was loved by his family and this man. He was capable and he was strong.

And when Miller pulled away and stared at Sandy as if his world hung on Sandy's every word, Sandy wanted to believe that future nudging at his heart was truly possible.

Miller popped a kiss on his forehead and trailed two fingers along

Sandy's jaw. "Geo's gone to Sam's for dinner and they're dropping him back later. We've got the house to ourselves." He waggled his eyebrows and Sandy almost dropped with relief. "I've got Chinese ordered. Figured it was a takeout kind of week. I'll pick it up and see you at home."

Home. How easily that sat in Sandy's heart. "Takeout and sex. You have the best ideas. See you there."

He watched Miller drive off and then called his mother. There wasn't a hell of a lot to say if you omitted the bit about the woman his father was seeing, but she was glad to hear from him. He mentioned Floyd might be contacting them, although not what about. She sounded curious but didn't push, tiptoeing around his mood like he might shatter.

And Sandy wasn't entirely sure that he wouldn't.

He did the same with Lizzie before sitting for a few more minutes to untangle his emotions from the knotted mess inside his belly. Epic fail. He spun the volume on his Adele playlist to slightly under ear-detonating and headed for Miller's.

Home.

Fucking hell.

Two hours, one fried rice, a chicken foo yung, a tasty teriyaki beef, an epic blow job, and a right royal fucking from Miller as Sandy rode him, and Sandy lay sprawled, almost comatose on Miller's bed. His finger drew lazy circles in the puddle of spill in Miller's belly button as he waited for his arse to recover so he could think about maybe moving. Next year should do it.

"Damn, that was good." He lifted his finger to his lips and licked it clean.

Miller snorted. "Are you talking the chicken foo yung or my dick in your arse?"

"The chicken foo yung, of course. Although I have to say that fried rice came a close sec—ow!" He leapt sideways off the bed as Miller's finger wrapped around his knee in a vicious horse bite. The man had sasquatch-sized hands, which was pretty damned fantastic, ordinarily. His good hand could wrap around both their cocks with a knuckle to spare.

He hopped on one foot to keep his balance and glared down at Miller who barely blinked an eye before scooting to the middle of the bed and lifting the duvet. "Get back in here. I'm getting cold."

"And whose fault is that?" Sandy grumbled, crawling under the covers and snuggling against Miller whose body heat could give an iron smelter a run for its money. "And how the hell can you be cold? You have a core temperature of at least 800 degrees."

Miller wiped the come from both their bellies, and then wrapped an arm around Sandy's waist and pulled him close. "Unlike you, whose fingers and toes give new meaning to the expression frozen most days."

"I can't help having long arms and legs. It's like trying to warm the last bedroom furthest from the lounge fire. I've always felt the cold."

Miller kissed his forehead. "I like that you feel the cold. It means you're always up for a cuddle."

Sandy tipped his head back to stare at him. "Who are you and what have you done with my boyfriend? The Miller Harrison I first met was *not* a hugger. He was the tree to my hug. Stiff and immovable."

"You've turned me to the dark side." Miller's hand sneaked down to fondle Sandy's soft cock and balls. "Speaking of stiff . . ."

Sandy wriggled under the onslaught of Miller's wandering fingers. "Mmm. Yeah, well don't think you're going to get another round out of me, there's nothing left in the tank." His cock twitched.

"Mmm." Miller chuckled against the back of his neck.

"Don't get excited," Sandy warned. "I merely hiccupped."

"Riiiight." Miller added a slow stroke.

Sandy nuzzled into Miller's neck with an embarrassing whimper, but he knew Miller wasn't really going anywhere with it. They were both exhausted and Sandy's cock had very little oomph remaining to back up its interest. Still, Miller's hands on him always felt good, and Sandy was all for that at the moment.

They'd talked a little more about the meeting with Sandy's dad while they'd eaten their Chinese food, and Miller had listened and said all the right things. Then he'd bundled Sandy into bed, which was exactly what he needed. Now, sated and loose-limbed, he felt in a much better place to be objective, or at least not a ball of seething prickly affront.

"Are you going to see him again?" Miller's lips brushed Sandy's shoulder and up his throat, raising goosebumps in their wake.

"Mmm." He angled his head to allow Miller better access and thought about the question. "I don't know. At the moment I can't get past my anger to think about the fact he's maybe trying. And I'm so pissed off that he's here for himself and not for us. Not because he feels guilty. Not to say sorry. Not really even to mend fences. But because he needs something."

"You were hoping for more?"

Was I? Of course I was. Kids of arsehole parents always hoped, right? He thought of Geo and the simmering anger ignited again. "I thought I wasn't. I thought I was over all that, but . . ."

Miller lifted his chin to look him in the eye. "He's your father, Dee. It's natural to hope."

Those beautiful freckles blurred. He went to scrub the tears away, but Miller got there first with his lips.

He tucked his head into the curve of Miller's neck and played with the red tufts of hair on his chest, twirling them into little fiery haystacks. "Maybe, but hope hurts. I spent years hoping he'd come back—call, write, anything so I'd know I wasn't to blame, but nothing. I thought I was done with hope as far as he was concerned. Guess not. What a chump, right?"

"Look at it this way." Miller nuzzled against Sandy's hair. It had become a Miller thing—naked, clothed, it didn't matter. Miller's nose in Sandy's hair on a regular basis was as sure as the sun rose and set each day. "You achieved what you said you wanted to. You saw him. You told him what you thought of him. And now it's your decision whether to take it any further. No one will judge you either way. But can I ask you to consider one thing?"

"Go ahead."

"Does it really matter *why* he came?"

Sandy bristled. "You sound just like him."

Miller threw up a hand. "Hear me out."

Sandy wasn't sure he wanted to, but he said nothing.

"All I'm saying is that regardless of what a prick he is, or maybe *because* he's such a prick, it was a pretty ballsy thing to do, especially knowing what you guys had to think of him."

"What the hell, Miller? Ballsy? You're sounding like you admire the guy." Was Miller trying to help? Because Sandy had a couple of choice words for him if he was. He didn't want to see it from his father's side. He didn't have to.

But Miller wasn't done. "Look, I'm not sticking up for him, but from what you've said, he's not the type of guy to have agreed to do this easily. It hadn't bothered him in the last twenty years, right? So he has to feel strongly about this woman. Maybe this is his Waterloo? Karma, if you like. She's bi and she's forcing him to face what he did. Would it be better if he'd gotten there on his own? Sure. But bigots don't usually change without personal investment."

"And, *I* wasn't personal investment enough? His *family* wasn't?" Sandy scoffed, wiping at his eyes and regretting the scathing tone as soon as the words were out. But he was so done with making excuses for his father's obnoxious behaviour.

Miller closed his eyes for a second, clearly trying to inject some calm into the conversation, which only pissed Sandy off more. He wasn't a child to be soothed. His anger was damn well justified.

"Of course you should've been enough." Miller leaned forward and kissed each of Sandy's damp cheeks, virtually ensuring the faucet was turned back on. "But that's not how guys like this operate. All

I'm saying is that your dad has to, at the very least, be thinking about shit, which is a lot more than he's done before. Just something to think about, that's all."

Sandy wasn't ready to be that noble-minded. "What I *think* is that *you* can afford to give him the benefit of the doubt because you've never experienced that kind of vicious homophobia from people close to you, ever. You have a wonderful family and you led a closeted sports life. You're a masc athlete; you've never been bullied about your sexuality in your life." It came out more petty than he'd hoped, but damn it, it was true.

Miller opened his mouth as if to protest, but Sandy kept going. "I'm not judging you for that, Miller, just stating a fact. People like Geo and me have lost a trust that I'm not sure can ever be replaced. Don't kid yourself that my dad is turning over some new leaf. He's doing this for himself, that's *all* he's doing. And I feel fucking filthy just thinking about enabling a happy future for him in *any* way. The worst of it is he's already got what he came for. He can go back and say he met with us—built some bullshit bridge—and she'll never know the difference. Meanwhile, we've just had our lives put through the fucking emotional wringer, and he gets to walk away . . . again."

"But you said he left the door open if you wanted further contact? He's not just walking away this time."

Sandy glared at him. "Don't do that. Don't be so fucking sensible and shit. I don't need your Mr Committee-Peace-Maker, Everyone-Makes-Mistakes persona right now. I need you to dig deep and pull out that Mr Sympathetic-Boyfriend, Maim-The-Bastard, and-Scorch-The-Earth-Under-His-Feet persona, if you can."

Miller snorted. "I must've missed that particular addendum in the boyfriend induction package. I told you I'd be shit at this."

Sandy bit back a smile. Miller couldn't help not understanding. Hell, Sandy barely understood himself. "And you told me to let you know when you were being shit at it. So, this is me telling you. Less peace broker, more righteous avenger, if you please?"

"God, you're adorable."

Sandy's glare turned icy.

Miller gulped. "I mean, yes, sir. Absolutely. I'll get right on that."

"Be sure that you do." Sandy's head dropped back and he closed his eyes. "I just wish . . ." He paused and shook his head. "Oh god, I'm so fucking ridiculous. Thirty-four and I'm still wanting his approval. What the hell is wrong with me?"

Miller reached for him. "You wish that he'd done it for you guys? That he'd maybe said he loved you or did a better job of an apology?"

Sandy sagged against Miller's side. "Yeah, all of that."

"I know, sweetheart. And you absolutely fucking deserve to hear those things. I guess you just have to decide how much you're prepared to compromise. I'll back you either way."

Sandy scooted to his stomach and propped himself on his elbows. "Thanks. I'm sorry for being on such a downer. The whole thing pisses me off and I'm so sorry to add to your troubles at the moment. You've got quite enough going on. But I'm glad I'm here. I needed this . . . I needed you."

Miller smiled and slipped a hand around the back of Sandy's neck, pulling him close for a kiss. "Where else would I be? I like you in my bed. I like you in my life. I like that you invite me into your life, especially on days like today. I like what we're doing with Geo, together. I love you so much."

Sandy's heart surged in his chest and he laughed, running his finger over the cute splash of freckles on Miller's shoulder. "I don't think I'll ever get used to hearing those words. I love you too." He lowered his head and immersed himself in the taste of this man who had come to mean so much to him, so much more than could possibly be wise or sensible.

When they broke apart, Sandy ran a finger over Miller's lips. "You give my heart a soft place to fall, do you know that? You're a good man. You're sexy as hell, and I couldn't be happier."

Miller grabbed his fingers and pressed a kiss to them. "I hope I don't disappoint you."

Sandy shrugged. "People always disappoint each other. It's life.

Getting through it is what matters. Speaking of which." He fell back on the bed with a sigh. "Something else happened today."

"I think I know."

"You know?" Sandy propped back up on one elbow. "Oh, shit. Of course. It's part of your job, right? Advising committees on that stuff."

Miller nodded. "I was copied on the complaint, but I didn't want to raise it until you were ready. It's bullshit, Dee, but that doesn't mean it won't be taken seriously. The family are bigots with an axe to grind, but they're also grieving and the hospital will want to be careful. It's not a good mix and the family may not back down."

Fuck. Sandy had hoped it might blow over. "So what's going to happen?"

"The hospital doesn't usually delay on these sorts of complaints about staff. They'll want a quick resolution to avoid media involvement. The meeting's set for next Thursday. You'll be seen separately from the family. The invite should already be in your inbox. You can take a support person with you."

"I want you."

"I . . ." Miller pulled a face. "I can't, Dee."

"What?"

"Like you said, it's my job to advise these committees. I won't be able to do that in this instance or be your support person. There's a conflict of interest: *you.* I'm your *boyfriend*, Dee."

Shit. Shit. Shit. "Of course. Fuck, sorry. I forgot. But . . . you mean you won't be able to say or do *anything* to help me?" Sandy's stomach dropped as he realised he'd been assuming Miller would be beside him.

"I'll copy them all the relevant policies and legalities, so you can be sure I'll make clear my *unstated* opinion, but gender and dress codes are grey areas, you know that. I hope they'll do the right thing and there'll certainly be options for you to appeal if it doesn't go your way, but I can't interfere."

Sandy's mouth fell open. "Interfere? How about just support?"

Miller gave him a look. "You know I support you."

Sandy said nothing because . . . well, fuck. "But they can't fire me for wearing a skirt, can they? That's discrimination."

"Ordinarily, yes. And no, they can't fire you without getting in a lot of hot water and they certainly have no say in your off-duty dress. But the hospital has uniform policies for on-the-clock time, and that complicates things, especially when employees are dealing with the public. Your department has a policy that stipulates the wearing of scrubs for clinical work and suitable dress for other departmental or court work. With only you and the pathologist most of the time, you've been pretty much free to decide between you what *suitable* means." He grimaced. "That might change after this, depending on what the committee finds."

Shit. "So I'm going to have to justify myself all over again. I mean, if I'd been wearing trousers, they wouldn't even be touching this, right? So this is clearly about the skirt. Can't I get them on that, somehow, if they try to screw with me?"

Miller looked pained. "I'm sorry, Dee. I just don't know. Every institution is facing these kind of gender considerations now, and none are ready for it."

"So we challenge it," Sandy stated. "We can't just let them get away with bowing to ignorant public pressure."

A worrying flush hit Miller's cheeks and he dipped his chin. "I don't know how much help that would be. Getting political is always threatening to committees like this. They might respond by digging their heels in. Creating waves might turn their opinion against you. Chances are they'll do the right thing if we just give them enough rope and tick their boxes."

"Chances are? Give them some rope? Tick boxes? What the hell, Miller? Our community never gets *anything* simply given to them, because people need their eyes opened to see what's right in front. Look at Geo. We've always had to fight." He stabbed his finger at his own chest. "*I've* always had to fight. It's what we do. We don't just trust the world to do the right thing. You should know this. People living with disabilities often have to fight to be seen and heard too."

"I know, I know," Miller said patiently, and Sandy wanted to box his bloody ears.

He wasn't sure if it was because he was already riled from his father or because Miller was being almost purposefully obtuse. He hated to think the latter because . . . well because that fucking changed so much in Sandy's world he felt sick to his stomach.

"There are policies in place." Miller was still talking. "Processes you can go through if the decision doesn't go your way." He ran his fingers through Sandy's hair, but Sandy just couldn't.

He pulled away. As ridiculous as it was, because he really did understand Miller's predicament, he felt monumentally let down. Why couldn't Miller understand that this complaint encapsulated Sandy's whole life struggle. Back down and trust someone else—a committee no less—to do the right thing? Was he fucking serious?

Down the hall the front door opened and closed, followed by sounds of plates and banging in the kitchen. Geo was home and had found the leftover Chinese. Sandy crossed to the bedroom door and pushed it closed, lowering his voice.

"What's wrong with doing our best to challenge and make sure that first decision is the right one?" he said, returning to sit on the edge of the bed, well away from Miller. "So we don't have to go through all your *processes* and waste everyone's time?" He heard the defensiveness and hurt in his voice, but he was past caring. "You know what, don't worry. Cam will come with me."

Miller didn't appear overly happy. "Okaaaay. Just . . . maybe warn him to be . . . diplomatic. Politics and subtlety aren't exactly his strong point."

Sandy's gut clenched and a cascade of disturbing emotions formed a solid ball in his throat. *What the actual fuck?* He stared Miller down who was starting to look more than a little uneasy. Damn right.

"Diplomatic?" he snapped. "We both know Cam doesn't possess that gene. And why the hell should he try? Everything about this is *political*. The politics of gender and sexuality. Cam has standing and respect in this hospital. He *also* happens to wear makeup, and I'm damn sure you won't find that in any dress code for the male nursing staff. And that means he has a vested interest in the outcome of this meeting. What if the next person complains about *him?*"

"No one would dare." Miller chuckled.

A wintry chill stole through Sandy's chest. "Don't you fucking dare joke about this."

Miller's smile disappeared and his eyes flew wide. "Dee, I didn't mean it that way. You know I love Cam. Look, I— Ugh. Why are we arguing?"

And Sandy was startled into realisation. Miller was genuinely surprised at the force of his reaction. Did he not get how important this was? And what did that mean for Sandy whose life went against the grain in this way, every single day? His looks, his sexuality, his dress, his gender.

He'd thought Miller understood. He'd believed Miller's hands were a safe place for his heart. But now he wasn't so sure. When push came to shove, rather than fight alongside him, Miller was dissembling. He was running. Blowing fucking processes and policies up Sandy's arse and hiding behind *vested interests,* of all fucking things.

Unfair? Maybe. But this mattered to Sandy. This decision threatened a huge chunk of himself he'd fought his entire life for. Miller was supposed to love him, and Sandy didn't know how the fuck to hold those two things together.

"Do you think Cam won't be worried how any decision might affect him?" He tried to make Miller understand. "Can you imagine Cam without his makeup? And you're sitting there saying it's fine for this committee to put my gender up for debate, but I can't get political in return and challenge their very right to do that? That I should play nice? Well, fuck that." *Shit.* He hadn't meant to shout.

Miller blanched. "I didn't mean . . . Fuck." He blew out a sigh. "Look, I shouldn't have joked about Cam. I'm sorry. I'm just saying that I know how these committees work. It's my job, Dee. If you get their backs up, you won't get the outcome you want. I know you don't want to play their game, as it were. But the bigger question is, do you want to win or not?"

"Not at *any* cost." Sandy couldn't believe he was having to defend himself. "Plus, I could play nice and still get slapped on the hand and told not to wear a skirt, right?"

Miller nodded. "It's a risk."

"So why the hell should I make it easy for them?"

Miller threw up his hands. "Okay, okay. I'll stay out of it. I shouldn't have said anything after everything with your dad. You're upset—"

"Don't you dare," Sandy warned in a low voice. "Don't you dare suggest I'm not thinking clearly."

"I'm not," Miller backpedalled. "I just really don't want to fight about it. I was only giving you an insider opinion. And I'm sorry I can't be there with you in the room."

Sandy was too, but for a lot more reasons than Miller was likely thinking right then. It was a huge crash from the warmth of their post lovemaking just a few minutes before, and Sandy wondered if they were on the same page at all, at least about what truly mattered to him.

"I don't want you to get hurt, Dee."

Too late for that. But he never dreamed it would be Miller, not his dad or the complaint, which inflicted the greatest hurt of the day.

"I only wanted to explain how these complaint committees tended to work, like it or not."

Sandy quietly seethed. "Okay, so just for the sake of curiosity, what else would you suggest I do other than muzzle Cam?"

"I didn't tell you to muzzle him."

Sandy arched a brow.

Miller held his palms up again. "Fine. For curiosity's sake, but don't hate me for this since you did ask. If I was advising anyone else in the same position, I'd suggest that between now and the committee's decision"—

Oh hell no.

—"it would be sensible to try and keep a low profile, avoid any similar incident. Keep it to scrubs in the department until after the meeting and just be . . . careful."

The worst thing about that bitch of an answer? The earnest look Miller wore, like he actually believed that what he was saying was okay.

"Careful?" Sandy's eyes narrowed, his voice flinty. "Careful? I want to make sure I understand exactly what you mean. You're saying no skirts or dresses?"

Miller looked like he'd suddenly discovered a pin-less grenade in his hand and wasn't sure where to throw it or which way to run. "Just until the decision."

"What about to the actual meeting? What would be your advice there, Mr Governance Coordinator?"

Miller's expression took on a slightly panicked look. "Look, I know you hate the idea—"

"Answer the question."

Miller sighed. "If it was me, I wouldn't."

The knot in Sandy's throat almost choked him. "I thought your job was to make sure *committees* followed moral, ethical, and anti-discriminatory guidelines?"

"It is. I just—"

"But you think telling me to toe the cis-gender line to *appease* the committee so they won't be *put off* by my dress is the way to encourage those guidelines?"

Miller's gaze skittered around the bedroom like a trapped blowfly. "I want you to have the best chance."

God love the man for trying, but Sandy was done. He exploded. "What the ever-loving fuck, Miller? Who the hell *are* you? I thought I knew you. I thought you understood what this meant to me."

Miller reached with his arms, but Sandy scooted back with his hands raised.

"Just listen, please?" Miller's eyes pleaded. "You *asked* what I'd recommend, and I *told* you. And remember, this is about me wanting you having the best chance to get the result you want so that you *can* wear skirts. It's not about what I personally believe, because you know I support you."

"Do I?" Sandy rolled away and started picking up his clothes. "Are you listening to yourself, Miller? Do you even remember telling me to wear what I wanted when I met your parents? That you wanted *me to be me*? That you were proud of *me* in any way I presented myself? And now you're telling me to hide that part so I can convince some bullshit committee—after ten years at this hospital with an unblemished record—that I can still be professional while wearing a skirt? A modest skirt and jersey, Miller? Not fishnet stockings and a fucking G-string."

"I know that. I told you. It's a bullshit complaint—"

"If it's bullshit, then why should *I* have to *tone down and toe the line*. Jesus, my father would be so proud of you." *Shit.*

The blood drained from Miller's face and his mouth fell open. "Don't you dare compare me—"

Goddammit. "I wasn't. I'm sorry. But even today, he accused me of wearing the skirt simply to irritate him."

"But didn't you, to a degree?" Miller slammed his eyes shut. "Fuck. I'm sorry."

But it was too late. The statement stung, and for a moment Sandy was struck speechless. It didn't matter that it was even partly true.

Sandy lifted his chin, his heart in pieces. "You don't get to judge me. Do you know how many times I've been asked to *tone down*, to please not wear a skirt today? Or how many times I've been given that do-you-have-to *look* by boyfriends, family, even friends, over the years?" He struggled to keep his hands from shaking as he stuffed the last of his clothes into his bag. "I thought you were different, Miller. You seemed to accept me exactly as I was. I never thought I'd be hearing those kind of words from you."

Miller swung his feet off the bed and reached for Sandy, but again Sandy brushed him off.

"Goddammit, I'm screwing this up," Miller pleaded.

"Yes, you are." Sandy snapped his bag shut and spun to face him. "I get that you can't be with me at the meeting, although I must admit I'd hoped if we were *that* important to each other, it might've been worth some professional risk. But I'm not going to pretend any of this other bullshit is okay. I think it's best if I leave."

"No! Shit. Don't do that." Miller reached for his canes. "Please, stay. I didn't mean to upset you, Dee. I just . . . fuck, I don't know what to say. I'm sorry, okay?"

But Sandy wasn't feeling it. He sat on the chair to put his shoes on and to avoid looking Miller in the eye.

"No, I don't think staying is a good idea," he said, getting up and walking to the door. "I don't know what just happened here, Miller, but I can't pretend I liked any of it, and I don't know where we go from here. I've got thinking to do. And I'm going to need to talk to some people about the meeting, my union rep, Cam, and get some legal advice as well. And you've got Geo, your training, the series, not to mention your *job*."

"At least let me give you some names," Miller offered quietly. "I'm so sorry, Dee. I didn't mean for this to happen. Please, let me help?"

Sandy wanted so badly to say yes, but the problem with having high expectations was the hellishly long fall. Miller might be sorry he'd hurt Sandy, but Sandy wasn't at all sure Miller truly understood exactly what he was sorry about. And that was a problem, a very big problem. Lesson learned.

"Thanks, but I'm sure Cam will have all that I need. I'll talk to Geo on the way out, tell him I've got work stuff to do or something. I'll drop by tomorrow to see him for a bit, but I'll call to check when it suits."

Miller stared at him in utter confusion and that said it all. "Dee, please don't do this. You know you can come anytime."

Sandy took a big breath and blew it out slowly. "I'll come while you're at training. It'll be . . . easier."

"Easier? Dee, what's happening here?" There was no mistaking the desperate sheen to Miller's eyes.

And Sandy wanted so badly to fall into his arms and tell him everything was going to be okay. But he couldn't.

"This is just a stupid argument, right?" Miller struggled to his feet and it was all Sandy could do not to race over to help. "We can talk about it when we've both had time to think. This is fixable, isn't it?"

God, Sandy hoped that was true, but his heart wasn't so sure. He stepped close and cradled Miller's chin. "I do love you. More than anything." He pressed a chaste kiss to the corner of Miller's mouth, steeled himself, and turned away.

"Jesus, Dee. I love you so much. We'll get through this. Remember what you said. We'll disappoint each other, but it's how we get through that really matters."

The anguish in his voice almost shattered Sandy's resolve, but he kept going, refusing to look, every weighty step a deep slice into his heart.

He reached the hall, pulled the bedroom door softly shut behind him, and prayed Miller was right.

CHAPTER TWENTY

THE SOUND OF SOMEONE BUSY IN THE KITCHEN STARTLED Miller from any attempt to add a few more minutes of sleep to his abysmal total for the night. That is if he'd even slept at all—a state of affairs somewhat borne out by the horror glimpse of his eyeballs in the mirror when he'd gotten up to take a piss, accompanied by a less than flattering ashen pallor. Oh, and an expression that screamed wretched fool with a side-order of miserable douchebag.

How the fuck had he managed to finally profess his love after thirty-five years, have the feelings returned, and then lose the fucking subject of it in the space of less than a week? There had to be some kind of fucking prize for that. A Guinness world record for boyfriend arseholery.

Because no sleep had left a lot of hours for thinking and not much room to hide. There was no escaping he'd fucked up epically.

He grabbed his phone and rolled to his back. No reply to any of his texts to Sandy. He suppressed the urge to chuck the device at the wall and instead typed his millionth apology for the night, added a **good morning** and a **please can we talk**, then willed the thing to buzz a reply as he waited. Yeah right.

He blinked back the tears. *Goddammit.* He was now officially *that* guy—hanging onto his phone, stalking his boyfriend, and begging for acknowledgement. He'd spent most of his life handling emotions on an equivalent scale to zits—the best course of action being to avoid their occurrence in the first place. And if the odd one sneaked through—cleanse thoroughly, adjust your diet, cover it up so no one else can see it, and carry on with your life. Problem solved.

Emotionally stunted? Hell yeah.

Effective? He'd thought so for too many years to count.

But then he'd never been in love. He'd never been out. He'd never had anything to lose that wasn't his choice, not really. He'd avoided relationships not only because he wasn't out, but because he'd known at some level they needed more attention than he was willing to give.

Emotions were soft things, things he couldn't so easily control, things that could derail his goals. Sporting success, getting mobile again, and overcoming his fear of being pitied or invisible were enough to deal with. Clawing his way back to the top in everything he did left no room for emotional entanglements. Emotions screwed with focus, and Miller was all about focus.

A quiet knock on his bedroom door sent his heart leaping. Sandy? Then a tentative voice called his name and his chest fell empty again.

"Come in." He wiggled up to a sit and dragged the duvet over his hips.

A flash of dark curls appeared as the door eased open. "I thought you might like a coffee." Geo shoved a steaming mug out in front of him. "I think it's how you like it. I wasn't sure which pod to use but . . ."

"Oh my god, you're a life saver." Miller waved him in. "Thank you so much. As long as it's caffeine, I'm not fussy."

Geo almost tiptoed across to hand Miller his coffee, like Miller might bite him or something. "It's seven." Geo backed away as soon as he took the cup.

Miller wrapped his hand around the mug and lifted it to his nose. "Mmm, you have no idea how much I need this."

"I thought you might want to be woken," Geo said from the safety of the doorway. "Dane's picking me up around eight thirty for school. I still want to go if that's okay?"

Shit. Miller had been so caught up in his own misery, he'd completely forgotten. When Sandy had gone, he'd crawled out of his bedroom and done his best to ask about Geo's day, but he hadn't really paid attention to the teen's answers.

"Sure," he said. "I'll pick you up after. I've got training tonight, the last one before the game on Sunday, but someone will stay with you. If you need to come home sooner, just let me know."

"Thanks. Dee said he might come while you're gone." Geo gave a weak smile and turned to leave.

"Wait a second." Miller stopped him. "Have you heard from Dee, this morning?"

Geo eyed him warily. "Yeah. He wished me luck for the day."

Fuck. Fuck. Fuck. Miller's world turned decidedly cool. It was clear Dee was up and about, close to his phone, and checking his texts. So yeah, Miller didn't feel ignored at all.

"So . . . you guys had a fight, huh?"

Miller forced a smile. "Yeah. You heard us?"

Geo shrugged. "A little. I'm sorry if my being here—"

Shit. "It wasn't anything to do with you, Geo. Please don't think that. And I'm not blowing smoke up your arse. It was something else, something . . ." He blinked slowly and blew out a sigh. "It was me. I screwed up. I'm not entirely sure of the ins and outs of it because I suck at this relationship shit, but I know at least that much. I just have to figure out how to fix it."

Geo leaned on the doorway and looked down, scuffing his feet on the carpet. "It must be hard for him sometimes, right? I mean the clothes thing, you know?"

He'd heard more than Miller thought.

"He's so fearless," Geo continued, lifting his gaze to lock eyes with Miller, almost like he was willing Miller to understand. "When we talked that first time, I was like, whoa—in total awe of the guy."

Join the club.

"And then there was Cam, and then you coming out to your team . . . and I figured, if you guys could do it, maybe I could too. But all this shit shouldn't be so hard, right? I mean, being bi, gay, whatever. It shouldn't still be so fucking hard. Sorry. I shouldn't swear . . . I guess." He hesitated. "I hope you guys are okay."

Miller tried not to dissolve into tears, because out of the mouths of babes. "Yeah, me too, kiddo. Me too."

Eight hours later and Miller sat staring at the positive affirmation coffee cup his father had given him that read, *I am a Powerhouse. I am Indestructible,* and he just wanted to throw the fucking thing through the window and destruct the ever-loving hell out of it. Like he gave a shit about any of it at that moment. *Powerhouse* and *Indestructible* were the go-to, fail-safe attitudes that had shaped Miller's thinking most of his life, but they did nothing to solve his current dilemma. And just knowing that was fucking with his head. He was flailing in unknown territory.

Powering through had always been his approach. Don't tell me no. Don't say I can't. But work within the system. Never draw attention to my weaknesses. Stay on top. Lead from the front. Never give anyone a reason to see me as anything other than strong and equal. And never be vulnerable.

Never be vulnerable.

He thought of Geo and wanted to mentally slap himself. He'd gotten everything so fucking wrong. All the work Dee had done to get to the point in his life where he was comfortable and proud of who he was, and Miller had pretty much told him to conform to get what he wanted. Yeah, way to go arsehole.

Not even a day had passed and he missed Dee so fucking much. They *always* texted each other in the morning, met for coffee at some point, or shared funny memes and hospital gossip. Without him,

Miller's day dragged, his mind constantly wandered. He missed Dee's voice, his laugh, the taste of his lips, his skin, the way he looked at Miller like he was his favourite person.

Miller had never been anyone's favourite person.

Arriving at work, he'd recused himself from the committee, which set off another round of raised eyebrows. They'd been surprised at Miller but were definitely less understanding of Dee and apparently shocked at them together. *Well, fuck 'em.* He didn't know whether to be royally pissed off or just amused at the wheels clanking in his colleagues' brains.

But it got him thinking again about what Dee said. How Miller's experiences were quite different, and he suspected that living with a disability and being gay was still quite different from being a guy wearing what people considered women's clothes. It was all bigotry, but there was never going to be a one-size-fits-all key to changing it.

Why should Dee have to gender conform to get the stamp of approval? What the fuck did it matter if he wore a dress or pants? Women wore both. What the hell was wrong with people?

He still hoped that at least having the committee aware that their Clinical Governance Coordinator was dating the subject of the complaint might help Sandy's case. And after recusing himself, he'd spent an hour cataloguing and forwarding the committee members as much supporting data in Sandy's favour as he could. After that, he'd begun his marathon desk-staring competition.

He dry-swallowed two more ibuprofens and shook the near-empty bottle. He was taking too many, but with the Aussie game coming up in two days, he couldn't afford for his hip to lock up now.

He glanced again at his phone and fired off another text. **Are you okay? I'm just worried.**

A few seconds later he got a reply.

I'm fine.

Six letters. You'd think there was a fucking shortage. Six letters that screamed Dee wasn't fucking fine at all. But there wasn't much

Miller could do about it until Dee was ready to talk. He risked another text. **Can we please talk? I'm sorry.**

A longer wait this time as the dots appeared and disappeared. Then finally.

I'll stay with Geo while you train but I don't know if I can stay.

Goddammit. The dots came and went again and Miller waited.

I know I'm being a prick not talking but the complaint hearing is stressing me out and I can't deal with anything else.

Miller grabbed the damn coffee mug and threw it in the bin, getting some satisfaction as it shattered. He texted back. **You're not being a prick. I understand.** He hesitated. *Fuck it.* He added, **I love you.**

Dots appeared and disappeared again and then . . . nothing.

It killed him that Dee was stressed and didn't feel he could turn to Miller. What did that say about their chances? Not much if Dee saw him as adding to his stress, not easing it.

He had no one to blame but himself, and he had to turn this around. Didn't matter that he'd only been trying to help, he'd gone about it the wrong fucking way. Boyfriend 101—*listen*.

His office door flew open, hit the bookcase behind, and he almost fell off his chair.

"What the hell's wrong with you?" Cam stormed into the room in his ER scrubs, hair spiked to within an inch of its life, heavily lined tawny eyes glittering with fury, and his, I-just-fucking-dare-you expression glued firmly in place—the one reserved for roaming packs of arrogant surgeons.

Reuben followed behind, looking a little sheepish and somewhat apologetic, but he needn't have worried. It wasn't like Miller hadn't been expecting the visit.

"Oh good Lord, it's an intervention." He threw his pen on the desk and waved them both to chairs. "By all means take a seat."

"Damn right it's an intervention." Cam ignored the chair and stabbed his finger on Miller's desk. "My friend, your *boyfriend*, needed support and what did you do? Tell him to toe the fucking party line and keep a low profile. And maybe, just maybe, they'll all think he's a nice little boy and condescend to *let* him wear whatever respectable outfit he wants to—just like ninety-nine per cent of other hospital employees do *without* needing to ask."

Damn. Miller was in trouble. His gaze sought out Reuben, who merely held up his hands.

"I came along to keep the bloodshed to a minimum and that's it," Reuben said. "This is Cam's show, but for the record, I think you should listen."

It was worse than he thought if Reuben was on board.

Reuben reached for Cam's hand. "Remember, sweetheart, the nice man needs to play against Australia on Sunday, so maybe not break his thick skull like you threatened?"

Cam maintained his furious glare and it was all Miller could do not to wilt.

"No promises." Cam threw himself into the chair next to Reuben, keeping hold of his fiancé's hand. "All right, I'm listening."

Miller folded his arms and rolled his eyes. "You obviously know what happened without me having to repeat it and look more of an arsehole than I already do. Also, I'm not sure it's any of your business."

Cam waved the comment aside. "I happen to like the idea of you looking like an arsehole, and I don't feel that particular imagery can be overdone, so humour me. Second, he's my friend and I care about him, unlike—"

"Cam." Reuben caught his fiancé's eye and arched a brow. "Remember what we talked about."

Cam opened his mouth, no doubt to argue, then closed it again, miracle of miracles. It might not be the eighth wonder of the world, but it had to be close.

"Okay, okay." Cam slumped in his chair, his lips pressed into a thin line, and stared at Miller. "You hurt him."

Miller sighed. "I know. I'm a jerk. I get that."

Cam's brows knit together like he didn't quite know whether to believe Miller or not. "So why the fuck did you tell him to just suck it up and look *normal* till the committee was done?"

"I didn't say anything like that."

"You may as well have."

Miller rolled his eyes. "Don't be so dramatic."

"Miller," Reuben warned.

Miller put his hands on his head and breathed. "Sorry."

"Cam." Reuben eyeballed his fiancé.

Cam's expression puckered like he'd just sucked on a lemon. "Yeah, okay, me too. I just . . . don't get it."

"I'm going to fix it," Miller said with a great deal more certainty than he felt.

"Miller's much more like me than either you or Sandy," Reuben said directly to Cam. "Remember what I was like?"

"Adorable and sexy as fuck?" Cam winked.

Reuben blushed brightly. "Nice of you to think so. But I was also a prize arse. Miller's new at this, like I was. Maybe he wasn't as deep in the closet, but he's hardly clued up about it all either. On the other hand, he's been fighting the stigma of living and playing sport with a disability, something *we* know *nothing* about. But I suspect that involves"—and he glanced Miller's way—"doing everything *not* to draw attention to any difference, exactly the opposite of what we're talking about."

Miller nodded, incredibly grateful for at least some understanding.

But Reuben wasn't done. "You and Sandy have fought this battle your whole lives; it's second nature for you to smell the rat of marginalisation and come out fighting. But in the closet, reactions are always to avoid being seen at all costs. Miller's barely been out a month. I needed some wiggle room too, if you remember? Hell, I asked you to be my dirty secret for too fucking long. It wasn't till later that I really understood exactly what I'd asked you to do and how it hurt you."

Cam leaned over and pressed a kiss to Reuben's lips. "I did it because I loved you."

Reuben palmed Cam's cheek. "Be that as it may, I still hurt you." He turned to Miller who was quietly in awe. The soft side of Cam was well hidden and kind of spectacular.

Cam digested that while still eyeing Miller like week-old fish. "Okay, so I get maybe you *thought* you were helping," he said with a shake of his head. "Newsflash, you weren't."

Miller glanced up at the ceiling, wondering what the fuck he'd done to deserve being counselled by Cameron Wano. "If you've ever thought about being a therapist, don't."

Cam snorted. "Hell no. Holy crap, could you imagine?"

Reuben looked about to have kittens. "Yeah, let's not put that idea in his head."

Miller's shoulders slumped and he let out a long exhale. "I *did* think I was helping. I didn't want him to risk the job he loves. I didn't want them to only see his clothing. And I thought by taking the clothes out of the picture would help do that, that it would let them see *him*. I didn't think past that and I should've."

"Yes, you should've. Because the clothes are also part of who he is," Cam shot back. "They might be background and unimportant in your life, but not in his. They help him process the shifts that happen on the inside. Shifts you know nothing about. Just like your chair and canes are part of who *you* are. Like my makeup. How do you help people see beyond the differences when you hide them? If Sandy was wearing something offensive or sexually revealing or I came to work looking like the lead singer of Kiss, then yeah, conversations might need to be had. But this, Miller? Really?"

Miller grunted. "As I said, I'm a jerk."

"You said it— Ow! What was that for?" Cam spun to Reuben who tucked his foot back under his chair.

"Nothing, my sweet."

Cam narrowed his eyes at Reuben who continued to look the picture of sweet innocence and then continued. "What if someone told you to keep a low profile and just use your chair if you wanted to avoid complaints about taking up an accessible car park?" Cam arched a brow. "And then what if they also wanted you to front up to a committee with all your private X-rays and doctor's reports to *prove* your mobility aids were valid. Would you be happy to play nice?"

Yeah, nah. Miller was spitting tacks at the very thought.

Cam waggled his eyebrows. "Exactly. Then my job here is done." He pushed to his feet, pulling Reuben up with him. "He cares for you, Miller. I've never seen him like this. Don't screw it up."

They locked gazes for a few seconds before Cam tugged on Reuben's hand. "Come on, gorgeous. Take me home and tell me again why I shouldn't be a therapist. I think I'd be awesome. I'd have them flocking to my door for pearls of wisdom. You could retire from chasing that silly little ball around the field and bask in my glory instead. I'd even pay you to run all my social media accounts and answer my phone. I could run couples' retreats and—"

Reuben clamped a hand over Cam's mouth, hoisted him over his shoulder, and threw a smile Miller's way. "We've created a monster." He slapped Cam's butt and headed for the door.

From the hallway, Cam fired Miller an upside-down wink while a hand slid down the back of Reuben's chinos.

"Cam!" Reuben's voice rumbled, followed by a sexy laugh and the slamming of a door that sounded suspiciously like the cleaner's supply closet just up the hall.

Miller closed the door and brooded on Cam's words and his own realisations. Since when had he been so seduced by working the system that he forgot sometimes you needed to grow some balls and just fucking confront it. He'd rarely been the subject of the type of judgement Dee faced. He'd spent a lifetime ensuring he wasn't, never giving anyone anything to question.

Dee had shown a ton of integrity. It was about time Miller measured up. He grabbed his phone and fired off a text. **Can you please stay until I get home from training at nine?**

A good ten minutes of radio silence later, he got a reply.

I'm not sure that's a good idea.

Fuck. Fuck. Fuck. Miller's fingers flew. ***Please don't give up on me.***

More drumming of fingers and gnashing of teeth.

Okay. I'll wait.

Yes! ***Thank you. I love you.***

There was no reply.

CHAPTER TWENTY-ONE

"How about I do that?" Geo grabbed the overflowing kettle from Sandy's hands and tipped half of it out. Sandy stepped back and let the teen take over—his mind was a jittering muddle of nerves as he waited for Miller and whatever that would bring. He should never have agreed to meeting. He'd been hurt and he didn't quite know how to move on from that. It was too soon. They both needed time.

At least Geo seemed happier. His day at school had gone well, and spending time with Jacob without fear of being caught hadn't hurt either. Not to mention there'd been no sign of his father.

"Sorry." Sandy stepped out of Geo's way as he reached for the cups. "Daydreaming." He glanced at the clock. Fifteen minutes till Miller got home. His belly flipped and the bacon and egg buttie he and Geo had cooked for dinner made an unfortunate reappearance in his mouth.

He studied the oven, the wall, the floor, anything to keep from looking at the very spot in the kitchen where he'd experienced some of the best sex of his life. Pathetic didn't even begin to cover it, but . . .

A finger tapped his shoulder and Sandy jerked around. "What?"

Geo bit back a smile. "I *said*, do you want tea or hot chocolate?"

Sandy sighed. "Sorry. Hot chocolate would be great, thanks."

Geo set up, talking as he worked. "You're as bad as he was this morning."

Sandy's ears pricked. "You mean Miller?"

Geo rolled his eyes in dramatic fashion and Sandy was reminded what it was like to have all those hormones raging and not an ounce of patience to go with them.

"Yes, Miller." Geo practically flounced. "Who do you think I meant? Honestly, guys! I thought girlfriends were bad enough, but at least they make you talk."

Sandy snorted and elbowed Geo in the ribs. "Don't try and out-queen a queen, sugar. You'll come undone in spectacular fashion. You're still a baby in this world."

Geo's turn to snort. "Hierarchies everywhere you look."

Sandy swallowed a laugh. "So, educate me about girlfriends, then. I'm a bit light in that area of expertise."

Geo turned and rested his back against the counter while Sandy took a spot opposite on the breakfast bar. "Well, I've only had a couple, although I'm guessing that's a couple more than you." He waggled his eyebrows.

Sandy chuckled. "Watch it."

Geo ignored him. "Still, in my admittedly limited experience, it is true that *some,* but not all girls, can drive you batshit wanting to talk everything to death. Then finally when you think it's all over, they resurrect the argument at a later date only to talk it to death again."

"Sounds positively hideous."

"You'd think so. And it is, I guess. But at least you know what they're thinking, right? You don't have to guess. With Jacob, I have no clue most of the time what goes on in that boy's head."

It was all Sandy could do not to hug the ever-loving shit out of the adorable teen.

"Honestly, I ask him to tell me what he's feeling, and he stares at me like I just asked him to recite pi down to the fiftieth decimal point. Jeez, I love the guy, but really?"

Sandy struggled to contain his laughter.

"Now, if you ask a girl the same question, then more often than not, you better have stocked up for a long winter and that'll just cover the bullet points. But let me tell you, and you better believe it"—Geo eyeballed Sandy—"they never, *never* stop with just the bullet points." He sighed. "But most of the time you don't even have to ask a girl. They can't help but keep you up to date in case you missed a half-second of their riveting emotional life." Geo switched off the boiling kettle and filled the two mugs.

"And your point is?" Sandy thought the boy had a potential career in stand-up if he played his cards right.

"The point is, most girls aren't that extreme, just like not all guys are emotional toddlers. Stereotypes, right? But I've learned something from having girlfriends who liked to talk. I would never have guessed half the shit that went on in their heads. We fucking suck at reading minds." He stared pointedly at Sandy. "All of us. Which brings me to the question of the hour. Have you guys talked yet?"

Sandy's toes curled in his socks. He'd been out grown-upped by a teen, and he couldn't formulate an answer without looking like the coward that he was. Not that he needed to.

"Hmph. Thought not," Geo grumbled. "He was gutted, you know? This morning." He handed Sandy his mug of chocolate. "He knows he screwed up."

Sandy arched a brow and studied Geo. "So I gather you heard a fair bit last night?"

Geo avoided his gaze and cleared the cocoa and milk away. "Enough."

Sandy took a sip of his hot chocolate and closed his eyes for a second to enjoy the dense sweetness. "This is perfect, thanks. And we are going to talk for a bit tonight when he gets home."

"Awesome." Geo almost vibrated in place.

"But no promises," Sandy cautioned. "I doubt you heard enough to know how complicated it is."

"Fair enough, I guess." Geo failed to hide his disappointment. "I just like you guys. You . . . fit, together. And maybe I don't understand but I do know complicated, and I know hurt. And I'd like one day to have something like what you guys seemed to have."

And if Sandy hadn't been leaning on the breakfast bar, he might've stuttered to his knees. He put his cup down, walked over, and rested his hands on Geo's shoulders. "You *do* know those things far too well for your age, and you're right to remind me. I promise Miller and I will talk. But whatever happens, you'll always be able to see me as much as you want, understand?"

The whirr of the electronic lock on the front door jolted Sandy's attention, and he dropped his arms to hide his shaking hands.

"I'm home." Miller's voice was thin and weary.

"I'll just take this to my room." Geo lifted his cup and moved away. "I'll have my headphones on, just so you know. Give you some privacy."

Sandy nodded. "Thanks for the pep talk."

Geo snorted and headed out of the kitchen with a glance to the front door. "Hi, Em. I've got homework. Talk later?"

"Deal." The thud of Miller's satchel hitting the floor made Sandy jump in his boots.

But when Miller rounded the corner of the breakfast bar, his heart squeezed almost painfully in his chest. A slew of conflicting emotions greeted him in Miller's troubled gaze—relief, fear, uncertainty, regret, hope. But underpinning them all, something Sandy didn't dare to acknowledge lest his own heart answer too soon.

"You stayed." Miller was clearly nervous, his hands white-knuckling his wheels, the veins in his neck beating a visible pulse just below the skin.

Sandy fought his instinct to wrap his arms around Miller, instead offering a small smile. "I said I would."

Miller sucked in a breath. "I know, I just . . ." His dark-circled eyes appeared overly shiny, their bright green, dull and leaden. They bounced around the room avoiding Sandy entirely, causing his breath to catch in his lungs. "Well, I wouldn't have blamed you if you hadn't." Miller let go his wheels, shuffled in his chair, and placed his hands carefully in his lap.

Sandy frowned. "You're in pain."

Miller looked surprised at the comment. "Oh, it's nothing. Just took an unexpected hit."

"You need to get out of that chair. Come on." Sandy brushed past him into the lounge and took a seat at the far end of the couch.

Miller spun and followed, transferring to the other end of the couch with obvious discomfort. Sandy handed him a few pillows to shove under his legs, which he accepted with a guilty nod.

"How bad is it?" Sandy already knew the answer from the tightness around Miller's mouth.

Miller broke eye contact to straighten his sweats. "It'll be fine for the game."

"That's not what I asked. One to ten, how bad?"

Miller groaned and looked up. "For a guy who wasn't answering my texts, you're pretty pushy."

Shit. Sandy acknowledged the point. "You're right, sorry."

Miller's eyebrows gathered in. "No, it's fine. I shouldn't have said that. It's a six, maybe seven. But that's only because it's fresh. I've taken something for it. I'll be right tomorrow."

"Uh-huh." Sandy couldn't help the frustrated shake of his head. "You can't keep doing this to yourself, Miller, you need—" He swallowed the rest of what he was about to say and took a slow breath. "Jesus, there I go again. I'm sorry. It's none of my business. Your body, your decision."

Miller flinched. "Don't do that, Dee. I want it to be your business. More than you know."

Sandy glanced away, his throat thick with emotion. This was exactly what he'd wanted to avoid. "Miller, I—"

"Just listen, please? Can you do that for me?" Miller dragged his fingers through all those red waves, still damp from the shower.

Sandy's pulse picked up and that jittery feeling returned to his belly. Like he might give in on the slightest puff of an apology. But it felt too soon. He wanted to hang on to his anger a while longer, wrap it around like a warm blanket to get some distance, just in case. He'd been here before, with other men struggling to understand. He was tired of the fight. Tired of explaining.

He was ready to leave when Geo's words came back to him—*we suck at reading minds.*

Fuck. He stayed in his seat and gave a half-hearted shrug. "Okay, I'm listening."

Miller visibly sagged with relief, and that hope in Sandy's chest burst back into life.

"Thank you." Pink flushed in Miller's cheeks, hiding all those spangled freckles. "I've missed you, Dee. I know it's only been one fucking day, but not having things right between us . . ." He hesitated. "Well, it made everything crystal fucking clear. Knowing I couldn't just pop down and see you, or call you, or have one of your nutty texts arrive to brighten my day? It did my head in, Dee."

Sandy laced his fingers to stop them creeping over to Miller's. He hadn't been alone in the feelings he'd fought all day, after all. Ignoring Miller's texts had nearly cost him his sanity, to the point that Ed had sent him off early to lunch with a flea in his ear and a warning to get his head out of his arse and get his love life sorted, or Ed would do it for him.

"I warned you I'd fuck this relationship up." Miller rubbed his hands up and down his thighs. "Shocker, right? I don't expect forgiveness, but I am so, so sorry. I could've, *should* have done and said better. But it came from ignorance and habit, and from the way I've lived my life.

"I've become part of the system I'm supposed to monitor, just like you said—"

A flutter started low in Sandy's belly.

"I didn't even try to see it from your side. I just barrelled in like I always do, looking for a quick solution that avoided any drama. I thought I was protecting you from unnecessary judgement, but I ended up hurting you instead. I forgot how fucking strong you are. Turns out I was the coward."

Sandy swallowed hard, blinking back tears. It was much more than he'd hoped for.

But Miller wasn't finished. "I hate being the centre of attention for anything but my successes, and certainly never for my differences. But it means I've forgotten that sometimes we need to fight too. I tried to take that away from you, something Cam reminded me of."

Sandy startled. "Cam? Don't tell me he— Ugh. Of course he bloody did." Sandy was gonna kill him.

"And Reuben."

"Reuben too?" *What the hell?*

Miller shrugged. "But that's a story for another time."

Sandy could only imagine.

Miller stared at his hands for a minute. "I'd already gotten there on my own." He looked up. "But they were still right. What I suggested would've taken your voice and everything you've fought for. I don't ever want to do that. I want to support you one hundred per cent, in every way I can. And I'm so sorry that it took this to wake me up, baby."

Sandy's throat closed over and he took a minute to let Miller's words sink in before responding. "I should've said more at the time and I didn't; that's on me. But I've trusted men before only to be let down, and I wanted to believe you were different. I *did* believe you were different. I believed enough that I fell in love with you." He looked directly at Miller. "That's why I was so upset."

Miller looked crushed. "I know. God, I was such an idiot. If I could go back—"

"No." Sandy reached for Miller's hand and he latched onto it like a lifeline. "You know, I think I was almost looking for it, waiting for it to happen, waiting to be proved right. So when I caught even a glimpse, I overreacted. I'm not denying it hurt, just saying I've been nursing the hurt when I should've just stayed and talked it through at the time. I'm sorry for that. Geo helped, actually."

Miller's eyes widened comically. "Geo?"

Sandy chuckled and squeezed Miller's hand. "Yeah, that kid's got potential. He said, and I quote, 'we suck at reading minds, all of us.'"

"Smart kid."

"Yeah, it was enough to make me realise I hadn't bothered to understand *why* you believed the things that you said." His thumb drew soft circles on the back of Miller's hand. "I'm sorry I avoided you, and I get why you said what you did, even if it wasn't the right thing for me. It's . . . okay."

Miller's frown eased but didn't go away. "But are we?" He searched Sandy's face, and this time, Sandy didn't even have to think.

"Yeah, I'm pretty sure we'll be just fine."

"Oh, thank fuck for that." Miller looked to where their hands were joined, shuffled sideways on the couch, and gave Sandy a small tug. "Come here."

Sandy stretched out in Miller's arms, the sense of coming home almost overwhelming. He buried his nose in Miller's chest and gave a small, contented sigh. "Thank you for keeping on telling me you loved me, even when I didn't say it back. I do love you, Miller, and I do still believe you're different from those other men. I just forgot for a minute that it didn't mean you were perfect."

Miller chuckled, the sound bubbling deep in his chest against Sandy's cheek. "Yeah well, hold on to that thought, because I might not make the same mistake again, but there are a million other ways I can still screw things up without breaking stride."

Sandy leaned back to look at him. "I dunno. I think maybe we needed this to make it real, yeah? We've got a lot of baggage between us, you and I."

Miller brushed a lock of hair from Sandy's eyes and tucked it behind his ear. "We do, sweetheart. But can we agree to unpack it together next time, without the in between needing to think bit?" He leaned forward to brush their lips together, just a whisper, a question.

"Yeah, I think we can do that." Sandy returned the kiss, groaning at the first taste of Miller back on his tongue, fresh and clean, a hint of mint with the sweet edge of that electrolyte drink he favoured after training. The jolt of familiarity punched hard—what he'd nearly thrown away.

A deep groan rumbled from Miller's throat as his hand moved over the swell of Sandy's arse to lift and pull him closer, the power of those shoulders.

Sandy's fingers trailed across Miller's back and up his bicep.

Miller crushed him to his chest, his body trembling. "Holy shit. I thought I'd lost this, lost you. I love you so fucking much."

"Me too." Sandy held on, giving in to his own tears. "Me too."

Dancing hazel eyes appeared over the back of the couch, and a wide smile lit up under a mass of dark curls and teenage intensity. "Oh, thank fuck for that." Geo regarded the two of them tangled in each other's arms with obvious relief. "Maybe now we can all get some sleep." His disappearance was closely followed by the sound of the refrigerator kicking in. "Anyone else for ice cream?"

Sandy pressed a hard kiss to Miller's lips. "Make it three."

CHAPTER TWENTY-TWO

"OH. MY. FUCKING. GOD," CAM SCREAMED IN SANDY'S EAR from the seat behind. "This game is the bomb. How have I never watched it live before? These guys are ridiculous!"

The screech of steel on steel reverberated around the stadium as three wheelchairs slammed together and someone hit the floor.

"Because you're usually at the drop-in centre on a Sunday," Reuben shouted equally loudly in Sandy's other ear. "And I . . ."

The rest of what he said was lost to a huge shout from the packed stadium as the Wheel Blacks scored again, thanks to Miller's lightning reflexes and another Mexican wave circled the crowd.

"Aussie, Aussie, Aussie, oi, oi, oi," screamed the defiant Australian contingent in reply, and Sandy couldn't keep the huge grin from his face.

His mother grabbed his hand as the Wheel Blacks made another charge for the goal, and then she, Lizzie, and Miller's mum all leapt to their feet shouting, "Go, go, go."

The two mothers had bonded almost immediately, much to Sandy's amusement and to the horror of Miller who saw endless teasing and mother arseholery in their futures. But then again Sandy was well used to that.

On Sandy's other side, Geo whooped and hollered while keeping his arm wrapped tightly around his boyfriend's waist. Jacob was much quieter. He had a polite manner and a shy smile, content to be held and fussed over by the more gregarious Geo. It was so damned cute it made Sandy's teeth ache in their sockets.

As time passed, and with no attempt at contact from his dad, Geo was looking more comfortable. His therapist was happy with how he was doing, although she warned it would all depend on his father. Geo had contacted a couple of relatives on his mother's side, people he felt safe with, and so far, that connection looked promising.

Sandy hoped the calm would last, and everyone was holding their breath for the social services appointment at the end of the week. It might only be a heads-up meeting to pre-empt any fuckery on behalf of Geo's dad, but it still sat like a prickle in their feet and Sandy couldn't wait for it to be over.

"Block him, block him," Sam shouted at Miller's team on the court. He and his father sat on the other side of Jacob, juggling a huge carton of popcorn that had been making its way around the group. Dane's wife had stayed back at their restaurant so he could watch his brother play.

"Penalty, penalty!" Dane's arm shot up, dumping a handful of popcorn onto the head of Michael, seated in front.

Oops. Sandy swallowed a laugh at the sight of the impeccably turned-out doctor smothered in caramel popcorn.

Dane apologised profusely, but Michael waved it off with a huge grin. He shook the sticky stuff free, turned, and caught Sandy's eye. "You have a very exuberant family," he barked. "Makes me homesick. It's as bad as ice hockey with about as many crashes. The doctor in me is horrified. The sports fan is fucking thrilled."

"Hey, ref. Put your glasses on." Mark shot to his feet in front of Sandy as the referee allowed a dubious Australian goal, and the small Aussie cheerleading section erupted in a roar.

"You're blocking my view." Sandy grabbed Mark's jacket and tugged him back into his seat.

Ed patted Mark's thigh affectionately. "Maybe you can ticket his car later if that makes you feel better?"

Mark replied with a dazzling smile and landed a loud smacking kiss on Ed's cheek. The poor man fired beetroot.

To Miller and Sandy's surprise, almost all their friends and family had turned out for the first game of the series. All except Josh, who was attending a police call out with Paris.

And the game hadn't disappointed. Miller was a demon on the court—racing from end to end like he had a fucking rocket up his arse and landing impossible catches—the top scorer by a long run. His dad was ecstatic, setting up a *Tap, Tap, Tap* chant that circled the gym every time Miller scored.

Sandy, on the other hand, cringed with every hit. He watched the way Miller protected his right side and it made him slam his eyes shut every time Miller hit the floor, quietly praying he made it through the game so Sandy could kill him in private for nearly giving him a heart attack.

Miller might look invincible—look like he owned the court—but Sandy knew better. The tightness around his mouth hadn't eased any since Friday night, and there'd been a pallor to his face before the game that Sandy hadn't liked one little bit.

Miller was hurting and Sandy ached for him. But until he'd talk about it, there wasn't much Sandy could do. But he wasn't forgetting Miller's promise to talk after the series, and he'd be holding him to that.

In the meantime he would cheer with the rest of them and revel in the fact they were back on track as a couple, and thank fuck for that. They'd parted Saturday morning after very little sleep and an aching arse on Sandy's part. Miller's day had been packed with official welcomes and a social event to attend with the Australian team. Sandy had dropped Geo at Jacob's for a bit and then taken him on another round of wedding lingerie shopping with Cam, followed by a visit with a drag queen Cam wanted to catch up with, Thelma S Dicksinim. It was the gay full-immersion equivalent of an induction to end all inductions, and Geo's eyes hadn't quite returned to their sockets a day later.

Sandy glanced at the time clock. Thirty seconds left and the scores tied. They were all on their feet, Miller's dad leading the Tap chant for his son who was indicating for the ball. Caught on the line, Jimmy was about to throw it Miller's way when he was slammed from the side and the pass went wild. It missed Miller to land in Australian hands.

Jimmy's curse was loud enough to reach Sydney, and Sandy screamed for a penalty along with everyone else. No such luck. In seconds, Miller had his chair spun and was hunting the ball, flying toward the Australian offensive player and dodging a defensive sandwich hit by centimetres.

"Go, babe, go, go!" Sandy shouted at the top of his voice, earning an amused sideways glance from Miller's dad and a clap on the shoulder from Reuben, who was holding Cam steady as he jumped up and down on his seat.

Miller caught the Aussie player within seconds, flying alongside before turning into him with a clash of wheels. The ball popped out of the player's hands and Miller grabbed it, spun, and barrelled back the other way. Jimmy and Benson headed off a two-pronged Aussie attack, and three seconds later, Miller flew through the goal to score. The full-time buzzer rang around the stadium and the crowd erupted.

On the floor of the gym, wheelchairs poured onto the court and Miller was lost in a sea of congratulations, back-slapping, and hoots of delight. The Australian team gathered in a huddle and, after some commiserations, offered three cheers to the Wheel Blacks and lined up to congratulate the winners, promising retribution at the next game.

Their friends and family rushed down to line up at the edge of the court and join in the rejoicing. A minute later, Miller's head popped up, searching the crowd. When his gaze landed on Sandy, a huge smile broke over his face and he hurriedly wheeled over.

Sandy pushed his coat into Lizzie's hands and raced to meet him, awkwardly straddling Miller's chair with his long legs to land a solid kiss, before peppering Miller's sweaty face with a few more and whispering dirty promises of late-night rewards when he got Miller into bed.

Cameras appeared like magic at their side and journalists pushed microphones in their faces, but Miller and Sandy ignored them. There was no avoiding the images that would hit social media, not to mention the game had been broadcast live on international television, so there was that. No point letting it get to you, and Sandy was damned if he was going to hide his love for his man. He'd even worn his best gauzy floral shirt tucked into skinny black jeans and sexy Doc Martens in anticipation.

But they couldn't ignore the crush of press for long, and eventually Sandy slid off Miller's chair to stand behind as Miller answered a few questions on the game, but none about Sandy. Not that the press let it go easily. They pushed and circled back to their relationship time and again until Reuben finally wandered over and drew them off with a wink over his shoulder. Bless the man.

With a final kiss, Sandy shooed Miller back to his team to celebrate in the locker room. He and the others chatted about the game and random stuff—Miller and Sandy's family getting to know each other—allowing time for the teams to shower and change.

Miller's dad then herded everyone out to the near-empty parking lot so they could clap the team as they exited the stadium on their way to the after-game function. Most players were travelling in their own vehicles accompanied by support people. Sandy was with Miller. He'd worried about assuming the role Miller's father generally filled, but James Harrison had made it clear he wanted Sandy to go.

They didn't have long to wait before a stream of jubilant faces started to appear amid much applause and cheering. Cam had jollied all the waiting friends and family into an honour guard for the Wheel Blacks, and the players' amusement was obvious. Sandy could only watch and laugh. Cam was a force of nature.

A few more rounds of hugs, handshakes, and piss-taking, and Miller was finally able to get free of the throng. Sandy sent him to the car while he headed across the parking lot to the main door of the gym where Geo was busy saying goodbye to Jacob—mostly with his lips and hands from what Sandy could tell.

He was halfway there, checking his phone, humming to himself, and stressing over his first official outing with the team as Miller's boyfriend, when loud shouts jerked his attention up.

A white Subaru Outback had pulled in on an angle in front of the two boys, both front doors wide open, and a man was dragging Geo toward the passenger side while Jacob yelled and tried to free him.

Fuck. Geo's dad.

The arsehole let go of Geo, turned, swayed for a second, then landed a punch to Jacob's jaw that sent him sprawling on the ground. Then he grabbed Geo again.

By then, Sandy was running, shouting Geo's name and calling for help. If Geo's dad got him in that car, there was no predicting what might happen, and Sandy wasn't letting the bastard get Geo someplace there wasn't an audience, not if he could stop him.

As he ran, Sandy heard Geo shout something he couldn't make out but which earned Geo a fist to his head and a thump on his back that sent him reeling toward the Subaru. His dad followed, shoving Geo into the passenger seat while he floundered for a handhold to stop him. Then Geo's dad leaned right in front of his son's face and said something that caused Geo's eyes to snap back to where Jacob still lay on the ground. Whatever was said drained all Geo's fight and he slumped in his seat, his eyes glued to Jacob while his father slammed the door shut and headed unsteadily for the driver's door. The guy looked plastered.

Sandy's heart hammered in his chest. He wasn't going to make it in time. It had all happened too quick and he just wasn't fast enough.

Then Mark sprinted past. "Let me deal with the dad," he shouted. "Try and get that bloody gate barrier down so he can't leave."

Thank Christ. The barrier was closer and Sandy immediately changed direction. To his right, Mark shouted for someone to call for the police and ambulance. Several people immediately pulled out their phones—one guy choosing to film what was happening rather than call anyone, for fuck's sake.

But Sandy was almost at the gate, his chest on fire, but he wasn't slowing.

Michael and Dane appeared from nowhere to join the chase. Dane veered to help Jacob who was struggling to get to his feet, leaving Michael to catch up with Mark.

But they were all still too far away, and before any of them could do a damn thing, the Subaru's engine roared and it took off for the still-open gate.

Sandy shouted and waved his arms at the people milling outside the gate's entrance, hoping they'd do something to stop the car, but everyone cleared out of the way instead and Sandy couldn't really blame them.

Tears filled Sandy's eyes as the Subaru drew level and he caught sight of Geo staring at him through the side window, eyes wide. He looked to be trying to work the door handle when his father backhanded him across the head and he slumped in his seat.

No.

The Subaru pulled past Sandy and his feet began to slow, lungs hungry for air, his heart ripping in two. Then an all-too-familiar Nissan shot by, heading for the Subaru, and a new terror lodged in Sandy's throat.

Miller!

He never even turned his head as he passed, laser-focused on the Subaru, and Sandy could only watch in horror as Miller headed to cut it off, putting himself right in harm's way.

"No!" Sandy's roar was lost to the engines and shouts echoing around the parking lot as Miller gained on his target.

Geo's dad caught sight of the Nissan's approach and tried to switch lanes, but the tall shoulder on the footpath threatened to roll him, so he simply floored it instead.

And Sandy could do nothing but watch in dismay—his hands on his thighs, gasping for air, as Miller cut the Subaru off with only metres to spare from the gate. With nowhere to go, the Subaru slammed into the side of Miller's Nissan with a sickening crunch before rebounding and coming to rest against the fence.

Miller! With his heart in his throat, Sandy sprinted for all he was worth.

The Subaru driver's door flew open and Geo's dad staggered out, but Mark and Michael had caught up and were right there to meet him. Stunned and holding his chest from the impact of the airbags, he was easily subdued, and Michael held the guy down while Mark headed for Geo still sitting in the passenger seat.

That meant Sandy could focus on one thing and one thing only. Miller. Goddamn the batshit, beautiful nut job. If he'd got himself hurt, Sandy was gonna string him up by his damn balls.

He made it to Miller's car and yanked hard on the driver's door, but it wasn't budging. He hammered on the window. Miller didn't move, but Sandy was sure he heard a groan. Miller's head was turned away, the activated airbag hanging limp in front of him. The back half of the Nissan had taken the brunt of the impact, the rear passenger door staved in while the driver's door was badly buckled.

Sandy hoped that boded well for Miller, but if the man didn't move his fucking head soon or say something, anything, Sandy was going to lose his freaking mind.

"Hey, he'll be okay." Jimmy's chair nudged Sandy out of the way. "He's a tough, stubborn son of a bitch. Don't you fret. Go round the other side. I'll keep trying here."

Sandy turned and stared, blinking in disbelief. Jimmy? Homophobic, dipshit Jimmy? "But you—"

The man flushed a bright red and began to work the door. "Yeah, yeah, I'm not a total arsehole, you know, although I'm not sure Vicki would agree about that at the moment. And I didn't key his damn car. That was David. But you can yell at me later. Now git."

Sandy scooted around the car, checking on Geo as he did, relieved to see the boy sitting on the ground with Michael in attendance. Mark hovered over Geo's dad, who was sitting a good ten metres away, grumbling drunkenly about his rights and some such bullshit that everyone ignored. Sirens rang in the distance as a crowd gathered, including Sandy's and Miller's families, and Jacob's mum who'd witnessed the whole thing from her car parked outside.

A hand landed on Sandy's shoulder just as he got to the passenger door, and he spun to find Miller's dad, his pale face racked with fear.

"Come on, son, let's get him out of there."

Between the two of them, they managed to finally get the passenger door open and Sandy scrambled inside.

"Miller!"

But Miller was silent, slumped in his seat, mouth hanging open, his face running with blood.

No! Sandy couldn't breathe, caught in a panic that threatened to swallow him whole. This couldn't be happening. Not now.

"Miller? Please, sweetheart, open your eyes." Sandy's hands shook like a leaf as he cradled Miller's face.

"Miller?" He pushed the blood-soaked hair back from Miller's eyes and glanced down, relieved to see his chest rise and fall. *Oh, thank God.*

The tears came unbidden. He spun to Miller's dad. "He's alive."

Miller's dad scrambled into the back seat as the Nissan shook with the force of Jimmy's continued attempt to leverage the driver's door open.

"Oh god. Son?" James Harrison pleaded in a desperate whisper.

Sandy wiped the back of his hand across his eyes. "He's breathing, but he won't open his eyes. We need Michael."

"I'll get him." He patted Sandy's hand, crawled back out, and shouted across to Michael.

In seconds, Michael was at the Nissan, demanding Jimmy get the driver's door the fuck open now.

Dane suddenly appeared beside Jimmy's chair.

"How's Jacob?"

"He's fine." Dane wedged a tyre iron into a gap, and the door creaked open a notch. In two more attempts it sprang wide and Michael was right there, running his eyes and hands over Miller while Sandy held Miller's face.

"Please, honey, open your eyes. Are you okay?"

But Miller was out of it, his head lolling in Sandy's hands.

"Goddammit, Miller, you open your eyes and talk to me now or I'm telling Merv about that hoard of Moro bars you've got stashed in your bedside table!"

Michael snorted and Miller's eyelashes flickered.

"Yeah, you didn't think I knew about them, did you?" Sandy stroked Miller's cheek. "I bet they're not on your pre-game nutrition list. That'll earn you a decent fine in the locker room."

Miller groaned and one eye flicked open, then closed.

Yes! Sandy's heart jolted in his chest. "Come on, baby."

"Keep talking," Michael told him. "And hold his head and neck still if you can. The ambulance won't be far."

Sandy glanced up at Michael. "But he's breathing, so that's good, yeah?"

Michael gave a tentative nod. "That's always a good start. The air bag's done its job, but I think his head must've ricocheted off the driver's window and knocked him out. You can see the smack he took here." He indicated a spot just back from Sandy's fingers. "Heads bleed like a bitch."

"But he's gonna be okay, right?" Miller's dad pleaded from the back seat, and Sandy was right fucking there with that particular question.

Michael hedged. "He needs to be checked out thoroughly before

I can promise anything. First impressions are promising, but head injuries are tricky. Let's get him to the hospital and take it from there."

Two ambulances drew alongside, silenced their sirens, and the paramedics quickly split between the two vehicles. "Hey, Doc. Fancy meeting you here," one of the medics teased as he opened his bag. "In the thick of things again, I see? And whaddya know? Mr Cameron Wano as well." Sandy looked up to see Cam standing nearby, ready to help.

"Yeah, yeah," Michael shot back. "We figured you needed the practice, Holford."

The paramedic laughed and jostled Michael out of the way. "How about you let the big boys take over while you tell me what we've got. You go round the other side if you want to be useful."

Sandy felt a tug on his arm and turned to find Miller's dad pulling him away. "Let them work, son," he said, his face ghostly pale, cheeks wet with tears.

Sandy figured they made a matched pair.

They sat down within sight and sound of the medics and were quickly joined by their friends and family as everyone hunkered down to watch the team work on Miller.

Sandy's mother grabbed his hand and squeezed. "He'll be fine, sweetheart."

But all Sandy could see was blood and Miller's slack face somewhere underneath it all.

CHAPTER TWENTY-THREE

GODDAMMIT. MILLER WAS TAKING NAMES. AT LEAST HE WOULD if he could open his fucking eyes to see who was responsible for hammering on his skull and jabbing needle shit into his arms.

"Stay still."

He jolted at the familiar voice as a hand clamped tighter on his arm.

"Fuck . . . you," he croaked with some difficulty.

The voice chuckled. "Well, hello there. Nice to have you back . . . I think."

Michael Oliver.

Arsehole.

"That's Dr Arsehole to you." Michael chuckled.

Fuck, he'd said that aloud?

"Now stay still so they can take this blood or I'll take it myself. And believe me when I say, you don't want that. Sharon here is way more skilled than I am in that department."

"Hos . . . hospital?" Miller tried to wrench his eyes open, but whoever was in charge of those things wasn't taking his call.

"Yes, you're in Auckland Med's ER, *my* territory, so behave. Now we're going to roll you to your side and get this bloody shirt out of the way."

Like hell. Miller fought the hands sliding under his shoulders.

"Miller, you have to let us do this—"

"No," he barked hoarsely.

Michael sighed. "Do I have to get Cam in here to help? It's his day off, but I'm sure he'd be delighted to kick your arse."

Fuck. Miller wasn't that far gone. "No . . . Cam."

"Well, apparently his brain's working just fine," Michael grumbled and a woman laughed.

Miller wasn't impressed. It was all coming back to him. Geo, his dad, the crash. *Fuck.* "Geo?"

"Just give us a minute," Michael said, and the hands disappeared from under Miller's back. A few seconds later one landed on his shoulder and there was the scrape of a chair by his head. "Geo is okay."

Miller felt Michael's hot breath on the side of his face.

Oh, thank god.

"He's shook up, but physically okay. His dad's in custody screaming blue murder. Jacob took a punch to the face, but other than that he's fine. Sandy is climbing the walls in the waiting room along with everyone else waiting to see you, and your team are driving our staff mad with enquiries, particularly someone named Jimmy."

Jimmy? Miller couldn't even. He didn't have the mental acuity to deal with that bag of unlikely snakes. But Geo and Sandy were safe. The air whooshed out of his lungs. His heart could settle with that news. But there was still one question that had his knees shaking.

"Sp-spine?" he choked the question out and one eye finally fluttered open.

"Hey, there you are." Michael smiled from the chair next to Miller's head. "You've got a good shiner in the other eye, so I'd get used to seeing one-eyed for a day or two."

Miller managed a weak smile.

"So that's why you didn't want us to turn you?"

"Yes."

"Okay, well let me reassure you. You took a nice whack to the head, which knocked you senseless for a bit, and you needed a few stitches, but the X-rays on your back and hips were clear—nothing broken, squished, or otherwise compromised. Wiggle your toes for me."

Miller focussed really hard and—yes!

"See, all in working order. Art took a look as well, but you were lucky. There's some bruising, but it's hard to know whether that's from the game or the crash. Either way, things look unchanged where it counts."

Miller gasped with relief and almost fucking cried.

Michael wiped his cheeks with a clean inch of sheet, and yeah, crying like a baby.

"I get it." Michael patted his arm. "Too fucking close for comfort, right? Being a hero isn't all it's cracked up to be."

Miller choked out a laugh through the tears, then eyed Michael and nodded. "Thanks," he said. "You can turn me now."

Michael slid his chair to the side and patted Miller's shoulder. "Good man. We'll get this done and you can have some visitors, a few at a time. We're going to keep you overnight until I'm happy with your head, and then it's home for at least ten days."

"But—"

"Don't even try." Michael narrowed his eyes. "Head injuries need rest. You were completely out to it for a good few minutes, so I'm not bargaining here. Understand?"

Miller nodded. "Sandy . . . first."

Michael grinned down at him. "As if I could stop him."

"Miller! Oh my god." Sandy raced into the room, his eyes going wide when he saw Miller semi-sitting in the bed.

Okay, so he'd needed a fair bit of help to get there, but Miller wasn't staying on his back a minute longer. That, together with the whole hospital thing, had altogether too many associations with his accident.

Sandy threw his coat on the chair and hauled Miller close for a long hug before peppering his face with kisses. "Thank god you're all right." He winced. "Ouch, your eye." He fingered the dressing on Miller's head. "Is it okay?"

Miller grabbed his hand, turning it to kiss the palm. "If having your brain feel like a sponge squeezed into a skull lined with porcupine quills is okay, then yeah, I'm doing okay."

Sandy's brow furrowed. "Yeah, I bet that sucks." He ran his fingers lightly over Miller's forehead.

It felt like heaven.

"Michael said they can't give you much pain relief because of the bang to your head." He pressed his lips to Miller's brow, then buried his face in his neck, sliding his arms all the way around Miller's shoulders. "Is this okay?"

"More than." Miller never wanted those arms to let go. He drank in that familiar citrus smell, let it fan across his face, and bring his body alive. *This.* This was what he needed, *who* he needed. He wrapped an arm around Sandy's lean body as tight as he could manage and held on, his entire body shaking.

He'd come close, so fucking close.

Sandy pulled back. "Miller? Are you okay?"

He looked wrung out and pushed to the edge, and Miller knew he was the cause.

"Sweetheart, what's wrong?"

"I'm fine." Miller gently pressed his bruised lips to Sandy's. "I just need to hold you. I just . . ." His voice broke into embarrassing sobs.

"Shhh." Sandy smoothed his brow. "I've been crawling the walls to touch you as well."

Miller melted against Sandy's chest, those long arms keeping him safe. "I love you, baby, so fucking much."

"I love you too." Sandy kissed his head. "I thought . . . god, Miller, I thought you were dead. You wouldn't wake up, and your face . . . it was covered in blood and—"

It was Miller's turn to reassure. He leaned back against his pillows and cradled Sandy's face. "I'm sorry I scared you. I didn't think. I just didn't want him to get Geo. I—"

"You saved him and you're okay, so that's all that matters." Sandy covered Miller's hands with his own and eyeballed him. "But if you ever, ever do something like that again, I will personally fuck you up. Do you understand me?"

Miller bit back a laugh. "Is that a promise?"

"Don't!" Sandy scowled and stabbed a finger Miller's way. "Just don't. None of this is funny. I can't . . . I can't imagine losing . . ." He ducked his chin and dropped his cheek to Miller's chest, his shoulders shaking.

Fuck. "Hey, baby. Shh. It's okay." Miller stroked those silky locks, thanking all the gods for giving him the chance. "Michael said Geo's okay?"

"Yeah," Sandy mumbled against his chest. "He's with our parents, who—" He pulled up with a distinct scowl on his face. "—are getting on altogether too well for my liking. Our mothers and my sister have bonded like damn superglue, and your dad has spent the last hour explaining the finer points of vegetable gardening to me, lauding the fact that he might finally have a *son,* a *son* in case you missed that little titbit, who showed any interest. All that while your damn brother Dane, watched on with a smug smile and did absolutely nothing to help. And I'm not positive, but I think I might've agreed to let him dig a starter garden in your backyard for my education. I'm a brussel sprout short of a fucking meltdown, I can tell you."

Miller snorted. "I'm impressed. You work fast."

"It's not funny. I have to go through with it now. You should've seen the look on his face." Sandy's gaze narrowed. "And I'd have thought you'd be horrified at the *son* part?"

"And yet weirdly I'm not." Miller's heart sang. "Are you?"

Sandy's mouth contorted oddly, then he sighed. "Not nearly as much as I think I should be."

Miller shuffled over and patted the bed. "Come here."

Sandy arched a brow and glanced at the door.

"Please. I need a full-body hug."

"Hah! Is that what they're calling it these days?" He studied Miller for a second, then a sly grin stole over his face. "All right. But just for a minute. I have to let the others come in or my Harrison family ranking will slip, vegetable gardening acolyte or not."

He eased himself onto the bed next to Miller, slung an arm over his chest, a leg over his thigh, and Miller's whole world settled on its axis. He sighed and let the feel of Sandy's long body ease his rattled soul—Sandy's breath warm on Miller's neck, his lips trailing kisses along Miller's jaw, murmurings of soft nothings and promises of love filling Miller's ears.

He sank against the line of Sandy's body and thought, *home.*

How had he lived without this? He'd been such a bloody fool. All those years living half a life.

He thought of the strange peace he'd felt looking up from the game to see their two families and their friends grouped together and watching. And the fear that had gripped his heart when he saw Geo's father dragging him away from Jacob. And the panic when he'd woken and thought his back was gone completely. And the burst of love in his heart when Sandy raced into his room—more, so much more than he'd ever imagined.

And with all those thoughts, Miller's head suddenly cleared like a fog lifting. The sharp angles and soft curves that made up his life appearing in stark relief. And with that understanding came a fierce clarity.

"We made the six o'clock news by the way," Sandy said, his head still on Miller's chest. "My blouse looked fucking awesome."

CHAPTER TWENTY-FOUR

SANDY STARED AT HIS REFLECTION IN THE MIRROR AND HIS mood soured. Maybe Miller had been right, after all. He should just wear fucking trousers and be done with it.

His phone buzzed and he glanced over to the bed. Yet another good luck text. All their friends and relatives who knew had called or texted. It meant so much, more than he could possibly explain.

But they couldn't help with this. He stared back at the mirror.

D-day for his meeting with the complaints committee. He plucked at the dark green pencil skirt, black fitted tee, black jacket, black tights, black Doc Martin's, and long jade necklace. His blond hair gleamed under the lights of Miller's bedroom, and with nothing but lip gloss on his face, he looked clean-cut and professional, or at least that's what he thought.

But was he just deliberately poking the hornet's nest ? Risking the decision he wanted for the chance of a big fuck-you to the system?

Maybe?

Probably?

He didn't have a damn clue. It was hard to see it objectively anymore.

"Stop second-guessing yourself." Miller steadied himself on his canes in the doorway and ran a heated gaze over Sandy. "You look bloody fantastic."

Sandy's cheeks burned under the approval and he flashed Miller a determined smile. "If I get an erection wearing this skirt, it's gonna be a bitch to hide. Besides, you've had your allocated quota for the day."

They'd started the morning with a lazy blow job followed by a slow, syrupy fuck—their first sex since Miller's discharge three days before, and Sandy's arse was aching nicely, thank you very much. He'd insisted Miller just lie there and think of England while he loved on him as he'd been desperate to do for nearly five days. Bloody epic.

The head injury was still messing with Miller's balance, but he was improving fast. There was colour in his face, a little too much bruising still around the eyes, but the eyelid was open and his hip pain was easing thanks to the enforced rest. He was benched for the remainder of the trans-Tasman series, and Sandy couldn't be happier, although he was careful not to gloat too hard. He wasn't looking forward to the return of Miller's heavy training schedule, even though he knew Miller was likely itching to get back even if he'd been quiet about it.

"I'm thinking I should wear trousers, like you said." He brushed out his skirt and centred the zip at the back.

Miller peered around Sandy's shoulder to look in the mirror. "Absolutely not. You look gorgeous, and so damn hot." He trailed his fingers up Sandy's thigh to palm his dick through the woollen material, and his eyes popped. "You're commando, you dog."

Sandy flushed. "It makes me feel . . . brave. Too much, you think?"

"No. If that's what you need, do it. Although you better keep those long sexy legs of yours crossed, or there'll be a little too much explaining to do, and I'm not sure you could dig your way out of that one." He buried his teeth into Sandy's shoulder, causing him to shiver. "And I think you should wear this to bed tonight."

Sandy pressed back into Miller's groin, smiling at the hard ridge that bucked up against his arse. "Got plans, have you?"

"Mmm." Miller nipped along the curve of his neck. "Lots and lots of plans."

Sandy hadn't been home except to get some clothes since the whole attempted kidnapping thing and, quite frankly, was struggling to find a reason not to keep it that way. Miller was dropping hints like crazy about Sandy renting his apartment and saving on two mort- gages, but Sandy worried it was still a bit too soon. Rollercoaster didn't even begin to describe the last week, and then there was Geo to consider.

Speaking of which, he caught a flash of colour in the mirror and—

"Oh my god, I'm scarred for life." Geo's pale face appeared in the doorway. "You guys need a warning sign or something on that door. Or, here's a novel idea: close it." He disappeared back up the hall, muttering something about bleach and old people making out.

Miller turned to the door with a chuckle. "He seems to be doing okay."

Sandy followed his gaze. "Yeah, for now. But I think we should keep those daily therapy sessions for another week, maybe more. It helps that his dad can't get bail—gives Geo some time. And if that social services woman plays fair tomorrow, we're in the clear."

"*We*. I like the sound of that."

"Oh, do you now?" Sandy turned and leaned into Miller's kiss. "I'm surprised you let him stay home from school today, Mr I Don't Need Any Help. Your mum offered to stay with you while I'm out."

Miller shrugged. "I don't need to be babysat by *anyone*, but I figured he could use the space at the moment. It was a good excuse."

"Hmm." Sandy ran his fingers through those beautiful red waves that had grown almost to Miller's shoulders. "Don't cut this." He pushed a disobedient few strands back from Miller's bright eyes. "Put it up at work if you have to, but I love it long."

"Anything for you." Miller popped a kiss on the end of his nose. "Mark thinks Geo's dad will go down for a good long while, which will give us all a break. They've got video from that guy's phone and all the witnesses to corroborate what happened. With a protection order, it amounts to kidnapping, plus he was driving drunk. He's screwed, and I doubt they'll go easy on him."

"Still . . ." Sandy's heart squeezed. "How do you recover from that sort of damage by a parent? Makes my dad look like a damn boy scout."

"Speaking of which, did Reuben get you those tickets?"

Sandy blew out a sigh. "Yes, but I still don't know if I'm doing the right thing. Am I being too naïve, giving him a chance like this, just because Geo's dad made me think things could've been so much worse?"

Miller shrugged. "Depends what you're looking to come out of it. And you won't know unless you try. Personally, I think it's a brilliant idea. You're in control, not him. Neutral ground. It's a damn All Blacks' game. He should be kissing your bloody feet to get given a ticket for free. Plus, you're making him bring this woman, which has to be awkward for him, and your mother and sister will be there as well, and me. So, if he's an arsehole in any way, he'll be in more trouble than he can wiggle his way out of. I won't let anyone hurt you, sweetheart."

And Sandy believed that. Believed it in his heart, which was a long way from the week before. Things had changed in Miller since Sunday, dramatically changed. Sandy couldn't pinpoint it exactly, but it was as if Miller had dropped his remaining walls between them, and Sandy couldn't be happier.

"I just thought after Geo's dad and everything that . . . fuck, I don't know what I thought, but I wanted to tick the box, I guess. Give him a chance so I can say I tried. Does that make sense?"

"Perfect sense. And there's nothing wrong with that." Miller ran his hands down Sandy's arms.

He'd become surprisingly good at making Sandy feel safe and supported, even in just a few days. Turned out when Miller decided something, he went all in. Stuck at home with nothing to do, he'd spent hours online, calling contacts for advice on the complaint against Sandy and forwarding document after document for the committee to consider. Not to mention a few meetings with Cam Sandy hadn't been privy to and about which Miller had been less than forthcoming.

"I really wish I could be there for you today but—"

Sandy pressed a finger to his lips. "Shh. Michael said no, end of story. I'll text as soon as I'm done. They've promised a decision within the day."

Miller wrapped his canes around Sandy's back and caged him in.

"Mmm, I love when you do this," he murmured against Miller's lips.

"I am so damn proud of you." Miller's gaze drilled right into Sandy as if he could make him believe the words by sheer force of will. "I know I got things wrong before, and I still have a way to go to prove my words, but whatever the committee decides today, you're *my* hero. You look professional and sexy as fuck. If I only managed half the warmth, care, and integrity you show every day, I'd be a good man. I love you, Dee. And I love everything about you, *everything*. So go show that fucking committee what real class is, and I'll be waiting to celebrate when you get home, regardless of the decision. In my eyes, you win either way, at least in what really counts."

Sandy blinked back the tears, his words thick in his throat. "God-dammit, Miller, you're gonna wreck me before I even get there. That means so much. It means fucking everything." He threw his arms around Miller's neck. "I love you too. I'll call." He pressed a hurried kiss to Miller's cheek and raced from the room before he ugly cried his face into a mess.

"Where are you?" Sandy hissed into his phone, eyes scanning the hallway for any sign of Cam. Ten minutes until the meeting started and he was standing outside the room on his own. "For a fucking support person, I have to say this is not a great start."

"Hold on to your knickers, we're almost there." Cam sounded breathless. "I picked up our union rep on the way and got caught in the ER trying to sneak through undetected."

"I'm not wearing any knickers," Sandy shot back. "And you're supposed to be here for *me* today, not your harem of doting staff."

"You're not wearing . . . damn." Cam laughed. "That's it. I won't be able to think of anything else while we're in there. You should drop your pen by the door as you leave so you have to bend over and pick it up."

Sandy snorted. "Hardly the look I'm going for."

"Hey. You're the one going commando. We're in the stairwell now, see you soon."

He pocketed his phone and nodded at a greying middle-aged woman about to enter the room. Her gaze dropped to his skirt and her lips pursed. She gave a weak nod and disappeared into the room.

Awesome. It was all he could do not to flip her off.

His phone buzzed with a call.

"We're here." Cam's voice rang in his ear and Sandy breathed a sigh of relief, catching sight of him coming up the corridor. They'd discussed dress tactics, and Cam had decided to support Sandy with his best face of makeup, a flash of jewellery, and some kick-arse clothes. Black skinny jeans, mesh shirt, leather bomber jacket, ear gauges, and his official Charge Nurse ER tags hanging front and centre. A definite statement. He wasn't on duty, but he was making a point and Sandy loved him for it.

Their union rep followed Cam, looking slightly askance at Cam's outfit, but with enough folders tucked under her arm to sink a ship. She'd be allowed to talk in the meeting, although Cam wouldn't. His role was as Sandy's support person/family/whānau only, and thank god in NZ, the terms family or whānau could involve an entire clan/tribe if Sandy wanted it. Or just Cam. The scales were even.

He met Cam with a huge hug, hanging on for as long as he possibly could. "I love you for this, you know that," he whispered. "I just wish Miller was here too." He straightened Cam's jacket and fixed the collar.

"Well, as it so happens . . ." Cam turned Sandy around and held him by the shoulders as a crowd of people approached from the other end of the corridor led by Miller in his chair, with Geo pushing, and Jacob and Jacob's mother alongside.

"But . . ." He spun back around to find Cam's eyes bright with tears. "What the hell, Cam? What's going on?"

"Did you really think Miller was going to let you do this on your own after everything that's happened? He did this, Sandy. Every last person. He asked me to help, but this was his idea, and I think it's fucking brilliant."

Sandy spun back. "But who . . . ?" His hand flew to his mouth as he recognised Michael, Josh and their daughter, Sasha; Mark and Ed; Reuben carrying Cory; Lizzie and their mother; Miller's parents; Dane, Sam, and Chloe; Thelma S Dicksinim in a stunning blue taffeta full-length gown complete with high heels and gloves to her elbows; Merv and most of Miller's team in chairs, including, god help him, Jimmy Richardson. The man was still a work in progress, but at least he was trying.

And that wasn't everyone. Sandy recognised hospital staff, some he knew to be gay or bi, others trans and NB, and others he had absolutely no idea about. Not to mention quite a few he knew were straight and married and maybe just there to support him. Even a few senior medical staff and administrative personnel had dusted off their university protest faces to join. Some wore ally tees; some rainbow pins; and a couple of rainbow flags were draped around shoulders.

He was so fucking moved he couldn't do anything but stand in place like a complete fool, with his mouth hanging open, and stare. Then his eyes landed on Miller and he knew exactly what to do.

He covered the distance between them in a heartbeat and flung himself into Miller's arms. "I don't know what to say." He peppered Miller's face with a million kisses. "You did all this?"

"Of course I did." Miller laughed and held Sandy's face. "We're in this together. Your fights are mine, right? And vice versa. I might've made a crap job of my first attempt, but you gotta admit, I know how to bring it home when it counts." He hauled Sandy down for a fierce kiss before letting him go.

Sandy's gaze swept the crowd. "But . . ." He was still trying to wrap his head around it, recognising more and more people as the throng grew and everyone came up to say hi.

He hugged family and friends, shook hands with people he hardly knew, and was set upon by Geo who couldn't wait to mock him about how easy he was to dupe.

"I can't believe this," he finally addressed them all. "But I am so, so grateful. Thank you, all." He dropped to his knees in front of Miller. "But mostly, thanks to you, baby. I love you."

Miller shrugged. "I love you too. But I didn't have to twist any arms, just so you know. When people heard, most were horrified. And there are lots who wanted to come but couldn't."

Sandy nodded to the closed door. "They're probably not going to like this, you realise that? I believe this is what you, Mr Harrison, would call *political*."

Miller snorted. "Touché. And fuck 'em if they don't," he answered without a hint of concern. "If they can't find their way to common sense and decency, not to mention the chance to get ahead of the game and be a leader in this kind of thing and not a bunch of cowards, then I don't want to work here. I can get another job. The dress code should reflect the need to be *appropriate for the job irrespective of gender*, and that's what I've unofficially counselled through the research and documents I've made available. If they can't read between the lines, it's because they don't want to, and I don't want to work for an employer like that."

A voice cleared behind them and Sandy turned to find the same woman as before, only this time a little wide-eyed and unsure. "Mr Williams?"

Sandy nodded.

"The committee are ready for you now." She registered the sheer number of people with wary concern on her face, eventually focussing on Miller. "Mr Harrison? We weren't expecting you. We thought you'd recused yourself?"

Miller wheeled forward. "I did. I'm not here in an official capacity. I'm here as a member of Dee's family, his whānau, his support. I won't be speaking. I think you'll find that's perfectly within his and my rights."

"Oh . . ." Her gaze skittered once again over the gathered faces, eyes going wide as she recognised a few of the more senior personnel. "This is very irregular. There's a lot of you. I'm not sure—"

"We won't all come in," Miller assured her. "Just a couple. The rest will wait outside. But I suggest you remind the committee that it's respectful for them to at least appear and acknowledge the full support group, journalists included."

"Journalists?" Her hand flew to her chest and it was all Sandy could do not to laugh out loud.

"We'll just wait here, shall we?" Miller eyeballed the poor woman who looked to be regretting a number of her life choices, primarily her place on this particular committee.

After a few seconds deliberation, her shoulders deflated. "Very well, Mr Harrison, Mr Williams. I'll take it to the committee."

When she disappeared back behind the closed door, a swell of murmuring ran through the group.

Sandy caught Miller's mouth in a hard kiss and whispered. "You are so getting lucky tonight."

Miller beamed and lifted his mouth to Sandy's ear. "Gotta be worth a garter belt and stockings at the very least, right?"

Sandy lowered his voice even further. "The leather gag thingy arrived in the mail yesterday."

Miller's eyes blew wide. "You . . ." His gaze darted to the few people close enough to hear. "Really?" he squeaked.

It was so fucking adorable. "Toss you for first go."

Miller looked about to swallow his tongue when the door to the meeting room suddenly swung open.

"Mr Williams, the committee will be right out."

Sandy turned to Miller. "Showtime."

With expressions ranging from embarrassed and flustered to just plain irritated, the ten-member committee duly filed out of the meeting room and took position along the corridor wall to welcome Sandy's support network. There were some smiles and nods of approval from about a third of them, including the chairperson who Sandy knew as a genuinely good-hearted woman, while the rest looked about as uncomfortable and out of place as only a bunch of mid-level bureaucratic put-upon suits could.

The fidgeting discomfort warmed Sandy's heart.

Wary gazes acknowledged him, including a few raised brows at his dress. He nodded, smiled sweetly, and dusted off his skirt. There were more raised brows and a few tight smiles as the committee members recognised representatives of the various senior management teams who'd appeared in support of Sandy.

Miller's hand slipped into his and squeezed. Sandy squeezed back.

Then just as the chairperson stepped forward to say something, a member of the Maori Nurses Group broke into beautiful song, quickly joined by several others. The traditional waiata rang down the corridor, turning heads and garnering interest from staff and public alike.

The committee listened politely with a few darted glances to the gathering throng and the camera flashes that punctuated the song.

The honour from his Maori peers was unexpected and moved

Sandy to tears. But in that, he wasn't alone. Kleenex appeared throughout the crowd while others joined in the singing.

Sandy's mother appeared at his side, her arm around his waist.

When the waiata was done, the nurse acknowledged Sandy in Maori as friend and co-worker, and then spoke for a little before stepping back. The committee replied appropriately and then motioned Sandy inside the room as everyone took a collective breath.

With half his stomach threatening to make an appearance in his mouth, Sandy swallowed hard and followed the members into the cramped room.

Miller, Cam, Sandy's mum, and the Rainbow Legal Liaison that Cam had recommended, all joined Sandy, leaving barely enough air in the room to breathe.

Sandy took a seat while the others stood behind him, their presence a solid wall of support at his back.

Miller's hand landed on his shoulder and suddenly Sandy's nerves vanished, and he could breathe again.

The chairperson repeated a brief welcome, read the complaint and a few guidelines, and then asked if Sandy would like to offer a brief reply before they got down to the discussion.

Surprised at the calm running in his veins, Sandy got to his feet.

"All of you know me, to one degree or another," he began. "I recognise most of you from meetings, the cafeteria, labs, X-ray, the list goes on. Most of it is only in passing, though. And that's because you go about your jobs without making the kind of professional mistakes that would draw attention to yourselves. I go about my job too, and so far, I've avoided making those kinds of mistakes as well.

"I'm good at my job." Sandy paused making sure his gaze landed on every committee member. "I'm very good at it."

"But I suspect you all recognise me for different reasons as well. In the way we remember anyone who doesn't fit the usual images we carry in our heads, someone whose appearance goes against the grain, whether it be because they use a chair like Miller or dress a little differently like me, or for any number of reasons.

"Believe me, most of us would probably rather *not* catch your eye, but we're not there yet. I'm not in this room because I made a professional mistake. I'm not here because I wasn't modestly dressed. I'm here because someone didn't like the clothes I chose to wear that day —clothes that many of you wear every day without having to think if someone will hate you for it or worse." Sandy nodded at the chairperson who glanced at her brown skirt and beige woollen jersey with a frown.

"We can't force people to change their prejudices." His gaze again swept the room. "But we *can* stop enabling them to spread those prejudices in our communities. And as a government institution devoted to free public health care, what are we saying if we're too scared of offending people to be the leaders we're meant to be? That's all."

A thick silence descended on the room. Sandy felt Miller's hand slip once again in his and he realised he was still standing. His cheeks grew hot and he mumbled his thanks, taking his seat while behind him, four pairs of hands clapped none too softly.

He wasn't sure how loud he'd been speaking, but more hands joined in from the corridor outside, enough to put a huge smile on Sandy's face.

And in that moment, he knew. It didn't matter to his heart *what* the committee decided. He'd be disappointed if it went against him, but he had all he needed right here.

He'd survive this like he'd survived everything else, by believing in who he was and knowing he was loved by the people who mattered.

And the fight would go on.

EPILOGUE

ONE MONTH LATER

"Miller, sweetheart." Miller's mum sidled close and slipped her arm through his.

"Uh, oh. What are you after?" He eyed her warily.

She flashed an innocent smile, which he didn't buy for a single minute. "Nothing. I was just wondering if you'd do the honours of a speech today. Your father will say a few words, but you know him. He'll get all choked up, and half of what needs to be said won't be. Just follow up and fill in the gaps, will you?"

Miller sighed. "All right. But you owe me. How about you take Geo and Sam to the beach house with you next week so Dee and I can have a bit of time?"

"It'll be our pleasure. Tell Geo he can bring Jacob if he wants."

Miller kissed her cheek. "Thanks."

She wandered away to schmooze and Miller took up position parked alongside the garden shed to scan the large crowd. They'd delayed Dane's fortieth for three weeks to allow Miller to heal, Geo to recover somewhat, and the rugby series to finish.

The Wheel Blacks had won the series two games to one, and Miller had watched it all from the bench, surprised at how that didn't come with quite the sting of regret he'd expected. That may have had something to do with Sandy cheering alongside and the welcome afforded him by Miller's team.

Everyone in the wheelchair rugby community had rallied around both of them after the incident and the publicity that came with it, and Miller couldn't deny it felt good. Even David was coming along in his attitude, albeit reluctantly. It was either that or be chucked off the team for keying Miller's car. Once Merv had found out who was responsible, thanks to Jimmy, he'd gone on the warpath, and it was Miller who'd insisted David be given another chance. He wasn't sure it would work, but whatever.

"Hey, you," Cam shoved a beer in Miller's hand. "Excellent party."

Miller clinked bottles and drew a long swallow. The sun had come out for the occasion, and although not exactly tropical, the temperature was bearable with a jacket and a half-dozen outdoor heaters scattered around. Miller's parents had opened up their invitation list to include all of their combined friends, *and* Dee's family. Their back yard was chocka—at least fifty people at Miller's last count, and catered had become BYO, which had worked just fine.

"Geo looks good." Cam nodded to the teen busy smooching Jacob over by the runner beans.

Miller snorted. "Those two are superglued together. It'd be cute if they didn't take up so much damn room in our lounge. I'm always tripping over shoes and feet. We have a clutter jar on the fridge instead of a swear jar, and it's jammed with dollar coins. I couldn't give a shit if they swear, but if I trip over one more damn sneaker or game controller on my canes, I won't be held responsible."

"Go on, you love it."

Miller couldn't hide the grin. "I do. God help me, I never saw myself with kids let alone a teen around the house, and I know Geo's not ours, but some days it just feels like it, you know?"

"I do." Cam's gaze followed as Geo led his boyfriend into the house. "I don't even want to think what they're about to do." He slapped Miller on the shoulder. "You've taken to this whole semi-parent thing like a duck to water, I have to say."

He had. Miller smiled to himself. "It's easy with Dee. He and Geo just click. Makes it pretty simple for me. And Geo's a good kid. Get him through this next year and on to university, and maybe we'll think about starting something of our own."

"A family?" Cam looked surprised.

"Yes." Miller frowned. "Is that so unbelievable?"

Cam smirked. "Not at all. Just . . . fast."

"You took on a kid pretty quick." He glanced at Cory, who was being kept busy with Josh's police dog, Paris, in a quiet corner of the garden away from the crowd.

Cam's eyes went soft. "Yeah, Cory came with the territory. I love that kid."

"You're a good dad." Miller eyeballed him.

Cam blushed prettily. "Thanks. But your mum is gonna be impossible once she knows you're planning a family, you realise that?"

"I know. And keep your voice down. It's a long way off. We just thought we'd start thinking about it, that's all. Anyway, how're the wedding plans? Less than two months now."

Cam blanched. "Shh. You'll fucking jinx it. We've finally decided on the menu, and the music, and the damn flowers. Well, I've decided. Bloody rugby season is screwing with everything. The honeymoon is still a thorn in my side. I want tropical resort and he wants winter skiing. I told him I can organise for an icy reception and a cold pole up his arse any damn time he wants."

Miller snorted beer down the front of his shirt.

"Luckily Reuben doesn't give a shit if we marry in a draughty barn with bagpipes playing and Josh's dog as the celebrant. I, on the other hand, have the bar set slightly higher. Oops, gotta go." He put his beer on a table. "Cory's heading for the herb garden. Your dad will have my arse if that kid uproots his brand-new plants."

Miller watched Cam move like lightning through the crowd, in time to scoop Cory into his arms and save a seedling's life with only moments to spare.

"In case I haven't said it—" Miller's dad appeared at his side. "—we're so damn proud of what you've done for Geo, so proud, son. He's going to be okay and it's all thanks to you and Dee and your friends."

Miller blinked rapidly and took a second to get his shit together. His father wasn't one for gushing or praise, and it threw him. "I guess it never occurred to us to do any different, you know? He's a cool kid."

"Mmm. Still, it was a good thing you did and we'll support you all the way. I hope you know that?"

Warmth filled Miller's heart. Family. God, they sure had their moments. "I do, and thanks."

"I also wanted to say, I like your friends, Miller. And I like how you are when you're with them too."

Miller looked up at his father and frowned. "Okaaaay? Can I ask you to expand on that?"

His dad's jaw worked. "Well, I guess I mean that you're more . . . relaxed, more . . . you. I don't know that I can explain it very well other than to say, I'm not sure I've seen you this way since you were a little kid. Maybe because once you hit your teens, you got busy with sport, training, all that. It was always . . . busy." His gaze slid away. "Did we push you too hard, son? Did *I* push you?"

Miller reached for his father's hand without thinking. He'd been finding himself doing those kinds of things more and more. Even Dane had started hugging him when they met, picking up on Miller's change. It felt . . . good.

"You only wanted to help, dad. And you were the best support I could've had when the shit hit the fan. I wouldn't have got through without you. Did you push too hard sometimes?" He shrugged. "Maybe. But I've never been a push-over, either. I could've said no, and I didn't. I did it as much to myself as anything."

He caught Sandy's eye across the yard where he was talking with Lizzie and his mum. He'd worn a dark blue tightly fitted dress with black tights—a combination that had Miller frothing at the mouth all fucking day—a soft blue and green scarf, and those ubiquitous Doc Martens.

Sandy quirked a curious brow and sent him a wave.

Miller smiled and waved back. "I should probably have come out earlier," he admitted, not looking at his father. "After the accident, at least. I would've had more balance then. He makes me happy, Dad, so happy . . ."

His father's hand landed on his shoulder.

"He's a good man, Sandy is. One of life's little gems, as your mother would say. You did well."

Miller snorted. "I was so fucking lucky, Dad. I came close to screwing it all up, you have no idea."

His father squeezed his shoulder, hard. "We all do at some time, son. Every damn one of us."

Miller took a deep breath and steeled himself, ready to share a decision he'd been avoiding telling his dad for three long weeks. "I'm done, Dad." He cleared his throat. "I'm not going back to the Wheel Blacks. Merv's asked me to consider coaching, but I'm not sure about that, not yet. I haven't decided about playing regional, but I'm done with top level. My body can't take it. And I want more time for Dee, Geo, all of us."

His dad was quiet for a minute, watching the crowd of people ebb and flow through the garden, talking, eating, laughing.

"I figured you would," he finally said, catching Miller's eye.

And to Miller's relief, he looked not the least bit concerned or disappointed.

"It's time for that, I guess," he continued. "Whatever you decide, your mother and I will always support you. Let us know if you need any help. We're proud of what you've achieved, and we'll be equally proud of whatever you do next, wherever your next venture takes you." He patted Miller's shoulder. "Now, I need to go mingle. I hear you're playing backstop to my speech. Doubt I'll need it. I've got the sucker nailed this time."

And with that, he headed in the direction of Sandy's mother, leaving Miller gaping and ready to puddle on the granite pavers in relief. Two months and his entire world had changed. He still couldn't believe it.

"Penny for your thoughts." Sandy bent down and brushed their lips together.

Miller pulled him close for a more thorough taste.

"Mmm." Sandy finally pulled up and licked his lips. "What was that for?"

"Because I love you, and you look so fucking delicious I can hardly stand it. Not to mention I just told my father I'd quit the Wheel Blacks, and he patted my hand and said well done."

Sandy's eyes popped. "Really?"

"Well, not in those exact words, but, yeah, pretty much."

"Well, how about that?" Sandy searched the garden till he found Miller's dad, waited till he looked over, and then blew him a kiss. The man blushed and looked away, and Miller marvelled again at the force of nature that was Sandy Williams.

"Oh, I meant to tell you I heard back from that guy who looked at my apartment." Sandy's eyes sparkled. "He's going to take it. A year for a start, and then if his company extends his time, he'll sign for another year."

Miller couldn't be more delighted. Sandy had been cautious about moving in at first, but since he hadn't actually slept in his own apartment in the three weeks since the incident, he'd finally caved and put it up for rent. Miller was pinching himself. They'd quickly become this strange little family, the three of them, and he loved it.

"Have you decided whether you're going to attend the inclusivity policy meeting next week?" He knew it had been a thorn in Sandy's side ever since he'd been cleared of the complaint and asked to help form an updated policy in keeping with the hospital's stance on non-discrimination.

Sandy pulled a pained expression. "I guess so. I really don't need the grief. Regardless of what they say and what happened in my case, some of the stuff we have to address is going to be a fight to get across the line. A couple of the nominated members are fucking nightmares. But as long as Cam keeps his promise to be part of it as well, I guess between the two of us we can deal with any arseholes."

"I have every faith. Now come a little closer." Miller tugged at Sandy's dress.

Sandy arched a brow but did as Miller asked, turning to allow Miller's hand to slide up the back of his dress.

"Damn, I love the feel of you through these things." He ran his hand over the sweet curve of Sandy's arse, keeping an eye on the crowd in front to make sure no one could see what he was up to and—huh. His gaze shot up to meet Sandy's smirk. "You're commando under those tights, you saucy tart."

Sandy drew his bottom lip between his teeth and batted his lashes. "I am. Wanna kick our teenager and his boyfriend out of that accessible and oh so roomy bathroom?"

Miller sucked in a breath and took a quick look around. "Yeah. Fuck it. Lead the way."

The End

Thank you for taking the time to read
AGAINST THE GRAIN
Auckland Med. 4

Please consider doing a review in Amazon or your favourite

review spot. Reviews help authors gain visibility and are hugely important.

Read the next in the series
YOU ARE CORDIALLY INVITED
Auckland Med 5

There's a wedding in the air at Auckland Med, but Reuben wonders if they'll survive the stress long enough to say, 'I do'. Cam is directing the entire operation with his combat eyeliner in place, whilst the wedding party is doing its best to ignore him. The pressure is mounting and the cracks are beginning to show.

There's a bachelor party to survive.

The paparazzi to outrun.

A wedding outfit to confirm.

A rugby game to win.

A jerk of a father to cope with.

A stunning opportunity to consider.

A relationship to untangle.

And a shocking event that could derail everything.

With the universe conspiring against them, Reuben and Cam will have to summon every scrap of belief they have in each other to make it to their vows.

Reviews

"If you were expecting this to simply be a *tacked on* epilogue of sorts to Jay's utterly brilliant Crossing the Touchline then think again. This is a full on novel with a deep emotional thread running right through which sees both Cameron and Reuben pushed to their limits by a myriad of different hurdles on their way to the aisle."

5 Stars—Mirrigold Book Blog

"You Are Cordially Invited exceeded my expectations in the best way and I loved every moment of it, even when it had me in tears!"

5 Stars —Amanda Amazon

"Easily the wedding of the year!"

5 stars—Vas Amazon

AUTHOR'S NOTE

Have you read Jay's
SOUTHERN LIGHTS SERIES?

An mm romance series set in stunning Queenstown, New Zealand, with lots of humour and heart.

POWDER AND PAVLOVA
by Jay Hogan

Southern Lights 1

ETHAN SHARPE is living every young Kiwi's dream—seeing the world for a couple of years while deciding what to do with his life. Then he gets a call.

Two days later he's back in New Zealand. Six months later his mother is dead, his fifteen-year-old brother is going off the rails and the café he's inherited is failing. His life is a hot mess and the last thing he needs is another complication—like the man who just walked into his café,

a much older...

sinfully hot...

EPIC complication.

TANNER CARPENTER's time in Queenstown has an expiration date. He has a new branch of his business to get up and running, exorcise a few personal demons while he's at it, and then head back to Auckland to get on with his life. He isn't looking for a relationship especially with someone fifteen years his junior, but Ethan is gorgeous, troubled and in need of a friend. Tanner could be that for Ethan, right? He could brighten Ethan's day for a while, help him out, maybe even offer some... stress relief, no strings attached.

It was a good plan, until it wasn't.

ALSO BY JAY HOGAN

AUCKLAND MED SERIES

First Impressions

Crossing the Touchline

Up Close and Personal

Against the Grain

You Are Cordially Invited

SOUTHERN LIGHTS SERIES

Powder and Pavlova

Tamarillo Tart

Flat Whites and Chocolate Fish

Pinot and Pineapple Lumps

STYLE SERIES

Flare

Strut

Sass

(Coming 2022)

PAINTED BAY SERIES

Off Balance

(Romance Writers New Zealand 2021 Romance Book of the Year Award)

On Board

In Step

STANDALONE

Unguarded

(Written as part of Sarina Bowen's
True North— Vino & Veritas Series and published by Heart Eyes Press)

Digging Deep
(2020 Lambda Literary Finalist)

ABOUT THE AUTHOR

JAY IS A 2020 LAMBDA LITERARY AWARD FINALIST AND THE WINNER OF ROMANCE WRITERS NEW ZEALAND 2021 ROMANCE BOOK OF THE YEAR AWARD FOR HER BOOK, OFF BALANCE.

She is a New Zealand author writing in MM romance and romantic suspense primarily set in New Zealand. She writes character driven romances with lots of humour, a good dose of reality and a splash of angst. She's travelled extensively, lived in many countries, and in a past life she was a critical care nurse and counsellor. Jay is owned by a huge Maine Coon cat and a gorgeous Cocker Spaniel.

Join Jay's reader's group Hogan's Hangout for updates, promotions, her current writing projects and special releases.

Sign up to her newsletter HERE.

Or visit her website HERE.

Milton Keynes UK
Ingram Content Group UK Ltd.
UKHW021308091123
432266UK00027B/1267